Praise for the DS Alexandra Cupidi Investigations

'A powerful, scary suspense mystery which had me swiping over pages at speed while savouring every word. This is a brilliant novel' Lesley Thomson

'Shaw never lectures; his crucial imperative remains ironclad storytelling and razor-sharp characterisation, both in evidence here' *Financial Times*

'William Shaw is an expert manipulator of his readers' emotions . . . each new torment provokes readers' sympathies more and more . . . The many stranded drama works, but it is the boys' story that is the most engaging' Natasha Cooper, *Literary Review*

'Shaw handles diverse plotlines brilliantly, demonstrating his ability to write about contemporary events with the same keen intelligence he used in his fine crime novels set in the 1960s' Joan Smith, *Sunday Times*

'Shaw expertly manipulates his readers' emotions, engaging their sympathies in a . . . tautly constructed thriller whose diverse plot-lines again demonstrate his ability to write about contemporary events with intelligence, well-drawn characters and sinister and divisive themes. Deadland is an ingeniously unguessable, often moving and always powerful story which brilliantly captures Kent and its social divisions' John Cleal, *Crime Review*

'Grips the reader by the throat and never lets go' *Independent*

'A first-rate police thriller' C. J. Sansom

'A gripping story, impeccably researched' *Guardian*

'A thrilling plot, recreating all the political tension of an explosive time' *Figaro*

'A superb, flowing writer . . . always intelligent' *The Times*

'The question of why a killer kills is always central. William Shaw delivers a perfect motive' *Spectator*

'Sensuous storytelling . . . Shaw goes from strength to strength' *Daily Mail*

William Shaw has been shortlisted for the CWA Historical Dagger, longlisted for the Theakston's Old Peculier Crime Novel of the Year Award and nominated for a Barry Award. A regular at festivals, he organises panel talks and CWA events across the south east. His books include the acclaimed Breen & Tozer crime series set in sixties London, the newest series featuring DS Alexandra Cupidi, and the standalone bestseller *The Birdwatcher*. He worked as a journalist for over twenty years and lives in Brighton.

BY WILLIAM SHAW

The Breen and Tozer Investigations

A Song from Dead Lips
A House of Knives
A Book of Scars
Sympathy for the Devil

The DS Alexandra Cupidi Investigations

Salt Lane
Deadland
Grave's End

The Birdwatcher

GRAVE'S END

William Shaw

riverrun

First published in Great Britain in 2020 by riverrun
This paperback edition published in 2021 by

riverrun

an imprint of

Quercus Editions Limited
Carmelite House
50 Victoria Embankment
London EC4Y 0DZ

An Hachette UK company

A CIP catalogue record for this book is available
from the British Library

Paperback 978 1 52940 176 9
Ebook 978 1 52940 178 3

This book is a work of fiction. Names, characters,
businesses, organisations, places and events are
either the product of the author's imagination
or used fictitiously. Any resemblance to
actual persons, living or dead, events or
locales is entirely coincidental.

10 9 8 7 6 5 4 3 2 1

Typeset by CC Book Production
Printed and bound in Great Britain by Clays Ltd, Elcograf S.p.A.

Papers used by Quercus are from well-managed forests and other responsible sources.

For Ellen

The earth does not want to keep secrets.

Vasily Grossman

PART ONE

PART ONE

ONE

There have always been a few people here, coming and going, passing through, usually in the company of dogs. But recently there have been many more, above his head, all the time. And they have started changing things, digging stuff up, messing with the way it has always been around here.

He sleeps through the day, but today sleep was hard. The earth shook. Tyres bit into the ground. Dirt fell on him. He could hear the cubs nearby, fractious and scared, quarrelling with their mother.

They are all hungry. It is spring; the season when they must eat all they can. If they do not, they will die when the cold returns.

It is poor land.

The badger sett is dug deep in this sandy soil. To the north, this group's territory runs alongside the road that leads out from the small town. To the south, it is marked by a line of old haw-thorns and stunted ashes.

Badgers have lived on these islands much longer than humans; they were here a half million years ago. They are part of this landscape. Prodigious shifters of earth, they have literally helped shape it. A sett like this might have moved twenty-five tonnes of earth over years.

Badgers are numerous. There are hundreds of thousands of them; they occupy Britain more densely than anywhere else in the world, but we rarely see them – at least not alive. The badgers we mostly see are dead ones, dirty shapes of dark fur lying by the sides of roads.

Though they have been here so much longer than we have, and though we live alongside them, we struggle to understand them, not only because they are underground creatures, and secretive, but because they don't appear to behave like we want them to, like other mammals we find easier to love.

They live by rules we don't really understand, in small fractious groups that can't be described as families; if they do cooperate, we often struggle to comprehend how.

Among mammals, our sense of smell is one of the worst; theirs is excellent. It is the main way in which they understand the world around them. We communicate mostly by sound; they, by scent. It is as if they are operating on entirely different wavelengths.

And most of their life is lived unseen; underground and in darkness.

The sun has dropped and it's time to go out. When finally the gnawing in his gut gets the better of him, he moves cautiously down the tunnel, to the bend where it turns up towards the surface, to where he would normally pause to sniff the outside air, but when he does there is nothing. No scent of anything fresh; just the usual earth around him.

This is wrong. By now the air should smell of fresh grass, hyssop, cow parsley, other badgers and dog shit.

He moves forward more cautiously in the blackness and his snout meets something hard. At the end, where darkness should change to dusk, he finds the tunnel blocked. He digs but there is something in the way, something so hard his big claws make no impression on it at all.

He sniffs. It smells rank.

People stink.

TWO

The key was shiny in Gram's hand, catching the evening sun as he held it up. 'Ready?'

When he slotted it into the lock in the huge blue door, it slid in, like a spoon into a baby's mouth.

Angela placed a hand on each side of her face. 'Oh my giddy God. You are joking?'

'Welcome to Guldeford Hall. You're going to love this place, Boo, I promise.'

It was a Saturday in early May. She looked up at the vast country house above her. 'It looks so . . . bloody . . . expensive.'

'Historic building, Boo,' he said. 'Five bedrooms, three en-suite. All modernised, obviously. Micro Combined Heat and Power system.'

She took both sides of his face and kissed him. 'I love it when you talk heat and power.'

Architects had transformed the Kentish oast house into an enormous luxury home. It sat in its own grounds, surrounded by heavy, dark trees, well beyond the noise of traffic. Gram turned the key. 'Should I pick you up and carry you over?'

'I'm going to slap you so hard you'll never know what hit you.'

Gram laughed. 'Ta-da!' The moment he pushed the door open the beeping began. He strode in, turned to face her.

Beep beep beep.

'You do know the code, don't you?' she said, still outside the door.

Beep beep beep.

He closed his eyes tight. 'Um . . .'

'Gram!'

Beep beep beep.

'Thought I'd remember it without writing it down, Boo.'

The noise seemed to be getting louder.

'It's OK. We've got at least thirty seconds before it goes off.'

'It's been thirty, you—'

He grinned, put down the plastic carrier bag he was holding, raised a finger ostentatiously and pushed the keypad four times. The beeping stopped. The sound of late spring reasserted itself; the fluty whistle of blackbirds and the humming of fat bees.

She stepped inside the doorway and punched him right in the stomach.

'Ooof.' He doubled, winded by her fist.

She laughed and walked past him, through the small inner hallway into the larger hall, a massive space, floor tiled black and white, a modern staircase soaring up from the left to right. A barometer on the wall. Small prints, at regular intervals.

'Oh Jesus, Gram. I bloody love it.'

She turned as he was straightening, put her arms around him

and squeezed him. 'I really love it. It's amazing. It's huge. You could fit all of my place in the hall, plus my car, and there'd still be space over.'

'You won't need your flat any more. We'll live here together. Five bedrooms, three en-suite. So we'll need lots of children. Plus there's a vinery and stables.'

'Will we have to get horses?'

'Obviously.'

'Hate horses. Always did. But I can cope. Especially if there's a vinery. Can we look around?'

'Llamas, then,' he said. 'Herds of them. Be my guest. You are the lady of the house, after all.'

She went upstairs first.

He took the bottle of Prosecco out of the plastic carrier bag and went to the kitchen, a huge room with a massive window that looked out onto the north lawn. The refrigerator was gigantic, but Gram realised the door had been propped open.

'Bugger,' he said, out loud. The fridge was off.

'Gram!' A loud scream from upstairs.

He dashed from the kitchen back into the hallway, bottle still in hand. 'What's wrong?'

'The bed in the main bedroom is ginormous.'

'Jesus. I thought you'd seen something scary.'

'Kind of scary because the bed is made up,' she said. 'As if someone's been planning this all along.' From the first-floor landing she looked down at him. 'What's that?'

He raised the bottle. 'It's to lower your defences.'

'Christ, Gram. You'll need more than a bottle of Aldi five-quid Prosecco to do that.'

8

'It was more than five quid.'

'And there's a bath the size of an Olympic pool, too.' She descended, approached, leaned forward, kissed him. 'You know what's bloody weird, though. I looked in the wardrobes too. There are all these suits. And—'

'I think there's an actual Olympic swimming pool too, somewhere.'

She took the bottle off him. 'I can't drink that anyway. It's warm.'

'The fridge isn't on. It'll take ages to cool it.'

'Do you know who I am? I own a herd of llamas. I have standards,' she said. 'Stick the fridge on.'

'It'll take for ever, Boo,' he complained.

'How much is it on the market for?'

'Two mil. Just over.'

'Great,' she said. 'I'll take it.'

'I'll draw up the paperwork,' he said, and then saw that she had sat down and was crying. 'Oh, Boo!'

Angela Booth, whom he liked to call Boo, sat in the middle of the black-and-white-tiled floor, holding her hands up to her face. 'Sorry,' she said. 'Give me a minute.'

He sat down on the floor next to her and put his arm around her. It only made the crying worse. 'What's wrong? I didn't mean to upset you. I was just trying to make you happy.'

It took a little while for her to stop. She wiped her red eyes with the sleeve of her shirt. 'I'm sorry, Gram. This is great. I didn't mean to spoil it.'

They lay down side by side on the cool tiles and looked up at the chandelier which hung on a chain from the ceiling two floors above. The crystals made rainbows of the early evening light.

Near the centre, a spider had woven a web between the shards of glass. A beautiful place for a spider to live, thought Gram. *Spectacular open plan, designer dwelling. Suitable location to raise a family. Plenty of flies available.*

'It's just so unfair,' she said. 'I'm thirty-two. I'm a school-teacher. I work my bloody arse off and I won't ever get to buy a one-bedroom flat, let alone something like this.'

'I'm saving up,' said Gram. 'I'm going to ask for a pay rise.'

'Pfft. You'll probably get the sack from the agency for sneaking into empty houses and having sex with your girlfriend.'

Gram sat up, interested. 'So we are going to have sex then?'

She shrugged. 'If we must.'

'I'll admit, I was worried.'

'Definitely not on warm Prosecco though. No sex without alcohol. Surely a place with three en-suite bathrooms has another fridge somewhere,' she said.

He lay back down again and tried to remember the details for this house. He placed his hands together in front of his face and closed his eyes.

Rolling onto her side, she nudged him with her knee. 'What are you doing?'

'I'm praying, obviously, to St Joseph, the patron saint of estate agents, for a fridge.'

'Have you really got a patron saint?'

'Actually, we have.'

'That's a waste of a saint. What I was about to say about the suits in the wardrobe was that they're all cut to ribbons. Classic husband-and-wife stuff.'

'You're kidding.'

10

'Whoever owns this house has been a naughty boy, don't you think?'

'The man who owns the house is dead. That's why they're selling.'

She opened her eyes wide. 'Oh God. She murdered him in a fit of jealousy.'

'Sorry, no. Just a brain haemorrhage. He was walking the dog, apparently. Dropped down dead. It was in the papers. He was quite a big deal.'

'Not big enough to have a second fridge,' she said, kissing him on the forehead.

He jumped up, grinning. 'Hallelujah. Yes. I remember now. I saw a freezer in the garage. Come on.' He offered her his hand.

The garage had originally been an entirely separate out-building. The architect who had converted the oast house had extended the kitchen out towards it, creating a vast space between it and the kitchen that had been turned into a games room.

'Ooh,' Angela said, as they walked through. 'Billiards.'

'No balls,' he said.

And she was still laughing, for no particular reason, when he unlocked the adjoining door and stepped into the large, empty garage that smelt of recently laid concrete. And there, in the corner, sat a white chest freezer. A red light shone in the gloom. 'Thank you, St Joseph,' he said.

'It's a miracle.'

They walked across the big floor to the white box. It hummed gently.

'And it's on.'

*

The bottle shattered on the grey concrete, covering Angela's bare legs in sticky warm alcohol.

'Oh,' was all Gram said, his face lit by the light inside the freezer's lid.

The man who lay inside was naked, knees bent, arms crossed over his chest. Long crystals had formed on his eyelashes, and on the soft, thin hairs on his head.

They stood in silence and stared.

In the end, it was Angela who spoke. 'Close the lid,' she said.

He did as he was told. The box closed with a soft *whump*.

'Do you think it's him?' she asked.

'Who?'

'The guy who owns the house.'

He looked at her, trying to process what she was saying. 'No. He was buried weeks ago.'

'Wait there,' she said.

He was still standing by the freezer when she returned with a kitchen cloth and a bottle of spray bleach, some plastic bags and a dustpan and brush.

'What are you doing?' he whispered.

She stopped and looked at him. 'We have a choice,' she said. 'If we tell the police we were here, you will lose your job. Or we can not be here at all.'

'But he's dead,' he said. 'We should call the police.'

'Yes. He's dead, Gram. And it's not our fault. We can't do anything about it. If we leave him like this, someone else will find him.'

He looked at her. She was older than him, more experienced.

'But . . .'

'If you call the police,' she repeated, 'you'll lose your job.'

There was a faint creaking sound from the freezer as it adjusted to cool the warm air they had let in.

'Look at these people,' she said, suddenly bitter. 'These people who own these houses. We have so little. They have so much. Let them deal with the shit, for a change.'

And he watched her, shocked by this darkness in her, as she knelt and started to sweep the fragments of broken glass.

THREE

Likes: dogs, good restaurants, people who can admit their falws.

'That's a shit joke, isn't it?' said Jill Ferriter, looking in the mirror.

'Give him a chance,' said Alexandra Cupidi, standing behind the younger woman. 'You've not even met him yet. He might be funnier in real life.'

'Don't know if I want to.'

It was a Saturday evening. The constable and the detective sergeant had finished a long shift; Alex had promised to help her colleague get ready for the date.

Jill pulled at a wrinkle beneath her eye. 'I look like a dog.'

'Harry likes dogs,' said Alex. 'It said so on his profile.'

'It's a mistake.' Jill picked up a different colour of eyeshadow and leaned forward towards the glass. 'You're the one who should be doing this. You've been single for ever.'

'Thanks so much.'

'I'm going to call it off. I'm not ready. What about I message him, apologise, you and me go out on the lash?'

'Cancel, for all I care, but I'm not going out drinking with you,' said Alex. 'My liver isn't up to it. I'm going home after this.'

'One drink, at least. I need it before I go out.'

'I'm driving.'

'One glass. C'mon.'

Jill stood up and led the way out of her bedroom towards the kitchen. There was an open bottle of Pinot in the fridge. As she poured two large glasses, Alex looked at the younger woman dressed up for a night out.

'Do I look frumpy? I never usually wear long dresses.'

'You look gorgeous.'

It was not useful to be as pretty as Jill was when you were a police officer. Alex, who was almost six feet tall and incapable of ever looking as well groomed, had never felt pretty herself. Jill gulped down her glass and said, 'Ready for a top-up?'

'Don't. You know what you're like when you've had a few.'

'I'm just nervous, that's all. The whole thing is a mistake. There's something desperate about it. I found an app that does double dating. We could do that instead.'

'Absolutely not.'

'See? You think it's a stupid idea, too.'

Alex held the glass to her lips and tasted the wine. Jill disappeared into the kitchen to refill her own.

Jill re-emerged, checking her watch. 'God's sake. I'm supposed to be there in twenty minutes. We'll be late.'

One of the toughest coppers Alex had ever known had worked herself into a bundle of nerves. 'Thing is, Alex, the men I meet who are my age are so immature. I don't know

15

why I bother. I'm an independent woman. I own my own flat, and everything. I should be perfectly happy without a man, shouldn't I?'

Jill lifted her glass and emptied it a second time.

FOUR

People stink.

Even underground they stink.

The sett doesn't need another entrance, there are over a dozen old ones, but the one he uses most has been blocked. Other badgers use other exits. That one was his.

To use other exits meant crawling through other tunnels. Only a few weeks ago, when trying to use an entrance he'd passed through many times in the past, the group's younger male, a three-year-old, bit him on the arse, drawing blood. Since the fight, he avoided that route, staying out of the path of the younger, stronger badger. And if he went the other way, he would have to go past the angry sow protecting her cubs.

It was easier to move earth.

So he digs now – a tunnel he has been working on for weeks, every day shifting soil, depositing it outside in untidy piles beyond the other entrances.

The digging makes him hungry. He is spending too much time

deep in the safe soil, not enough outside searching for worms and beetles. But the darkness is reassuring. Darkness is his element, protecting him. It is light that is dangerous.

Today the hunger begins to rouse him early; it is hours before he dares to go outside. The two cubs are shuffling somewhere down the tunnel. They are hungry too; fatten or die.

And then the dull noise of footsteps above jolts him fully awake.

The humans are back. They are close. He lies still in the darkness. In another chamber, he hears the old sow and her cubs moving. They have heard it too.

Tonight he will dig some more, bringing old earth up to the surface. The soil here is sandy; tunnels collapse and have to be re-dug. He digs deeper.

This is not the usual scent, though; below the surface, there is an old stink of bones. People stink. Even when they are underground.

Footsteps again, closer.

And then a noise he doesn't understand.

'Stop what you're doing. You're under arrest.'

FIVE

'Stop what you're doing. You're under arrest.'

The security guard was still a long way off, running across uneven ground towards them.

'Stop. You two. I can see you.'

'Run,' shouted the older of the two, a rangy young man of twenty.

'No,' said the girl, nervous, standing her ground. She was obviously younger, a teenager, thin and angular, with short, uneven hair that looked as if she cut it herself. She remained where she was, crossed her arms. The man opened his mouth to object, but said nothing. The scrubland they were trespassing on had been recently fenced; thin, hummocked soil, fringed with stunted willows, it ran for a quarter of a mile alongside the B-road.

The man roaring towards them stumbled on a rabbit hole, fell forwards, but managed to keep his footing, swore, then regained his pace moving on towards them.

'Only way out,' said the girl quietly, 'is through the hole we cut in the wire. If we go that way he'll know we made it. Criminal damage.'

The boy was dark haired, with a thin black beard. 'Yeah, Zoë, but . . .' He was dressed in an army jacket that was too big for him. Zoë wore khaki trousers too, and an old white Pikachu T-shirt. 'I've still got the bloody cutters in my pocket,' the boy muttered.

'Don't panic. He's not a copper. He can't arrest us. He's not allowed to search us.'

'You'd know, Zoë, wouldn't you.'

'Calm down.'

'It's all right for you. Your mum's a bloody fed. She'll probably get you off if we get done.'

'Shut up, Jay.'

The guard had finally reached them, out of breath. 'You know this is private land?'

'No such law as trespass,' said Jay, smirking.

'That's not actually even true,' muttered Zoë.

'How did you get in here?' asked the guard, looking around him, as if to reassure himself that there weren't more intruders.

Neither of them answered.

'What are you doing here anyway?'

'Looking for our cameras,' Zoë answered.

'That you nicked,' muttered Jay.

'What cameras?'

'We left trail cameras to film wildlife here. They're gone.'

'What's a trail camera?'

20

'Like you don't know,' said Jay.

The guard looked sceptical. 'I'm going to have to ask you to leave.'

'What if I don't want to?' said Jay. 'You can't actually make me.'

'It's fine,' said Zoë. 'We'll go.'

But the guard had already grabbed Jay by the elbow.

'Fascist,' Jay shouted. 'Keep your hands off me.'

'We're going,' said Zoë. 'Leave him alone.'

The guard was trying to walk back towards the main gate with Jay, dragging him along.

'I said we were going,' shouted Zoë. 'There's no need for this.'

The guard ignored her.

'Leave him alone.'

The guard turned to look back at Zoë, frowning when he saw that she had taken her phone out and was pointing it at him. 'No filming here. This is private land.'

The guard let go of Jay, raising his hand towards the camera to obscure his own face as he approached Zoë.

'Don't you touch her!' Jay reached for his own phone, but as he pulled his hand out of his pocket, something fell out.

Zoë looked down and saw the wire-cutters they had used ten minutes before to cut through the security fence.

The two exchanged an anxious glance, but the security guard hadn't noticed, though the blades lay glinting in the fading summer light. She dodged to one side, holding the camera closer to the guard's face, distracting him.

'No filming. You don't have permission.' Though he was a

21

young man, his face was red from the exertion of running from the small cabin near the entrance on the far side of the site.

'Why do I need permission?' she demanded.

Instead of answering, he reached out and snatched the phone from her.

'Ow.' The girl tried to get it back, grabbing hold of the man's arm. 'Give it back.'

'You have no right,' shouted Jay.

'Get out of here,' the guard yelled back. 'That's confiscated.'

'That's illegal,' protested the girl. 'You can't just steal things.'

'Tell you what's illegal. You're on this land without permission. Now get out.'

The man shook the girl off and she fell backwards onto the long grass.

The fields lay to the east of Lydd, a little north of the small airfield that was optimistically called London Ashford Airport, though the city was over two hours' drive away. Zoë and Jay sat on the verge of the track that led north from the B-road to the security gate. She was gnawing on what was left of her nails as she watched a damselfly hovering a few metres off.

The security guard had shut himself in his cabin with her phone.

'This is fucked,' said Jay.

Red-eyed damselfly, thought Zoë. The start of May and they're already here. She would have made a note of it on her phone, a record of the species that were appearing earlier each year as the world warmed, only the guard had it.

'I bet they probably found the other cameras and confiscated them too. Such a fascist.' Jay sniffed. 'Bet he's got all them cameras right there in his office.'

Zoë said, 'Might have.'

'It's why they put the fencing up. They're clearing the site before anybody gets a chance to record what's there. It's an outrage.'

'We don't actually know that, do we?' Even before the planning application had been agreed, the developers had ringed this part of the site, building a chain-link fence around what had been open land.

'But I bet they're planning to.'

Zoë wrinkled her nose, nodded.

'Be much cheaper for them that way. There are probably newts. Bet you there are.'

'Bet there aren't. Way too dry.'

Jay looked offended. The evening sun was warm on her skin, but air was cooling as the sun dropped. She turned. The guard was looking at them through the small window on the edge of the cabin.

She stood up. 'Give me back my phone,' she called.

The guard slid the small glass opening shut. A light came on.

'What are we going to do?' Jay said. 'About your phone?'

She didn't answer.

'Your mum will go nuts,' he said.

It was true. She would. The green of the world around them deepened as the sun went down. They would be walking home in the dark.

She stood and strode up to the door of the site office

23

and banged on it. 'Let me have my phone,' she shouted. 'It's mine.'

There was no answer. Inside, the man turned up a radio.

Jay watched her from where he was sitting. 'Tell you what,' he said, standing. 'Wait just there. I've an idea.'

SIX

In the end Alex had agreed to drive Jill to Folkestone to meet her date. 'Just so you can identify him when my body ends up in a trunk somewhere.'

'He could fit you in carry-on luggage,' said Alex.

'Thanks.'

They parked the car and walked through the small town centre. It was Saturday night. Things would be getting lively soon, but it was still early. They were walking down the steep Old High Street, past the tourists eating ice creams, Jill taking small steps because of her heels, when her phone pinged.

'Bogging hell. I bet that's him cancelling.' They stopped by a shop called 'Vintage and Vinyl' and she pulled it out and frowned at the screen.

'Is it?'

'No it's not.' She looked up, made a face. 'It's McAdam asking if I can come in. Somebody found a body in a freezer.'

Alex went to check her own phone, but there was no message for her.

Jill's fingers hovered over the phone. 'I can always cancel the date,' she said.

'Yes, you could.' Alex nodded. 'Or you could tell McAdam you can't do it. It's your day off. You don't have to go in. Which would you rather do? Go out with a nice-looking young man or spend time with a cold dead one?'

'Honest?' She looked back towards where they'd parked the car. 'Right now I'm actually not sure.'

'You're going on a date, Jill. The body will keep.'

Jill set off ahead down the narrow road again towards the wine bar, heels clicking on the paving. 'Was that supposed to be a joke?' she called over her shoulder.

Zoë had waited. It had taken a while for the guard to notice that Jay was back inside the perimeter.

She had been pressed against the side of the cabin out of sight when the door had burst open and the man had emerged again, heading for the site gates. 'You,' he shouted. 'You!'

The guard had left the site-office door swinging wide.

Zoë stepped straight into the empty cabin, where a radio was playing an old rock song. A half-eaten sandwich curled on the table, but her phone wasn't there. She looked around for a hiding place. The only drawer was in a small cabinet on which a kettle and some tea bags were perched. She opened it but there were only a few dirty spoons inside, and a roll of Sellotape.

It wasn't there. He must have it in his pocket. Where were the trail cameras, then?

On the walls were the plans for the site. A large printed sheet, with all the new roads and houses marked on it in thin white lines. The map was covered in rectangles; each one a new house, each with its own tiny garden. Imagined roads wound around the estate. Hundreds upon hundreds of houses that would obliterate the land beneath them completely. The development was huge.

She was still standing there, gazing up at the plan, when the guard came back.

'What are you doing in here?'

'Looking for my phone.'

The guard smiled. 'What phone?'

'The one you just stole off me. And the other cameras too.'

'What cameras?'

The man stepped inside the cabin and locked the door behind him. 'You're a troublemaker, you are.'

'Hey,' said Zoë, anxious. 'Let me out.'

His smile was triumphant. 'You're the one who wanted to come in here in the first place.'

'You can't keep me in here. You've no right.'

'Who says?' he asked, and Zoë could smell the sweat on him.

The wine bar was on Church Street in the old town. They paused outside the window. Jill checked her watch. 'Twenty minutes late. That's not that bad, is it?'

There were couples, sharing olives and canapés; a group of young women sharing a jug of Pimms. Only one man sat alone at a table. He was dressed in a blue jacket and new white T-shirt; his black hair was gelled but not so much that he looked like he was trying too hard.

'You think that's him?'

'Not bad,' said Alex. 'If I'm honest, a little better than in the picture.'

The man looked up, saw the two women in the window, raised his eyebrows quizzically.

Alex pointed at Jill and nodded, as if to say, 'This is the woman you've been waiting for, just in case you're disappointed.' His smile was quite nice too, actually, she thought.

'Sorry I'm late,' said Jill when she was inside. 'This is my . . . my friend Alex. She's just dropping me off . . .'

' . . . to make sure I'm not an axe murderer.' Harry stood to greet them.

'Are you?' asked Alex.

'And now she's leaving,' said Jill.

'You wouldn't like a drink before you go?' Harry asked Alex. He was older than Jill; maybe in his early thirties she guessed. A small hint of grey among the black.

'She's driving,' said Jill. 'Aren't you?'

'Shame,' said Harry, standing to go to the bar.

'I know. But she has a daughter to get home to – don't you?'

'I could stay for a quick one, just to make sure you're safe,' said Alex. Joking, of course, but at that point, her phone vibrated. She expected it to be McAdam calling about the body in the freezer, but instead it was a number she didn't recognise.

She swiped the screen.

A man's voice. 'Mrs Cupidi? Um. It's about your daughter . . . I'm a friend of hers. Something's happened.'

'Nothing wrong, I hope?' asked Harry.

'Oh dear,' said Jill. 'What a shame. Do you need to go?'

SEVEN

The badger hesitates at the entrance to the sett and sniffs. Everything is smell; smell is everything.

There are six badgers in the group. Two sows, two males and two cubs. The older of the two sows has passed this way recently. This February she gave birth to a single cub, but the younger female killed it; ate it too, probably. It was the way things are. Even in a good year, a sett can only raise a few babies, and this year she was not the fortunate one.

The two cubs have been out playing with their mother. He can smell they have been here, though they are probably safe below now.

He recognises the bitter scent of foxes, too. They are no danger at all. A fox would never be foolish enough to bother a badger, though the vixen has her own babies too in her earth on the other side of the ash trees, and would chase badgers away if they came close.

And of course he smells the humans too. They have been around.

As he emerges cautiously, the younger male, fat and confident, trots over, sniffs. The older badger reciprocates, sniffs back and is rewarded with the reek of freshly chewed worms on the younger male's breath, which makes him even hungrier.

There is something dangerous about this younger one's scent. A warning of more fights to come. The older one has had fights in his day and old scars to prove it, places where the bristles are no longer dark. He must avoid fighting now. He is not as strong as he was.

Sensing this, the younger male turns and rubs his back flank against him, imprinting him with his smell. It's a stamp of his dominance.

Losing a fight is too much to contemplate. The badger is too tired, too old, too hungry. So he grunts quietly and moves on.

This is home; but home is changing.

He sets off to find food, but discovers old pathways have been blocked. The new fences themselves are not a problem. They are diggers. They ignore fences. They can always go under. Build roads, they'll cross them. Build walls, they'll find a way through.

The only way to stop a badger going somewhere you don't want it to is, basically, to kill it.

In the darkening evening, he travels alongside the fence, where other badgers have left their scent. Sure enough, he finds a hole, a place where the wire has been parted.

This is new. This hole was not there yesterday.

As he pushes through the hole, he smells humans, too, on

the wire. They have been this way as well, using this fresh new track.

Humans crawling through holes. This too is new.

He gives a shiver, grunts, but only pauses for a second out here in the open. It is early summer. He is hungry.

EIGHT

By the time Alex got to the site at Whiteland Fields it was getting dark. A rather mournful-looking young man in a green army jacket sat on the grass outside the site office.

'Was it you that called me?' demanded Alex.

The young man stood, unfolding himself slowly. 'You Zoë's mum?'

'Are you her boyfriend?'

'No,' he said a bit too suddenly. 'I mean . . .' Under the long hair, he seemed to blush.

'Is she in there?'

He nodded.

'What happened?'

'He nicked our gear. She wanted it back, that's all.'

'What gear?'

'Cameras for filming wildlife. We've been doing it a few days.'

The office was a Portakabin installed at the gates, three metal steps leading up to a closed door. She tried the handle, then knocked.

'If you don't get lost, I'll call the police,' said a voice.

'No need,' said Alex, knocking again.

The security guard yanked the door open. 'What?'

'My name is Alexandra Cupidi. I'm that girl's mother,' she said, pointing past him towards the seventeen-year-old girl behind him.

'So you going to pay for the criminal damage she caused, then?'

'What damage?'

The guard looked Alex up and down, then disappeared back into the site office, re-emerging with a black torch. 'I'll show you.'

'Wait in the car,' Alex told her daughter and the stringy young man.

Walking with the swing of a man who felt he owned the air around him, he led Alex up the lane, following the fence until the line of posts turned a corner away into the scrubland.

'Here.' He shone the torch at the bottom of the fence, where the links had been parted to make a hole about a metre wide.

'Did you see them do it?'

'No. I found these, though.' He dug in his pocket and pulled out a pair of blue-handled wire-cutters. They looked new, barely used.

She looked at them for a second, then said, 'So you didn't see them do it?'

'Not actually see them . . . no.'

'Did you see them with those?' She pointed at the tool.

'No. But I'm sure the police would be interested.'

Somewhere close, a large animal rustled in the undergrowth, as if panicked by their voices. Alex peered into the blackness, but could see nothing.

'Doubt it,' she said. 'Not these days, with all the cuts. They say you've stolen two trail cameras. And an iPhone.'

'That's bollocks.' The guard switched off the torch. 'And they know it. They were pestering me about that yesterday. But I haven't seen any cameras around here.'

'Two trail cameras, apparently about a hundred and fifty pounds' worth each.'

'Never seen them.'

'And the iPhone?'

The guard paused. Alex pulled out her own phone and showed him the screen. The blue dot of Zoë's iPhone pulsed gently on the map.

'They were filming me without permission.'

Alex asked, 'And have they shared the film for criminal or terrorist purposes?'

'What you mean?'

'Because if they haven't, then they were completely in their rights. The only crime I can see that's taken place here that would stand up to any scrutiny is the theft of an iPhone and several trail cameras. Go ahead, call the police.'

'What are you?' he scoffed. 'A lawyer?'

'No,' said Alex, peering into the undergrowth. 'I'm a detective sergeant. Can I borrow your torch?'

Less certain of himself, the man handed it over and Alex pointed it away from the fence, towards a low, dark copse.

Two eyes shone back. Then the head turned and the large, dark creature waddled away.

NINE

'That guard. He's lying. He would have sold my phone too if you hadn't turned up.'

'You don't know that, Zoë.' Alex handed her daughter back her iPhone. 'He says he doesn't know anything about the other cameras.'

Jay snorted.

Alex dropped him at the nearest bus stop, then drove down the long, straight road to the headland, lights on full beam.

Zoë made a face. 'Bill's going to be mad. I promised we wouldn't lose them. They were, like, top-of-the-range ones.'

'I thought they were your boyfriend's.'

'He's not my boyfriend, Mum,' said Zoë angrily. 'We borrowed one off William South and another off his friend Vinnie.'

'Oh, Zoë. And you just left them out there, unattended?'

'They're wildlife cameras. That's what you're supposed to do with them.'

'What were you filming with them?'

'Foxes, pine martens, badgers, toads. Anything that moved. Why do you think they've fenced off that land?'

'To stop people going on it?'

'Probably so they can get rid of anything rare, Mum, without anyone noticing. That's what developers do. All the time. We've been trying to record what's there so they can't. There's a bunch of us been doing it.'

'Oh please. It's a massive development. They wouldn't risk doing something illegal.'

'Considering you're a cop, Mum, you're so naive.'

Her seventeen-year-old daughter was obsessed with wildlife. It had started with birds, now it was pretty much anything that grew or crawled. She wrote lists. She took photographs. She made detailed maps and notes, comparing what she'd found with other enthusiasts. She went on protests and signed petitions. Alex had once opened a Tupperware box in the fridge to find a dead vole inside, put there by Zoë, who said she had wanted to study it later.

They drove through open marsh, past the deep water of the old pits. The English Channel lay ahead of them, beyond the wide stretches of shingle.

'Definitely not your boyfriend?'

'You have got to be joking. I'm not into boys.'

'What about girls then?'

'Mum!'

'Well, I don't know. You never talk to me about that stuff.'

'Why do you think that is?' Muttering now.

At the Pilot Inn, the car turned right into the private estate of Dungeness, onto a foreshore littered with dozens of old cabins, converted railway carriages and huts. Only a few of their windows were lit. Rising above the ramshackle buildings, the silhouette of two lighthouses, one old, dark and sturdy, the other made from concrete, new and functional, lit from beneath to show its black-and-white bands. Beyond that, the bright industrial bulk of the nuclear power station, incongruously vast on the wild shoreline. Dungeness B was venting steam, which drifted inshore, a dramatic pale cloud illuminated from beneath by the hundreds of sodium lights that covered the nuclear site.

The track narrowed as it approached the power station, turning to the north alongside the fence dotted with signs: *Nuclear Installations Act 1965. Licensed Site Boundary.*

A little way along the track sat a small cabin, its planks woodstained red. Alex stopped outside it.

'Maybe we should tell him in the morning,' said Zoë.

'We?'

'Aren't you coming in?'

'You lost them. You need to tell him.'

'I didn't lose them. They were stolen.'

Arum Cottage was where William South lived. It was a small, low bungalow that sat just outside the fence. Once the views it would have had across the flat shingle to the sea would have been magnificent. Now they were obscured by the power station.

Alex switched off the car's engine and got out, walking behind her daughter.

William South must have heard them. He opened the door before she reached it. Alex didn't like beards much, but the one William South had been growing since his return to Dungeness suited him, even if the salt-and-pepper hair was just an attempt to make himself more anonymous.

He smiled when he saw Zoë, then saw that she wasn't smiling back. 'What's wrong?'

'You know those cameras you and Vinnie lent me?'

'Oh.' Was all he said.

The small shack smelt of garlic. He was cooking mussels.

He put some more in the pot for Alex, and dug out some more oven chips for her vegan daughter.

'So you think they stole them?'

'He tried to nick my iPhone too,' said Zoë. 'Mum had to get it back off him.'

'But he didn't admit to the cameras?'

'Stands to reason. You can trace an iPhone, can't you?' said Zoë, dipping a chip in ketchup. 'He knew he couldn't get away with that.'

Alex would have very much liked to be drinking one of those nice glasses of white wine that Jill would probably be consuming now, but Bill South had gone dry. After leaving prison, he had become too fond of drink; now he had given it up completely. He no longer kept it in the house. Even the mussels weren't cooked in wine.

'I'll pay for them, I promise,' said Zoë.

'With what?' her mother asked.

'Gran gave me money.'

'That was for when you go to university.'

'I don't want to go to university anyway.' Before her mother could object, she turned to Bill. 'I saw the drawings. They were on the walls of the security man's place. It's going to be hundreds and hundreds of houses.'

'Plan's going to the council next week,' said Bill, pulling a mussel from its shell, then dropping the remains onto the growing pile in the bowl in the middle of the table. 'We'll probably be getting quite a bit of work out of it.' Bill had found work with an ecological survey company, counting species on sites which were about to be developed. He said the work suited him.

'That's hypocritical. You shouldn't do it,' said Zoë. 'You're helping them destroy the environment.'

'What if we find something rare on there? Nightingales.'

'You know there's no nightingales there. Even if there were, they'd probably bulldoze it. You're just being paid to rubber-stamp it.'

Alex waited until he had left the table to go outside to empty the bowl of shells onto the shingle, then said quietly to her daughter, 'You're being rude. It's his job.'

Bill returned. 'Want a cup of tea?' called Bill from the kitchen.

'It's true, though.'

'What is?' Bill asked, teapot in his hand.

'Mum said I was being rude.'

Bill shrugged. 'Zoë's right. Mostly they just build the houses anyway. The best we can do is to stop it being too bad.'

'There's a badger sett there. It might have been there hundreds of years,' said Zoë. 'What right do we have to destroy it?'

'We'd move the sett,' said Bill. 'Relocate it somewhere else. It can happen with a licence.'

'I can move homeless people on, I don't need a licence for

41

that, but I'd need a licence to move a badger,' said Alex. 'Keeps you in your new job, though.'

Bill looked down at the table. 'Law's the law. Isn't that what you say? Same as when you put me inside.'

'Yeah, Mum.' There was an accusatory tone in her daughter's voice.

Alex held up her hands in self-defence. 'Can we drop it?'

After a second of silence, Bill continued. 'They're a protected species. Illegal to hunt them. Illegal to disturb their setts. First we get a licence. But that's the easy bit. It takes months to make the move. We have to map the sett, find a new location where they're not going to infringe on any other badger territories, build a new one in a safe place, and then begin the process of trying to move the badgers to it, so—'

'Don't you miss being a copper sometimes, Bill?'

'Mum!' said Zoë. 'You said *I* was being rude.'

He turned to look at Alex. 'Not so much, to be honest.'

Another awkward pause. It was because of Alex he wasn't a copper any more. She was the one who had investigated him and arrested him; she was why he'd gone to prison and lost his job as an officer.

Later, when they were at the door to go home, Zoë said, 'I'll get the cameras back off him, I promise. And if I don't, I'll pay for them, I swear.'

'I'll put them on the house insurance,' said Bill. 'Say someone broke in. They'll believe me. Police round here are useless.'

'Mum will probably arrest you again,' said Zoë.

Bill snorted quietly, but said nothing.

*

42

Though it was only a hundred metres or so further up the track to their house, Alex drove the car there. Deep in the heart of the sunken woods out to the west, strange lights glowed among the stunted trees. Trapping moths, Zoë had explained, the first time Alex had seen them. At this time of year the place was crawling with them both: nature-lovers and moths.

Alex pulled up outside their house, one in a long line of solid-looking brick cottages that had been built here a century earlier by the navy. Now, fewer people seemed to live in them permenantly. Some had been bought as holiday homes. Others were rented out. The one at the end was a hostel for birders; that one was always busy.

'I worry about him, that's all. I think he's a bit lost,' said Alex as she locked the car.

'Shame you didn't worry about him before.'

Alex knew better than to argue. 'Promise you won't try and get those cameras back?'

Zoë got out and let herself into the house without saying anything.

PART TWO

TEN

'So?' said DS Cupidi.

Monday morning, back at work.

'What do you mean, "so"?' Jill said. She was driving to an address in Rye where they were going to interview a witness who had found the body of an unidentified dead man in a freezer.

'So . . . Harry, obviously.'

Jill looked up and whistled, little-girl-innocent.

'You didn't? On a first date?' demanded Alex.

'Do you think it was too early?'

'You slut.'

Jill's laugh was a nice, big-bellied one. It was good to see her happy again, thought Alex. Her experience with men had not been great. 'Oh God,' Jill said as the lights changed. 'Maybe he thinks I'm a slut too. Do you think I've put him off?'

'Because men are really put off by good-looking women who enjoy sex.'

'But he's really classy, you know? He wasn't pushy at all.'

'So the sex was all your idea?'

'You think I'm a slag?'

'No. Just envious. His place or yours?'

'His. It's gorgeous. He had this penthouse flat near the Quarterhouse.'

Rye was a pretty little medieval town; all cobbles and tiles, small streets and posh shops, but the part they were driving to was a less than pretty housing estate to the west of the old town. They were going to interview a man called Gram about a body he had found in a freezer in a locked room. The crime scene investigators had said there were no signs of forced entry.

'Harry was really nice and gentle. And he has really nice wrists.'

'Enough, Jill.'

The body had been frozen; they had no way of knowing how long it had been there.

'Gram Hickman. What kind of a name is Gram, anyway?' asked Jill.

'What's got me is that Gram says he discovered the body on his own.'

'Gram sounds like a drug dealer's name.'

Alex checked the map on her phone. 'Next left. What does he do, this Harry of yours?'

'He's not "of mine". He's a property developer.'

'So he's well off?'

'Oh God yeah.' The constable grinned. 'Stinking.'

Alex did feel a little jealous. Not of her having a boyfriend, or of him being rich or good-looking. Just because Jill had finally found someone, the kind she had always wanted, and now she would want to spend her time hanging out with him. Alex didn't get on well with that many people in Kent Serious Crime; the young constable was the one real friend she'd made in the force in the two years since she'd moved from London – apart from Bill South, and their relationship had never been the same since she'd been the one responsible for putting him in prison.

They pulled up outside a former council house. The red-brick buildings in this street all looked identical except for the front doors; they had all been upgraded, mostly in white PVC. Gram's one was dark wood, with a brass-effect knocker.

'Gram. Is Gram short for Graham?' Jill asked the young man who was boiling the kettle.

'No. My dad was a music fan. Gram Parsons?'

'Your dad's name was Gram too?' Jill blinked.

'No. Gram Parsons. The musician. My dad liked him. That's what I was christened.'

'Sorry. Never heard of him.' Jill shook her head.

'My mother too,' said Alex. 'She's crazy about all that twangy stuff.'

'Apparently he died of a drug overdose in the seventies,' said the young man called Gram. 'Not much of a role model exactly.' The young man was good-looking in a boy-band kind of way, his dark hair swept across the forehead. He put down two cups of tea on the table. Jill had hers black; no dairy.

Alex picked up her cup. 'So you're off work, your boss said?'

'Is that how he put it? Truth is, he gave me the sack.'

Jill left her tea on the table. The cup was old and chipped, and she was fussy. 'Don't suppose you left him a lot of choice, breaking into a client's house.'

'It wasn't like I was planning to trash the place,' Gram said.

It was a shared kitchen. A note, pinned to the fridge with a magnet, read: *Whoever is stealing my yogurt BUY YOUR OWN.*

'So why were you in there?' Jill frowned.

The young man looked away. 'Just wanted to look around.'

'Seriously?'

'I don't know. I just like the place.'

Jill leaned forward conspiratorially. 'Are you sure you didn't go in to nick something?'

'No!'

Alex tutted.

Gram turned to look at her, spooked. 'What?'

She smiled. 'You're a really awful liar.'

The man coloured. Looked away again. 'It's the truth.'

'Oh really?'

The man nodded.

'OK.' Alex shrugged, and stood. 'Odd thing to do. Just go to a house to look at it.'

'Isn't it?' said Jill.

'A house that happens to have a dead body in it.'

Gram smiled nervously. 'I didn't know that, did I?'

Alex put her cup down, half drunk. 'And we believe that because . . . ?'

Gram looked uncomfortable. 'Look. I was the one who phoned you, remember? I was a responsible citizen. I could have just left the body there and walked out.'

'That's one plausible explanation of your behaviour,' said Alex. 'Though others are available.'

He was lifting his own cup to his lips to drink but seemed to miss, sloshing tea onto his shirt. 'You don't seriously think . . . ?'

As he stood and went to the sink to find a cloth to wipe himself down with, Alex winked at Jill who was trying her hardest to keep a straight face. *Told you*, Jill mouthed.

'Of course we seriously think,' said Alex. 'It's kind of our job.'

'Look. Just don't tell anyone, OK?' said the man, miserably. He turned. 'I promised I wouldn't tell anyone she was there.'

'Oh!' said Alex, with the grace to act as if this was all a surprise.

And the young man told them about why he had really gone to the house. 'You'll need her name?'

'Yes.'

'You sure? She teaches in secondary. She's kind of worried that this will get out.'

'She's a witness. We'll need her name.'

'She'll kill me.'

'So you took the key from your office and used it to access the property?' Alex asked him.

Gram nodded. 'Borrowed.'

'Bit naughty, isn't it?'

'Not like I'm the first estate agent to do it.'

They had found a broken bottle of Prosecco in the bin outside. It hadn't been that hard to guess the rest. 'So it's easy to do?' Alex asked. 'Borrow a key.'

'I mean, as long as you don't find a dead body in the freezer.'

'So other people from the estate agency could have got into that building?'

'I suppose.'

'You can just take the keys? You don't have to write it down anywhere?' demanded Jill.

'You're supposed to. The point is, no one's going to know if you didn't. They've all done it. I was just the one who found a dead body.'

'How did you know how to switch off the alarm?'

'It's always in the notes.'

Alex leaned down, picked up her shoulder bag, dug out a small police notebook and wrote down some details while the young man looked on anxiously. When she'd finished, she looked at what she had written. She had underlined 'They've all done it'. Twice.

'You didn't recognise him?'

'Jesus, no. I mean . . . I hardly looked. I just shut the lid, moment I saw him.'

'The garage door was definitely locked?'

'Yes.'

'Who else do you think might have taken the keys, then? Apart from yourself,' she asked.

'Well, no one's going to admit to it, are they?' said Gram. 'Obviously. Looks bad enough for them, me getting caught doing it, doesn't it?'

ELEVEN

Alex recognised the figure standing by the road into Lydd long before she was close enough to see her face. She slowed the car.

There was something about the way she stood: fragilely thin, but chin held slightly up, as if to say, 'So?'

Alex pulled up alongside her, and wound down a window.

'Are you spying on me?' demanded her daughter. She was standing on the verge between the road and the new fence that surrounded Whiteland Fields.

'I was just coming back from work. Thought I'd drive by to take a look at the place in daylight.'

'Why?'

Alex didn't answer because she wasn't sure herself. 'What are you doing here?'

'Nothing.'

'Nothing?' Alex glanced down the road towards the security guard's cabin.

Her daughter looked down at her own skinny legs. 'I was going to go in and try and survey the badgers.'

'On your own?'

'I asked Jay, but he says he's going to see a movie.'

'Lightweight.'

'They nicked the cameras to try and stop us.'

'Don't be daft. We don't know who stole them. You'll get into trouble with that guard again.'

'He won't see me. It'll be getting dark in a while. He just sits in his cabin watching telly all the time.'

'You don't have to save the world all on your own, though, love. Bill South pretty much said his company would be doing all this as part of the planning process.'

'But what if they really are planning on digging them all out first? It happens, you know. Why else did they fence it all off?'

Alex stared at her daughter. Often she puzzled her. As a younger woman, she had never imagined having children, and now she had one, she was always surprised by it. Especially to find herself the mother of this strange and fierce girl. She was so unlike other teenagers she knew. Around her neck hung the binoculars she had given her for her sixteenth birthday.

'Sure you don't want a ride home? I'll cook something.'

'It's OK. I can walk.'

They were four miles from home. The lanes here were dark, and the locals drove fast down them. Alex would worry. 'I can wait.'

Zoë looked away and said, 'If you want.'

'Maybe I could help you?'

Zoë snorted.

'What's so funny? You never know. I might enjoy it.'

'You'd be trespassing, for a start. You're a police officer. You'd never break the law, would you?'

'You have to go in there? Can't you see them from out here? With those?'

'You have to get close if you don't have a camera.'

Alex looked along the length of the fence. 'How do you get in?'

Zoë looked away. 'They haven't fixed the hole in the fence yet. I checked.'

'The hole that someone deliberately made.'

'We just found it,' said Zoë, but she was trying not to smile as she answered.

'Course you did. What if I come back later? I can pick you up then.'

'If you like.'

Zoë turned away, raised the binoculars to her eyes. Some bird in the far distance had attracted her attention.

'Make it nine,' she said, without lowering them.

'Be careful, won't you, love?'

Her daughter didn't answer. Alex started the engine and drove away. When she looked in the rear-view mirror, the teenage girl had already disappeared from view.

Alex pulled up at the Pilot and ordered fish and chips. She took it outside and sat on one of the old wooden picnic tables, watching container ships creep along the horizon. The summer was beginning. There would be tourists here soon. It was nice to have the place to themselves for now, at least.

The sun had already dropped behind the power station when one of the locals joined her, a pint of lager in his hand. He nodded, then silently sat a few feet away.

'Been fishing, Curly?' she asked.

He shook his head, pulled out a cigarette and lit it without asking if it bothered her.

Curly was one of the handful of fishermen who still ran inshore boats off this beach, though he spent more time tinkering with his trawler than he did out on the water.

He smoked the cigarette in silence. When he'd finished it, he drained his pint and disappeared without saying anything.

When she went into the pub to return her empty plate, Curly was sat alone at the far end of the bar and already at the bottom of his next pint.

'What's wrong with him?' asked Alex.

The woman behind the bar was in her twenties. 'What's wrong with him is that he's a miserable fart.' She put some dirty glasses into the dishwasher. 'Plus, somebody just told him that the house on the beach that he grew up in is on the market.'

'Oh,' said Alex, who knew the one she was talking about. One of the squarer-looking bungalows on the north side of the track, made from board, with a black tin roof.

'Don't know why he gives a toss. It's not even his. His dad sold it years ago.'

Curly had always called it 'our house', despite the fact that, as the barmaid said, his family hadn't lived there for over thirty years.

'How much is it on for?'

'Three hundred grand,' she said. 'Practically falling apart.

You'd have to pay me that to live out there. Don't know why he's so fussed. He's got a cosy little place up at Greatstone.'

Alex glanced down the bar. Curly was staring into his empty glass. 'It's just the idea of it, I expect,' she said. 'Rich people being able to buy it just like that.'

'Welcome to it, ask me,' said the young woman.

Alex rolled along the road slowly in the darkness until the pale figure of her daughter showed up, her face white in the headlights.

'See what you wanted?'

Zoë nodded. 'Yeah,' she said, buckling her seatbelt.

Alex moved off. 'You saw badgers?'

She was shivering, Alex realised, turning up the heating. It must have been cold, lying out there in the long grass.

'Six,' she said eventually. 'Two cubs. Watched this old one for a bit, and he was digging out earth.'

'How do you know he was old?'

'He had old scars on his back. They fight, sometimes. Only way you can really tell most of them apart.'

'So that's useful? If they try and move the badgers, you can show evidence that there were some there?'

Again she nodded. 'Maybe. Better if I'd had them on camera, though.'

She didn't seem particularly excited. She was more preoccupied.

'Anything wrong?'

Zoë shook her head. 'Actually. Can we stop in Lydd a minute?'

'Why?'

'I want to tell Vinnie about it.'

57

'Aren't you hungry?' Then: 'Vinnie who?'

'The one I borrowed the camera from. He studies badgers. And he's part of the protest. I want to tell him I saw them there.'

Alex sighed. Zoë gave directions to a narrow street on the south side of the town's big church. She told her to stop outside a small terraced house covered in white weatherboards. 'Are you going to be long?'

'I can walk home,' Zoë said, knowing what her mother would answer.

'I'll wait outside.' She watched her daughter, dressed in combat shorts and jacket, get out and ring the doorbell. There were no lights in the house; none came on.

The window that gave out onto the street had a poster in it: *Say NO to Whiteland Fields Development.*

Zoë rang the bell again, shrugged, and got back in the car.

'Not in,' she said.

'Leave a message.'

'Already did. Called him earlier. He's not answering.'

As Alex drove out of the town, she noticed more of the posters. They seemed to be everywhere. Zoë was silent as they drove on towards the sea. Only when they reached the Dungeness estate did she speak again.

'Mum. They were watching me,' said Zoë.

'What do you mean?'

'While I was out there, there were people watching me.'

Alex slowed. A rabbit was sat in the middle of the track ahead of them, eyes pink in the headlights. It made no attempt to move. 'What sort of people?'

'Them. The same people that stole the cameras.'

58

'Did you see them?'

'Not exactly. But I know they were there.'

'You didn't see them?' She stopped the car.

'You're in another world, Mum. These people exist. They're watching us.'

Alex switched the headlights off. 'Who are they, then?'

'The government, probably. Agencies.'

'Jesus, Zoë.'

'Stop laughing. It's real.' Crossing her arms tightly, tightening her lips, Zoë had clammed up.

Sometimes it wasn't just the people her daughter hung around with that worried Alex.

TWELVE

'How blue?' Jill asked, looking at the black-and-white photo of the face of the dead man. 'Blue like in *Avatar*?'

Alex was at the wheel for a change, driving to Canterbury to interview the owner of the house where the body had been found in the freezer. 'Never seen *Avatar*,' she said.

'What do you mean, you've never seen it? Aliens who are deep blue and have these huge eyes. Everybody's seen it. Don't know why, it's boring as hell, even in 3D.'

'No. Not like that. Just a faint pale blue, under the skin.' The victim's lips had been blue, his skin an unusual pink.

'Is that suffocation?'

Alex followed the satnav around a roundabout. 'The pathologist said it was possibly a symptom of poisoning. They won't know for sure for a couple of days. Same as with the time of death. They're still defrosting him.'

'Ugh.'

Jill's phone buzzed.

'Him again?' said Alex.

Jill grinned. 'As it happens.'

'Keen.'

'Too keen, do you think?'

Alex shrugged as Jill examined her phone. 'He wants to know if I want to go to the opera. I've never been to an opera in my life.'

'You should go, then.'

'What if I hate it? He'll think I'm common.' She replaced the copy of the photo into the envelope and put it back in Alex's bag. The body in the freezer remained unidentified.

They parked in London Road in front of a large Georgian town house. A neat-looking woman in her sixties dressed in a grey Chanel suit opened the door. Alex held out her ID. 'Belinda Utting?'

She nodded. 'You'd better come in.'

Belinda Utting wore plain silver jewellery; a chain with an amber pendant, two small teardrop-shaped earrings. She led them into a large ground-floor living room and told them to wait there while she made tea. There was a wall of books, spines arranged by size and colour, coffee-table art books, respectable fiction and wide-looking biographies. A few landscape oil paintings. A silver-framed photograph of a younger-looking Belinda Utting and a man, standing next to Prince Philip and the Queen like they were old friends.

Jill peered at it. 'Oh my God. Is that . . . ?'

'Mr Utting. Yes.' Alex looked over her shoulder.

'No. I meant . . . Oh, very funny. He's dead, isn't he? Her husband.'

'Several weeks ago, of a brain haemorrhage. He was something big in the judiciary, I read. *Sir* Andrew Utting, not Mr. I wonder if that's why she put the house on the market. She probably didn't like living alone in that big house.'

'She must be minted if that one's still for sale and she can afford this. If he's a Sir, does that make her something too?'

Belinda returned with a wooden tray, mugs of tea, and a plate of biscuits. 'I find it all quite upsetting,' she said. 'Do you know who he is yet, the man in my freezer?'

'I'm afraid we don't.' Male, mid-forties, as yet unidentified. No obvious signs of a struggle on the skin, no bruises, no abrasions. No tattoos. Minor scars on his hands. May have been some kind of manual labourer. No matches on the Missing Persons database.

'We were wondering if you might recognise him,' said Jill.

'Oh.' Belinda picked up a jug. 'You want me to go and see him?'

'We have a photo.' Alex pulled the envelope out of her bag and showed it to her.

'Milk?' asked Belinda, peering at the picture. 'No. Don't recognise him, I'm afraid.'

'You sure?' Alex watched her face for any signs; all she could see in it was the sad smile, a patrician sympathy for the dead.

'Poor man. Not from the photo. But it's hard to tell. I could look at him if you like. I don't mind that kind of thing. I used to be a doctor in a former life.' She handed each a cup of tea, then offered round the biscuits.

'The estate agents tell me the house isn't selling because of Brexit, which is simply ridiculous.' She handed back the photograph, and took a biscuit herself. 'I may well also take legal action.'

'The body appears to have been placed in the house by someone who had a key.'

'Exactly,' said Belinda.

'You think it would have been someone from the estate agency?' interrupted Alex.

'Well, who else could it have been?'

'No one else has keys?' Jill resumed the conversation.

'Obviously I have a key. The gardener has a key to the garage, I suppose, but it couldn't be him.'

'So they could have got in via the garage door?'

She took the tiniest bite from her biscuit. 'I suppose. But they'd have had to know how to turn off the alarm, even then.'

Alex looked at her. 'So whoever put the body in the freezer would have had to have known the code?'

'Obviously. Yes.'

'And where do you keep your set of keys?'

'In my dressing-table drawer.'

'Check that they are there, please,' Alex said.

The woman frowned, then left the room and returned with them two minutes later. 'Here,' she said. 'What was that young man from the estate agency doing there in the evening anyway?'

'We believe he was trying to impress a young woman,' Alex said.

Belinda Utting snorted.

'This is a beautiful house,' Jill said.

Alex looked around the carefully ordered room. 'Two beautiful houses, in fact. One in Rye, one here.'

'My husband preferred the countryside. I favour the town. We are lucky to have been able to have one foot in each.'

'You lived separate lives?' Alex asked.

Belinda Utting tightened slightly. 'We just preferred to live like this. Separate, but together.'

'How separate? He may have had friends who used the house that you didn't know about?'

'Of course not,' she said, frostily. 'Are we finished?'

Back in the car, Jill said, 'If her husband had been a Sir, shouldn't we have been calling her "Dame" or something?'

'Probably,' said Alex.

'Only, I've never met a Dame before,' said Jill. 'I'm a bit embarrassed now. I feel like I was doing it wrong.'

Alex ignored her. Traffic had built up on the M2, and they had to be at the HQ in Maidstone for a team meeting on data management, which nobody wanted to be at anyway.

The meeting made a long afternoon longer. The house in Dungeness was empty when she got home; it was dark.

She called Zoë's mobile but there was no answer.

Fixing herself a salad from the fridge, she took the photograph of the dead man's face out of the envelope and stared at it. The Dame had clearly not recognised it.

She tried to figure out what the dead man told her. A good-looking face that gave no clues of why somebody might have murdered him.

A blob of dressing flicked from a spinach leaf onto the photo. She stood, found a piece of kitchen roll and tried to wipe it off, but it left a long smear on the shiny surface.

Her phone buzzed.

Trapping moths with Bill by the sunken woods. Come see.

Alex walked into the night outside. It was easy to see where her daughter was from the shine of electric light from the moth traps. The two of them were sat on the shingle by one of the devices, bright faces lit in the blackness around them.

Approaching the two, boots crunching on the ground, she peered inside the traps, and saw, under the perspex cover, a dark moving mass of bugs, fluttering and crawling on the empty egg boxes that lined the bottom, put there to give the trapped insects somewhere to settle. She shivered. Her daughter dipped into the trap, caught one and sealed the lid of the small plastic jar, then picked up a lens to examine it with.

'Having a good time?' asked Alex.

Moths were everywhere. They crawled on her daughter's clothes, on her face and in her hair. The evening was still and warm. 'Like they're all out for a big party,' said William South.

A tiny one landed on Alex's hand, then another. She felt their legs crawling on her skin and resisted the urge to brush them off her.

'Look,' her daughter said, holding up the small jar for her to peer into. Crawling inside, a smallish moth the colour of bright green moss.

'Sussex emerald,' said Zoë.

'You sure?' said South.

'Yeah. Look.' She handed the older man the jar and said, 'It's very rare. You only find it here in Dungeness.'

'Really?'

'Yes. You can find them on the Continent, but this is the only place in Britain where they breed.'

Alex looked at it through the perspex.

'Beautiful,' said South, holding the jar in the light. 'Isn't it?'

Alex looked at him. 'I thought it was just birds you were into?'

'Birds are just the gateway drug,' Zoë said.

'I could do my kitchen that colour,' Alex said, looking at the green of the moth. 'How's work, Bill?'

'Busy, busy, busy. Always new places being concreted over.'

'Don't,' said Zoë.

When they finally switched off the lamp, the land they stood in seemed to vanish.

Alex shivered, felt suddenly cold. 'Hot chocolate?' she said.

'Go home,' South told Zoë. 'I'll pack up the lamps.'

She was in the kitchen, heating almond milk for Zoë, when an old Beastie Boys song came on the radio and she turned it up and started dancing to it, relishing its joyous stupidity.

It took her a while before she realised that someone was shouting.

She turned down the volume.

'Mum!'

There was something wrong.

She put her head around the living-room door and saw Zoë holding a piece of paper. It took her a moment to realise that it was the photograph of the drawing of the dead man.

'What's happened?'

Zoë's face was pale. She knew enough about her mother's work to understand what a photo like this would mean.

'Do you recognise him, Zoë?'

There was a loud hiss as the milk boiled over onto the cooker, and Alex dashed back out to the kitchen to stop it burning on the hob.

THIRTEEN

It has been a dry, cold spring.

In dry weather, the worms go deeper. The badgers forage for bugs, widen their search for food or go hungry.

In the chamber further down the tunnel, the older one can hear the cubs complaining.

Tonight, nose raised, the badger samples the air outside the new entrance he has dug.

He smells a scent that should not be there. Another male badger is in the territory. He recognises it; one from the neighbouring group has trespassed onto their land in his own search of food.

Badgers fight fiercely to protect their home. While other mammals have been hunted to extinction here – the bears and the wolves – badgers are tenacious. They have held their ground; it's what they do. There will be fighting tonight. Territory must be protected.

But not by him. He is old. He turns and heads back into the safety of the earth.

FOURTEEN

They ran back into the darkness outside, holding the picture.

Bill South was standing in the dim light at the end of the row of houses, still shaking out the last of the moths from the boxes.

Alex held up the drawing. 'Do you recognise this man?'

South looked, then said, 'So he's dead, then?' Bill South was an ex-copper; he knew what a photo like this would mean.

'Yes.'

'I told you, Mum. I told you a million times. It's Vinnie Gibbons.'

'How was he killed?' asked South.

'We don't know yet. Did you know him well?'

'He was one of the people you'd see around, you know. Out and about. Not a big talker. But one of us – do you know what I mean? One of the people who got the bug young.'

'The bug?'

'Like Zoë. People who get into the world outside of TV and magazines.'

'I don't think young people have TV and magazines any more, Bill.'

'You know what I mean. People who find themselves in the natural world, not the artificial one.'

He set about carefully coiling the electric lead that had lit the traps, twisting each kink out as he turned, concentrating hard.

She watched him working. 'I'm sorry, Bill. About your friend.'

He nodded.

It was after midnight now. The three of them sat around the kitchen table, staring at Alex's laptop. 'It's him, definitely.'

In a Facebook photograph Vinnie Gibbons held a slice of pizza; there was a shyness about his smile.

'Told you, Mum,' said her daughter. Zoë looked shaken, her face white. She had put three sugars into the black tea that South had made for her.

'He's a naturalist,' said South. '*Was* a naturalist. Sometimes the company I work with employed him to help out. Only, he hasn't been answering his phone for a few days, and now we know why.'

'It was him who told me about that sett at Whiteland,' said Zoë.

'I'm sorry, love,' said Alex. She put her arm around her daughter.

'He was one of the first protestors against Whiteland Fields. Badgers were his thing.'

'He was involved in a big case involving baiters last year. We got a conviction out of it.' He still says 'we', thought Alex.

70

'He was planning to write a book about them, Mum. He thinks that badger trails and setts can be, like, really old. Badgers don't move for anything. They stay exactly where they are. They'll fight just to stay put.'

'I know people like that,' said Alex, looking at South, thinking of her mother.

'Mum,' Zoë chided. 'Vinnie's thing was that people used to think some setts were, like, maybe a hundred years old, but it's turning out that some are way older than that. Some are *hundreds* of years old. And he thought if he could map badger trails and setts, he could build a kind of map of the ancient landscape, where old woodlands used to be, and stuff like that.'

Alex said, 'That doesn't sound like a reason for someone wanting to kill him.'

'What happened to him?' South asked again.

'We're not sure, but it could have been poison.'

'Poison?' South blinked. 'So it was planned?'

He still thought like a policeman, thought Alex. 'We don't know enough to say yet.'

'This is nuts, this is really nuts,' said Zoë, rocking back- and -forwards on her chair. 'I knew him.'

Alex called her boss, DI McAdam, at seven in the morning with the victim's name and address.

'I'll be in at eight,' McAdam said.

Alex left her daughter still in bed and drove off with a slice of toast in her lap and a coffee in the cup holder. The road north took her out of Lydd, so she stopped at Gibbons's house, just

71

where she and Zoë had parked the night before, and looked in through the window, coffee in hand.

The curtains to the front room were open. On the window was the yellow poster. *Say NO to Whiteland Fields Development.* She peered inside. A small living room with a TV and a three-piece suite. Ordinary pictures on the walls. A forensic team would be arriving soon, to go through the place. Until they discovered where Gibbons had been murdered, it couldn't be ruled out as the scene of crime.

'You can't park there,' a woman's voice said.

Alex turned away from the window. A tall woman with a shopping trolley stood a couple of metres away.

'He's not in, anyway.'

'How do you know?'

'He's been gone a week,' the woman said. 'Without having the courtesy to tell anyone.' She had short grey hair, and lips that sat in a straight, red line.

'A week? How do you know?'

'Because my cat is dead and it's all his fault.'

Alex placed the cup on top of her car, lifted her wallet from her bag and showed her ID.

'Oh,' said the woman. 'Has something happened?'

Her name was Vera May, and she was his next-door neighbour but one. Vera had gone to visit a sister in Inverness. Her cat was old and didn't go out any more. Her lodger was away on business, so Vinnie Gibbons had promised to feed her cat and to clean the tray. When she got back two days ago, the cat was dead and there was no sign of Vinnie. 'And he's supposed to be the animal lover.'

'Do you have a key to his house?'

'Naturally. We are neighbours. Is everything OK?'

'I'm afraid not.'

She broke the news.

Vera May's mouth fell open. 'Now I feel awful.'

'That's your house there?' Alex pointed to another house, also with a protest poster in its window. 'Was Mr Gibbons very involved with the protest?'

'Of course he was. We all are. It's horrible. We will be swallowed up.'

'And does everyone here agree with you?'

Vera May drew back a little. 'What are you suggesting?'

'Did he have enemies?'

'Obviously the developers and everyone who supports them. There are people who will profit from this, and people who believe that it's fine to just build anywhere.'

'Was that what Mr Gibbons thought too? Not In My Back Yard?'

Mrs May's voice dropped a few notes. 'That's a very offensive label, Sergeant. This is not a back yard. This is a historic village whose origins go back to Roman times.'

'From my understanding, Mr Gibbons was more interested in the welfare of animals.'

'On the contrary. Mr Gibbons had a great interest in local history. He was as committed as we all are to keeping the barbarian from our gates.'

'Everything OK, Mrs M?' An unshaven man in running gear unplugged his headphones, stepping between Alex and Vera

73

May like a nightclub bouncer anticipating a fight. He looked around fifty, but in good shape. 'Having any trouble with this woman?'

Alex stepped towards him, holding up her warrant card. 'You knew Mr Gibbons too Mr . . . ?'

He studied her ID for a second, then stepped back, as if stung. 'Only through Vera. I'm her lodger.'

'Can I take your name?'

'What's this about?'

'Vincent Gibbons is dead, Richey,' said Vera May.

The man's mouth fell open. His name was Browne. 'Browne with an "e". First name Richard,' he said.

As Alex was taking Vera May's phone number, a constable arrived, parking next to her on the pavement. Vera May strode off towards his car to disapprove.

'You're local, Mr Browne?'

'Used to be. Thinking of moving back. Been in London twenty years. Come to stay a few weeks to see if I can cope with country life.'

'And how are you finding it?'

'Challenging.' He nodded towards Vera May, who was saying in a loud voice to the newly arrived police constable, 'You can't park there.'

'Know exactly what you mean,' said Alex. She turned to Vera May. 'Can you give this constable your key, Vera? We'll need access to Mr Gibbons's property.'

Neither of them would go in, though; he was just here to protect the place until a forensic team arrived. Alex left the constable on duty outside the house and got back in the car. The toast was cold on her passenger seat; she didn't feel like eating it.

The Facebook photo was projected onto the screen in the incident room when she entered, bag slung over her shoulder: Vinnie Gibbons, the slice of pizza, the shy smile. She abandoned thoughts of a fresh coffee and stared at it.

McAdam saw her standing there and approached. 'This isn't good. The pathologist confirms he was poisoned. It was hydrogen cyanide. He almost certainly breathed it in.'

'Zyklon B,' said Alex. 'Hydrogen cyanide. It's what the Nazis used.'

The half-dozen people looking at the screen all looked at her. 'What?'

'They dropped hydrogen cyanide into the showers at the concentration camps. It wasn't instantaneous; it would have been agonising.'

They were silent for a second. It confirmed that this was an unusual kind of violence; premeditated and cruel.

'I should tell you. My daughter had met the victim on one occasion. Do you want to rule me out of the investigation?'

'Did you ever meet him?' McAdam asked.

'No.'

'Do you want to recuse yourself?'

Alex looked at the photograph. 'Absolutely bloody not.'

McAdam nodded. 'The gas is most effective in a confined space. We need to find the crime scene. We've secured his house. We're waiting for a specialist unit to arrive to find out if that's where he was killed.'

Constable Ferriter arrived and looked at the face on the screen. 'That the man in the freezer?' she asked.

She was wearing a new gold necklace with 'J' for 'Jill' hanging from it.

'A local wildlife enthusiast. He lived in Lydd. Zoë seems to have known him fairly well.'

'Oh. She's upset?'

'Yes.'

Alex pointed at her new jewellery. 'Harry been buying you presents?'

'God's sake,' Jill protested. 'It's not that serious.'

'I'm going to find a coffee. Want something?'

'God, yeah.'

'Hungover?'

'I think I fell asleep, too, in the third act.'

But before she could leave for the coffee, one of the civilian staff who had been going through the records stood up and called across the room, 'Alex? You should see this.'

Alex weaved through the chairs and desks over to the workstation. The young woman was peering at a computer screen.

'Vincent Gibbons of New Street, Lydd?' she said.

'Has he got a record?'

'Er . . . no. The opposite. I just found him on a search. Vincent Gibbons. He was a key witness in a case we brought last year.'

Alex peered at the screen. She had found an online newspaper report: *Convicted Badger Baiter Faces Jail*:

> Kent farm worker Francis Collins, 46, has been convicted of offences including causing a badger to suffer

and keeping premises for an animal fight. He has also been disqualified from keeping dogs. A second man, Julian Epps, was acquitted of all charges. Local man Vincent Gibbons, who had witnessed the initial incident and reported it to the police, told the court he had come across the men who were digging up a badger sett while he was walking in the countryside near Tenterden. When police arrested Collins, they found footage of badger-baiting on his phone.

'Reckon it's relevant?' the woman asked.

Alex was already halfway across the room, heading to her own screen to look up the case notes.

FIFTEEN

The economy was uncertain. The window of Kidder and Fish, Independent Estate Agents, was full of unsold properties. Alex searched among them for Guldeford Hall, the Uttings' house, but couldn't see it. She wondered if Belinda Utting had already removed it from the market, or whether the agency had discreetly removed it from the window. Selling a property where a dead body had been discovered might not be good for business, especially given how the body had been found.

Inside, the estate agency was brightly lit. A customer was sitting opposite a young man whose hair shone with product. 'It's a very friendly, community-minded street, close to very good schools,' the young man was telling her. 'I think you should see it.'

There were eight elegant desks in the office, each with a silver iMac on it. Only three were occupied; the others didn't look as if they had been used for a while.

'Kent Police,' she said to the perky young woman who was rising to greet her.

The customer swung around in her seat, curious, but already an older man in a well-cut dark-blue suit had stood, and was now striding across the room towards her, anxious to intervene before she said more.

'Michael Kidder,' he said, extending a hand. 'I was expecting you.'

'Is there a Fish?' Alex asked.

Alex followed towards a smaller room with a bigger desk, shiny with polish. On it sat a glass trophy: *Estate Agent Awards 2015. Runner-up.*

'I usually tell people Mr Fish is retired,' said Mr Kidder, sitting down in a modern leather office chair. 'Though in truth, there was never a Mr Fish. Our branding agency thought it up. Apparently two names are thought of as more reliable in this business.'

'I spoke to Gram Hickman. He tells me you sacked him,' said Alex, taking the chair opposite him, putting her bag down beside her.

Mr Kidder steepled his fingers. 'Obviously we can't allow our employees to use customer properties in that way. If we get that sort of reputation, nobody will ever trust us again.'

'Mr Hickman feels a little aggrieved. He claims he's not the only one who has used customer properties. Is that true?'

Mr Kidder drew his chin back a centimetre. 'I certainly bloody hope he's not saying that. If he's demeaning the name of our agency, I may have to take legal action. It would be defamatory.'

'Only if it's not true.'

'Obviously it's not,' said Mr Kidder. 'If I were to find any of my staff abusing their position in the way he did, I would sack them immediately, just as I have Mr Hickman. If he has any other names of people who have abused our trust in the way he did, I will have no hesitation doing the same to them.'

'I should imagine you're slimming down anyway.'

The man smiled as brightly as he could under the circumstances. 'We remain optimistic about the second quarter of this year.'

'You don't rule out the possibility that someone else could have taken the keys from this office and used them to access Guldeford Hall?'

'Of course I do,' said Mr Kidder.

'But Gram Hickman did.'

She let that sink in for a second.

'Well, obviously, yes,' the estate agent said. 'But . . .'

'So?'

'You'll want a list of everyone who could have had access to the keys.'

'Please.'

'I'll compile it, yes.'

He tapped his keyboard.

'How much do you know about the Uttings?'

'I only met Belinda Utting a couple of times, and briefly. Between you and me, I think she just wanted to be rid of the place. We dealt mainly with the family lawyer. We were pleased to get the business, of course. To get a house like that adds to our prestige, obviously. Though it's rather blown up in our faces now, hasn't it?'

She thought of the empty desks. 'On that list, you'll need to include former employees as well.'

'How far back?'

'From when you put Guldeford Hall on your books. Is that a lot of people?'

The man nodded. 'A few, yes,' he said sadly. 'It's not been good lately, frankly, what with the internet, and then with the downturn . . . and Brexit. And now we're in the news because one of our staff wanted to impress his girlfriend.'

And though it meant there were more people on the list of those who could have left the body in the freezer, Alex found herself feeling a little sorrier than she'd expected to feel for an estate agent.

She stood on the pavement outside the office, waiting for Jill to pick her up in the car, looking through a copy of the details for Guldeford Hall.

This historic house in extensive grounds features large picture windows, high ceilings, fireplaces in many rooms, and modern amenities throughout. The property was recently extensively remodelled to a high standard. The annexe was added to the house in 2012, and accordingly provides additional flexible accommodation, all presented in first-class order.

£3.2 million.

A car horn honked. She looked up. Behind the wheel, Jill sat with a scowl on her face.

'What's up with you?' Alex asked as she got in.

'Headache,' she said.

'Was that the opera, last night?'

'It was in Italian. And they sing the same words over and over. Any joy with Kidder and Fish?'

'Six names. Three of them former employees. It's just like Gram Hickman said. If he had got his hands on a key to the house, so could any of them. How did *you* do?'

Jill had been interviewing the Guldeford Hall gardener who visited the property every week, and who also had a key to the garage.

'The man looked pretty genuinely shocked by the news that there had been a body in there.'

'Doesn't he read the news?'

'I think he's one of those people who talk to plants more than they do humans. He has no obvious connections with Vincent Gibbons, has never seen him visiting the house. Hadn't noticed any unusual goings-on there. Said he hadn't seen anybody else visiting, either. I'm not sure he'd notice much if it didn't have roots. On the upside, he gave me some good tips for perennials I could grow on my balcony. You don't have any paracetamol, do you?'

'That bad?'

She nodded and turned the ignition key.

The secondary school where Gram's girlfriend taught was also in Rye. Her name was Angela Booth, and she arrived in the head teacher's office from class looking flustered, carrying a pile of what looked like essays.

'You wanted to see me again?' It was a small room, pictures

of children on trips on its walls; smiling, eager pupils in canoes, at art galleries, on cliff faces.

'This time it's these police officers who need to speak to you.' The head teacher's voice was terse.

'Oh,' said Angela Booth.

Alex stood, gave what she thought was a friendly smile, introduced herself.

'How long will you need?' demanded the head.

'Ten minutes. Maybe fifteen,' Alex told her, and the head retreated, leaving her office for them to use.

'How did you find out where I worked?'

'Your boyfriend Gram told us.'

She nodded sadly. 'Course he did. I bet it was him who told the papers too. He's such a . . . boy.'

'The papers know about you being at Utting's house?'

'Oh yes. They called the head this morning. Thank you very much.'

That would explain the head teacher's frostiness. 'Wasn't us,' said Jill. 'We don't do that kind of thing. More likely to be someone from the estate agency.'

The teacher slumped down into a low metal-framed chair with a sigh. 'Bloody brilliant.'

'He was right to tell me about you. This is a murder investigation.'

'Of course I know that,' said the teacher, scrabbling in her bag. She had dark almond eyes and smooth skin and Alex could see why the young man was so in love with her. 'And if there was any point at all in admitting that I'd been there, I would have.'

Angela Booth found the plastic pack of nicotine gum she'd been looking for and put one into her mouth.

'I just want to know anything you saw that evening that might help us.'

'The journalist was asking if the head thought I was a fit teacher. I'm a brilliant teacher. That doesn't matter any more.'

'I'm sorry.'

'Can't be helped. I split up with Gram too.'

'I'm sorry for that, too. He seemed like . . .'

'A nice boy? Yeah. Too nice for me, apparently. Did he tell you I didn't want to call the police that night? I knew it would come back on me like this.'

'Stupid idea.'

Angela shrugged. 'I honestly don't see how anything I say is going to help.'

'Sometimes it's amazing how just one detail that seems irrelevant at the time can change everything.'

'What I saw,' she said, 'was a really beautiful house of the kind I am never likely to have myself.'

When Alex showed her the photo of Vincent Gibbons, there was no sign she recognised him. 'Who was he?' she asked.

Alex told her. 'We have no idea how his body ended up at Guldeford Hall. He has no connection with the house.'

'I don't know anything, I swear. All this is just one big mess.'

She chewed her gum slowly and methodically. Alex gave a card with her number on it, just in case she remembered anything.

*

From Canterbury, they drove back towards the flat wetland of Romney Marsh, where they had an appointment with the local Wildlife Crime Officer.

'Never seen the point of them, really,' said Jill. 'Political correctness, isn't it?'

The officer lived in one of the villages that edged the marsh. At the end of a lane, by a woodland, sat a pair of houses, one with a pristine garden, lawn neatly cut, the other surrounded by weeds, hedge choked with brambles.

Jill got out and peered over the gate at the one full of dandelions and grass so high it was already going to seed. 'His garden is a wildlife crime, if you ask me.'

'You here about Vinnie Gibbons?'

They turned. A young man was striding towards them from the woodland opposite the house, holding out his hand to shake as a black Labrador trotted beside him. He was good-looking, pink-faced, with a shock of fair hair across his forehead, and it looked as if he had something stuffed down his fleece.

'Constable Tony Skinner?' Alex called out to him.

'I'll put the kettle on.' Unzipping his fleece, he revealed a small infant strapped to his chest in a blue baby-carrier.

'Aw,' said Jill. 'A baby.'

The baby started crying immediately.

'Meet Oscar,' he said.

'How old?'

'Two weeks.'

Close to, you could see the darkness under Skinner's eyes. He hadn't shaved in a while, either.

Kent's Wildlife Crime Officer was on two weeks' paternity leave, which was why they were visiting him at home. Followed by the dog, he led them through a cluttered kitchen into an equally cluttered living room, damp baby clothes hanging on a dryer by the fireplace. Squares of muslin hung on a radiator. Another, older Labrador with milky eyes got up on unsteady hind legs and growled. The room smelt of dogs and baby milk.

On a large sofa his wife Marisa was just waking, bleary-eyed from an afternoon nap. He unstrapped the tiny child and handed it to her. She unbuttoned her cardigan to feed him. 'I'll go in the other room,' she said.

'Don't mind us,' said Alex.

While Tony Skinner boiled a kettle, she wrapped a blanket around the child.

'He's beautiful,' said Jill.

'Surprisingly loud, considering,' said his mother.

'Terrible news,' said the officer, returning with a tray of mugs of tea. 'I'm gutted. Totally gutted.'

'He was a friend?'

'Just a good man, that's all. Very knowledgeable. Very reliable. Very passionate about things. Bit of a mammal specialist. Did a lot of work bait-marking badgers.'

'Sorry?' said Alex.

'It's how you can see how far they travel. You have to collect the faeces—'

'Oh my God,' muttered Jill.

'Sorry. You didn't say how he died though?'

Alex took a mug of tea. 'He was poisoned with hydrogen cyanide.'

Skinner was just handing a cup to his wife. 'You're kidding me?' he blurted, his voice suddenly loud. The mug sloshed hot liquid on the carpet.

'Look out,' said Marisa. The baby wailed. 'You almost poured that all over him.'

'Hydrogen cyanide? You serious?'

'Ssh, shh, shh,' whispered Marisa, calming the little one.

'And you think there might possibly be a connection between the death of Vinnie Gibbons and Frankie Collins?' His voice suddenly indignant.

'Maybe I will go to another room.' Marisa stood, holding the squalling baby.

'You know what hydrogen cyanide is, don't you? It's Cymag,' said Skinner.

'What?'

'They used to sell it for killing pests. Rabbits and rats. It's a pellet. You bung it down the hole. The moment it gets even a bit wet it gives off gas. Back in the day, farmers and game-keepers used to keep a store of Cymag to kill anything they didn't like the look of. It was banned in 2004, but look in any old farm shed and you can always find a few tins of the stuff. Illegal, but you can't just chuck it in a bin, 'cause it's toxic. And besides, some farmers find it handy, even if it's not legal. There's a kind of farmer who just likes killing anything. But rust gets at the tins and you have a nasty situation on your hands.'

'Rabbits, rats . . . and badgers?' asked Alex.

'Oh yes.'

In the kitchen next door they heard Marisa singing to her baby. '*In a cabin in a wood . . .*'

'This is crazy,' said Jill.

'Wait here,' the officer said, standing. 'I've something you should see.'

SIXTEEN

Alex sat waiting for Skinner to return; Jill checked her phone.

'He must think I'm such a twat.'

'I'm sure he doesn't.'

From next door came the sound of Marisa's song. *'Help me, help me, the rabbit cried . . .'*

'You fancy him, don't you?'

'Yeah. But I'm bollocksing it up, aren't I? I always do. I didn't mean to get drunk, but it was all so posh and I felt such a dick there. And it's not just that. Afterwards he dropped me back at mine. I guess I wanted to make up for falling asleep and not being sophisticated. I was kind of all over him. In his car. I was so drunk. I'm really embarrassed.'

Alex lowered her voice. 'You tried to have sex with him in his car?'

'Sort of. And now he hasn't been in touch all day. I think I've fucked it up. He doesn't like me any more, now he knows I'm like that.'

'I'm sure he's just busy.'

'Scared, more like.'

Skinner returned a minute later with a battered black laptop under his arm. 'Who's scared?' he asked.

'Nothing,' said Jill.

'Right.' He put the computer on the kitchen table and opened it up. It took another minute for him to find the right file, then he pressed PLAY and turned the screen towards them.

At first it wasn't clear what they were looking at.

In a dapple of sunshine, in the middle of a sloped woodland, three men were standing, backs to the camera, looking at the ground in front of them. The video was shot from what looked like a long way off, so it was hard to see what they were doing. Only when one of the men stood back, and you saw that he was holding a shovel, was it obvious that he had been digging. Four dogs trotted impatiently around.

It didn't look like much. Just some men and dogs in a wood. You could hear the man who was filming breathing as he tried to hold the camera steady. Alex suddenly realised whose breath she was hearing. 'Vinnie Gibbons filmed this,' she said.

'He was making maps of the setts all over this bit of west Kent.' Skinner stopped the video. 'It was kind of a citizen science project he was running.'

'Is that all he shot?' asked Jill.

'It was enough to convict one of those three men.'

'What were they doing?'

'He had a theory that you could reveal the layout of ancient landscapes by mapping where badgers lived,' said Alex.

Jill and Skinner looked at her. 'How did you know that?' asked Skinner.

'Bill South knew him. He told me.'

'So he was trying to make his own maps of the territory by bait-marking them, which is a long job,' Skinner explained.

'Enough said,' said Jill.

'He turned up one day in this woodland near Tenterden, pure accident, and saw these men digging up a sett. Daylight. Bold as anything. He had to make the choice of whether to protect the sett by letting them know he'd seen them, or gathering evidence. Problem with wildlife crime is, most of the time we know it's going on, but we never get enough evidence to prosecute. We can find a poisoned hen harrier on an estate, but that doesn't prove the gamekeeper did it.'

He pressed PLAY again and the small video repeated.

'So he sat there for about an hour watching them.'

'Did they get any?'

'Nope. They gave up when it got dark. But he got their number plate and called me up, sent me the footage. The car belonged to a man called Frankie Collins. Lives not far from here. I didn't expect much to come of it. You never do. I found his address, went up to his house, and first thing I heard was the dogs. About half a dozen terriers. He kept them outside in a pen. Collins was out, but I took a look at the dogs anyway, and that's when I knew that Vinnie was on to something.'

He clicked on another file. A photograph popped up on the screen.

'Oh God.' Jill gasped. 'That's awful. What's wrong with it?'

The photograph was of a black dog. It was impossible to tell what breed it was, because its muzzle was scarred so badly; it looked like it had melted. The fur on the bottom of its jaw was completely gone, leaving just raw, red flesh.

'That's what a badger will do to a dog in a fight. It literally tries to bite the dog's face off.'

'Jesus. Badger-baiting? I didn't even know it existed any more.'

'You'd be surprised.'

'Jesus God.'

'The state of the dogs, plus Vinnie's video, meant we had enough to do a full raid of the place. Six o'clock the next morning, with a full team. Took his dogs, his hard drives, everything. From them we got a list of his associates, and Collins turned out to have a video on his phone, stupid bastard. It was of badger-baiting. Setting the dogs on badgers and watching them fight. The dogs looked like the ones we'd seen at Collins's house, but we couldn't prove anything. From his bank records, we were pretty sure they'd been live-streaming the fights and making a tonne of money out of it. There are betting syndicates out in Asia that pay a lot of money these days for that kind of thing.'

'Kidding?' said Jill.

'Nope. Animal fights are worth a lot. Unfortunately the Crown Prosecution Service said we didn't have enough evidence to convict them on that. But with Vinnie's video of Collins digging the sett, we had him on that at least. We had a whole gang of them, in fact. Eight names, altogether, once we'd done our work, including the three in Vinnie's video.'

He closed the laptop.

'The Crown Prosecution Service said we only had enough to charge the two of them. The odds are stacked against us. It takes a lot to prove they set out to do this. And the CPS are scared of these cases because they know the defence always has deep pockets when it comes to animal crime cases.'

'That lot, deep pockets?' said Jill, looking at the closed laptop. 'They look like a bunch of benefit scroungers.'

Skinner snorted. 'They are. But when it comes to anything to do with hunting, all sorts come out of the woodwork and chip in for lawyers. Not just small change. These are people who like to stir it up and say it's about townies trying to stop country people having their honest clean fun.'

Next door, the baby grizzled.

'There's a lot of people who don't mind people killing badgers, however they do it. There are some farmers who hate them. They don't think it's a real crime, either.'

Alex looked at Jill, grinned, and said, 'They probably think it's just political correctness.'

Skinner nodded. 'Yep. All that.'

'I didn't say that, not exactly,' Jill muttered.

'The other one got off. Claimed they were just out for a walk with their dogs. Only Frankie Collins is actually filmed digging. But that, plus the videos they found on his phone, meant we had him. He would never have gone down if Vinnie Gibbons hadn't had evidence enough to let us raid his place.'

'It's, like, so primitive,' said Jill.

'I think that's the point.'

'So you think killing Vinnie Gibbons is revenge?'

'Don't you?' Skinner asked.

'Bit bloody extreme, isn't it?' said Jill.

'Yes.'

The grizzle developed into a sudden wail of pain.

'Just wind,' said Skinner. 'One more thing. The trial was last summer. I bumped into Vinnie a few months ago. Every year there's a big conference put on by the Badger Trust. Vinnie's always there. At it, I gave a bit of a speech about the trial, and how we'd got a conviction this time, and he came up to me afterwards and told me that back in May last year, a couple of weeks or so before the trial started, someone had dumped a dead badger on the pavement outside his house.'

'A threat?'

'Oh, definitely. He said there was a note left in the badger's mouth – a screwed-up ball of paper. It said, "You're next".'

'I didn't see that on any of the records,' said Jill.

'He didn't bother to report it. It was the badgers he was concerned about, not himself, see? And after the trial there wasn't much point, he thought.'

'Well, he was wrong,' said Jill.

'Did he keep the note?'

'I asked, obviously. He said he'd chucked it away. He didn't think it was serious.'

Alex thought for a while. 'He said he'd come across them digging by accident. Do you think that's true?'

'What are you saying?'

'Did he have a particular sense of mission against badger baiters?'

'Wouldn't you? He was a good man, that's all. It's a bloody shame.'

'I just need to know whether he was the kind of man who went out looking for a fight.'

'Not Vinnie.'

The baby was howling now.

'We better go,' said Alex. 'Let you get on.'

'Do you have to?'

'Your turn with the baby, isn't it?' Alex stood.

'First adult conversation I've had in a week,' said Skinner, staying in his chair.

On the way out, they stopped, and Alex took the baby for a while. She could never remember Zoë being this small. She felt awkward holding Oscar, as if she had forgotten how to do this. The baby's cries grew louder.

'You want a go?' she asked Jill.

Jill wrinkled her nose. 'I'm no good with babies really,' she said.

Later, as they drove back towards HQ, Jill said, 'I can't see myself ever having one myself.'

'What?' Alex was trying to read her notes as they drove down the country lanes. It was making her feel sick. She stopped and looked out of the car window at passing hedgerows.

'Don't want a baby. Mess my life up even more.'

'Yep,' said Alex. 'So true.'

'I didn't mean . . . Just, saying I'd be useless at it.'

'Same,' said Alex.

'Bollocks.'

'I had Zoë when I was younger than you are. I hadn't a clue what I was doing. Still don't.'

Jill was silent the rest of the way back, occasionally glancing down at the phone in her lap.

SEVENTEEN

'Fuck,' said Jill, checking her phone.

'Call him then.'

They sat on the beach with the basket of blankets, a bottle of wine and a Chinese takeaway. Jet trails made big white lines in a pinkening sky.

Zoë sat on her own, further down the slope of the beach, throwing stones towards the sea.

'I can't,' said Jill.

'And what was he like in bed, anyway?'

'Shut up.'

'Want some food, Zoë? If you don't, Jill's going to finish it all. She's binge-eating.'

'Not hungry,' her daughter shouted back from the shoreline.

'Not funny,' muttered Jill.

'Oh come on, Jill. I'm just jealous. I haven't had anything resembling a boyfriend since I moved here. Single mother. And a copper. The men run a mile.'

Zoë stood and slowly walked back up towards them, head down, kicking stones.

'I just wish I hadn't got so bloody drunk,' said Jill. 'It's so embarrassing.'

Zoë stood in front of them, silhouetted in the evening sky, and said, 'I'm fed up. I'm going to go home.'

Zoë and Jill; both miserable company. 'Face it, Zoë. They are probably going to approve that application anyway, whatever you do,' said Alex. 'Councils need to get homes built.'

'I emailed all the councillors,' Zoë said bitterly. 'Most of them didn't even bother replying. The ones that do just pretend to listen. I hate them all. It's corrupt. They all want to make money out of it somehow.'

'It's not really like that,' said Alex, pouring herself more wine and holding out the bottle for Jill.

'Of course it is.'

'I shouldn't,' said Jill, lifting up her glass.

'It's all about greed. The estate they're planning to build is massive. It's, like, huge. It's going to swamp the place.'

'People need houses,' said Alex.

'It's OK for you,' said Jill. 'You've got a house here. Out of everyone I went to school with, I'm the only one who has a flat of their own. Half the constables I joined the force with are living in dumps and paying nearly everything they earn for the privilege. I'm the lucky one.'

'Lucky' was an odd way to put it, thought Alex. Jill's mother had been an alcoholic. Her only other relative, her grandmother, had died when she was six. Jill had no memory of her at all. All she knew was that the woman had been wise enough not to leave her money to her mother, who would have drunk it. Instead she left it to Jill in a trust fund. Only after her mother had died had she taken the money out of the bank and put a deposit down on a flat.

'Every time people try to build houses around here,' Jill was raging, 'the Nimbys get up in arms. It's always the people who already have houses who don't want us locals spoiling their views.'

'You can't just build all over the countryside.'

'Plenty of it,' said Jill. 'Don't see why not.'

Zoë went pale. She stood still for a second, biting the inside of her lip, then turned away without saying anything and set off walking back towards the house. Alex watched her go. She was going to be in a dark mood all evening now.

'Are you drunk again, Jill?'

'I'm miserable,' she answered.

Alex lay back, looked upwards at the dark azure of the evening sky.

'Any more in the bottle?' the constable asked.

'No.'

'Fancy going to the pub?'

'We've got work tomorrow, Jill.' Alex sat up again. 'Come on. I'll make up a bed.'

Alex woke in the night. Jill was snoring, though even her snoring seemed graceful. It was more like a purring. From below she heard the noise of a kettle boiling.

Alex crept downstairs. Zoë was standing in the kitchen in a T-shirt she recognised as one of her own. It looked huge on Zoë.

'Can't sleep?'

Zoë shook her head.

They sat on the sofa under a blanket, drinking herb tea. 'She's such a cow. I don't know why you're friends.'

'Jill? She didn't mean it. She was drunk,' said Alex. 'And in a bad mood.'

'They're bad people. They killed Vinnie Gibbons.'

Alex put her mug down on the coffee table and turned to examine her daughter. 'You honestly think that?'

Her daughter sipped from her mug. 'He'd been studying the badgers there. He would have been at the meeting tomorrow. If *he'd* objected, maybe they would have listened. That's why they didn't want him there.'

'Who's saying this?'

'People I know.'

'Like Jay?'

She should be used to her daughter's friends by now. She squeezed her daughter's bony shoulders tightly and leaned forward to pick up her mug.

'I mean. What's wrong with Nimbys anyway?' said Zoë.

Alex thought of Vera May. 'Don't you want to put a bomb under people round here sometimes?' she said. 'They can't accept that the world has changed.'

'Badgers are Nimbys.'

Alex laughed.

'Shall I tell you something pretty amazing?' said Zoë.

'Go on.' Her arm was still around Zoë and her daughter hadn't shucked it off yet. 'Tell me something pretty amazing.' She was relishing the moment. Mother and daughter; they lived in the same house, but they rarely talked any more like they had when Zoë was younger.

'In the seventies there was this guy, Hans, who studied badgers. He cut up all these coloured plastic bags from supermarkets and he put the bits in badger food.'

'Lovely.'

'Shut up.' Zoë let go of her mother and punched her on the arm. 'This is brilliant.'

'Go on.'

'Badgers use latrines. They don't just poo anywhere. They use special places. They're like little scrapes in the ground.'

Alex held her tongue.

'This guy, Hans, he was in these woods in Oxfordshire, and he wanted to understand what role these latrines played in marking badger territories. Because we'd known for years that something was going on, but we didn't know what.'

'What did he add the plastic bags to?'

'Like ... peanut butter and honey. They love peanuts. Anyway, he left bits from a different-colour bag at each sett and then waited a couple of days and went back and looked at the poo, and what he found was that each group left their own colour in the latrines inside their territory, but also something else pretty fantastic.'

'Thrill me.' She pulled her daughter closer.

'Shut up. At the edge of every territory were latrines with two colours in. Or maybe three if there were three territories that joined at a corner.' Zoë grinned. 'You see?'

Alex smiled at her wide-eyed girl. 'Actually, no. I haven't a clue what you're on about.'

'Mum! Don't be thick. They were borders. The ones where there were two or more colours were like border markers. It's like both groups are posting sentries along the border. Each group has a borderland. Each badger understands where it is.'

'That is amazing.'

'Are you being sarky?'

'No. I get it. It's clever. Sometimes you can't observe things directly. You have to find other ways to find out what is happening.'

Zoë pushed away, but put both hands on her mother's shoulder and talked quietly, almost into her ear. 'Think about it, Mum. All the time there was this secret map of the land right there. Something that badgers understood, but we couldn't see it, all that time. This vast tessellated pattern of territories. It's been there for centuries, shifting a bit here and there, moving when one population declines and another grows. Pretty cool.'

Alex turned and kissed her daughter on the forehead. 'How come you know all this . . . stuff?'

'I read books, Mum.' Her daughter flinched away from her. 'You should try it sometime.'

EIGHTEEN

The smell of blood hung in the air when she emerged from the police car the following afternoon.

GW Farm Meats smelt like every bad crime scene Alex had ever been to. Her stomach churned, and she wondered if she was going to vomit.

'You OK?' asked Jill.

Until recently, Alex had always been OK with the smell of blood. It was never nice, but it had never upset her that much until recently. 'Yeah. Fine.'

The abattoir was fifteen minutes north of Ashford. From the outside, it looked like any other farmyard save for the refrigerated lorry waiting to load up that morning's animals. Francis Collins was in prison because of Vinnie Gibbons's evidence, but his associate Julian Epps wasn't. He worked here as a slaughterman.

At the small reception office, behind a glass door, Alex identified herself and asked to see Epps.

'What's he done?' the woman behind the desk demanded.

'Nothing, we hope.'

'Can't it wait? He finishes at two.'

'No,' said Alex.

The woman glared at her for a second, then disappeared through the door at the back of the room. They waited, standing in the empty office until she returned. 'He'll be out in a while. We can't just stop because somebody wants to talk to one of the men. And then he'll need to clean himself up.'

Alex's stomach heaved again. A light sweat broke out across her forehead.

'Does he work here every day?' asked Jill.

'It's piece-work. We call him when we need an additional slaughterman,' said the woman.

'Do you have a record of when he's worked?'

'Why do you want to know? Has he been up to something?'

'Just procedure,' Jill said blandly.

'Only, we like to know what the people we employ are up to.'

'Ask him. We're about to.'

Alex felt as if she were about to pass out. This was not like her. She would have stepped outside, but the smell of death was just as strong there.

She found a chair and sat down, pulled out her phone and called Zoë, who answered truculently, 'What?'

'Just calling to say hello. I didn't have time to say it this morning.'

'Hello,' said Zoë impatiently. Last night's intimacy had vanished again. In the background she could hear people chattering and shouting.

'I know you're upset at the death of Vincent Gibbons and I

just wanted to say I understand and I wish I was better at saying things like that at the right time.'

'All right,' said Zoë, non-committally.

'What are you doing?'

'Nothing.'

'What's that noise then?'

'You actually found out anything about Vinnie Gibbons yet?'

'Not really. I wouldn't tell you even if I had. You know that.'

'I got to go, Mum.'

The voices in the background grew louder. 'What's going on?'

'I'm at the council offices in Folkestone. There's a protest and I'm here because Vinnie's not. He should have been. The planning meeting is this evening.'

'You're at the council meeting?'

'Outside. It's not till later. We're here all day. They say they wouldn't let me in anyway.'

She imagined her daughter standing at the council offices, thin and fierce, as the councillors filed in to the meeting.

'What are you doing?'

'I'm just holding a sign.'

'What does it say?'

'It's not exactly original. It says, "Your houses on our land? No thanks!".'

'Our land?'

'The people's land. The animals' land.'

'Are there police there?'

'A couple.'

'Promise you won't get arrested again.'

The woman at the desk raised her eyebrows.

'It's a council meeting, Mum, not an Extinction Rebellion protest.'

'Are there many others there?'

'Nobody I know. Jay's supposed to be here, only he hasn't turned up.'

'What will you be doing?'

'We're just here to talk to any councillors who come in or out.'

'On your own?'

'What's wrong with that?'

At the desk, the woman's phone rang. 'You're on,' she said, pointing to the exit door. A young man stood on the other side of the glass wearing jeans and a checked shirt.

'Got to go.' Alex ended the call. The man turned and walked away slowly. Alex left the office, hurrying to catch up with him.

'I'll just be a minute,' said Jill. 'Just making a note of his shift dates.'

Alex felt grateful for the fresh air. Twenty paces from the door, Julian Epps stopped and turned. 'I know why you're here,' he said, firing up a roll-up cigarette with a single flick of his lighter.

He smiled, breathed smoke through his nose. 'You're so predictable. Knew you'd be down here, moment I heard about Gibbons. I knew you lot would put two and two together and make five.'

'I apologise for being so dull,' said Alex.

'Course you had to come to my workplace, didn't you, just to make absolutely sure I got in maximum shite.'

Alex said, 'I take it you also don't know anything about the death of Mr Gibbons?'

'You know how hard it is getting a properly paid job around here? Proper job. Apart from driving an Uber, that is.'

The stink of blood had followed her. Alex could smell it on him, feel it infiltrating her clothes, her skin. 'We're police officers. We know exactly how hard it is to get a properly paid job.'

'Amusing. At least you've got a fat pension at the end of it.'

'If you have any information about the murder of Vincent Gibbons, we'd like to hear it.'

Julian Epps examined the end of his cigarette; knocked a little ash off with a fingernail. 'No. Don't know anything. Not that that would ever stop you lot from noseying around my business, would it?'

'Do you know of anyone who might have had a grudge against Vincent Gibbons?'

'Define "grudge",' demanded the man. 'When we were up for trial there were plenty of people who had some things to say about him. Me included, I suppose. Just talk. But what do you expect?'

'Frankie Collins committed a crime.'

The man smiled again. 'Kids are stabbing each other on the streets, and people like you, Tony Skinner and Vincent Gibbons are chasing people like me. Really? I'm just trying to make an honest dollar.'

Alex was finding it hard to concentrate. 'When did you last see Vincent Gibbons?'

'Oh my God. Jools! I thought I recognised you.'

Alex looked round. Jill had left the small office and was walking towards them, a grin on her face.

Julian Epps looked towards her.

'You don't remember me, do you?'

'Sorry?'

'You were in the year above me, weren't you? CCS School. That sheep in the girls' lavs. That was you, wasn't it?'

He peered at her face. 'Ferret?'

She grinned. 'Yeah.'

'Bugger me. Little Ferret.' He smiled back. 'How are you doing? Well, obviously OK.'

'What about yourself? I didn't recognise the name. Julian. Nobody ever called you that.'

'Excuse me.' Alex attempted to interrupt.

'Heard about your mum,' said Epps. 'Sorry.'

'Yeah,' said Jill, her grin vanishing. 'She wasn't well for a long time though, with the drink and everything.'

'Hard, though.'

'Bit of a shitter.'

'Never expected you to be a copper, leastways. Of all people.'

The friendliness vanished from Jill's face. 'Well, you didn't know me very well then, did you?'

Epps's face hardened too. 'Come on, Ferret. I know it's a job and everything, but you lot have never been on our side. And it's a shame if you're part of it.'

Jill said, 'Grow up, Jools. You were with Frankie Collins when he was committing a crime. You were lucky to get off, what I heard.'

'Lucky?'

'Yep. I saw the photos of his dogs.'

108

'Frankie was doing something people round here have been doing for hundreds of years.'

'Like incest and sheep-shagging, you mean?'

'I don't expect her to get it, she's a townie, isn't she?' He nodded towards Alex. 'You, though. You should understand.'

'Excuse me,' Alex said. 'Get what?'

'I'm right, aren't I? You're a townie.'

'East London born and bred. Does it show?'

'So you don't get how we live.'

'Which particular "we" are you talking about?'

'Country people. People who live on the land. Who have done for generations. Who know that dogs are working animals, not fashion accessories. Who are despised by townies like you. You got a dog?'

'Not keen on them, to be honest. I was bitten by an Alsatian once as a kid in Clissold Park. I still have the scar.'

'Probably didn't even like the taste.'

'Hope not.'

'You wouldn't get it. I'm just surprised that Ferret doesn't get it. We look after the place. Always have. Ever noticed how there are badgers everywhere? In the past, a bit of hunting and we kept 'em down a bit. Now all the bleeding hearts that have got all shouty about people hunting foxes and badgers are upset that all the hedgehogs are disappearing, you heard that?'

'What are you on about?' said Jill.

'Why, Ferret? 'Cause the badgers have eaten them all, that's what. Badgers scoop out the innards of a hedgehog and leave the bristles, like skinning a banana.' He flicked the butt of his cigarette away and mimed scooping out the meat with one hand, fingers curved like an ice-cream scoop, raising the imaginary innards to his mouth and licking his lips. 'Stop people like us hunting badgers, and you end up with too many of them. It's the way it is. Same with the TB. Badgers are nasty little things that spread disease. Now farmers are having to slaughter their herds.' He stepped on the butt lying on the gravel between them. 'More work for a slaughterman like me. Shit for the farmers, though.'

Alex stepped forward between the two of them. 'Remember me? I'm here to ask you about Vinnie Gibbons.'

Julian Epps stuck his hands deep into his jeans pockets. 'Might have seen him around a few times. Can't remember when. Never spoke to him. Nothing to say to him. Bit of a sad-sack, you ask me. He was out to get us from the start.'

'He said that he came across you and Francis Collins in the woods that day by accident.'

'What? And happened to start filming us? If he actually cared about the badgers, why didn't he try and stop us digging?'

'Maybe he was frightened of you?'

Julian Epps didn't answer. 'OK to go now? Only, the cows won't bloody kill themselves.' He smiled again. 'See you around, Ferret. Don't be a stranger.'

He turned and strode away, arms swinging, towards the slaughterhouse.

Two minutes down the road, Alex abruptly pulled the car into a turning off the A20, a small track that led to a field, and opened the car door.

'What are you doing?' asked Jill.

Alex got out, stood, leaned forward, placed her hands on her thighs and emptied her stomach. Vomit spattered at her feet.

NINETEEN

'Jesus,' said Jill, getting out of the car. 'What's wrong?'

Alex stayed, face down for a second, the taste of acid in her mouth. It was done now. When Jill offered her a tissue, she took it, wiped her face. 'Something I ate, I expect. Or a virus.'

When she was sure she had finished, Alex reached down, grabbed a hunk of grass and used it to wipe small splashes from her shoes.

Jill offered her a mint. 'Sugar free.'

Alex took one and put it in her mouth to try and get rid of the taste of vomit.

'I used to fancy him rotten when I was in Year Twelve.'

'Julian Epps?'

'Yeah. All the girls did.'

'A man who does impressions of badgers eating hedgehogs?'

Jill laughed. 'He was a bad boy. Had his own motorbike. He had interesting muscles on his arms and was a bit tanned from working outdoors, helping his dad out. He always had a bit of cash on him from working weekends which helped. We were all jealous of him, to be honest. Looking back now, you can see all the ways guys like that were always going to fuck it all up, can't you?'

Lorries thundered past on the narrow road.

'I mean, look at him now. Killing diseased cows for a day job. Super.'

'What was that about the sheep in the girls' toilets?'

'He put one in the girls' toilets at school. As a prank.'

'Short of entertainment, were you?'

'God, yeah. You get in the passenger seat. I'll drive.'

But before she started the engine, Jill's phone pinged and Alex noticed her taking a surreptitious glance at the screen.

'Is that him?' asked Alex.

'Who?' She turned her phone upside down on her lap.

'Harry.'

'So I texted him last night because I hadn't heard back from him and told him to get lost basically.'

'When you were drunk at my house?'

'A bit drunk, yeah.'

'Now he's been apologising all day, making up that he had a big work thing on today, because they just got this massive project going through planning, but it wouldn't have taken him much to just pick up the phone, would it?' Alex knew from experience with Jill that it was best not to provide an answer. 'I shouldn't give a crap. Sending him drunk texts. It's juvenile. I'm twenty-five.'

'Are you going to see him again?'

Her phone buzzed again.

113

Alex said, 'Well?'

'I don't like feeling like I'm a total fuck-up.'

'So that's it. It's over already?'

The hedges around them shook as another lorry roared past. 'You don't have a boyfriend, do you? It's not like everyone has to have one. I mean, you're perfectly happy, aren't you?'

Alex looked at the flatland around her. 'Oh yeah. Perfectly,' she said. Jill started the engine. 'His company. It's September Homes, isn't it?'

'Yes. He's a partner in it.'

'They're part of the consortium developing Whiteland Fields, aren't they?'

'Are they?'

'You know perfectly they are. It's on the signs on those great big fences they put around the place.'

'Yeah. The one Zoë is so upset about.'

'So he probably is a bit busy.'

Jill turned her head to look at her boss. 'Yeah. I know, but.'

'Don't be so proud, Jill. Just give him a call.'

'I can't. Not now.'

'Don't be an idiot. Live a little. He's been trying to get in touch with you. You like him.'

Jill looked miserable. 'It's never going to work. He's rich. He's cool. I just fuck it up. Like Jools. It's what we do.'

'It's an order,' said Alex. 'Besides. I want a word with him.'

'What?'

'If his company is developing Whiteland Fields, I want a word with him about Vinnie Gibbons.'

'Why would you want to do that?'

'Because if Vinnie Gibbons was observing a badger sett on the site he might have seen him there, that's all.'

'Know what?' said Jill, looking at her phone. 'I think I'm coming down with that virus too.'

Alex sat silently in the passenger seat, window slightly open, trying to get the smell of blood out of her nostrils.

Alex logged out the key to Vincent Gibbons's house and drove back through Lydd on her way home. The forensic team had done their work. Dust was already starting to settle evenly everywhere.

The investigators had left the old mail in a pile by the door. The earliest unopened letter had been dated late April, a week before Gram and Angela had discovered his body in the freezer; it was the best indicator they had so far of the approximate date of Gibbons's death.

Alex walked through the small empty house, trying to get some idea of who the man was, taking photographs for reference on her phone. The Extinction Rebellion sticker on the fridge; the bad painting of a naked angel, purple-skinned, kneeling beneath an oak tree. The books were a mixture of history, mythology and natural history. The food in the cupboards was basic and functional; a lot of lentils, rice and tinned tomatoes.

His desk had no computer on it – it had been taken away for analysis – but was piled with notebooks and sheets of printed paper. She spent a while looking through them but found nothing about Francis Collins, Julian Epps or Whiteland Fields.

The last place she looked was under his bed. Half a dozen shoeboxes were piled there.

She pulled one out. It was neatly labelled. *Golf Club 3. Marsh-lands. Dennes Lane.* She lifted it and shook it. Something rattled inside. When she opened it, it seemed to be full of small animal bones, sticks, stones and what looked like lumps of earth.

Kneeling down, she pulled out several more, all similarly labelled, all full of odd bits of debris. The last she looked at was labelled *Lydd Area & Whiteland Fields.* She lifted the lid. A bird's skull. Some fragments of stick. A pale, round shape that she thought at first was a stone, but then realised when picking it up that it was too light.

She held up her phone and took another photograph, but thought no more about it.

TWENTY

It has still not rained.

To find enough to eat, they now have to venture further. Like the male who came two nights before, they must trespass into the territories of other badgers, which means they may have to fight. Last night he tried to head south, beyond the ash trees, but was confronted by the same male who had invaded their territory. The other male smelt him first, stood high on his paws, nose down to display his black and white stripes, daring the older badger to come any further. Too old to risk the battle, he ran and went hungry.

Tonight he will try to forage in the opposite direction. But to the north of their territory runs the road. Beyond it there is old farmland. These neglected fields are part of the planned development too, but for now they are fallow. The land here is low-lying. It often floods in winter so there have never been setts there. This low earth is rich and often damp long after their own land has gone dry.

To reach it he must cross the road. Though their smell is good, their eyesight is poor, their hearing worse – and these days cars drive so fast. We see the results of this carnage everywhere at this time of year.

The old badger leaves the sett when it is almost dark and pushes through a newly dug scrape that leads under the new fence, past the cabin in which the security man sits up alone watching *Love Island*, oblivious to the dark shape that moves, low to the ground.

At the tarmac's edge the badger pauses for a second. And then sets off across it, unaware of the supermarket van, carrying produce for home delivery, roaring towards him.

TWENTY-ONE

There was a recycling bin outside the front door. Several empty bottles of something sparkling poked out of the top.

The offices of September Homes were in the Glassworks in Folkestone, a converted factory in the centre of the town, an old building that now looked coolly contemporary. Buzzed in, she walked up the stairs to the second floor, where vaulted brick ceilings had been painted a cool white.

Even from a metre away Harry French's aftershave was citrusy and expensive.

'You're Jill's boss, aren't you?' He grinned, extending his hand. 'I met you at the wine bar. She said you were coming in. Is she not here?'

'No. This is business.'

It was a small office. A glass box carved out a rectangle of space big enough for several desks. French looked surprisingly young, dressed in thin-leg jeans, brogues and a plain crisp white shirt.

'You've been celebrating.'

'Oh yes. Somewhat.' He looked around, sheepishly. 'Jill's a bit pissed off with me, isn't she?' French leaned against the edge of a desk, half sitting, pulled out his phone, checked it for messages, replaced it in his pocket. 'Got a bit caught up last night . . .' He tailed off. Smiled again, apologetically. 'Sorry. I don't expect that's why you're here, is it?'

'She thinks it's the other way around. That you were angry at her.'

'Oh.'

Alex perched on the corner of the desktop opposite, placing her shoulder bag beside her, looking around the big empty room. 'You've just been granted planning permission to build several thousand houses on Whiteland Fields and the surrounding area.'

'Yes. Not just me, obviously. Just a small cog. Us. The consortium. Yes.'

'Good news?'

'Tremendous news. For us it's a major, major project. It puts September Homes on the map. We've been working for years to get here. It's just a preliminary stage, of course. We'll have to fulfil a lot of conditions. And there will be objections still. But they shouldn't be problematic now, so yes.' That smile again. 'Sorry. Do you want coffee?' Alex shook her head. 'Is Jill angry at me?'

Alex held her palms up. 'It's not for me to say.'

'So, she is, isn't she?'

'Confidentially, more at herself than you.'

'You're good friends, aren't you? She talks a lot about you.'

'Can I ask you, did you ever meet a man called Vincent Gibbons?'

120

'Sorry. Business.' Shook his head. 'Gibbons? Don't think so. Why?'

'He had an interest in the land you are going to build those houses on.'

Harry French looked puzzled. 'As a competitor?'

'As a naturalist.'

Harry French paused, then smiled. 'Ah. One of the protestors.'

'You hadn't been aware of him?'

'No. At the start of a process like this, there are always a lot of people who raise their voices.' He shifted his weight forward a little. 'Does this person . . . ?'

'Vincent Gibbons.'

'Is he making some kind of official allegation against us?'

'Not at all. He's dead,' said Alex.

Harry's face flushed suddenly. 'This is a murder inquiry?' He paused. Considered for a second. 'Oh. That guy in the freezer in Canterbury? The one Jill told me about . . .'

'Yes. Him.'

'And you think his death has something to do with Whiteland Fields?'

Alex didn't answer. 'You fenced off the land and have a security guard there already. Is that because of hostility to the project?'

'God, no. You can't do a project like this without a certain amount of preliminary work. We've had to get plant on there, equipment for monitoring groundwater in order to be able to put in the planning application in the first place. You can't just leave stuff like that unattended.'

'That must have been a substantial investment, considering you hadn't got planning permission.'

'That's the nature of the game. It's all risk.'

'So you've bought the land. You've invested in it. No wonder you were cracking open the bottles. If you hadn't got planning permission, all that would have been wasted?'

'Well, we have a more than reasonable expectation that we will be granted permission to build. Councils have a legal duty to meet housing targets these days. Around here, the need is desperate. A single project like ours goes a long way to helping them do that. So yes, you can say we've been pretty positive about it. Of course, with planning committees you never know. It can always go wrong. They're just local councillors.' His grimace was deliberately comic. 'Their decisions can be . . . eccentric. So yes, we were pleased we had the result we did.'

'What would have happened if you'd have lost?'

'We'd have appealed. The appeal goes to the Secretary of State for Housing, who's got a, let's say, less emotional view of housing need than some local councillors. The local wildlife trust have already announced that they're planning to try and get the development called in by the Secretary of State. We expected that. Their membership would be up in arms if they didn't try.'

'Which means?'

'Well. If they get their way, the Secretary of State has the power to overturn the council's decision and halt the project. But that's highly unlikely . . .'

'So the odds are well stacked in your favour.'

'You make it sound like that's not a good thing. Do you know how desperately we need housing in this country? England needs to build four million more homes—'

'There's a petition on the council website asking them to reject the development. It has over six hundred signatures on it. Some of the comments are pretty bitter.' Including one from Zoë, she thought. *This is a crime*, she had commented.

'Vincent Gibbons? He was a signatory?'

'Yes. He also had a poster in his window about it.'

'As you say, there will always be people who are not happy about new houses being built. It's impossible not to upset people, in this industry. What can I say? Whiteland Fields will bring work, housing, and hope, even. It's not just a new town. This is an integrated future village that brings rural life into the twenty-first century. Some people don't like change, others have a vested interest in opposing it.'

'If Vincent Gibbons discovered some rare species on Whiteland Fields, would that have made a difference to your application?'

'What? A crested newt. Or a dormouse?' He had a small smile on his face.

He pushed himself away from the desk, stretched, leaned back again.

'You know what the sad truth is? These days, semi-urban environments like ours often have more diversity than most of what's there in the countryside. We make sure of that. We build them in. It's not like we don't give a damn like the protestors say. We care about the countryside as much as they do. But obviously you're not going to please everybody. Is there any evidence that this man's death is somehow connected to our development?'

'To be honest, nothing I know of, except for the fact he was interested in it.'

Harry French swept his fringe back. 'Making that connection

is not great for us, obviously. We've got planning permission. Our next stage is to try and engage the extra investment to make this development reality. That work starts now.'

'You need more money?'

He laughed. 'If we could back it out of our own pockets, believe me we would. I've put all I have into it. Every last bloody penny. We've done all the work up to now, but we're going to have to share the profit to get the extra investment. A housing development of this size requires millions in order to get off the ground.'

Alex smiled. 'And a police investigation into a murder of an objector may not help you attract the millions you need, is that what you're going to say?'

Harry had the grace to look embarrassed. 'I shouldn't have even suggested that. It makes me look ugly and venal. But it's true. And it's stupid of me to ask. Because you have to do what you have to do.'

'Chances are it's nothing,' said Alex.

'Right,' he said. 'Chances are. Thing is. I'm not one of those big multi-millionaire developers. We've built this from the ground up. I was working for a bigger outfit but then I heard of this opportunity. When they showed me Whiteland Fields I knew it was gold. So I quit, and we've been trying to get it off the ground ever since. We've done a few small projects on the way, but nothing like this. With planning about to become a reality, we needed to look like the kind of company others wanted to partner with.' He held out his arms.

'So this has been a good week for you, then.'

'The best. Until now.'

She picked up her bag, put it back over her shoulder to leave. 'Do you like Jill?'

He eyed her a second. 'Did she ask you to ask me that?'

Alex laughed. 'No. She wouldn't bloody dare.'

Alex opened the car door.

'Well?' asked Jill.

'Are you all right to drop me home later?'

'But what did you think?'

'The office is very swanky.'

'No. Of him.'

'He's got quite nice teeth.'

'You do my head in sometimes. What did he bloody say?'

Alex turned to her younger officer. 'He obviously likes you. He says he wants to smooth it over with you and he's sorry he took you to the opera. It was a mistake. He was trying to impress you.'

Her phone buzzed. Jill laughed. 'It's him. It says, "Your boss seems nice".'

'Seems,' said Alex.

'He's asking if we want to go to the cinema tonight.'

'You know what that means, don't you?'

'He doesn't think I'm a total fuck-up?'

'It means you've got to leave this part of the inquiry well alone. Not if you're going to go out with Mr Property Developer with the nice teeth and wrists.' Alex had pulled out a notebook and was writing in it. 'Are you?'

'Yeah. I suppose I am. Serious?'

'If it's something to do with Whiteland Fields, then he's on our list of people we need to keep an eye on.'

'That's ridiculous, though,' said Jill. 'It's nothing at all to do with him. Just because Vinnie Gibbons happened to be interested in the place . . .'

Alex was never keen to rule someone out of an investigation, but she didn't disagree. 'This is procedure. It's not about whether Harry French did it.'

Jill put the car into gear. 'You liked him though, didn't you?'

'It's not about whether I like him,' said Alex.

'Yeah, but you do, don't you?'

'Yes. Of course I do,' said Alex as convincingly as she could.

It was spitting gently as they approached the coast; Jill switched on the wipers, but it stopped almost as soon as it had started. It hadn't rained properly in a long time, thought Alex.

A gust of wind buffeted them. Alex tried to remember whether she had put the blanket box back inside from the night when they had sat out on the beach together.

Jill drove past South's cottage, down the single-track road to the Coastguard Cottages, then pulled up behind them. 'What's that?' asked Jill. 'By your back door.'

The moment she braked and killed the engine, Jill had thrown open the door and was jumping out of the small car, running towards the back door.

Puzzled, Alex looked towards the back of the house and saw what she'd seen. The door that she and Zoë used most of the time to go in and out of the house, which led into the kitchen, was painted white. Except it wasn't white now.

The door was pink. It was smeared in something that looked

like blood. Big red arcs of it had been swiped over the panels, from top to bottom.

And Jill was standing looking down at something Alex couldn't see from inside the car, holding her hands to both sides of her face in horror.

TWENTY-TWO

The badger lay on the back-door mat.

Its belly had been sliced open and its innards had been dragged out. They lay in a bulbous red and brown pile at the bottom of the door. Whoever had pulled out its guts had smeared the woodwork with them, before letting them drop to the ground.

'Christ.'

An atavistic, brutal act; deliberately spreading the blood over Alex's property. Her house had been marked; a warning of some sort.

'Mum? What's happening?'

Alex looked around sharply. Her daughter was running towards her.

'Stay there,' Alex warned.

Too late. From where she was, Zoë could already see the dead animal. She ran forward, dropped to her knees in front of it.

'Scene of crime. Keep back,' said Alex, quietly.

Jill dropped beside her, putting her arms around the teenager, lifting her away.

'Who did this?' Zoë wailed.

Jill and Alex exchanged a glance. 'We don't know,' said Alex, despite the look she had just shared with her colleague.

Another police car arrived within fifteen minutes, dropping a copper off whose job it would be to guard the scene of crime.

'That?' The lanky lad, who looked dwarfed by the utility vest he was wearing, pointed at the dead animal. 'I'm supposed to stand over that? What is it, anyway?'

Tony Skinner turned up in a Toyota pickup not long afterwards.

'Thought you were on paternity leave,' said Alex.

'Bastards,' Skinner said, getting out of the cab.

William South had arrived now too, striding up the road from his little bungalow to find out why the police vehicle had passed, light flashing. They stood around the dead beast, unable to touch it or move it away from the doorway. Its hindquarters had been crushed almost flat by something.

Skinner kneeled down close to it. 'How did they kill it?' Alex asked.

'I'd guess it was dead by the time they picked it up. Roadkill probably. Not dead long. Last night, I'd say.'

'Smells like it's been dead for ever,' said Jill. 'Poor Zoë's really upset.'

'Not surprised,' said South. 'Poor girl.'

The young constable was squatting down by it, taking photos on his phone.

'Excuse me,' said Jill. 'What you doing that for?'

'I don't know,' said the man, embarrassed. 'Crime scene, isn't it?'

'Leave him alone, Jill,' said Alex.

South turned to Alex. 'Who have you offended this time?'

'Frankie Collins.' They turned and looked at Skinner, who'd said the name out loud. 'Or one of his mates.'

Jill shivered. 'Because of us investigating them over Vinnie Gibbons?'

Skinner squatted down to take a picture of the dead animal on his phone. 'Any CCTV?'

Some of the houses along the track had cameras, but few of them were pointed onto the road.

'You better go,' said Alex. 'You'll miss the film. And the posh meal.'

'I can't go now.'

'Yes you can. Go on.'

Jill shook her head. 'I can't,' she said. 'I'm not going to leave you like this.'

The wind gusted hard. They walked around the row of houses and entered by the front door instead.

In the kitchen, Alex opened the window and passed a mug of tea out to the copper who stood in the rain, standing guard over the animal corpse. 'Come inside,' she told him. 'Nobody's going to touch it. You can keep an eye from here.'

She looked at Jill. 'Go out for your movie and your meal. There's nothing you can do here.'

'Not sure I feel hungry now,' she said.

The policeman had come in the front door and was shaking the rain off his vest.

'They're warning you off, aren't they?' said Zoë. Everyone turned to look at the teenage girl.

'Obviously,' said Jill, leaning down to put her arms around her. 'But that's no reason to be scared. They won't do anything to you, we'll make sure of that, won't we?'

'I'm not scared,' said Zoë, shrugging Jill off. 'I'm bloody angry.'

'Go,' said Alex. 'You'll miss the film.'

'No. I'm going to call it off.' She took out her mobile and stepped outside, out of the front door, so she could have some privacy for the call.

'New boyfriend?' asked William South as they watched her emerge into view, hair blowing in the wind. She waved once, then jumped into her car.

'Yeah. A guy called Harry French.'

'I thought she was off boyfriends.'

'He's part of the development company called September Homes,' said Alex. 'The one your company are going to be doing the surveys for, Bill.'

'He's evil,' said Zoë. 'I bet he killed Vinnie Gibbons.'

The uniformed constable, mug of tea in his hand, observed the conversation with nervous bemusement.

'You can't say things like that.'

'What if he did, though?'

'You don't even know him. '

'He's a creep. 'Cause he's trying to build on Whiteland Fields.'

'It's the company he works for, not him,' said Alex.

131

Zoë had raised her voice now. 'Have you even looked into it? The whole thing is ultra weird. The board is full of people with connections to the government. Lords and stuff. It's immoral.'

Her daughter surprised her constantly. 'Who's saying that?'

'That's what they were saying at the protests. One of them is, like – an advisor to the government on housing or something. How can they lose? Whatever we say they're going to build it. It's totally corrupt. And he's part of it.'

Alex turned to William South. 'Is that true?'

South nodded. 'Lord Michaels is on the Whiteland Fields consortium's Board of Directors. Derry Michaels was one of the government advisors on the last planning consultation. He practically wrote the latest planning framework for the government. He's the one who says we have to streamline the planning process and create new towns in the countryside.'

'See?' said Zoë, standing angrily.

'It's not illegal,' Alex told her daughter. 'He's allowed to be on the board. They always sign up people like that to the board because of their expertise. They know what's possible and what isn't. It's normal.'

'And they write the laws that allow them to bulldoze that stuff through.'

'Nobody's bulldozing anything through. It went through the council. It's normal.'

'And local councils are scared stupid that they're going to be fined billions if they come to the wrong decision,' said Zoë. 'Bet he's making a mint out of it.'

'If he's a shareholder, he'll have declared it as an interest.'

'It's ridiculous,' said Zoë. 'It's so unfair.'

132

'It's not illegal,' said Alex again.

'That doesn't mean it's not shit,' said Zoë.

There was a silence in the room.

Jill came back. 'Why's it so quiet?' she demanded, looking round.

'Fancy a biscuit?' Alex asked the constable.

'Is that not illegal, then?' asked the young constable. 'Being a government advisor who makes the law, and then making money out of the result?'

'Don't you start,' said Alex. 'What's your name again?'

'Colin,' he said. 'Colin Gilchrist, Sarge,' he added as an after-thought.

Behind his back, Zoë rolled her eyes and mouthed, *Sarge*.

'I don't see it,' said South quietly.

'See what?'

'People like that don't go dumping dead badgers around the place. I know it round here. This is local.'

'Julian Epps,' said Jill.

Alex nodded. 'How did it go?' she asked. 'With you and Harry?'

'I told him it was an emergency. He was a bit offhand, to be honest.' She looked disappointed. 'Said maybe another time then.'

Constable Gilchrist looked up from his phone. 'I think there's something in its mouth,' he said.

They all turned and looked at the young man. 'What?'

'Look.' He zoomed out on his screen and held up the phone. 'There. Just poking out.'

Alex leaned in. A small triangle of white poked out between evil-looking teeth.

A flashing blue light lit the rain out over the beach. It would be the CSI team, coming to examine the remains of a dead badger.

Alex watched as they moved the dead animal, then, with a pair of tweezers, opened his mouth and extracted a tightly rolled ball of paper. With gloved hands, the young woman carefully unfolded the small sheet.

'I think I know what it says,' said Alex.

'Really?' The CSI officer frowned. She held it up.

The paper had been torn out of a small spiral notebook. There were two words in biro: *You're next.*

'The same as Vinnie Gibbons's,' said Skinner.

'Yes.' Alex looked up to see Zoë staring down at her from her bedroom window, eyes red, and knew her daughter would have seen the anxiety in her own face. Quickly she put on as reassuring a smile as she could, but Zoë's expression did not change.

TWENTY-THREE

Last night, the van missed him by a whisker. He barely noticed it; made it across the road and spent time feasting on worms like he had not for days. But on his way back to the sett, he smelt blood.

Approaching cautiously, he dimly saw the dark lump on the edge of the tarmac.

The younger male, the dominant one, had followed his scent towards the fields rich with worms. But he had not been so lucky when it came to his dash across the road. His body lay among dandelions and sweet wrappers.

The older badger sniffed for a second, then returned to the sett. He was going to go in by one of the other holes, but instead he used the entrance the younger badger had marked for his own use.

This evening, tempted out again by the worms, he returns to cross the road, despite the dangers. Badgers are stubborn creatures. But when he gets to the spot where the younger badger was killed, only his smell remains, and the old sweet wrappers. The body itself has gone.

TWENTY-FOUR

The 1950s-built house had a neglected air. The original wooden windows had rotted, turning black. There was a roll of sodden carpet outside the front door, next to an old grey mattress.

'Tasty,' said Constable Gilchrist, peering out past windscreen wipers towards the red-brick terraced house.

'Don't be a snob,' said Jill.

Needing a uniformed officer to accompany them, Alex had put in the request for Gilchrist to work overtime. He had been keen.

An elderly white Fiat van sat on the paving where a front garden had once been. There was rust on the sills and one of the headlamps was cracked.

'Check the number plate,' said Alex.

Jill called it in. The answer came straight back. 'Yep. Registered owner is Julian Epps at this address.' Gilchrist zipped up his stab vest.

'Let's go,' said Alex, emerging from the car into twilight.

*

A dog started barking the moment Gilchrist knocked; the kind of monotonous, regular noise that would drive any neighbours crazy. A young woman in a tracksuit and slippers answered the door, took one look at Gilchrist's uniform and called above the noise in a resigned voice, 'Jools. It'll be for you.'

Inside, a man shouted something and the barking stopped as quickly as it had started.

Julian Epps came to the door with the unfocused eyes of a man who had been drinking.

'Where have you been all day today, Mr Epps?' asked Alex.

'Oh. It's you. Back so soon?' He peered out into the darkness behind them. 'Hi, Ferret. Couldn't stay away?'

'Where were you today, Mr Epps?'

He stood at the door, not inviting them in, arms crossed.

'What's this about? Someone parked on a double yellow line? Someone drop a Mars bar wrapper on the pavement?'

'It's cold, it's late and we want to go home. Can you just answer the question?'

'I was here. All day. Wasn't I?' He turned, but the woman had shuffled back inside.

Alex nodded. 'No work today?'

'Thereby hangs a tail. Boss sent me home after you two'd been round. Told me to stay away. He doesn't like police coming to our premises. Scares people into thinking that something dodgy's going on, and you can't have that in his line of work.'

Alex said, 'I'm sorry to hear that.'

'I'm sure you are,' said Epps, nodding slowly. 'He'll be sorry. Not many people want to do that kind of work. Hard to get good slaughtermen. Why are you here again? No actual miscreants to catch, or do you just enjoy harassing a working man?'

'Was that your partner who answered the door?'

'Girlfriend.'

'And she'll confirm you have been home all day?'

Epps rolled his eyes. 'Of course I've been home all day. I've been laid off, thank you very much. Think about that next time you just roll up to a workplace.'

'If you could just ask your girlfriend—'

'Lucy,' he called. 'Come here and tell the woman that I've been in all day.'

Gilchrist took a step back from the front door, looking around the front of the house. Alex was conscious of him switching on a torch and shining it at the van.

The woman re-emerged. She sighed, looked at Epps, then at Alex. 'He's been here all day.'

Alex looked at her. 'And you've been home all day too?'

She glanced down at her slippers. They were worn. Wool was fraying at the toe. 'Yes,' she said, not meeting Alex's eye.

There would be other ways of checking.

'Sarge?' said Gilchrist. 'I think you should take a look at this.'

Alex looked round. Gilchrist, the lanky constable, was squatting down, all knees and elbows, shining the torch at the back of the van.

'What you looking at now?' called Epps.

Alex left the front of the house and joined him.

'I'm surprised at you, Ferret,' said Epps. 'You've changed.'

'Can't say the same about you, Jools.'

'There,' Gilchrist said, shining the torch on the rain-spattered rear bumper, just below the door. Small but definite streaks of red ran down the white paint.

'Keep your hands off my van.'

Alex ignored him, went to the front of the van and placed her hand on the bonnet. It wasn't exactly hot, but nor was it as cold as the evening air. In the centre, there was an unmistakable warmth in the metal.

'And you haven't been anywhere today in this van?' asked Alex.

Epps didn't answer. Inside, as if sensing something was wrong, the dog started barking again.

'Can we have the keys, please?' asked Alex.

'Just fuck off and leave me alone.'

'What they want that for, Jools?' asked the woman.

'Because it's their life's work to give me a hard time.'

'We can impound it if you like. We'll have to tow it away though.'

Epps stood at the door, arms crossed. His girlfriend said, ''K sake, Jools.' She disappeared back inside, re-emerging to throw the keys onto the concrete at Alex's feet.

'Why did you give them?' Epps shouted.

''Cause I can't bear the bloody martyr act for one more minute. Let them do their job and then get out of our hair.'

Epps stood at the door, open-mouthed.

'Thanks, love,' said Jill.

And as Alex bent down to pick up the keys, Epps shouted at the dog to shut up, then slammed the front door shut.

★

They stood guard over the van until the forensics people arrived, fresh from Dungeness.

'Doing swabs for badger blood twice in a day,' Gilchrist said. 'Makes a difference from the usual, eh?'

'We live for moments like this,' said the CSI woman, unsmiling, as she put on her gloves.

The girlfriend watched from the living-room window, a resigned look on her face. She had lied, and she knew Alex knew that.

There wasn't much blood in the back of the van, but enough for them to get samples from, to try to match it to the animal dumped at Alex's back door. The smears ran towards the back of the van, as if something had lain there, then been dragged out.

Afterwards, Alex dropped Jill off, then drove Gilchrist back to the station.

'Well done,' she said, pulling up in the car park. 'Nice work.'

'That was great,' said Gilchrist. 'I've been meaning to say all evening. I always fancied being a DC.'

'You should give it a go. We're desperate on Serious Crime.'

He gave her a look.

'Stupid fucker, though, 'scuse my language, wasn't he? Not even bothering to clean out his van.'

Epps had admitted nothing. He had stuck to his story that he'd been in all day.

'We'll be able to pick up his van on ANPR, won't we?'

Alex nodded thoughtfully. If they were lucky, they would be able to pick up some of the van's movements on the number plate recognition system, though all that would prove was that Epps had lied about taking the van out. The blood could be enough to charge him with, and it would give Alex some leverage over him, another way to get under his skin to work out if there was some connection between Frankie Collins's people and the death of Vinnie Gibbons.

Constable Gilchrist was still sitting in the passenger seat.

'I need to drop the car off and head home,' she said.

'Right,' Gilchrist said, sounding disappointed. 'Time to knock off, then.'

'Yep.'

'Jill working all the time on this one with you?' Gilchrist asked.

Alex raised an eyebrow. 'Some of it, yes.'

Gilchrist gave a small nod. 'She single?'

'Out,' ordered Alex.

He opened his mouth, thought better of it, then opened the car door and stepped out into the dark street.

TWENTY-FIVE

Their territory was vulnerable now the younger badger was dead. The surviving male would have to fight intruders alone now.

That evening, before feeding, he patrolled the latrines on the southern flank of their land, sniffing scents of the younger ones who would be challenging him soon. There would be fighting now. It was impossible to avoid it.

Between two ash saplings, he stopped and sniffed the air.

Someone alien was there, between him and the hole in the fence.

The smell of engine oil. A dark shape, still in the darkness.

People stink.

TWENTY-SIX

On Monday morning she stopped in Lydd on the way to work.

Vera May was expecting her. 'Tea?' she said.

Vincent Gibbons's neighbour was in her early seventies, Alex guessed, the kind of woman who probably wore woollen layers even on the hottest day. Her living room smelt of woodsmoke. A tidy house, with a few watercolours and dark old carpets on the old stone floors; shelves full of porcelain figurines.

'You're here to ask about poor Mr Gibbons?' she said, returning with a teapot on a tray.

'I wanted to know about the campaign.' Alex pointed to the poster in the window: *Say No to Whiteland Fields Development*. 'Mr Gibbons was involved, wasn't he?'

'Of course he was,' said the woman. 'Passionate about it. We all are. I'm on the parish council, you know. We're appealing, obviously, but we don't stand much of a chance. The whole system is rotten.' The woman perched on the edge of an armchair and poured. 'Very buggering angry about it,' she said.

Alex looked up.

''Scuse my French.'

'My daughter too, as it happens,' said Alex.

'You're Zoë's mum. I recognised you. You're the spitting image.'

'Don't tell her that. She'd be furious.'

The woman laughed, then her laughter turned into coughing for a while and she pulled a handkerchief from the fraying sleeve of her cardigan. 'Great girl,' she said when the fit had subsided.

'I know,' said Alex.

'The bloody housebuilding lobby. They have the government wrapped around their finger. So in this region we're expected to identify locations in which to build three hundred and fifty new homes a year. And when the housing developers get planning permission on those bits of land almost on the nod, half the time they don't even build. They just bank the land because it's now worth many times more because it has planning permission on it, which forces the District Councils to allocate even more land for housebuilding in order to comply with government targets, which frees up more land for the money-men to buy.' The woman started coughing again, dabbing her mouth with the cloth. 'It's a giant scam. It's about ruining the English country-side for profit. It makes me furious.'

'I can tell.'

The woman's mouth fell open. 'I do apologise. You probably hear all this from Zoë anyway.'

'On and off,' said Alex.

'I am so sorry. What did you want to ask?' Finally she lifted the teapot; one of those fussy porcelain ones with gold swirls and pictures of peasants on the side.

'In the campaign, was there anyone that Vincent Gibbons might have argued with?'

The woman missed the cup and poured straight into the saucer. 'Vincent never argued with anyone. Some of the things he believed in I didn't agree with, and I told him so, but he never argued.'

She passed Alex the cup. Alex tipped the tea from the saucer into the cup and stared at the pale brown liquid.

'Such as?'

'If I'm honest, he was one of those anti-hunting save-the-whale types.'

'Like my daughter.'

'Yes,' Vera May said, sympathetically. 'But I'm sure she'll grow out of it. She has a good heart.'

'What do you think about the Whiteland Fields Consortium?'

Vera May snorted. 'Do you even know where the money is coming from? A town like ours would be changed for ever if they built something like that.'

Alex looked down at her tea. She smiled. 'Is that necessarily a bad thing, changing this town?'

Vera May looked shocked. 'It would be a terrible thing. It would be horrifying.'

'My daughter claims the whole consortium is corrupt.'

May, perched knees together on the edge of her fringed armchair, looked puzzled, as if trying to work out whether Alex was supporting her or mocking her.

'Well, she's right.'

'You think?'

'It's foreigners, buying into our country with crooked money.

They own half of London already. Our MP pretends he's on our side but that's just so he gets our votes at the election. He's desperate to stay at the Westminster trough like the rest of them. All the time, his bosses are stacking the rules against people like us.'

'What about the presence of Lord Michaels on the board?'

'Exactly,' she said. 'We've written to the Communities and Local Government Secretary to investigate it as a conflict of interest, but they'll say there's nothing wrong with it. They're all on the take from lobby groups.'

'Surely it's not a conflict of interest if he's unpaid.'

'He doesn't have to be paid, does he? All his friends who invest in the scheme are. All his financier friends. And they scratch his back and he scratches theirs.' There was venom in her voice. 'How is that not absolutely one-hundred-per-cent criminal? You should investigate him about it.'

'I'm going to see him tomorrow, as it happens. He's being very helpful.' After talking to Zoë, Alex had spent a little time over the weekend looking up Derry, Lord Michaels; he was the kind of man who appeared in photographs, standing a step or two behind famous public figures. It was no surprise that in several that she found, he was there alongside Sir Andrew Utting, the late owner of Guldeford Hall. Lord Michaels seemed to belong to a generation who spent their lives in politics without ever being elected to anything. He was connected. Interested, she had emailed asking if she could discuss Andrew Utting and Whiteland Fields with him, expecting a starchy reply; instead he had invited her to tea at the House of Lords. She rather liked the idea of that.

'Good for you,' said Vera May. 'Give him bloody hell from us.'

'It's a friendly chat, Vera, that's all it is.' Alex looked down at her notes. 'I wanted to ask about the badger-baiting case that Vincent Gibbons was involved with last year. Did he talk to you about it?'

'They threatened him, you know. They left a dead badger on the pavement just outside his door. I mean, I didn't agree with everything poor Vincent said about hunting, but that was taking it much too far.'

'Were there other threats?'

'There were places he was no longer welcome, let me put it that way.'

'Did he ever talk about a man called Julian Epps?'

'I'm not very good at remembering names, I'm afraid. I'm better with faces.' A few years ago, there would have been a photo of Epps on file; but he had been acquitted. The police were no longer allowed to store the images of supposedly innocent people. 'Did your people find anything in Vincent's house?'

'Nothing helpful, I'm afraid.' Alex stood to leave.

'He had always believed there were Saxon remains on the site. The day I went away, he told me he thought he might be able to prove it, but now he's dead. And then I never saw him again.'

'If he had found something on the site, would that have been useful to you?'

'Of course,' she said, 'though who knows what would stop these people? They're fanatics.'

Alex stood. 'Your lodger. Mr Browne. He's not around?'

'Richard? Most of the time he's in London. He does something with computers in the city. He comes and goes. It's a very convenient arrangement. Even when he is here, I hardly notice he is. He's looking for somewhere more permanent in the area. I'm rather hoping he doesn't find it.' She laughed. 'It's nice to have a man around.'

'Of course, if they built the new development, that might make it easier for him.'

'That's the thing. People like him, you can't object to him wanting to live here, can you? After all, he's local, more or less, born and bred. He grew up around here, apparently. His father used to have a farm, I believe. That's what's drawn him back. People like him – that's perfectly legitimate. But there's simply not the infrastructure here for everyone else.'

Alex saw herself out; Vera May returned to writing emails on her computer. As Alex closed the door, she reflected that it seemed unlikely that Vincent Gibbons was killed simply because of his opposition to the development on Whiteland Fields. If that had been the motive, it would have been much more effective to kill Vera May.

TWENTY-SEVEN

Alex was in London, enjoying herself as a tourist in the city she had been born in. She had turned up early for her meeting with Derry Michaels and walked in the Victoria Tower Gardens, looking out over the river, a high tide after the turn sending water rushing under Lambeth Bridge. Now she was sat at a table with the man, who was younger than most of the other diners. Handsome in a kind of tousled rugby-playerish way. Public school, Cambridge graduate, formed think tanks, wrote papers, joined lobby groups, advised and cajoled, then, after a decade, was relocated upwards to the House of Lords.

The Peers' Dining Room at the House of Lords in the Palace of Westminster felt like a place that had barely entered the twentieth century, let alone the twenty-first. The great and the good seemed to be mostly elderly, and sat on straight-backed chairs, prodding at the kind of food their nannies had probably served them.

'I'm completely transparent,' said Lord Michaels, smiling

at her in a way that she already found annoying. 'Ask me anything.'

If she had expected tetchiness about being asked to take part in a police investigation into a murder, there was none. If anything, there was a schoolboyish fascination with the case.

'I read about it in the papers. Found in a freezer at the Uttings' house. How absolutely ghastly,' he said with a smile. 'Shall I be mother?'

A waiter had brought scones. They looked huge.

'Now, what's the connection between Andrew and September Homes? I don't understand.'

She ignored the question. 'You knew Andrew Utting?'

'Awful loss. He was only a few years older than me. I've been there, you know? Guldeford Hall. Where the body was found. Marvellous house. Years ago, though. Do you like it here?' he asked.

'The cream tea?'

'The room. It's really something, isn't it?' He waved his arm around the long room, walls covered in sombre portraits and smeary landscapes. The ceiling was dark wood. To one side, there was a long table, around which several people sat silently, ignoring each other. 'We are from all political sides here. This is where we mingle. Hence the long table. We are forced to come together here. Of course, the House is not as important as it once was, and it probably won't be much longer before somebody abolishes us, which, for ideological reasons, I'm all in favour of, though I confess I have become rather fond of this place.'

'That wallpaper is like dropping acid,' Alex said. It was bright yellow, patterned with red thistles.

He laughed. 'An original design by Pugin. What would a serving police officer know about taking illegal drugs?'

'It's the only way to get through the day, believe me.' She took a sip of tea. His laugh deepened.

'I hadn't seen Andrew for several years. He was rather more of an old-school High Tory than me.'

'I've been trying to find out what kind of man he was.'

'You don't honestly think he was connected to this ghastly affair, do you? Andrew was a sweet man of great integrity. And he was dead long before your fellow was found.'

'My fellow was found in Andrew Utting's freezer. I want to know why he was there.' She took another sip of tea. 'It would help to know a little about him.'

'Different generation, really, from me. A senior figure in the judiciary. Obviously I came across him a few times. He was one of the ancients.' He looked around the room with a knowing smile.

'The ancients?'

'The aristocratic families who like to think they still run everything. They congregate in these corridors. The Uttings were one of them.'

'As opposed to the new people who think they run everything?'

Michaels paused, as if unsure whether to take offence or not. Eventually he said, 'Precisely,' and laughed again. 'I'm not talking ill of the dead. I loved him. We all did.'

'What about his wife?'

'Ah. Belinda. "Belinda smiled and all the world was gay." If only that were true. She was always quite hard work, as I recall. I don't think there was a lot of genuine affection in

152

that relationship. She was always more interested in his status than his soul, if you understand my meaning. It was always something of a paradox, I thought. Andrew was such a sociable fellow, always throwing parties, always making connections. He was a genius at bringing people together, and yet privately I think he was rather lonely. I don't think he loved his wife at all but he stuck by her because, like I said, he was a man of integrity.'

'There are several lines of enquiry into the murder of Vinnie Gibbons. One of which involves Mr Gibbons's interest in the piece of land known as Whiteland Fields.'

Derry Michaels looked shocked. 'His interest?'

'You didn't know? The dead man was a naturalist. He had been studying wildlife on that land. When the planning application came around, he was among the protestors.'

'Christ. I had no idea.' Derry Michaels took a scone, split it in two and placed a dollop of cream on it, then leaned over the table towards her.

'Are you surprised by the strength of feeling there has been against the Whiteland Fields development?'

'Not at all,' he said, as if the idea were ridiculous. 'All developments such as this produce strong reactions. It's one of the problems we face. Within the planning system, local people have the ability to abuse their power. After all, they are the people who already have houses.' He spooned a lump of strawberry jam on top of his scone and popped it whole into his mouth. After he'd finished chewing, he said, 'When the English buy a house in the countryside, they think they've bought the view, too. They want to keep other people out.'

'Passions run high. On both sides.'

He grinned, and she noticed a crumb lodged on his lip. 'Yes. As you can tell, it's something I am just as passionate about as they are. It's a matter of national survival. The housebuilders must be allowed to build. We're having a big reception for the development in London next week. Big fanfare to celebrate getting through planning. All the great and the good invited. You should come.'

'Police officer. Probably not wise to invite me.'

'See what you mean.' His laugh dislodged the crumb, which landed on her side of the table, but he didn't seem to notice.

'Do you know the area well?'

'Of course. I spent a lot of time there. I don't just agree to become a director of a company and pay no interest at all.'

'Did you ever meet any of the objectors?'

'A few. Yes. Though I have no memory of meeting anyone like Mr Gibbons. I may have. It's the same story everywhere. Everybody thinks their own place is special. Their own place is the exception. They can't all be the exception, can they?'

'I want to ask you a question,' she said. 'It's entirely hypothetical.'

'Go ahead.'

'If the murder was connected to the development in some way, would that affect the value of people's investments in the project?'

He leaned forward again, lowered his voice. 'You think this murder might have been some attempt to derail this project?'

A woman on the opposite side of the room started coughing. 'I don't have any idea why Vincent Gibbons was killed. I'm just trying to think things through. Somebody went to a great deal of trouble to kill him in a very unusual way.'

'I know passions run high, but I don't think they'd run that high. Would they?' The woman was still coughing as he pressed his fingers together. 'Would it affect the value of the project? The thing is, by this point in a development, there are many millions involved. The scale of something like this is enormous. There is very little that can stop it at this stage.' More coughing. 'I don't mean to belittle a man's death,' Michaels was saying, 'but in the scale of things, it's not going to make much difference. But I don't suppose that would necessarily mean that some of the nut jobs wouldn't try it on. It's quite boring. We come up against this stuff in some form or other all the time. Local democracy, so called, is a joke. We'd be better off without it. It's just an excuse by busybodies to stop anything good happening in this country. But really . . . No. I can't see that his death is connected with the development. What do you think?'

She avoided the question. 'It's early days.'

'Of course. How's the scone?'

The woman finally stopped coughing. The room was quiet again. 'On the stale side. '

'Yes, it is, isn't it?'

Alex looked at the people around her. Several she thought she vaguely recognised, wondering if they had been ministers in Thatcher's or Blair's cabinets. Though he had claimed not to be particularly worried by the investigation's implications for the development, Derry Michaels seemed to have brought her here to try and impress her, in the way these people did, and to see what he could learn from her. Michaels, she realised, was one

155

of those who enjoyed the feeling that they were on the inside; a person for whom being in the know was a constant reassurance that they were at the centre. 'Some of the objectors think it's an issue, you being both on the board of the consortium and also a government advisor who's helped write the procedure which enables them to build.'

His eyes narrowed. 'I thought this was a murder inquiry?'

'Yes. It is.'

He dropped his voice a little lower. 'So what is the question?'

'As I said. I'm trying to understand the passions. On either side.'

He reached into the inside pocket of his jacket and pulled out a small Moleskine notebook. 'There is no conflict. I don't stand to profit from it. I am simply there to help make sure the development happens. Can I ask your superior officer's name?'

'Detective Inspector Toby McAdam.'

When he'd written the name carefully in the book, he replaced the elastic around it and put it back into his pocket. Then he spoke, again calmly, choosing his words with care. 'It's a great sadness to me that the world has become so cynical. I'm just surprised to hear it coming from someone who is in public service.'

His voice rose against the chink of cutlery on crockery, the low murmur of conversation.

'Of course passions are running high, but it's a passion of mine to get houses built. That's why I was so eager to help reform a planning system which has for decades now been failing to get houses built. It's a duty. And that's why I advise schemes like this. Only by getting my hands dirty can I really understand how

156

we can get ourselves out of this mess.' He paused. He handed her a business card, then said, 'Are we done?'

He walked her back to the exit where she handed in her pass to a young man at the desk. Lord Michaels shook hands formally, then turned his back, and she watched him disappear behind the large doors.

She stood outside the entrance in Old Palace Yard, looking up at the ridiculous statue of Richard the Lionheart on horseback, holding his sword vertically. There was something of the football hooligan about him, she thought.

It had been an entertaining visit but not particularly useful. Michaels, she realised, had summoned her to ask for information, not to dispense it, because he was the kind of man who couldn't bear not to be at the centre of everything. It was how these men held on to what power they could. He didn't know anything about the death of Vincent Gibbons; he cared even less about it.

'Sergeant Cupidi.' She was aware of someone shouting her name. 'Sergeant Cupidi. Wait.'

She turned to see the man she had handed her pass to running towards her, holding a small yellow piece of paper.

TWENTY-EIGHT

'Sorry,' the man panted. 'I was supposed to give you this on the way out.'

He handed Alex a note. The yellow paper was written on in red biro, the letters big, round and girlish: *Please see me on your way out. Need to talk to you. Important. Tamsin Porter.* And a mobile phone number.

Who was Tamsin Porter? Alex looked around and tried to think who might have known that she was here. There was no indication of who the note was from, beyond a name she didn't recognise. But presumably it was someone who worked here. Beyond the black security fence, a tourist was pointing a phone at her, taking photographs.

Curious, Alex called the number. 'DS Cupidi,' she said, as she stood below the Lionheart's horse. 'You wanted me to call.'

'Where are you?'

Alex paused. 'What's this about?'

The woman's voice was bubbly and loud. 'I can't say much now. Can we meet face to face?'

Alex looked around her, as if expecting to see the caller among the crowds of tourists. 'Who are you and how did you know I was here?'

'Wait a minute. Let me close the door.' The phone was quiet for a second, then the woman spoke again. 'I work in the office of the Secretary of State for Housing. My minister just wanted me to have a discreet word. Can you spare a minute? We're just at Portcullis House around the corner. Two minutes' walk away. Can you meet me at the doors?'

Alex noticed she hadn't answered her second question, *How did you know I was here?* But she said, 'OK.'

'Super. I'm wearing an orange top.'

The entrance to the parliamentary offices faced the river. Alex walked the crowded pavements under Big Ben, crossed Westminster Bridge Road and made her way to the entrance.

There, sure enough, a young woman with curly hair and a bright orange cardigan waited by the revolving doors. She grinned at Alex, gave a little wave as if they were friends. 'Easier to have a quick chat out here. It takes a bloody age to get anyone through security these days, even in your line of business.'

'What's this about?'

'Can I just check your ID? Sorry. Can't be too safe.'

Irritated now, Alex hesitated. Then pulled her wallet out of her shoulder bag, opening it at her warrant card.

'Super. Let's go and sit somewhere.' Without waiting to see if Alex was following, the young woman in the orange cardigan set

159

off across the busy lanes of Victoria Embankment. Alex caught up with her on the other side, where she had wandered past the Millennium Pier, with its crowds of tourists queuing for river boats, to an empty bench that sat with its back to the bike lane, looking out towards the London Eye.

'I work with Howard Roteman,' said the young woman.

'Bully for you,' said Alex.

'He's the Minister for Housing,' she explained, as if she felt that Alex had not looked impressed enough.

'And that makes you . . . ?'

The woman laughed. 'Just a humble assistant. One of several.'

'How is the minister? Still drink-driving?'

Tamsin Porter rolled her eyes. 'For obvious reasons, he doesn't drive at all these days.'

'The many advantages of a ministerial car.'

'Exactly.'

Shortly after he had been appointed to the government front benches a few years ago, Roteman had been caught speeding in an expensive car; when they breathalysed him, he had been over the limit. It had played into a public narrative of the government being over-privileged and out of touch. Roteman had done a round of hand-wringing TV interviews apologising for his behaviour, looking as contrite as he could. The *mea culpa* had worked as well as it had been intended to. He was now seen as one of the more honest members of the Prime Minister's cabinet.

'Howard wanted me to have a quiet word.'

'A quiet word?'

'About the Whiteland Fields development.'

The hairs on Alex's neck prickled. 'Seriously?'

160

'Mind if I smoke? I shouldn't, I know.' She pulled out a packet. When the cigarette was alight, she said, 'Yes. Absolutely seriously. We want to be kept informed about any developments in your investigation that might affect the public view of Whiteland Fields.'

A tourist couple were dragging a tired, weeping child along the pavement. 'No,' the woman was saying. 'Daddy's not going to carry you.'

'Say that again. You want me to update you on the investigation?'

'Yes. When there are developments.'

Alex looked directly at the young woman. 'Why?'

She looked surprised. 'Because he's interested.' She puffed on the cigarette as if unfamiliar with it, taking tiny mouthfuls. Then, when she realised from Alex's frown that that wasn't going to be enough, she added, 'Look. It's all very hush-hush but we're building up to a major new announcement on housing policy. Obviously it's good to do it in some sort of context. With some sort of backdrop, if you prefer.'

'Ministers in hard hats and shiny jackets, standing on factory floors.'

'Exactly,' said Tamsin, obliviously. 'We are announcing a new era of next-generation housing. Whiteland Fields is an integrated development of low-energy housing. It's perfect. But obviously if there's a risk of any negative press surrounding the development, we need to be aware of it.' She smiled. Took another micro-puff. 'And, given his own history with bad press that you alluded to earlier –' a conspiratorial smirk – 'he is always cautious about public image. Well?'

Alex looked at her. 'Why didn't you ask Derry Michaels to ask me?'

'Oh God. It's Derry's pet project. We certainly don't want to give him the impression that we're not a hundred per cent behind it.' The big wheel across the water moved slowly. 'I love a bloody cigarette,' said the young woman. 'I know I shouldn't.'

'Derry Michaels didn't seem to think there would be a problem if it turns out that the protests against the development are connected to the murder of Vincent Gibbons.'

'Didn't he?' she said, as if considering this. 'No. I don't suppose he would. Different priorities for us, though. We need flagship projects to celebrate they need to be pristine. All I've been told is that the minister is extremely keen to make sure that he knows what's going on, so that he can avoid any risk. You do understand that, don't you?'

Alex nodded.

'Super.' The woman stood and dropped the remains of her cigarette onto the grey London paving. 'And you will keep this under your hat, obviously? It's sensitive.'

'I'll need to tell my boss.'

The woman's brow lowered a millimetre. 'Your choice, obviously.'

'Super,' said Alex. 'I'm a public servant, just like you are. We have our ways of doing things.'

The woman chewed her lip for a second, pulled out a business card with her name and her contact details on it, and handed it to Alex. Alex took the card, examined it.

'So I can tell Howard you'll be in touch?'

'This is your card. What if I want to speak to him directly?'

'Why would you want to do that?'

Alex shrugged. 'If someone is interested in inside information on an investigation that may not yet be in the public realm, I want to be sure I understand exactly what they plan to do with it before I tell them.'

The woman laughed, as if Alex's concerns were absurd. 'He's a minister. Believe me, he understands the need for discretion better than any of us. I am happy, obviously, to pass on any request.' She pulled out her phone, checked the screen. 'Look. I have to go now. I have a meeting.'

'One other thing,' said Alex. 'How did you know I was going to be here, visiting Lord Michaels?'

'Sorry?'

'You left a message for me at the security desk. How did you know I was going to be there?'

Tamsin Porter, Assistant to the Secretary of State, frowned. 'That's a very interesting question, isn't it? You know, I'm not actually sure. Howard just told me you were going to be there. I suppose he must have had some kind of conversation with Derry, mustn't he?' And then the puzzled expression was gone again and she was smiling, holding out her hand to shake.

She remained on the bench after the perky young assistant had gone, thinking, watching khaki-coloured Thames water flow past.

Eventually she stood and walked to Westminster Underground station. In London for the day, she knew she should catch the Circle Line east and visit her mother who still lived in the family home in East London. It had been weeks since they had seen each other but she couldn't cope with the chaos of her mother's life, so instead she travelled three stops to London Bridge and ran for a train heading back to Ashford.

She sat with her head against the cool glass to the window, relieved to be leaving the city, heading back to her home.

It had been a strange, absurd day. She was imagining telling Zoë about it. She would make light of how she had taken tea with a Lord and been hunted down by a minister. But by the time her train was passing into the green Kent countryside, none of that felt so funny. Politicians looking over a police officer's shoulder was never a good thing. There would be more to this. There always was.

PART THREE

TWENTY-NINE

People stink.

Tonight, when the older badger goes to visit the latrines, he smells it again.

Engine oil and something else, lurking in the hump of ash trees.

Instead of going any further, he turns, scurries back and lies in darkness in the sett, waiting for the smell to go away.

One good thing, though. Now the younger badger is dead, he is claiming the older tunnel for himself again, marking the entrance as his own, as the scent of the dead one fades into the past.

THIRTY

This was Bill South's idea. A Friday night, almost two weeks now since Gram and Angela had found Vincent Gibbons's body. Nothing else going on. 'Come and see the badgers. It'll help.'

Alex was less than convinced. 'Help what?'

'Just help you understand what kind of man Vinnie was.'

Alex put the bottle of wine back in the fridge.

The security guard was the same young man who had taken Zoë's phone. He had the grace to look sheepish as he unlocked the gate to Whiteland Fields for Alex. 'Boss said it was OK.'

Alex had phoned Harry French in advance to ask if he minded them going on the land.

While they talked, South stood with his finger in the air. 'What do you think?' he asked Zoë.

'From the west,' she said.

South nodded and, without needing to discuss it any further, headed off along the fence line close to the road, heading east,

Zoë following on behind. Alex sighed, then trotted after them. Against her better judgement, William South had persuaded her to join them badger-watching.

The light was disappearing fast, tussocks of grass dark under Alex's feet. The landscape was mostly flat but the ground uneven. Alex stumbled, swore. Zoë hushed her. They had explained that the idea was to keep downwind of the sett, to prevent badgers from noticing their scent.

South had brought a canvas to lie on. He unfolded it carefully, flattening it onto the grass. The three of them lay side by side, propped up on their elbows, watching in the direction of the main sett.

'Where is it?' Alex whispered.

Zoë pointed towards the rise in the land ahead; a darker smear of earth, presumably one of the entrances to the sett. Fresh dirt, newly dug. Alex was surprised how close they were to it. She tried to remember when she had last seen badgers that weren't dead by the roadside. It must have been in her childhood; her grandparents' farm in Devon.

Zoë and South, one on either side of her, raised binoculars to their eyes. With Alex between them, they lay waiting for something to happen.

Stars appeared in the sky overhead. Something tiny rustled in the grass next to them. At one point, South whispered, 'Hear that?'

'Whoa,' breathed Zoë.

'Hear what?' said Alex.

'Ssh,' South mouthed.

'What?' said Alex, a little louder, irritated by the fact that her

169

teenage daughter and this man, who was so much older, seemed to be communicating by some kind of code she didn't recognise.

'Quiet.'

Alex heard nothing in particular. Just the noise of traffic along the main road. She peered more intently towards the sett. Nothing seemed to be moving there at all. Long minutes passed. The evening grew darker still.

South moved so that his head was close to hers. His voice low, breath against her ear. 'Anything from forensics about the body?'

'Nothing useful. No signs of anyone else's DNA. No evidence to suggest where he was killed. It looks as if the body was thoroughly cleaned first. Maybe put in a bath, literally. They've been through the drains at the Guldeford Hall to see if there are any DNA traces there, but they found nothing. We're in the dark. Nothing so far to link it to Frankie Collins and his mates, but we'll get there.'

South nodded. 'Difficult,' he said.

In the dark, trying to make out vague shapes. She still had no idea where Vincent Gibbons had been killed or how the poison had been administered. 'Is this the kind of thing Vinnie Gibbons did? Lying here like this, waiting for something to happen? Did you ever come here with him?'

'No.'

'You?' she asked Zoë.

'No, but I know he came here.'

'What if nothing happens?'

'It just did. We just heard a nightjar back then.'

'Whoop-de-doo,' said Alex.

'Mum. Behave.'

Far away at the edge of the field, a light came on in the Portakabin.

'Don't let her wind you up, Zoë. She loves it really.'

She didn't love it; she loved the idea of being out here, but it was unnatural to her to lie so still for so long. She was an impatient person. She had never been good at stake-outs, even when there were criminals to be watched. This stillness and silence made her want to leap up and scream. Her teenage daughter's effortless patience amazed her.

South eventually spoke, almost inaudibly. 'Zoë says you were treading the corridors of power this week.'

'I thought I told you you weren't supposed to tell anybody,' said Alex.

A whisper. 'He's not "anybody".'

'I knew I shouldn't have told you.'

They lapsed into silence again. Nothing moved. Nothing appeared from the holes in the ground they were looking at, which became harder and harder to see in the disappearing light.

'Do you think they've gone, the badgers?'

South laughed softly. 'No.'

'With all this stuff going on around them?'

'You don't get rid of badgers that easily. That's the point. Nothing shifts them easily. Build a housing estate on top of them and they'll dig the place up.'

'So what was Vincent Gibbons doing here? Why was he so fascinated with these badgers?'

'He was all over the place looking for them.'

'There are too many badgers,' said Alex. 'They're eating all the hedgehogs. So a man told me.'

'Oh yeah, Mum. Now you know all about badgers? Too many, says who?'

'Can't say. Can't trust you any more.'

'Bet it was a farmer.'

'Close.'

'It's total rubbish anyway. Reasons hedgehogs are declining is because of pesticides, habitat fragmentation and climate change. People blame badgers for everything.'

'Like bovine TB?'

'Exactly.' Zoë was trying to whisper, but her voice was slowly getting louder.

'I expect you reckon they don't spread TB to cows?'

South rolled over, sat up facing them both, an amused look on his face.

'It's the other way round,' Zoë hissed angrily. 'Cows are spreading it to badgers. I mean, deer have it now, foxes, even cats.' Alex loved her daughter when she was like this. She lay in the gloom, listening to her angry passion. 'Why aren't they killing cats? They're not shooting them like they are badgers. Maybe they should.'

'Now you want to kill cats?'

'Stop laughing at me, Mum.'

'I'm not laughing, I promise.'

'They're blaming badgers because it's easier than admitting that dairy herds are riddled with the disease. A cow's, like, a billion per cent more likely to catch TB from another cow than a badger. It's why we should all be vegans.'

'Ssh.' It was South's turn to try to quieten them.

South dropped onto his elbows, raised his binoculars to his

eyes and stared at something to the left of where the main sett was.

'What?'

'Something moving there.'

They all strained to look into the gloom, but Alex saw nothing. She was uncomfortable now, and wanted to stand and bend her legs.

'Clue's in the name,' said Zoë. 'Bovine TB. Cows, not badgers.'

'Bill. I was thinking, you've been to Vinnie Gibbons's house, haven't you?'

William South nodded.

'I took some photos there after the forensics people had left. Wonder if you could take a look. Maybe there's something out of place, something missing.'

'If you like. Can you email them?'

'Can I stand up?' said Alex. 'My leg's gone to sleep.'

'Wait,' said South.

'Doesn't look like we're going to see anything tonight anyway,' said Zoë. 'I'm guessing they're nervous because of all the people coming on site.'

'There. Again,' South said quietly.

Alex looked, but saw nothing at all. But then a car drove up the small lane that led to the airport behind them. As the car turned at the fence, its headlights swept across the grassland in front of them and Alex saw it. A tiny double flash of light. 'Binoculars?'

'Yes,' said South.

'More badger watchers,' she said.

'Maybe,' said South.

There it was again. A small glint in the woods to the left, beyond the fence. She stood.

'Where are you going, Mum?' hissed Zoë.

Alex's legs were stiff but it felt great to be moving again. She was off at a slow trot across the grass now, towards the fence. She didn't run straight towards where she'd seen the reflection, but headed towards the west, where she remembered there had been a cut in the fence.

It was still there, unmended. She crouched her way through it and sprang up again. In another few seconds she was among the thicker vegetation. Stopping suddenly, she called out, 'Hello?'

Nothing. Only her own breath.

She stood still for a second, wondering if it had just been a trick of light.

And then, a little to the south, the unmistakable crack of a stick.

'Who's there?' she said.

Another rustling, and then she saw him. Clearly silhouetted against the lighter western sky, the shape of a man.

'I want to talk to you.'

But the man, whoever he was, did not want to talk to her; he turned and ran. Alex sprang after him towards the trees.

Almost at the place where he had been standing, an unseen bramble snagged her ankle and she fell face first into the under-growth, thorns pricking her skin.

Trying to push herself up, more spines punctured her hands. She had just managed to get herself back on her feet when she heard the roar of a motorbike, close by. She looked up. A small unpaved track ran the far side of the trees, back out to the lane that led to the airport.

The bike braked briefly at the corner, its rear light painting the dirt behind it red, but he hadn't switched on his headlights. And then there was darkness again, and the bike was roaring off towards the main road.

She turned to see someone on the far side of the fence she had just come through. 'Who was it?' called South.

'I don't know.'

Alex turned back to where she had seen the man watching them, squatted down and examined the ground around where he'd been, but found nothing; no sandwich wrappers or cigarette ends, not even footprints.

'Anything?' called South.

She made her way back to the hole in the fence and crawled back through. 'Nothing.'

'Bloody hell. What happened to you?'

Alex raised her hand to her face and felt dampness. It was not just her legs and hands that had been scratched; she must have cut her face on the thorns too.

'Who was it?'

'I didn't see.'

'You spooked the hell out of them, anyway.'

'Maybe,' she said.

'Does Julian Epps ride a motorbike?'

'He has a white van.'

'Him or one of his mates,' said South, looking around.

Zoë caught up with them. 'Mum!' she gasped, switching on the torch on her phone to examine her face.

'It's fine.'

'I told you. I told you they were watching us.'

'It's why you brought me here, isn't it, Bill?'

'Zoë had said she'd seen people watching her at night.'

'You didn't believe me, Mum.'

Stung, Alex walked in silence back across the ground, past the badger setts, Zoë clinging on to her arm. The man at the gate said, 'What happened?'

'Have you noticed anyone hanging around on the far side of the fence?'

The man shrugged, shook his head. 'Only interested in what happens inside the fence,' he said. 'People who shouldn't be here.' Inside the cabin, the TV was turned up loud.

Back inside the car, she pulled down the rear-view mirror and examined her face, dabbing it with a paper handkerchief. A long scratch ran down past her right eye.

Zoë looked at her. 'I've got some aloe vera in the house.'

Unsettled, Alex looked at her reflection, a red line down the side of her face. Her daughter believed in conspiracies; she always thought people were watching her.

THIRTY-ONE

Saturday night, and Alex didn't feel like cooking. She arrived early at the Pilot, found a table free at the window looking out towards the Channel and sat on her own with a large white wine, reading the newspaper.

Her phone buzzed, and when she looked at the number, she saw it was DI McAdam's. She put down the paper, lifted her glass to her lips, took a generous gulp and answered it.

'I've just had a very interesting phone call,' he said.

'Let me guess. A young woman who works for the Secretary of State for Housing.'

'A Tamsin Porter called me up to inform me of a meeting she had with you.'

'Was she charming, and did she say "super" a lot?'

'Are you out somewhere?'

'In the pub at Dungeness. Come and join us. Constable Ferriter'll be here in a minute. William South is coming too.'

'I can't. Dinner party.' There was resignation in his voice.

Alex knew his wife, a tightly wound woman who kept a perfect house. 'She said she had asked you to keep her up to date with the inquiry.'

'Probably because I told her I'd tell you.'

'On the surface it seems an innocent enough enquiry . . .'

'On the surface,' she repeated.

'Yes.' DI McAdam was a cautious man who would like this kind of interference from on high even less than she did. He ran things well, was young, sensitive, clever, and was marked down as a high-flyer. 'Do you think there's anything else behind it?'

'It's perfectly plausible that Howard Roteman would want to know that everything was OK before he uses the housing development as the backdrop for a press conference, isn't it?'

'Yes,' McAdam said, though he sounded no more convinced than she was.

'So?'

'Does he have any say on whether the project goes ahead, Alex? I'm trying to work out whether there's a political dimension in this – something that might come back and bite us in the arse?'

In the background, McAdam's wife's voice: 'Toby. Don't you ever turn that phone off? Our guests are here.'

'In theory, that's the Secretary of State's decision, not his,' Alex said, 'but he must have some influence. But it's not commercial information, is it?'

'Isn't it? The victim was a protestor against the development.' A young gull landed on a picnic table just outside her window, pecked at a cigarette butt, then dropped it in disgust. 'Let me handle them,' he said.

'Thanks.'

Alex heard his wife calling his name in the background.

'Everything OK with the rest of the investigation?'

She was about to tell him about the man she had chased at Whiteland Fields, but thought better of it. She wasn't sure if it was important. And it was the weekend; he would only worry.

After the call, she returned to the paper. A migrant boat had sunk in the Channel; everyone was feared drowned.

'What happened to your face?' She looked up. Curly was standing next to her with a pint of lager in his big, callused hand.

She nodded at the chair next to her but he stayed standing.

'Gardening accident,' she said. 'I heard they're selling your family's old home.'

'I always thought I'd buy it back one day. Might still try.'

'What with, Curly?'

'Sell my boat, maybe.'

Curly kept an old fibreglass double-hulled trawler on the beach.

'How much is that going to raise?'

'Not enough, that's for sure,' he said, and returned to the bar.

By the time William South and Zoë arrived, half an hour later, she was already on a second glass, made a mental note to go easy, but then Jill arrived and bought a bottle of house white for them both to share.

'I thought you'd said you were going to slow down with the drinking?' said Alex.

'I am,' said Jill, pouring a glass. 'So you didn't get to see this bloke who was spying on you then?'

'We don't know that he was spying on us.'

Zoë said, 'I told you there were people watching us, Mum.'

'I don't get it,' said Jill.

'Ask your boyfriend about it,' muttered Zoë.

'I don't get it either,' said Alex. 'I hear there's going to be a big event up at Westminster about the new houses.'

'How did you know about that?' demanded Jill. 'That's supposed to be embargoed.'

'Are you going?' asked Alex before anyone could answer.

'I am invited, actually.' She grinned. 'Don't know if I will, though. It'll be a bit posh. After the opera, I'm worried I'll show him up.'

'It'll be a bit posh, and you of all people don't want to go?' said Zoë.

'I don't even understand what he sees in me.'

'Oh shut up,' said Alex.

And then they were all huddled round the table trying to persuade her to go; even Zoë.

The four of them walked the quarter-mile back to Alex's house in the dark, talking nonsense, Zoë arguing with everyone. Alex wasn't that drunk, just a little warmer inside than before. She felt good.

'Oh shit,' said Jill tipsily. 'Meant to say. Gave my card to the gardener at Guldeford Hall and he called me back yesterday. Turns out Sir Andrew Utting was a bit of a ladies' man.'

'Ah,' said Alex. 'Maybe that's why they lived separately. So why did the gardener call you back?'

''Cause you'd said to ask him about who knew the code to the alarm? Apparently this woman used to drive up and let herself in sometimes. Middle-aged woman.'

'Any description?'

'Never saw her close to, so. Apparently she drove a red Mazda,' she was saying as Alex went to put her key in the lock.

But the back door was already unlocked and open, and swung wide as she pushed it.

Holding up her arm to stop the others from going in, she hissed, 'Quiet.'

It took a couple of seconds for the chatter to die.

'What's wrong?'

Alex stepped inside, put her hand on the switch and the kitchen was suddenly bright with light. Her eyes darted around the room, looking for signs that someone had been there: open drawers, footprints on the floor.

'Sorry, Mum,' said Zoë. 'It was probably me. I was last out. Didn't shut it properly.'

Alex forced them to stay on the doorstep while she went inside.

'There's no one there, Mum.'

Even later, after she had gone through each room, checking wardrobes and the spaces under beds, checking her computer and her daughter's laptop, checking the drawer where she kept her father's gold wristwatch, did she join them downstairs.

Zoë had probably left the door open by mistake, that was all, Alex told herself.

THIRTY-TWO

On Sunday morning, Jay arrived on a moped, and Zoë already had the helmet on before Alex made it out of the kitchen door to ask her what she was doing.

'He's just taking me to Folkestone, Mum,' muttered Zoë.

'What are you doing there?'

'None of your business,' said Zoë. 'I'm seventeen.'

'Is it legal?'

'Mum!'

Jay smirked. 'Borderline,' he said.

Zoë punched him on the arm. 'If you want to know, I'm going to a creative protest and civil disobedience workshop, OK?'

From behind came a laugh. Alex looked round and glared at Jill, who was standing in the kitchen doorway, one hand over her mouth. 'Sorry.'

'Have you got a licence for that?' Alex asked Jay. 'And insurance?'

'Shut up, Mum, for Christ's sake.'

'I'm going to tell all my colleagues in traffic to keep an eye out for you,' Alex said. 'If anyone sees you speeding or driving dangerously, I'm going to ask them to come down on you like a tonne of shit, OK?'

'Mum. Your pushbike goes faster than this thing.'

Alex watched them putter down the track alongside the fence, cursing boys and motorbikes.

'Creative civil disobedience workshops,' said Jill. 'I love that girl.'

'It's your boyfriend's development they're protesting about.'

'He's a big boy.'

'If she so much as scratches her knees, I'll kill him.' She turned to Jill, and saw she had put a coat on, ready to leave. 'You seeing big boy today?'

'He's away somewhere at some mega business meeting,' she said.

After she'd gone, Alex made a thermos of coffee and wandered down the track towards William South's shack.

He was splashing red preservative onto the wood.

'Want a hand?' she asked.

The two of them spent an hour together touching up the wood-work, not talking much. You had to keep on top of it in this place. The wind off the sea could be fierce, picking up debris and flinging it across the flatland. The buildings here took a battering whenever storms hit the shore, which they seemed to more often every year.

It's why she liked it here. It felt precarious. 'Why is someone keeping an eye on Whiteland Fields, Bill?'

South was standing on a ladder propped against one of the gables. 'Why are you asking me?'

Alex dipped her brush into the can. 'You're the one that believed Zoë's conspiracy theory.'

He grunted, climbed down the ladder to pick up a hammer, then returned to bang in a loose nail, so hard the whole house seemed to shake. When he had put the hammer down again, he said, 'Birders have a word for pretending you've seen something when you haven't. It's called "stringing". I trust Zoë. If Zoë says she's seen something, then she has. You should know that.'

'I barely understand her at the best of times.'

A sudden burst of sunshine lit the land around them. 'I don't go for the conspiracy, though.'

'So why is somebody watching them?'

'That Epps man. I know his kind. I was a community copper round here. Local lads who missed any chance of getting out of the place. I wouldn't put it past him to be after the badgers. They're a nasty bunch. Probably think they'd be doing the developers a favour. He's the one you should be gunning for, ask me.'

They took a break for coffee, sitting on a bench improvised from a plank and a couple of ladders.

'So Jill's in love,' he said.

'She deserves a break. She's been through some shit.'

South wasn't a man who talked much normally; his spell in prison had left him even less conversational than he had been when she had first known him, though today there were a few words. 'What about you? You ever think about . . .'

'About what? Love?'

'If you like.'

184

'Nope,' Alex said. She picked up her cup and took a gulp.

'You never lonely?'

'With Zoë? Never a dull moment. Did you see her just now? She's disappeared off down the road with an animal rights protestor. What about you, Bill? Anyone?'

He looked away. 'No.'

'You ever lonely?'

He turned again and looked straight at her. 'Always,' he said.

There was an uneasy moment in which she wished she had never asked the question. Then he stood suddenly and said, 'I should caulk the flue. Water getting in up there.'

She was grateful when her phone rang. 'Sergeant Cupidi? It's Colin Gilchrist. You remember me? Sorry to disturb you on a Sunday, but I'm at the offices of a company called September Homes.'

'Is there anything wrong?'

'There's been a break-in here. We were just looking through the keyholders and the name of Harry French came up. Then I remembered you mentioning his name when I was at your house, so I thought I'd better give you a call, just in case . . .'

'What kind of break-in?'

'Somebody nicked some computers, by the look of it.'

Alex put down her coffee. 'Did you contact Harry French?'

'Left a message.'

'Apparently he's away somewhere at a business meeting. I'll be there in about half an hour,' she said.

'No need,' he said. 'I can manage.'

In truth, she wasn't sure she needed to go either, but working would stop her worrying about Zoë on the back of a moped, and

185

William South had disappeared up a ladder onto his roof and was pretending she wasn't there.

She had been to worse scenes of crime. The burglars appeared to have known what they had wanted. The Apple computers had all gone.

'CCTV,' said Gilchrist, pointing at a camera. 'But I bet they knew it was there.'

The crime scene officer had arrived; she was dusting for prints. 'How professional a job does it look?'

'It's not like we have a Trustpilot rating for burglars,' said the woman, then stopped and added, 'Yet.'

'But it's not just some druggie feeding a habit?'

'Whoever it was, they've certainly had enough practice not to leave prints, or bleed in useful places,' she said.

'Bastards,' said Alex, looking around.

'I know.'

Alex put on gloves and went to look at Harry French's empty desk. No photos. No ornaments. No computer now, either.

'Do you think they wanted the computers, or what was on them?' she asked out loud.

'Couldn't say at this stage,' said the CSI.

'Any luck getting hold of Harry French?' Alex asked Gilchrist.

'I'll try him again now.'

'No matter. I'll do it,' she said, pressing his number.

He answered after a couple of rings. 'Sorry to disturb you, Jill said you were away at a meeting . . .'

'Yes,' he said, 'I am.

'. . . but I'm afraid to say that your offices in Folkestone were broken into last night.'

French swore. 'Did they make a mess of the place?'

'Not at all. A broken window lock on the ground floor. A couple of broken doors. It looks like yours wasn't the only office they went into, but they stole all your computers. I wanted to ask . . .'

A woman's voice: 'Who is it, Harry?'

The phone muted for a second, then he was back. 'What was that you were going to ask?'

'Apart from the computers themselves, is there anything of value on those computers?'

'Everything's on the server, so we haven't lost anything. Is that all?'

'You don't seem very concerned. Is there any material on any of the computers that could be valuable to someone?'

'There's commercially sensitive information, obviously, particularly around what we expect as a return on investment from this development. But it's a crude way to steal information. More likely they were just interested in the computers. Are you worried about anything in particular?'

Outside, an ambulance was moving loudly up Tontine Street.

'No,' she said. 'Just checking.'

'Of course. I'll arrange for someone to come and make the office secure,' he was saying.

And that's when she realised that she could hear the same ambulance on her phone, slightly out of sync with the one whose siren was coming through the windows. At first she thought it was some trick of technology, a phantom echo. And then she remembered that Jill had told her he had a flat near the Quarterhouse on Tontine Street, yet he'd said he was away.

After the call was ended, she called Jill. There was no answer. She would still be doing her mammoth Sunday yoga session.

'Do you have an address for the keyholder?' she asked Gilchrist.

He gave it to her. It was in the Old High Street, the narrow road leading up from the sea that had filled with cafes and art shops.

'Call me if you find anything,' she said, pushing her way out through the door.

The house was only a minute away, a plain, Victorian brick building, perched on the thin street's slope beside an older, weatherboarded building. The ground floor was an interiors shop; Harry French's flat had to be the top two floors, accessed through a discreet side door.

A little way up the road on the opposite side there was a coffee house and second-hand bookshop. She asked a couple who sat holding hands across the table in the window if they wouldn't mind her sharing with them. They looked put out, but were too polite to refuse. She sat, drinking a double Americano as slowly as she could, keeping her eyes fixed on the pale blue door on the left side of the shop.

Without taking her eyes off the door, she reached into her bag and took out her phone, then dialled her daughter.

'What?' Zoë answered.

'You didn't fall off the motorbike then?'

'Thanks for caring, Mum. It's very sweet.'

'Good . . . workshop?'

'We've just been learning how to resist arrest by police officers. What time are you home?'

She was just telling her daughter she wasn't sure, when she saw the door to Harry French's flat opening.

THIRTY-THREE

'Look at it,' said Jill, grinning up at the gilt-edged card:

Ms Jill Ferriter
is invited to an Evening Canapé Reception
to celebrate the launch of Whiteland Fields
at St John's, Smith Square, Westminster
RSVP

'Me. Born from absolute shite. You know what my mother
was.' Jill had grown up in and out of care; her mother had
been a sex worker. 'And look at me now. Canapé reception in
Westminster.'

Alex had said nothing to her about the woman she had
seen emerging from the blue door of Harry French's flat that
morning. She had been in her late twenties, perhaps a couple
of years older than Jill, stylish, thin, in a citrine yellow dress
with a white leather shoulder bag; beautiful, in a wealthy kind

of way. It was not so much the woman as the fact that he had lied. He was not away on business; he was at his flat with a woman who wasn't Jill.

The constable was in a towelling dressing gown, fresh from a shower, sitting on the sofa in her flat with her phone in her lap.

'Have you spoken to him recently?'

Jill shook her head. 'I wouldn't want to seem like the needy girlfriend or anything.'

Alex nodded.

'You want to see the dresses I ordered?'

'Plural. Dresses?'

'Course. You can help me pick one if you like. I'll send the others back. Wait there.'

Jill stood, and returned with a pile of plastic bags.

'How many have you ordered?'

'Six. Shall I try them on? Give you a fashion show.'

She disappeared back into the bedroom and reappeared in a long black dress. 'ASOS,' she said. 'Do you think it's a bit booby?'

'A bit?' said Alex.

Jill disappeared again.

'Does Harry ever ask about the investigation?'

This time it was a dress from Net-a-Porter.

'Too pink,' said Alex.

'What's wrong with pink? What did you say about Harry?'

'I just wanted to ask. When you're with him, does he ever try and steer the conversation round to the Vincent Gibbons murder?'

Jill stared at Alex. 'What are you asking that for?'

'I just wanted to make sure that . . .'

'That what?' There was colour in the younger woman's cheeks.

'You know how sensitive investigations like this are. I just want to make sure that you're not discussing the case with him. Does he ever talk about it?'

In her pink dress, Jill put her hands on her hips. 'I don't know what kind of officer you think I am. You know I wouldn't talk about it, even if he did ask. Which he doesn't.'

She turned, and flounced out of the room.

Alex looked around Jill's flat. It was spotless and spartan. She wasn't a reader, so didn't have shelves crammed with books; she had grown up a single child with a mother who had struggled with alcohol and drug addiction, so she didn't have photographs of relations on the table. The main decoration was a framed poster on the wall that said: *Live Well, Laugh Often, Love Always*. A couple of coffee-table books sat on a glass table; one Banksy, another on handbags. On the windowsill was a ceramic cactus, and propped up next to it, the gilt-edged invitation. The party was a big deal for her.

She came back in a high-necked dress – 'from Boohoo.com' – with black sleeves and a yellow body that descended into a pleated skirt. 'Seriously, Sarge. What's going on?'

She only called her 'Sarge' when she was in a mood.

'Nothing. Don't worry about it. You know me.'

Jill stared at her, still angry.

'You look amazing,' said Alex. She did. The dress lent her a sophistication that Alex had never seen in her before.

Jill softened. 'I've never spent this much money on a dress,' she said. 'Do you think Harry will like it?'

192

'Why do you care what Harry will think?'

'What's got into you?'

'Nothing. You look gorgeous in it,' Alex said. 'Treat yourself.' And then wondered if the yellow in the body of the dress was the same shade as the one the woman she'd seen leaving French's flat had been wearing.

She spotted Zoë and Jay by the side of Littlestone Road as she drove home.

'Motorbike's cocked,' said Jay. 'Pile of shit.'

'Get in,' said Alex, through the open window.

'Can't. Someone will nick it.'

Alex looked at the machine, propped against a tree by the side of the road. 'I rather doubt it.'

'Cost me good money.'

'Really? You want to come home with me, Zoë, or do you want to wait here while Jay works out how to get his moped home?'

'I can't leave him here on his own, Mum.'

Alex sighed, then pulled out her phone and called Curly, who had an old Ford Ranger pickup truck. 'He said he'll take it to your place in Folkestone for thirty quid,' said Alex.

'Haven't got thirty,' said Jay, shrugging.

Alex rolled her eyes.

She waited by the side of the road until Curly's yellow pickup arrived, and helped lift the bike onto the back of the truck, paid him £30, then watched Jay and his motorbike drive off towards the main road.

'Lucky I passed by.'

'Otherwise you wouldn't have had a chance to patronise us,' said Zoë.

'Good day?' said Alex, trying to sound nice.

'Tired, though.' Her daughter, the teenage, animal-rights, eco-warrior, leaned her head against Alex's left arm, and closed her eyes as her mother drove.

She was driving along Coast Drive, sea on the left, bungalows on the right, when her phone pinged.

'Read it,' she said to Zoë.

Her daughter opened her eyes, sat up straight and lifted the phone from her bag. She unlocked the phone and found the message. '*Have emailed you report on blood sample. Surprising, no?*,' Zoë read. 'Is that from forensics?'

It was; it was from a crime scene investigator called Francis Joyce. The blood sample from her front door; and the one in Julian Epps's van. The report would be waiting for her on her computer.

'Slow down, Mum,' chided her daughter. 'You'll get busted for driving too fast.'

Alex looked at her speedometer which was registering over forty in a thirty zone and took her foot off the pedal. Zoë, the child who went to civil disobedience workshops, looked smug all the way home.

THIRTY-FOUR

'It's not badger blood,' said the crime scene investigator on the phone. 'It's one hundred per cent not a match for the swabs we took from your door.'

Alex blinked. She had read the report, last night, but hadn't been sure she believed it. 'Human blood?'

'God, no!' A laugh. 'Definitely not human either.'

'What is it then?'

'Not absolutely sure, to be honest.'

'What does that mean. It's werewolf?'

'Not possible to rule it out at this stage. Actually, no, we can rule out werewolves. Werewolf blood would have human characteristics. I'd assume so, anyway. Sorry. I messaged you a preliminary report from the lab because I thought you'd want to know. If you've any more of these challenges, send them our way. They're way more interesting than most of what we get.'

Alex was puzzled. If it wasn't badger blood in the back of

Julian Epps's van, then there was no way of linking him to the carcass left at her door.

Alex made it into the office by 8.30; she liked to be there before the office got too busy.

She took out a sheet of paper and wrote names on it; in the middle, Vincent Gibbons's. They weren't sure when exactly he was killed, but they knew he'd been gassed with the same poison people used to kill badgers with. He had been involved in a case prosecuting Francis Collins and Julian Epps. She wrote their names in a column on the left of the page, then crossed them out. Gibbons had also been protesting against the development on Whiteland Fields, but that line of enquiry seemed vague and elusive. Bill South's reproach rang in her ears; she should trust her daughter. She certainly didn't trust Harry French. So she wrote *September Homes* on the right-hand side of the page and next to it: *Harry French?*

'What's that?'

Jill had been standing behind her all this time. She turned. Jill was frowning at her. 'Jesus, Jill. You made me jump.'

Jill reached past her towards the sheet of paper Alex had been writing on. 'Is Harry a suspect?' she asked.

Alex turned towards her.

'Why? What are you going to tell me?' Her voice was loud. People in the office pretended not to look.

Alex stood and put on her coat. 'Let's get out of here,' she said.

When Jill's mint tea had arrived, she said, 'This is absolute bollocks, Alex.'

'Did he know you were a copper before he picked you from the dating site?'

It was a pretty basic cafe, white tiled floors and black metal chairs, but the only half-decent one near the police station. 'Why are you asking?'

'Is there any way he could have known?'

'He didn't pick me. I picked him. It's an app where women pick the men, not the other way round. If you have something to tell me, bloody tell me, Alex.'

'But he could have known who you were and what you did when you approached him?'

'It was on my profile. Why?'

'Show me.'

'So he is a suspect? And you think he's been pumping me for information? God's sake, Alex. You think I was born yesterday? I asked him out, not the other way round. I'm not telling him anything about the case, swear to God.'

'Show me what he saw when you did.'

Jill rolled her eyes, pulled out her iPhone. She opened the app and looked up her profile. 'It's kind of embarrassing, actually.'

She passed the phone across the table.

Jill, 25.

'Nice photo,' said Alex. It was hard to imagine a bad photo of Jill. A tiny scar above one eye, recently inflicted, still slightly red, was the only sign of a blemish on her perfect skin.

Jill stabbed her tea bag with a teaspoon.

'*I like cool bars and hot yoga,*' read Alex.

'Shut up. You have to say stuff like that.'

197

'Here you go . . . *I'm a copper. Looking for murderers by day, for non-murderers by night and weekends.*'

'Everybody puts what they do on it. It's how it works. It wouldn't be hard to find out, anyway. There's a Facebook link so he could go and look me up. My job title's right there. It would take five minutes. Oh Jesus, Alex. You seriously think he went out with me because he was trying to find out about the case? That would have been impossible. You're being weird. You've been a copper way too long.' She half laughed, nervous now. 'It's twisting you up. The body hadn't even turned up when I swiped him.'

'I know that.'

Jill looked at her for a long time, trying to read what she was thinking. 'You know something about him, don't you? This is why you're acting like a weirdo.'K' sake, Sarge. If you know something, you have to tell me. I'm going out with him. We've had sex.'

'I just have to ask, that's all.'

'I know you're my boss, but you're supposed to be my friend. And you're turning into this weird, creepy fucking person, Alex. Is it that you don't think I'm good enough for him?'

'Don't be daft, Jill.'

'Is it, though? Too good to be true, is it? Like, 'cause he's really handsome and charming and well-off and I'm some kind of chav? You think there's got to be something funny going on if a guy like him is after a girl like me.'

'Shut up, Jill. I just want you to be careful.'

'What does that mean, Alex?'

Alex handed the phone back. 'Ignore me. You're right. I'm just a copper. I can't help being suspicious of everybody.'

'Think about it, Alex. It would be pretty weird to date a copper just on the odds someone found the body, wouldn't it?'

'You're right,' Alex said, deciding to keep her suspicions to herself. There could be a perfectly simple explanation of why Harry French pretended to be out of town, of why the woman was in his flat. It was none of her business.

'Funny,' said Jill, frowning. 'His profile is still active.'

'What?'

'I thought he'd snoozed his profile. I snoozed mine after our first date.'

'He's still inviting people to get in touch with him?'

'I suppose he hasn't got round to it yet. Or maybe I'm not perfect enough for him.' She gave a tiny smile, stood up. 'You're not going to tell me anything, are you?'

'It's nothing,' said Alex. 'Like you said. I've been a copper way too long.'

'Actually, maybe you have.' Which stung.

Without another word, Jill left the cafe to walk back to the station alone.

The only car that was available for Alex to book out at the station was one of the old marked Escorts. It always felt different, driving in a marked car; traffic slowed around you, like they thought you might not have noticed them speeding. People annoyed her today. Jill annoyed her. She annoyed herself.

She drove north to Julian Epps's house. It was exactly the

same as the last time she had been there. The damp mattress was propped against the wall; the van was parked on the paving stones, though the stain below its rear doors had been wiped away.

'You again.'

Epps stood at his doorway again.

'Mind if I come in?'

'Yeah. I do, actually.'

'I can talk out here, but the neighbours might be listening.'

Arriving in a car covered in the word POLICE had an effect here, too. It made people nosey. Across the street, a young man had come out and was leaning against the fence, watching them, arms folded.

'Yeah. They do a lot of that round here. Especially after your gang of coppers came round the other day.' He stepped back. 'What is it this time?'

'I'll be honest. I jumped to conclusions. Somebody dumped a dead badger on my doorstep. When we saw your van, we put two and two together.'

'And made three.'

A dark-brown terrier of some kind that had been asleep in a basket by the kitchen door stood up and gave a low, menacing growl.

'Shut up, Nigel,' snapped Epps.

The dog quietened, but remained standing, looking up at Alex. 'What? So you come to apologise?'

'Why not?' said Alex.

'Because you lot never do.'

Alex looked around. The flat looked messier. Empty beer cans lay on the floor. 'Girlfriend not in?'

'She's gone to stay with her mum.'

'Classic,' said Alex.

'Yep. Pissed off at me for losing my job. Which was all your fault in the first place.'

He hadn't offered a seat, but Alex sat down anyway in an old black leather armchair and looked around. 'You didn't have to go badger-baiting in the first place, Julian.'

'You didn't have to be a bunch of nosey bastards. Besides, I got off, didn't I? Still. Enough of this banter,' he said sitting opposite her, legs splayed at a forty-five-degree angle. 'What are you really here for?'

'We had the blood tested and it wasn't badger.'

'Which I could have told you for free. Though obviously glad to see our tax dollars are being put to such good use. How much did that cost. Five hundred quid? A grand?'

'Not far off, actually.' She looked around her again. A large TV screen was hung on the wall; the others were bare.

'Good,' he said. 'Because it's our money you're wasting.'

'It wasn't human either, you'll be glad to know.'

He reached in his jacket pocket for a packet of cigarettes. 'Yeah. That would have been awkward, wouldn't it?'

'So I got to thinking, what would it be? You want to tell me, Mr Epps?'

'Not really.'

'I have a theory. There's you, laid off from your job at the abattoir. I reckon you took it into your hands to take a little bit of payment in lieu. That's what the blood in the back of your van was.'

Julian took out and lit a cigarette. 'Here we go,' he said. 'Two and two make three.'

'Do they? I reckon you took a beef carcass. Worth a bit, I'd imagine.'

'Can't prove anything, can you?'

The dog finally settled, walking in a circle a few times in its basket, then lying down.

'I don't really have to, do I?'

'What do you mean?'

'All I need to do is ask the boss at your work if you might have removed some meat from the abattoir. Probably something that had been condemned as unfit. That's what it was, wasn't it?'

'OK. Out,' said Julian Epps.

The dog's ears pointed upwards.

Alex held up her hands. 'Calm down.'

'Is that what you've come to tell me?'

'I want you to tell me who dumped a dead badger outside my house.'

'What? And you'll call off the dogs if I do?'

'I don't have dogs. Never liked them, remember? But I think you know who did it.'

Julian Epps looked at her. 'Look.' His voice was weary now. 'I know I like to come over as a bit of a dick, but I swear I didn't do it. And I swear to God I don't know who did. Since you came along, I've lost my work and probably my girlfriend. I just want you to leave me alone.'

Alex sat for a minute longer. 'But you can probably find out who did, can't you?'

'Out,' he said.

The dog stood again, and this time it growled.

THIRTY-FIVE

The younger male is dead.

Things change.

Its marker scent at the boundaries grows weaker. It's as if the walls around them were starting to thin, and more badgers from the neighbouring setts are beginning to trespass on their territory.

When he can, the older badger chases them away. So far, it has been easy. Last night, by the clump of gorse bushes, he came across a yearling male whose scent he recognised from one of the border latrines.

The older badger had barked, raised himself on his legs, shook his fur, leaned towards the other animal, ready for a fight. The other badger mirrored him, growling quietly, but then turned and trotted away, backing down.

A fight is coming, though. It is inevitable now, for another reason.

This evening, waking, he smells another signal, rich and pungent. It excites him.

It is a scent that tells him the older female is ready to mate. But there's danger in this, too. He won't be the only badger around here who understands the promise of this signal.

PART FOUR

THIRTY-SIX

At just gone 10.30 in the morning Evalynn Doubek was watching *Queer Eye* on the work computer in the reception office of the Golden Sands Holiday Park. The holiday season was a long way off and mid-week there was nothing much to do and nobody to complain about her watching TV when she should be working.

It was cold for May. She had a fan heater trained on her legs, and had turned the sound on the computer up high to hear the show over the noise. It may have been some kind of movement that made her look up from the screen.

When she did, she saw an elderly man was running towards her, down Long Beach Landings. His mouth was opening and closing. His progress seemed impossibly slow.

She recognised him.

He and his wife were one of the many couples who owned a static caravan on this site. The old people here complained all the time. They complained about the noise of the summer visitors; they complained about others leaving their laundry out to dry; they complained that the kerbside recycling bins were full so they had nowhere to hide their empty vodka bottles.

Mr McKenzie, she remembered. That was his name.

She was puzzled. It was unusual to see men of his age running like this. As he got closer, she saw his face more clearly. He seemed to be scared of something, his eyes and mouth were wide, but she couldn't see anyone chasing him. There were no obvious wounds on him.

And then, just about twenty metres from the office, the man's legs gave way and he fell forward with sickening speed, slapping face down onto the bare tarmac, out of view behind a parked Hyundai. She watched to see if he would get up again, or to see if anyone would help him, but he didn't, and they didn't.

She stood, leaving the warmth of the office to go and see what had happened. As she approached, she could see him, a dark shape lying between the kerb and the car wheels. She picked up speed.

She stayed with him there until the ambulance she had called finally came. He was breathing with great difficulty and his face was strangely pale. There were flecks of white around his mouth. Even semi-conscious, clearly confused, he seemed agitated, trying to speak.

She reached out to hold his old, liver-spotted hand, and realised she was shivering, not just from the cold.

Old people frightened her. She preferred this place in summer, when younger people came.

★

It was only as he was lifted into the back of the ambulance that she thought she ought to check the static caravan. He might have left the door open. He would only complain again if something had gone wrong.

She went back to the office, wrapped herself in her scarf and locked the door behind her.

One of the residents rapped on her window as she passed. She paused. The woman opened her window and called, 'Who was it this time?'

'A heart attack. Mr McKenzie from Maple Ridge.'

The woman nodded, shut the window, pulled net curtains across.

Evalynn Doubek walked on, past the small roundabout, past the endless rows and rows of small homes, propped up on supports, some with small white picket verandahs, others with fresh spring bulbs blooming outside. The worst were the people who lived here all year round. She didn't know how they could stand it. It would drive her insane.

Everyone wanted to live near the beautiful seaside; they had ended up here in little tin boxes. The disappointment made them bitter, she thought. They were always angry – at the caravan park for not being tidy enough, at the holidaymakers for having too much fun, at her for being foreign.

The door to the caravan was slightly ajar.

'Hello? Is there anyone here?'

No answer.

'Mrs McKenzie?' She opened the door and peered in. The first thing that struck her as she did so was the smell. Like old trainers, she thought.

She stepped back, recoiling from the odour, letting go of the door. And as the door swung back, closing again . . .

It took a second more to realise what she'd seen in that second.

Gingerly, heart thumping now, she opened the door again. Monster feet, claws pointing upwards. She blinked again, tried to process the scene.

The feet were at the end of a pair of legs that were clad in light tan tights. On the feet were a pair of comic slippers shaped like a creature's claws. Behind the beige three-piece suite someone lay on the floor, not moving.

She stepped inside, said, 'Are you OK?' but just speaking made her feel instantly nauseous and she recoiled, gasping for air, steadying herself on the handrail of the steps that led to the door.

THIRTY-SEVEN

That morning, Jill hot-desked at the other end of the room, as far from Alex as possible.

'We're struggling, aren't we?' said McAdam, pulling up a chair next to Alex.

'Sorry?'

'With the Vincent Gibbons murder.'

'Oh, that. Yes, we are.' Alex glanced over at Jill. She was staring doggedly at a screen. 'The fact is, we have no idea of when or where Vincent Gibbons was killed. Until we know that, it's hard to make progress.'

The latest reports from the lab confirmed that the corpse had been unusually clean. No unknown DNA traces; no fibres, no dirt, no indications of where the body had been moved from or where Vincent Gibbons had been murdered. Pathologists were wary of making estimates of any time of death; a body that had been frozen made any such calculation impossible. The question of how he had ended up in a freezer at the Uttings' house remained unanswered. There had to be something, but she felt she was blundering blindly.

'You're convinced it's either something to do with the part Gibbons played in sending Francis Collins to prison, or his involvement in the Whiteland Fields protests?' McAdam asked.

'Yes.' She wondered if her answer was too abrupt, as if trying to convince herself of it.

'And there's no other possibility you're considering at present?'

'If there was anything else, yes, obviously, we'd be looking into it.'

A pause.

'And you? Everything all right with you?'

'Fine, yes,' she answered.

'Right,' he said, looking unconvinced. 'Good.'

He strode around the room, trying to find someone to volunteer to go out to a holiday park at Camber Sands where a woman had been found dead. It would be routine stuff; just an accidental death, but it would still need to be investigated. It was the kind of job nobody wanted added to their workload. Afterwards, he returned to Alex's desk. 'And what's up with Jill?' he asked. 'She's been in a strange mood all morning.'

She looked across the room. Jill, who had clearly been watching them converse, turned quickly back to her screen. 'I have no idea,' said Alex.

Belinda Utting looked older than last time. Maroon lipstick seeped into wrinkles around her lips.

'I have never heard of it. What's it got to do with the man in my freezer?'

214

'It's a major housing development on a new town model. It's created a lot of unhappiness from local residents. Mr Gibbons was one of the opponents. What about a company called September Homes?'

Belinda Utting had made tea again. 'No. I don't think so.'

'Or a man called Harry French?' She handed over a photograph she had downloaded off Facebook.

Mrs Utting looked at it for a while. 'My memory isn't what it was, but I don't recognise him at all. You're no closer, are you?'

'Sorry?'

'No closer to knowing why somebody dumped that poor man in our freezer. You can't be, otherwise you wouldn't be back here.'

'No. I don't think we are. We have a lot of leads that go nowhere.'

'How frustrating for you,' said Mrs Utting, as if she were commenting on a bad bridge hand. 'It can't be good for you dealing with murderers all the time. It must corrode the soul.'

'I suppose it does.'

'There must be other types of police work you could do.'

'I'm good at what I do.'

'Are you?' said Belinda Utting, as if surprised.

Which was enough to snap Alex out of her sullen mood.

'Your husband had a mistress. She visited him at Guldeford Hall.'

Belinda Utting raised her chin. 'I beg your pardon.'

'We have information that he had a mistress.'

Mrs Utting leaned forward, lifted the lid of the teapot and stirred the contents with a teaspoon. 'I have no idea where you heard that from. It's obviously untrue.'

'I need to know her name.'

Belinda Utting stared, openly hostile. 'You are mistaken. My husband never had an affair.'

'There was one woman who visited him at Guldeford Hall. She drove a Mazda. I need to know who she was.'

She replaced the teapot lid with a *chink*. 'You are wrong,' she said. The woman put her cup down on the small white table. 'I despise women who have affairs with married men. It is not a sisterly way to behave.' She looked up at Alex, speaking directly to her. 'And I find it ironic that it's you asking me that question.'

Alex was taken aback by the bitterness in her voice.

'Andrew was in the judiciary. I know people. They know people. I asked them about you. You used to be in the Metropolitan Police, didn't you?'

Alex frowned. 'Yes?'

'I checked up on you. Apparently you had an affair with a senior officer when you served with them.'

'Whoever told you that is breaching confidentiality,' said Alex.

Belinda Utting gave an unladylike snort. 'My husband, unlike you, did not have affairs.'

Alex put down her cup. 'What you think you know about my personal life is neither here nor there. We've eliminated everyone who knew the key code to Guldeford Hall apart from a woman who drove there to meet your husband. It's vital we find out who could have had access to your home.'

Belinda Utting straightened her back. 'You're wrong.'

Alex stood. 'That's funny. You've just convinced me I'm not,' she said, and made her way to the front door before she said anything more offensive.

Alex drove back in a worse mood. Nothing seemed to be going right. Any hopes that they could link Julian Epps to the murder through the blood in his van had been dashed.

She realised she had changed her route home.

Before, she had driven alongside the sea, past the bungalows, caravan parks and Martello towers. Now she was more frequently travelling inland through Lydd, slowing as she approached the site by the airport.

The security guard was out pulling something off the fence, bad-temperedly tugging at it; as she got closer she saw it was coloured string, or possibly wool. Letters spelled out *MES FOR EVERYONE NOT JUST THE RICH.* She guessed he had so far just removed the first two letters.

Creative civil disobedience.

Further down the fence there were a group of people standing in front of the wire; she recognised Jay. Alex pulled the car over onto the verge and got out.

Someone had printed off Vinnie Gibbons's Facebook photo and pasted it to a piece of cardboard that had been attached to the fence with cable ties. It read: *VINCENT GIBBONS R.I.P. HE LOVED THIS PLACE.*

'Is Zoë here?'

Jay was standing talking to Vera May's lodger. Jay pointed. 'She's over on the low fields, other side of the road.'

'Whose idea was this?' She pointed at the poster of Vincent Gibbons.

'Zoë wanted to do it.'

Alex looked north across the road towards the farm buildings and fields and recognised her at once, tramping towards them, thin legs in wellingtons that looked huge on her.

'Tell me, have you noticed any people watching you, or photographing you?'

Jay shook his head. 'Press, you mean? No. The mainstream press aren't interested.'

'Not journalists, no . . .'

'Oh, everybody knows about that,' blurted Vera May. 'They've been photographing us, watching us for days now. Because they're frightened of us.'

'Who do you think it is?'

'The developers, of course.'

'How do you know that?'

'Well it would be, wouldn't it. They hate us.'

The lodger was standing on his own now, apart from the others. He looked out of place. 'It's Richard Browne with an "e", isn't it? I didn't take you for a protestor.'

'I'm Vera's lodger. She's very persuasive. I didn't exactly have a lot of choice,' said Richard Browne with a small smile. 'And it's one way to get to know the local community, isn't it?'

'Extreme measures,' said Alex.

Browne laughed. 'Yeah. Feels like it too. But here I am.'

'You object to new housing, Mr Browne? I thought you were looking to buy somewhere?'

He shrugged. 'Call me a hypocrite. There's a lot of it around.'

'Ouch,' said Alex. 'You mean all those people who have

moved here, bought nice houses, and want to keep other people out?'

Browne chuckled quietly. 'Don't know who you mean.' He picked a long stalk of grass. 'Some days I don't think they should be building on a pretty little place like this; other days I think they should just concrete the whole bloody lot over.'

'Yet you're here, with all the protestors.'

'Vera May asked me, so I came. Easier to keep the peace sometimes.'

'Vera says you grew up around here.'

'Is this some kind of interrogation?'

'I'm just interested in anyone who says one thing, but does something completely different.'

'It's about fitting in. Go under the radar. It's what you have to do in places like this.'

'That's what I've been doing wrong,' said Alex.

'There's always a code. You have to live within it or hope nobody notices.'

'This is where you're from?'

'My parents lived close to the town. As soon as I could, I got the hell out.'

'But now you're moving back?'

'I've made a bit of money. I'm looking for somewhere I can settle down. Maybe here,' he said. 'Maybe somewhere else entirely.'

'What business are you in?'

'Information security and analysis,' he said, leaning forward. 'Sounds absolutely thrilling, don't you think? But I lucked out. It's given me a pretty fair living.'

When there was a gap in the traffic, Zoë trotted across, wellingtons slapping her shins, a large bunch of red and blue flowers in her hand. She joined the small huddle, shoulders hunched, looking down to avoid people's gaze.

'You shouldn't go poking around there,' ordered Vera May. 'It's private land. This is a lawful peaceful protest. You'll get us a bad reputation.'

'There's a badger trail that runs over there. I wanted to see where it went.'

Vera May huffed a little, then said, 'Your mother's come to join us, it seems, at least.'

'God forbid,' muttered Zoë and walked to the fence and started carefully threading valerian and viper's bugloss into the chain links around Vinnie Gibbons's picture.

She went to bed but couldn't sleep. She hated days like this, when nothing moved. The air around them, too, was still. She got up, opened the window wider.

At around one her phone buzzed gently. She reached across to her bedside table and unplugged it.

A message from Jill:

Are you awake?

'Were you?' said Jill when she called her back. 'Awake, I mean.'

'Well, I am now,' said Alex.

THIRTY-EIGHT

At the main sett, the older female has come into oestrus. Without a younger badger to protect the territory, she is now free to mate with others who arrive. It means there is danger. Males from all around will smell her rich scent and come. This is when the worst fights happen.

One of many strange things about badgers is that – like humans – they can mate at any time of the year. Unlike humans, though, they only give birth in the early spring. That's a trick, in itself.

It is an unusual biology that makes this possible. Over the course of a year, the female might mate with many males, but instead of giving birth several weeks later, she retains the fertilised eggs inside her, storing them until mid-winter. The embryo waits as a tiny cluster of just a few cells until then, when it becomes implanted in the uterus and the cells start to multiply again until the female is ready to give birth to cubs, usually only one or two, just as winter is about to give way to spring.

Nobody really knows why badgers reproduce in this way, but there's a theory that might explain it. It may be because so much of badger evolution has been about surviving lean times. To survive for their first year, it's best if babies are born at the end of winter, giving them three seasons in which to fatten up before the next cold season. Without this delayed implantation of the embryo, males would all have to breed in December. They'd have to fight each other for the right to breed with females at a time when they should be preserving their energy to survive the winter.

Tonight, before the other badgers start to sniff the younger female's condition, the older badger will take his own chance. She is deep within the sett in her own chamber. In the outside dark, he walks from one entrance to the next; he sings to her, a low growl. With his sharp claws, he digs through the earth that lies outside each sett, dug from underground. Squatting, he adds his own signal to the smell, then rakes it towards the hole so that the smell of his desire will drift down towards her. He does everything he can to woo her.

In the dark, he waits. But she does not come for him.

THIRTY-NINE

The Ashford International Truck Stop never closed. This part of the world, on the edge of England, was constantly in transit. Trucks lined up in the vast car park, drivers resting in their cabs. The restaurant was handy for any copper on a night shift. At two in the morning, there were only a couple of truckers pecking away at plates. The carvery was closed, but the grill was still open.

Jill ordered chips, Alex a decaf Americano. She had left a note for her daughter on the kitchen worktop: *Had to go out.*

'Sorry,' said Alex.

'What made you sure?'

'I wasn't sure. I just realised he wasn't being honest with you and I wondered why.' She told her about the phone call she had made from his office; how he had told her he was away on business when he had been at home all the time. She didn't mention the woman she had seen leaving his flat.

'You should have told me.'

'You seemed so happy. So how did you find out?'

'I catfished him. After you said all that to me yesterday, I thought I'd prove to myself he was not who you thought he was so I made up a profile. Called myself Sandra, which was my mother's name, as it happens. Sandra O'Shea. Found a photograph on Facebook; nice-looking woman in a polka-dot tankini taken on a holiday in Greece somewhere.'

'Identity theft,' said Alex.

'I know. Bit naughty. I put up a profile and in about two hours, he'd swiped me. Honest to God. Creep. So I messaged him. *Hi. I read your profile. I think you look nice.* Kind of flirty, you know? He got back in touch with me in less than twenty minutes. Asked if we wanted to meet at the same bloody wine bar.'

Alex put her hand on Jill's.

'I thought he was different,' Jill said.

A driver took the table next to them, deliberately facing them, as if he were hoping to catch their eye. He looked Polish but he could be from anywhere. The whole of Europe passed through here, hauling goods.

'I was really looking forward to that party in London tomorrow, too.'

'It would have been dull. Lots of businessmen in a room.'

'I don't care. I've never done anything like that. You know what my background is. You know what I've come up from.'

When the chips arrived, she ate them one by one while Alex watched, dipping each into brown sauce before chewing it.

'You should keep the dresses anyway. They looked amazing .'

Jill looked up. 'So basically, you think he was just dating me because I was a copper? Because he knows something about this murder and he wanted to find out what we knew?'

Alex thought for a while and said, 'No. I don't think that. He can't have known you were going to be investigating this case. I think he's just a man who likes dating attractive women. Unfortunately, not one at a time.'

'He's a liar and a cheat.'

The driver called across to them: 'You look sad. You shouldn't be sad. You are pretty.'

Jill glared at him, then said to Alex, 'For ten sweet minutes I actually thought I'd found a decent one.'

'How did he react when you told him?'

'I haven't told him. For a second I thought I'd arrange a date as Sandra, see the look on his face, but I can't be arsed. He's not worth it.'

Rebuffed, the man took a gulp from his cup.

Jill leaned forward, lowered her voice. 'But maybe I don't tell him. Maybe I pretend I don't know. If he is up to something . . .'

'He's not. Besides, you can't just do covert policing because you fancy it.'

'It wouldn't be official covert policing. Not technically.'

'No,' said Alex. 'Just no.'

The man at the next table stood and approached them. 'Sugar please or you sweet already?'

'What's wrong with the sugar at the next table?' snapped Alex.

Defeated, the man shuffled to the next table instead.

'What if I go to the party, though. I mean, I'm actually invited? Make a tit of myself. Shout at him a bit.'

'No, Jill.'

'No no no,' said the trucker, grinning. 'You should not be arguing.'

'And you should be minding your own bloody business,' said Jill.

'I apologise. I just drive all day on my own and sometimes I want to talk. No offence,' said the driver. 'A little conversation to improve my English.'

'Do you know the English for bog off?' said Jill.

'Sorry. Sorry,' said the man.

'I just want vengeance. I was really falling for him, Alex.'

Alex laid her hand on top of Jill's again. 'I know.'

For a second, Jill's eyes watered, then she pulled her hand away. Her face hardened again. 'Actually, you should go, instead of me.'

'What?' said Alex.

'Why not? It'll be a laugh. That would freak him out.'

'It's not me that's invited. It's you.'

'But seriously, you should go. Just in case.'

Alex looked at her closely. 'In case what?'

'Look. There are two lines of enquiry, aren't there? One, that it's something to do with the arrest of Frankie Collins for badger-baiting. Two, that it's something to do with Whiteland Fields and Vincent Gibbons's opposition to the development. Sounds like you've got nothing firm on either of them, no? So why not have a nosey?'

'Can I remind you that you're not actually part of the team

looking into any connection between French and the murder of Vincent Gibbons?'

'I'm allowed an opinion, though. Or aren't I even allowed that?'

'What are you two fighting about?' asked the truck driver.

Jill turned to him. 'I have an invite to a very important party. I don't want to go, so I say my friend here should go in my place. But she doesn't want to.'

'Of course she should go to the party,' said the lorry driver. 'Nobody should ever miss a party.'

'There,' said Jill.

The truck driver finished his coffee and stood. He gave an odd little bow, then said, 'I must go to work. I want to show you one thing, please.' He pulled out his wallet and opened it.

'My wife and my daughter. They are beautiful ladies like you.'

In a yellowed plastic wallet, a picture of two women, dark-haired, smiling back at a camera.

When he'd gone through the revolving door, Jill said, 'He's hitting on us one minute, then showing us his wife and daughter the next. Men are so weird.'

'He was just lonely.'

'Aren't we all?' said Jill. 'What are you going to wear?'

Alex looked at her watch. It was three in the morning. There seemed little point in going back to bed now.

'No way,' said Alex. 'No way at all. I'm not going.'

FORTY

'Jill. Welcome,' said the tuxedo who stood at the red rope at the top of the steps of St John's, Smith Square, and handed her a glossy information pack. 'There's a cloakroom on the left.'

Zoë's father – Alex's ex – had used to bring her here to listen to contemporary orchestral concerts. She had hated trying to sit still for two hours while the players worked their way through the spiky, oddly shaped music, but she had loved the building. A short walk from Parliament, its pale stone columns and baroque towers were more frivolous and joyful than the city's other churches.

They had lit the interior purple, and draped tables in cloth. A woman in a black minidress offered her something sparkling; another raised a tray of canapés towards her. Alex tucked the welcome pack under her arm and took both, one in each hand.

She had taken the train up to London. Jill was sleeping over at her house to keep Zoë company. It was a stupid scheme, she knew.

In front of the altar, a projector was shining artists' impressions of what the Whiteland Fields development was going to look like onto a large screen. Alex had seen worse. The houses were small, but they had attempted to make them look like they were part of a village, each slightly different from its neighbour. Some were clad in wood, others in rich red tiles; some had windows in their sloping roofs, others had tiny Juliet balconies. The design was a little like a Toy Town village, thought Alex. Leafy trees had been imagined on corners. Oddly generic children played on the pavements, bright sunshine shining down on them. Healthy-looking people rode on bicycles. Electric cars were plugged into charging points.

The guests were well-dressed, huddled in groups, conversing. Alex found a small purple-draped table, put her bag under it and started leafing through the welcome pack for something to do:

Whiteland Fields is *the* Integrated Village. Welcome to a bold new vision to create 4,000 extraordinary places to live over six years. A new home for many in the Garden of England. Join us. Invest in the infrastructure of a great new place and help build a better, sustainable long-term vision for Britain.

The party seemed to be mainly for potential investors. It would be easier to attract new capital now the plans had been approved. The women were all uniformly better dressed than she was; the men in duller suits would be the ones with money. Those in the more fashionable ones, with red-framed glasses and recently trimmed hair, would be architects. As she clearly didn't look like a member of either the capitalist or the creative class, she was being ignored.

She picked up her bag and walked around the room. Her glass already seemed to be empty, because a young woman was approaching her with a smile and a bottle. Alex held it out.

'I thought it was you,' said a voice behind her. She turned to see Tamsin Porter, grinning as if she had chanced upon her oldest school friend among the crowd. 'What are you doing here?'

'A friend passed me an invite. I thought I'd come and take a look.'

'You've not been in touch with us yet,' said Porter.

'Because there's been nothing to tell you.'

Porter looked around. 'But you're here, so there must be something about this gathering that interests you.'

'Is your minister here?'

'God. They desperately wanted him to be. It would obviously be great for the project to have Howard Roteman here to make a speech. It would mean it was anointed. But –' she leaned in so close, Alex got a waft of floral perfume – 'as I said when I saw you last week, we would need to make sure it's something that we can get behind, one hundred per cent.'

There was something about politicians and those around them that relished the conspiratorial nudge and wink. Alex leaned in too. 'And you're not sure?'

Tamsin just smiled knowingly, giving away nothing, held out her own glass towards the waiting staff, and just as she did so,

Harry French pushed through the crowd in front of them and stood in front of Alex.

'Hello?' Confusion in his voice, as if he were trying to remember if he had invited her.

'Do you know Tamsin Porter? She works with Howard Roteman,' said Alex.

'Of course I do. Where is the minister?' He checked his watch.

'I'm so so sorry. Just had a message. Howard can't make it for the speeches,' Porter said, sweetly apologetic. She gave Alex the tiniest of winks. 'Called away on some urgent constituency business.'

French's face fell just a little. 'We were expecting him . . .'

'He wants me to tell you he's awfully sorry. He would have so loved to have been here to find out more about this project. Super do. And so many terribly important people here.'

'We were very much hoping—' said French.

'Of course you were,' beamed Porter. 'Can't be helped. Awful shame.'

'Of course.' French's eyes flicked sideways, back to Alex. 'I'm surprised to see you here, Sergeant Cupidi. I didn't know you were invited.'

'I thought I'd come and take a look.'

He looked around. 'Jill's not here, is she?'

'No. She's not coming. Just me.'

'She told me. You know she's split up with me?'

'Yes.'

'It's a misunderstanding,' he said.

'Is it?'

231

From the small dais, set up in front of the altar, a woman spoke through a microphone. 'Good evening, ladies and gentlemen. We'll only take a few moments of your time, but there are a few things we'd like to tell you about this really thrilling development. Where's Harry? We need Harry up here.'

'Why were you talking to Tamsin Porter?' Harry French demanded, pulling her away. 'Why are you here? I don't understand what's going on.'

'Harry French?' the woman's voice came over the PA. 'Where are you? We can't start without you. Probably chatting someone up.' A small laugh went around the room.

'Coming,' he shouted finally, giving Alex one last puzzled look before turning away.

'He's quite good-looking, isn't he?' said Tamsin Porter, curious.

Harry French was finally up on the small stage. The woman was listing the names of the heads of the various parties of the consortium. 'And finally, please, a special welcome to board member Lord Michaels of Dawlish.'

'Oh God,' said Tamsin Porter. 'Speeches. Let's go. Desperate for a fag.'

Outside they sat on the cold stone steps. Tamsin Porter smoked; the square around the church was quiet.

'Why didn't Howard Roteman come?' asked Alex.

'Other business, like I said.'

'Really?'

'They wanted him to get up there and give a speech telling everyone how fabulous this all was. He messaged me an hour ago to say he wouldn't be coming. Could I go in his place? Grovel a little.'

'Were you expecting him to cancel?'

Tamsin Porter blew smoke, thought for a while, then said, 'I can't say I'm surprised. Between you and me –' lowering her voice – 'he's had reservations about this one all along. I'm not sure why. I thought it would be right up his street. But . . . you know. Politics.'

'Surely it's exactly the kind of scheme Howard Roteman is supposed to be cheering on? The market building new houses for the people.'

'There you go. That's what I'd say. It is a bit weird, isn't it?'

'So what kind of reservations does he have?'

'I've been trying to work that out, but I can't. Besides, you think he'd share them with a minion like me?'

'I think a minion like you is clever enough to second-guess him.'

'Flattery, flattery,' said Tamsin. 'Honestly, I like you. I would tell you, but I don't know.' Her phone buzzed. She took it out and answered the message two-handed, cigarette dangling from her lip, squinting in the smoke. When she'd sent her reply, she removed the cigarette and said, 'Why don't you ask him yourself?'

Tamsin Porter took another tiny pull on the cigarette then dropped it at her feet and ground it out with her heel. 'He'll be here in a minute. He said to ask you to wait for him.'

'He knew I was here?'

'I just told him.'

'He wants to see me?'

'Apparently so. He won't be a minute. He's just around the corner.'

'You said he had urgent business with his constituents.'

'Did I? I misspoke. In fact, here he is now.' And she smiled as a shiny black tinted-windowed Jaguar XJ pulled up behind a taxi.

'Come on,' Tamsin Porter said, standing and picking up the fag end she had dropped with one hand, reaching her other out to Alex.

FORTY-ONE

That night a male from the south arrives, drawn by the scent of the female.

The older male is caught out; he is already at the hole in the fence when he first smells him. The younger one is fat and heavy; the older male has no option but to challenge this interloper.

Growling, he faces the other badger, legs raised, fur prickling.

Nose to nose, half a metre apart, they stare at each other. It is a clear night. The moon is almost full and their white stripes seem to glow.

They stay like that for minutes, still, both raised up to make themselves look as big as they can, warning each other in low, ill-tempered voices.

Finally the younger badger makes a cautious move forwards.

Provoked, the older badger lunges, hoping to make the first bite.

But for all that weight, the younger one is fast. His jaw closes on almost the same place as the older one was aiming for – the back of the neck.

The enemy's teeth sink deep.

The older one squeals in pain and shakes his head free, ripping his own skin away beneath the fur. He turns, but before he can run, the other one has struck again, this time in his rump.

It is a complete rout. He retreats underground to a hole far away from the main sett, bleeding heavily.

In the darkness he licks his wounds.

He can smell the new male's scent now. The message carried on the air is not intended for him, though, it's meant for the young female.

Her scent grows stronger too. She has left the burrow, drawn to the victor.

FORTY-TWO

When Howard Roteman got out of the car, the first thing that Alex thought was that he looked smaller than when she had seen him on TV. 'Fashionably late,' he called out to Tamsin. 'Did you make my excuses?'

'The speeches started about a quarter of an hour ago.' Tamsin looked at the screen on her phone. 'They should be over now. I think you'll be safe.'

'Excellent.'

'This is Detective Sergeant Alexandra Cupidi.'

'Ah.' He held out his hand to shake.

'You were avoiding the speeches for diplomatic reasons?' she asked.

He put on the face of a child who'd been caught sneaking an extra sweet from the tin. 'They'd love to have my fulsome endorsement. Obviously it would help get the scheme off the ground, but it's tricky. I'm not sure it's in our interest to fully get behind it. So if I just show my face for a few quick minutes, I'm doing my duty without actually saying anything that might look stupid in six months' time.' He pulled out his phone, checked the screen, put it back in his trouser pocket. 'Come on. Have you had a drink? I would bloody love one. Shit day . . .' He took the stairs two at a time. 'As per usual.'

This time, as she walked in with the minister, people paid attention.

'Stay close to me,' Roteman muttered. 'Will you do me a kindness? Engage me in earnest conversation about anything.' People turned, approached him, hands extended. 'You're my excuse,' he told her. 'OK? Just feel free to interrupt anyone who talks to me. That way I don't have to talk to them.' He grasped one of the hands, air-kissed a woman. 'Jacob. Good man . . . Oh how lovely to meet you, Jacqui. Everything well? Excellent.'

He turned back to Alex, waiting for her to say something. 'What am I supposed to talk about?' asked Alex.

'Anything. Just make it look earnest and uninterruptible. Hurry up. The time has come to talk of many things.'

'The police services are massively underfunded by this government, don't you think?'

'Very good.' He grinned. 'Not my department, obviously, so I can't possibly comment. But if it was left to me, everything would be different, you understand. Keep going.'

'Rising gang violence in the UK is the direct result of the government's failed austerity policies. Even the Inspectorate says so.'

'You're enjoying this, aren't you, Sergeant?'

'Very much. Some police forces have given up investigating around half their domestic abuse cases because they don't have enough staff. You have any idea what it's like to work in a police force where you can't even get around to investigating crimes like that because you don't have the resources? We feel like we're useless.'

'Obviously I deplore that.' The ring of people who had come to press their claims on the minister, or to seek his approval in some way, were holding their distance. 'But we have to put the economy on a sound footing.'

'The underfunding of the care system is putting extraordinary strain on the NHS but it's crippling the police services too. Every day we're dealing with people who're addicted, or mentally ill, who should be being looked after by health professionals. It means we're now so stretched we can't provide anything other than a basic service that's failing the real victims of robbery and violence.'

'Keep going. It's working.'

Though some people still stood around them, hoping for a chance to talk to the minister, Alex could see, from the corner of her eye, others losing interest and turning away.

'The growth of county lines drugs gangs is stretching rural police forces to their limit. We're short of even the most basic resources to deal with organised crime on that scale, and we're lacking in even basic intelligence on some of the bigger gangs. As a result, our departments know they're failing young people everywhere. On a daily basis we're dealing with young people who've been coerced into working with these gangs. The levels of violence are unbelievable. It keeps us awake at night.'

'How many more of these have you got?'

'How long do you need?'

239

Lord Michaels finally broke through the line of watchers and interrupted. 'Howard,' he said. 'Thank you so much for—'

'Unavoidably detained.' Roteman smiled. 'Important business. You know how it is.'

Derry Michaels took a second to recognise Alex, a flicker of confusion in his face. 'Can I introduce you to my colleague Harry French? He's one of the real dynamos behind the project.'

'If you must.'

Harry French was approaching the minister, a fixed smile on his face. 'Good to meet you at last,' he said, hand extended.

Howard Roteman's right hand was holding a glass. He avoided his handshake. 'Charmed.'

'There are a few people here that I'd love you to meet,' said French, looking round the room anxiously.

'Do you mind if I don't?' said Roteman with practised blandness.

'It'll only take a second.'

'Another time, perhaps?' said Roteman, turning back to Alex. 'The phenomenon of county lines gangs is extremely concerning. I would be fascinated to hear more about it.' Taking her arm, he led her away from the throng to a corner of the room.

Harry French stood, stung.

'Thank you,' said Roteman quietly. 'You are such a sport. You saved my life. And I know the government are the enemy at all times, but I would genuinely like to hear more about your opinions.' He looked around for his assistant. 'We've done our duty. Now I need to get out of here.'

'You're not going to give the project your support, then?' Across the room, Alex could see Harry French and Lord Michaels in deep discussion, looking over towards them. Alex realised that what she had just witnessed was a minor political drama, of a kind. They were expecting a favour; he had very publicly declined to give it.

'It's complicated,' Roteman said.

French and Michaels had been hoping this visit from a minister would have given their project a kind of blessing from on high; a promise to use their project as a backdrop for some new policy. The support of a minister – even a junior one like Howard Roteman – would have put wind in the project's sails. It would have made investors more eager to pledge their capital. But the minister had ducked the opportunity by deliberately arriving late and leaving early, talking to no one, doing the bare minimum.

'I need to know why,' Alex pressed him. 'This is the kind of initiative your government is supposed to be totally behind.'

Tamsin Porter appeared, perky and bright-eyed. 'All done, here?' she said.

'What's changed?' demanded Alex. 'Why aren't you backing Whiteland Fields?'

'Tamsin. Can you check whether the car's still there?'

Tamsin scampered away.

'Of course I'm behind the project. One hundred per cent. However, for various reasons, we can't afford to get too close to it right now.'

'Why?'

'It's nothing sinister, I promise.'

'Then tell me.'

'I'd ask that the conversation remains in confidence.'

'I can't promise that. I'm a police officer.'

'I don't need a promise. I just need to know that you won't discuss it with anyone outside the investigation, and then only when it's relevant to this discussion and that you ask whoever you have to tell to keep it under their hat.'

She nodded warily. 'OK.'

Tamsin was back. 'Car's ready.'

'I'm going to give Sergeant Cupidi a lift,' he said. 'You can make your own way, can't you?'

Tamsin looked disappointed. 'Oh. Right.'

He walked to the car swiftly. The front steps were more crowded now. People were leaving. As he approached the vehicle, cameras flashed. He opened the door for her, then strode around the back of the car and got in on the other side.

'Where do you live?'

She buckled her belt. 'Dungeness. Fancy driving me there?'

'Improper use of a ministerial vehicle, I'm afraid. You actually live there?'

'Yes.'

'Wow,' he said. 'Bleak.'

'Only tourists ever say that. The landscape keeps the faint-hearted away. We like that there. But I'm staying at my mum's tonight in East London. Perhaps you could drop me there.'

'That's a bit easier than Dungeness.' He looked at his watch. 'OK. We'll talk on the way. I like to drive round London at night. It helps me think.'

Alex leaned forward and told the driver her mother's address, and then leaned back into her seat while Roteman made a couple of calls. She watched through the tinted windows as they drove out towards Parliament Square, then down towards Victoria

Embankment heading north. Nobody paid them any notice. In London cars like this were commonplace.

'I'll be with you in just a sec,' said Roteman.

'No hurry,' she said, settling into the soft leather, gazing out of the window. Everywhere cranes dotted the London night skyline, their red lights punctuating the black sky. She had lived here most of her life. It was bleaker here than anywhere she knew.

FORTY-THREE

'You live in Dungeness,' Howard Roteman said, finally, as the traffic slowed at Ludgate Circus. 'So you are local. You know the area.'

'Yes.'

'And you know the government's in trouble. We're in a time of considerable instability.'

They were stopped now at a red light. A man approached them with a McDonald's cup. He stood a foot away, beyond the dark tinted glass, waiting for someone to wind down a window. Invisible to him, Roteman had the grace to look slightly embarrassed.

'We may be fighting another election sooner than we hoped. We saw off wingnuts at the last election but the right is split again now. We're going to be losing seats.'

This was a different man to the ebullient politician who had cornered her at the launch event. He suddenly looked very tired, his eyes a little deeper in his skull. The grey at his temples that was striking in photographs looked as if it needed a trim.

'I get it,' she said.

'You do?'

'You don't want to endorse the Whiteland Fields development because you're worried it's going to alienate the rural middle class and you'll end up losing the next election there.'

He nodded. 'Exactly. Not that we are going to lose, of course.'

'You wouldn't even be doing this unless you were worried about it.'

'Strange times. Nothing is certain any more. Anarchy is loosed upon the world. Our MP there is one of the saner ones. He's campaigned against the development, but of course his hands are tied. He can't be seen to go against party policy, so we proceed by stealth. We must do what we can to keep him.' He held out his hands, palms up. '*Mea culpa*. I'm a politician.'

'I noticed.'

'You must be a little disappointed in me. I think you were hoping for some dark reason why I didn't want to touch the development with a long stick.'

'I was, actually,' said Alex. 'I was hoping for something that would make sense of this murder.'

'Tell me about it. Distract me.'

'A man who had been protesting about the development turned up dead in quite strange circumstances.'

'Everyone wants there to be some conspiracy nowadays. It's exhausting.'

Alex nodded; thought of her daughter. 'So what happens when the locals appeal the decision and it ends up on your desk?'

He looked away. 'Not my desk. It'll be the Secretary of State's.

245

Obviously I'll make strong representations to him, but he will rule on the case with total impartiality.'

'And back the appeal.'

'Absolutely.'

'Because you'll tell him it's an electoral liability.' She thought of Vera May and her grey-haired protestors.

'I never expected politics to be this cynical either,' he said. 'These days we're on such a knife edge. The barbarians are at the gates. If we start losing seats like Folkestone and Hythe, where you are, there's not much left for us as a party. And opposition to the development down there is fairly vigorous, I gather. Which side are you on? For or against?'

'I'm not on any side. I'm a copper.'

'But you think that man's murder may have been something to do with his involvement in the protest movement.'

They slowed on Farringdon Road. A bus had broken down at traffic lights.

'There are a couple of lines of enquiry. He had made some enemies, but, yes, I keep coming back to his connection with the development.'

'You have a hunch?'

'We can't afford hunches.'

'Can't even afford hunches these days. I expect you blame the government for that?'

'We don't call them hunches, we call them lines of enquiry. There was someone watching the site the other day. How close an eye have you been keeping on it?'

'I assure you, the Ministry of Housing, Development and

Local Communities does not employ spooks. Tell me about this person you saw.'

'I was there taking a look. We were being watched. A man on a motorbike who clearly didn't want to be seen. When I approached him he disappeared. But the thing is, it wasn't just an idle observer. It was someone who knew what they were doing.'

He leaned forward, interested. 'How do you know that?'

'Because of the way the person left when I approached. And the way they hadn't wanted to be seen.'

'Tantalising.'

Strange, the experience of sitting in an official car chatting with a minister; a man she had seen on TV.

'You enjoy your job, don't you?'

'Not sure I enjoy it, but it's what I do. My father was a police officer. My mother too, once. And I'm not sure what else I would be qualified for.'

'Same here,' he said.

He lapsed into silence. They were in Canonbury now, approaching the London Alex knew well. She had grown up in these Victorian streets.

'How did you know I was visiting the House of Lords, that day I went to see Derry Michaels?'

'Parliament is full of little birds that tell me things.'

'Well they must be quite random little birds if they are telling you about junior officers from Kent who happen to be visiting.'

'Derry let it drop, if you must know. He does so love to talk. We had one of our endless meetings about planning process last week and he mentioned that a police officer was coming to see him about something to do with Andrew Utting and September

247

Homes. I called up one of your senior officers to ask if there was any particular concern about Whiteland Fields, and it turns out there is. Sorry to be sneaky.'

Her phone buzzed. Jill had texted:

Zoë gone to bed. How did it go? Did Harry say anything?

Alex would call her later and tell her everything that had gone on.

'It's very kind of you to go out of your way like this,' said Alex, putting the phone back into her bag.

'No trouble. I wasn't going home anyway. When you're a minister, it's surprising how many letters you get that say, "I wonder how you can sleep at night." As it happens, I can't. I seem to have developed insomnia. So I ask my drivers to chauffeur me around until I'm exhausted. I find it strangely comforting. I sleep better in a car than I do anywhere.'

'A guilty man never sleeps well,' said Alex.

'Exactly.' His smile was a nice one, she decided. Wrinkles appeared on the sides of his eyes when he grinned.

Her mother Helen opened the door, blaring rock music out into the street from behind her as the Jaguar was reversing out of the small cul-de-sac.

'Posh car,' Helen said, disapprovingly.

'You'll never guess whose it is,' said Alex, taking off her jacket.

When she told her, her mother didn't look impressed. 'He was on the telly the other night. A bit too smooth. One of those politicians who will tell anyone anything they want to hear.'

'I quite liked him.' Her mother raised her eyebrows

disapprovingly, and though Alex had said it to annoy her, she realised it was probably true, too. 'What's that smell?'

Her mother sniffed. 'What smell?'

'Have you been smoking cannabis?'

This time her mother didn't answer. She went to the CD player that was playing a song by Lou Reed and turned it up a notch. 'For my arthritis.'

'Mum.' The scolding tone in her voice, like talking to a child.

'Oh, stop being so sanctimonious,' said Helen.

'Cannabis, Mum.'

Her mother scraped a half-eaten plate of scrambled egg into the bin. 'Fancy a glass of wine?'

'Go on then.'

Alex walked across the messy kitchen and turned down the music, wondering if her mother was going deaf. Her father was the one who'd kept the place tidy. Now there were pans and plates in the sink, and a pile of paperbacks on the table next to an ashtray. Alex picked it up and examined the contents. Under it lay a pile of unopened letters; bills. She put the ashtray down and leafed through them; one was marked *Final Demand*.

Helen poured herself a glass and took a sip from it.

Her father had preferred jazz; her mother had liked rock. It was a particularly gloomy tune from the *Berlin* album. Alex recognised it now. She remembered hearing her mother playing it when she was a child.

'You look tired,' Helen said. 'You should wear brighter colours.'

Alex opened the final demand. It was from the electricity

company who said they were going to cut her off if she didn't pay her bill; dated three weeks ago.

'You can't just come in here and open my mail,' said Helen.

'Mum. It's overdue.'

'Well it's a mistake, then. I paid it ages ago.'

'If it's a mistake, why are they sending you this, then?'

'Besides. I'm a pensioner. They can't just cut off my electricity.'

Alex held another letter in front of her mother.

'I can't see it,' Helen said. 'I can't find my glasses.'

'You have a mammogram next week.'

'Really? I thought I was too old for that kind of thing. Did I offer you wine?'

Alex found her mother's glasses in the freezer eventually, when trying to pull out the ice to cool the wine with. When her mother put them on, they misted over immediately, and she burst out laughing like it was the funniest thing that had ever happened.

When she stopped laughing, she said, suddenly serious, 'You think I'm losing it, don't you?'

Alex lay awake most of the night in the bed she had slept in as a child. For a while she thought she heard her father moving around downstairs; he had always been an early riser.

She dressed, went downstairs to the kitchen, put the kettle on for coffee and started washing the pans in the sink. Her mother was a night owl. She would not be awake for hours. She could sneak off, closing the front door quietly behind her.

Over the roar of the kettle, she didn't at first register the buzz of her phone. When she looked down and saw who was calling she knew it would not be good news.

'There's been another cyanide murder,' Inspector McAdam was saying as she pressed the phone to her ear.

FORTY-FOUR

The static home sat on grass next to a stretch of tarmac that had been grandly named Maple Ridge, though there were no trees anywhere around. A large metal box of a home, surrounded by blue tape that fluttered in the cold easterly.

'Can't go in,' the crime scene manager told Alex. She stood looking down at Alex from the doorway of a neighbouring home that they had commandeered as a temporary scene of crime office. 'May still be dangerous.'

It had been two days since Evalynn Doubek had seen the screaming man running towards her, and discovered Mrs Phyllis McKenzie dead on the floor of her home. Her husband was still in hospital.

At first it had been easy for the police to conclude she must have been killed by a gas leak from a propane cooker, or a faulty heater emitting carbon monoxide. Such deaths were commonplace in caravans and homes like this. That there had been a carbon monoxide detector fitted inside the home didn't jolt anyone's faith in the theory. It must have been faulty, people reasoned. These static homes were well sealed. They were often occupied by the poor and the elderly, and this was exactly the kind of accident you'd expect, so nobody thought any more of why Phyllis McKenzie had died in her small front room, next to the beige three-piece suite. As part of the investigation, the detector was sent away for testing, but the results had not come back yet.

It wasn't until yesterday afternoon that anyone had suggested that there might be something very strange about her death.

It was pure luck that the pathologist who cut her body open was the same one who had completed another autopsy on a victim of cyanide poisoning only a couple of weeks before, otherwise he might not have been quite so alert to pinkish lividity of her skin. It was similar to the colour Vincent Gibbons had been. If it had been carbon monoxide, Phyllis McKenzie would have been redder. As a precaution, he had taken blood and urine samples, removed her liver and sent them away for analysis.

At first, he didn't pass his suspicions on to the police. The chances of two cyanide poisoning cases crossing his table would be infinitesimal. He did, however, add a note to the samples asking them to be processed as quickly as possible, 'as a favour'.

Police had sealed the caravan the previous night after he told them the results. Crime scene officers, dressed in hazmat suits, went in after midnight and confirmed that there were residues of cyanide coating surfaces throughout the static home – which would have accounted for the smell the receptionist had noticed.

To have one victim of cyanide gas poisoning in the area was unusual; two – not even including the husband whose heart attack was almost certainly brought on by the presence of cyanide in his blood – set alarm bells ringing very loudly. Lydd, where Vincent Gibbons had lived, was only around five miles away.

Alex turned away from the crime scene manager and walked slowly around the taped-off area.

'When can I get in there?' she called.

'Don't know yet. They didn't say.'

The caravan park was the other side of the road from the high sea wall that had protected the low marshland behind it. They were shoring the wall up again with steel and stone. The sea was rising and the old walls would not be robust enough.

The McKenzies' home was at the north end of the big site, presumably a cheaper pitch, far from the sea, close to the ancient drainage channel known as Guldeford Sewer. The land here was criss-crossed by these unprepossessing ditches that had been dug centuries ago to claim fertile ground from the salt marsh. They separated the land like hedges, dividing fields with an uncrossable width of slow-moving water.

Alex noticed that the site had these drains to the north and east, but there was a causeway at the north-east corner, running across the water, which meant that anyone could walk in here from the fields beyond if they wanted.

Alex stood with her back to the house where the body had been found, looking north past the waving reeds, their stems still green and fresh, towards the fields dotted with sheep. Everything looked so calm, so peaceful, so English.

★

'Do you have a record of who the first responder was to the original incident?' Alex asked.

The scene manager checked her notes. 'A Constable Gilchrist.'

'Did he go into the home?'

'Apparently, yes.'

Alex guessed he would have done. He seemed a good copper; he would have gone in to drag her out and attempt resuscitation.

Alex looked around. The site had hundreds of similar homes on it, but only a very few of them were occupied at this time of year. It would prove hard to find anyone who had seen anything. The place wasn't completely deserted, though. Across the road a woman in a towelling dressing gown and slippers had emerged from her home and was watching them. Alex approached her, holding out her ID.

'Did you know Mr and Mrs McKenzie?' she asked.

The woman nodded. 'It's awful. These places can be bloody lethal.'

News about how the woman had really died had not been released yet.

'Do you know, were either of them interested in wildlife?'

The woman looked like Alex had said something rude. 'Wildlife?'

'Badgers, maybe?'

'What you talking about?'

Alex tried again. 'What about politics? Would they have had anything to do with local politics around here?'

The woman tried to be helpful. 'I think he was into model railways. She collected autographs. She had Bruce Forsyth and

Anton du Beke. They both raised money for a donkey charity in Spain, is that what you mean? They were very caring people.'

Alex turned. A car was driving down Maple Ridge towards them. She recognised DI McAdam; he was not a man who usually left the office unless things were bad.

He got out of the car, and looked around. 'Just you here?'

'Calm before the storm,' she said, walking over to him. 'All the other units are on the way.'

He nodded. The place would be swarming soon.

'Anything?' he asked.

'Nothing obvious.'

She knew what he was going to say. He spent a long time standing, hands in his raincoat pockets, looking around, before he said quietly, 'Do you think you've been wrong on this one, Alex?'

She had focused the investigations on the two strands of enquiry; that it was either about payback for the arrest of Frankie Collins or that it was somehow about Whiteland Fields and the protests against the development. Now there had been another killing by what looked like exactly the same method – but it didn't fit the pattern at all. There was no connection at all with the McKenzies.

'Maybe it's there, but I can't just see it yet,' she said.

He nodded. 'Or maybe it's time to start rethinking this whole thing and admit that we might have been wasting our time looking in the wrong place.'

The woman wandered towards them, tugging her dressing gown tighter. 'What is going on?'

'It's not your fault, Alex,' DI McAdam was saying. 'There's no blame. You were acting on the best evidence you had.'

'Are you going to tell us?' the woman butted in.

DI McAdam stepped forward. 'I'd like to reassure you that as far as we can ascertain, there's no risk to other residents.'

'What do you mean, risk?' said the woman.

Other locals were approaching. A man in a golf cap started taking photographs on his mobile phone.

Backing away, McAdam smiled as reassuringly as he could, saying that Alex would take their numbers and would send an officer round to talk to them as soon as one was available, then nodded towards his car where they could talk more privately.

Watched by the growing crowd who stood around the woman in the dressing gown, Alex got into the passenger seat.

'So. If there's nothing obvious to link this to your other lines of enquiry, what have we got?' he asked.

'Honestly? I don't know. Except this doesn't feel right to me.'

'Have you considered the possibility that somebody just found an old stash of this stuff and is playing with it?'

The idea had already occurred to her, and it was terrifying. 'I know,' she said.

'Are we going to see more of this, Alex? There's going to be a hell of a lot of criticism if we've cocked this up. And what are we going to tell them? We have to tell them something. We've got no choice but to say this might be much worse than we thought. I think we're going to have to announce something to the press. Anything else would be irresponsible.'

The woman in the dressing gown had crossed her arms and was glaring at them.

★

As Alex walked down the narrow road towards the entrance, vans of uniformed coppers were arriving. The hazmat team were back, donning their chemical suits and breathing apparatus.

She reached the site office; three static caravans that had been joined together into a U-shape.

Evalynn Doubek was sitting in the reception office, a fan heater blowing at her legs, tapping her fingernails on the desktop. She offered tea, but Alex shook her head. 'The tenants here are our people. We look after them. They want to know what's going on,' she said.

'Believe me, so do we,' Alex said. 'To start with, I need to find out if there has been anybody unusual hanging around the site, anyone you didn't recognise, over the last few days.'

'This time of year, middle of the week, it's dead round here.' Eyes big, she clamped her hand over her mouth the moment she realised what she'd said.

'Don't worry. I'm like that all the time. But if it's quiet, that means people are more likely to be on site unnoticed.'

The woman nodded, face serious. 'Yes. Like the burglary.'

'You've had burglars on the site?'

Evalynn Doubek looked puzzled. 'You don't know about the burglary?'

'What burglary?'

'Your people were here on Monday because of the burglary – at the McKenzies' home. The day before she died.'

Alex was aware of a sudden ringing in her ears. 'So the McKenzies were burgled last Monday?'

'They came down from Birmingham to open up their place.

Every year they come down, give it a spring cleaning. They found it had been broken into.'

'So it had been broken into before Monday. How long before?'

Ms Doubek shrugged. 'We don't know.'

'And did they steal anything?'

'I don't think so. But Mr McKenzie was very angry that we had let this happen. We even gave them one of the luxury rentals to stay in until they could tidy their own home, but they were still angry.'

'Which others did the burglars break into?'

The woman shook her head. 'None. Only this one.'

'And you said you don't think they stole anything. Nothing was reported missing?'

'The police think they must have been disturbed.'

Alex thought. 'Let me get this right. On Monday night, when they arrived, the McKenzies didn't sleep in their own caravan?'

'We call them homes.'

Alex flicked her notebook onto a new page and wrote the days of the week out in order, from Monday to today, Thursday. She put an 'X' by the Tuesday, the day of the poisoning. Why had the burglars chosen this particular caravan in amongst the hundreds that were empty at this time of year?

While Evalynn Doubek tapped her fingers nervously on her desk, Alex stared at the page for a long time, hoping that something would reveal itself to her – and thought about what Zoë had said about the patterns that you can't see. She wanted something that would prove that McAdam was wrong, but she could find nothing.

FORTY-FIVE

When she got home that evening, Julian Epps's van was parked at the back of her house.

She got out, slamming the door of her Micra, and marched across to it. He was in the front seat; a pile of cigarette ends lay on the ground outside so he had obviously been here a while.

She leaned down towards the window. 'For someone who's trying to prove they haven't been harassing me, turning up here is a really stupid idea. How did you find out where I lived?'

He smiled. 'You know what it's like round here. Everyone knows everyone else. You come to my house. Thought I'd come to yours for a change.'

He looked towards the kitchen window; Zoë was silhouetted, looking back at them.

'People like you depress me. Everything you do just gets you into deeper shit, doesn't it? I'm calling the police.'

'Thought you were the police.'

'The big ones with tasers.'

'Yeah. I know them.'

She turned away to walk towards her house.

'Wait. Sarge. You wanted me to find out who dumped that badger on your step.'

Alex stopped, looked round, nodded warily. 'OK then. What have you got?'

'I asked around. It's a small world.'

'You know what it's like round here,' said Alex.

Julian Epps laughed. 'Yeah. That's it.'

Zoë opened the back door. 'Mum?'

'Funny thing, nobody knew anything.'

Alex watched as her daughter crunched along the shingle path from the back door. 'You came to me to tell me that you hadn't found anything out?'

'You OK?' called Zoë. 'That man's been there a couple of hours waiting for you.'

'I'll be in in a minute. Go back inside.'

Zoë hesitated, then turned and went back to the kitchen.

'She looks like she could do with a proper meal,' he said.

She leaned a little closer; smelt the stale smoke on his breath. 'Never come here again.'

'I'm just being sociable, that's all. Really, though. You may think I'm the scum of the earth, but I don't like being accused of things I didn't do. If I did it, fine. But I didn't. So I started asking around. And like I said, nobody knew anything.'

'You think I'd believe you, just because you tell me that?'

'Suit yourself. You asked me to help you. I just have. To be honest, I thought it would be someone I know, same as you. Stupid prank, you know? Townie copper sticking her nose into

261

our business, into our way of life. I mean, no surprise. We are all short of entertainment round here. But this wasn't anyone I know.'

Zoë was back at the kitchen window, keeping an eye on them.

'So?'

'Don't you think that's a bit weird?'

'Go on.'

'Thing is. The way I see it, somebody harassed you because they wanted us to look bad,' said Epps. 'They knew you'd come running straight over to me, thinking it was me that had something to do with killing Vinnie Gibbons.'

'Tell me just how you work that one out.'

'Because you fell straight for it, didn't you? Fake news. And as result I've lost my job and you're still wondering if I'm your man or not.'

He turned on the van's engine. The exhaust rattled noisily. 'I'm the victim in all this. Remember that. Somebody wants you running round thinking it was us that killed him.'

'This is all a giant conspiracy against you?'

'Think about it. It wasn't any of us.'

'I'd feel sorry for you, but you were the one digging up badgers and setting them to fight each other so you could film it and stream it on the internet.'

'That,' he said, 'was never proved.' And he put the van into gear.

In the kitchen Alex said, 'If you ever see that man again, call me right away. Or call the police.'

Zoë pulled a cucumber out of the fridge and chopped off a chunk. 'He was hanging around here waiting for you for hours.'

'Well you should have called me, then.'

'Brilliant. Now it's all my fault. You're the one who's never here.'

'Ow,' said Alex.

'Don't make me feel guilty. You started it, Mum.'

'Sorry. Bad day.' Julian Epps had just been the straw on the camel's back. She had drunk too much at the party, and then at her mother's house. And now a woman was dead. All along, she had been the one who had driven the investigation towards the theory that this wasn't a random killing, but a carefully planned one. Now it looked like she had been completely wrong, looking for a pattern in the killings where there might not even be one, and now another person was dead and for all she knew, there might be more. She put her arms round her daughter and squeezed. 'Missed you,' she said.

'Good party?'

Alex ran her fingers through her daughter's short hair. 'Gran says hello.'

'How is she?'

'Oh, you know,' Alex said vaguely. 'What if she sold the house and moved down here?'

'Jesus, Mum. She'd hate it here. We tried that before. You know that.'

'She won't be able to look after herself for ever, though.'

Zoë wrinkled her nose. 'She is enjoying herself. She's happy, Mum. She's finally living life how she wants to.'

Alex wasn't sure which she resented more: the fact that her

mother had been so happy these last few years, or the suggestion that her unhappiness had all been her father's fault for holding her back. Alex had always loved her father unconditionally; it was her mother she'd always found difficult.

Around six, she went for a cycle ride to clear her head, to work off her anger at Epps, at her mother and at herself for getting things so wrong.

She rode for about an hour until her limbs burned. Living in the city with a small child, she had felt herself growing old. Out here now, she felt younger and tougher than she had for years.

FORTY-SIX

Sweating as she heads for home, the woman on the bicycle does not even see the badger lurking in the dusty scrub by the side of the road.

People stink.

The older badger, wounds still raw, has been feeding on the low land on the far side of the road again, risking the cars, now that the younger badger has been hanging around their sett.

As he returns home, passing under the new fence, scurrying over the uneven ground, he goes to enter by the same hole he has been using for the last few days, but something is different here. The smell of it has changed.

The younger badger has left his own scent here, a strong, virile odour that stops the older badger in his tracks; scares him.

It is not just that the young one has come to mate with the sow; he has marked this part of the sett as if it is his own.

The older badger makes a chittering sound; he spends a long time sniffing at the hole in the sandy ground, returning to it again and again over the course of an hour or so, but never actually entering through it.

Eventually he returns underground, but this time by another way, through old tunnels that lead him instead past the chamber where the cubs are sleeping underground. Luckily their fractious mother is not here. Both cubs are male. Next year, if they survive the coming winter, they will be old enough to fight too, though with such a dry spring, the chances of them making it are slim.

By the north side of the sett, he starts to dig again. He is making a new exit of his own. He starts moving earth from the tunnel he had started weeks earlier. Once again he thrusts claws into that ground that smells of old death, encountering the human bones that obstruct his path again, that need to be dug around. Or shifted out of his way.

FORTY-SEVEN

Jill was one-finger typing at the desk next to Alex's at the same time as whistling 'Human' by The Killers, neither very accurately.

'What's got into you?' Alex asked.

'I'm not miserable all the time,' said Jill. She paused, looked up at Alex and said, 'Thing is, the original CSI say they found nothing in the caravan when they went after the burglary. And the CSI team weren't poisoned. Obviously. So we know whoever put the poison there must have done it between them leaving and the McKenzies going back in there on Tuesday morning to clean up the place.'

'Yes.'

'So the burglary didn't have anything at all to do with it.'

'It's got to have something to do with it.'

'Coincidence,' said Jill. 'You're barking up the wrong thing.'

'That's exactly what McAdam thinks. They're preparing a

267

press statement to say that there might be a random killer out there killing people with cyanide. Can you imagine the shit that's going to kick up?'

Alex looked again at her notebook. On Monday the McKenzies had discovered their caravan was broken into. On the following morning one of them had died. To be burgled one day and then poisoned the next, and for the two events to be unconnected, seemed unlucky in the extreme. Alex said, 'There was nothing stolen. I checked. That's on the report. No other caravans or homes on the whole site had been broken into. There has to be some connection.'

Jill shrugged. A phone buzzed and she picked it up.

'New phone?' asked Alex. It was a gold iPhone XS.

'Nice, isn't it?'

'Splashing out?'

'Harry gave it to me, matter of fact. He's trying to say sorry.'

'You serious?'

'Trying. Not saying he's succeeding. He sent me flowers and stuff. Said he learned a lesson. I don't really know, though. I have trouble trusting people, best of times. Knob.'

'But you kept the phone?'

'God, yeah. Why not?'

'Must have cost a fortune.'

'I expect it did. He can spare it.' Jill wiped the screen of the new phone with her sleeve.

Alex leaned back in her chair. 'Are you sure that's wise, taking his present, if you've no intention of going out with him any more?'

Jill put down the phone and started typing again. 'I don't care if it's wise. He owes it me, basically.'

She was still typing when Gilchrist appeared in his uniform, holding a mug of tea in one hand. 'You wanted to talk to me, Sarge?'

Alex fetched a chair from the other side of the room.

'You were the first one to arrive at the caravan park. I read your statement. I just want to hear what you saw.'

'It's just what I wrote. Turned up there a couple of minutes before the ambulance, she was flat out in the caravan not breathing. I pulled her out and tried mouth-to-mouth but I knew it wasn't going to work. She was already going cold.' A slight twitch of the lips. These moments left an impression on officers, chipped a little away each time. Alex knew that.

'That must have been tough. And you didn't suffer any of the ill-effects of the cyanide?'

'They took me to the hospital to check me out but, yeah, I was fine. The gas must have dispersed enough by the time I got in. Still smelt a bit though, but that was all. The door was ajar. I reckon that must have helped.'

'I want you to think about anything you noticed that wasn't in the report.'

He frowned. 'I put it all in.'

Jill paused in her typing. 'I heard you were thinking of joining CID, Gil?'

Gilchrist looked past Alex, grinned at her. 'Think I should do the Investigators' Exams?'

Jill didn't even look up. 'Prove you're up to it first. Tell the boss what you noticed.'

'Right,' said Gilchrist.

'Give it some time. Just put yourself back there and tell us what you saw,' said Alex.

The office was quiet except for a couple of civilian staff staring at their screens.

'Obviously noticed that CSI had been in. They left as much of a mess as the burglary.'

'Always do.'

He closed his eyes and concentrated. 'Door handle was covered in powder on the inside. I can remember thinking: That's weird, forensics have arrived even before I got here. He laughed. 'Only after did I hear that the poor bastards had reported a burglary the day before.'

'Anything else?'

'Just how brown the decor was. Velour three-piece.'

Jill started stabbing her keyboard with her index finger again. 'Try harder.'

Gilchrist stared at the carpet tiles at his feet for a full minute, trying to concentrate. Eventually he shook his head. 'Sorry, no,' he said, as if he'd disappointed himself as much as them. 'She was there on the carpet and that's what I focused on.'

'Think. What did it smell like? What else was going on?'

'The smell was rank. Like old laundry. That was the cyanide gas, apparently.'

'Anything else?'

He lifted his head, smiled. 'Running water. The shower was running. I'd forgotten that.'

There was a pause while they digested that. 'Why the hell would that be relevant?' asked Jill.

Gilchrist looked hurt. 'I don't know. It just was, that's all. And you asked me if there was anything I hadn't put in my report. The water was on. Am I done?' he said.

'Why would they have switched the shower on?'

'They were cleaning the caravan, obviously,' said Jill.

'Cymag is dry,' said Alex slowly. 'When you add water it gives off cyanide.'

Jill pushed her chair back. 'So somehow she must have released the gas when she turned on the tap? Some bastard put it in the shower so that whoever came along gassed themselves?'

The thought of being gassed in a shower had too much resonance. Alex closed her eyes. 'What if . . . ?' said Gilchrist eventually. Alex opened them again. They both looked at him.

'It's just an idea,' he said.

'What?'

'They went to the caravan site to open up their home after winter, right?' He looked tentative. 'So the water would have been turned off outside the home. What if she was inside, then Mr McKenzie goes outside and turns it on at the stopcock. I mean, it's always the bloke that does that, isn't it?'

Jill said, 'If someone had left the shower tap on, it would have released the stuff automatically . . . she would have got the full blast and he would have gone inside and found her on the floor.'

Alex nodded. 'Good . . . very good.'

She saw the next thought appear on Gilchrist's face too. 'Oh. So the burglar didn't take anything. They left the poison.'

'Handsome boy might make a detective yet,' said Jill.

'Whoever it was, they could have left the poison behind weeks ago,' said Alex. 'This wasn't an attempted poisoning. It was a mistake. And I think we know where Vincent Gibbons was killed.'

The expression she saw on Gilchrist's face was one she had seen on other officers' faces at times like this: he was pleased with himself, but he was trying to hide it. Discoveries as gruesome as this were not supposed to make you happy.

FORTY-EIGHT

'It was a gas chamber.' Just saying it felt bad.

McAdam followed them into a small conference room that wasn't being used and closed the door behind them. 'You're sure it's where he was killed?'

'Those static homes are like sealed units,' said Alex, sitting on the edge of the table. 'I'm guessing the killer somehow got Vincent Gibbons into the static home with some Cymag left on the floor of the shower. Then the killer turned the water on from the outside, just like Mr McKenzie did. Afterwards they cleaned out the place and took the body away, thinking that the shower would have washed it away, but I'm guessing there was still a residue of cyanide in the pipes.'

Jill stood next to her. 'Mr McKenzie goes outside, switches on the tap and ends up gassing his wife. Poor bastards.'

McAdam took a chair and sat at the end of the big table.

'She was old, I guess,' Alex continued. 'So it probably only took a little of the Cymag that was left in the drains to kill her.'

Despite the horror, it was hard not to feel a sense of thrill when facts like this started to show themselves.

'So the body was taken from there to Guldeford Hall, while the killers waited to dispose of it, which is where it turned up by pure accident. All we know about time of death is that Vincent Gibbons disappeared at the end of April, when Vera May last saw him. We've got to figure out how he got to the caravan site, then how his body was removed and taken to Guldeford Hall. We'll try and get our hands on all the CCTV in the area but a lot will have been erased by now – so it's not going to be simple.'

'And how someone managed to take his body and place it in Guldeford Hall without triggering the alarm,' said McAdam. He turned to Jill. 'Have you had any luck in narrowing down the number of people who might have known the code?'

'Trouble is that Belinda Utting and her husband lived entirely separate lives, but she doesn't like to admit it. We know of at least one case where Andrew Utting shared the entry code with a woman who he may have been sleeping with but his wife still swears blind that never happened.'

He had his phone out and was calling the public relations team. 'Have you sent out that press release yet?' His face fell. He muttered something to himself. As he was leaving, phone clamped to his ear, he was telling the PR officer, 'Well put a lid on it as quick as you can.'

The killing of these two people was not a random act after all; the two deaths were connected, if by accident rather than design.

Back at their own desks, Jill said, 'The look on his face. You showed him.'

'It's not about that,' said Alex.

'A little bit, admit it.'

She called across the room towards the man who'd been charged with compiling all the CCTV that showed traffic passing through the entrance to the site. 'Got anything?'

'Too much. Loads more to go through yet.'

They'd check each registration; track down the owner of every vehicle that had driven in and out of the caravan park. It was a mammoth task.

That afternoon, Alex left the office early and drove out to Camber Sands. It wasn't exactly on the way home but it wasn't too much of a detour.

The home had been entirely shrouded in white canvas now, a structure built around it. Inside, a team was slowly taking the whole place apart, looking for any other chemical residues – as well as any evidence that Vincent Gibbons had ever been there.

The latest news was that Mr McKenzie was recovering. He had confirmed what Gilchrist had guessed. He had gone outside to switch on the water and had sat on the step outside after-wards, smoking a cigarette. His wife hadn't liked him smoking inside. When he had finally gone back in there, he had found her unconscious on the floor and been unable to revive her.

Alex took wellingtons from the back of the car and walked to the north, towards Guldeford Sewer. The farmers found these ancient ditches useful. They acted as natural barriers, separating one farm's sheep from the next, but they made getting across this land hard unless you knew the layout of the network of causeways that joined one field to the next. It was like negotiating a maze.

Alex examined the gate on the causeway at the north-east corner. It was chained, but there was no lock on it. She climbed over and followed a rough track to the next gate. This was locked; but the padlock was shiny and new. She looked at it for a while. Again, she jumped over.

A flock of greylag geese, grazing in the field ahead, honked at her.

Looking around, she saw the next gate lay to the north-west. On this one, neither the chain nor the lock looked new, but something shone in the new grass near the post. When she parted the stems she saw the old links of a chain, one link bright where its metal had been cut through. The track on the other side of it was gravel. It looked as if it was heading out towards the Camber Road, or maybe the A259 beyond it.

She pulled herself up on the gate, trying to see which way the track led, and saw a short-wheel-base Land Rover kicking up a mist of dust as it drove along the lane towards her. Pulling out her ID, she stood high on the gate until it was close.

A man in his sixties, head red and shiny from the sun, a dog panting on the seat beside him, put his head out of the window. 'What you think you're doing? This isn't a public right of way,' he called out of the window.

She jumped down on his side of the gate, holding her card up. 'Somebody broke the locks on your gates.'

He pulled glasses out of his pocket and peered at her warrant card. 'Police? You found them?'

'Found who?'

His collie leaned across him, tongue flapping. 'The rustlers.'

'Rustlers? Stealing sheep?'

'Yeah.'

'Did you lose much?'

'Nope,' he said. 'Nothing at all, this time. I think they must have been disturbed, but they cut all the chains between here and Lowhold Farm up the road. Six gates. Stupid bastards. Left them wide open. Sheep were everywhere in the morning.'

'Around the end of April?'

'Yeah,' he said, a puzzled look on his face. 'Why? What's going on?'

Alex called the incident room and told them not to bother with the CCTV from the entrance to the site. It wasn't going to show them anything at all. She now knew why the killer had chosen this caravan; it was closest to the track that ran way across the fields. The killer had not arrived – or left – through the front gate at all.

That evening, Alex and Zoë went for a walk along the seafront, then cut inland to walk among the ponds of the bird reserve.

From the beach came the sound of the mechanical diggers, clanking and grinding over the shingle, piling it high on the beach in front of the nuclear power station, to defend it from the waves which were a little higher each year. They had built the power station on this vast, shifting landscape and would always be battling the moving stones it sat on.

A light rain was spitting, and it was still cold for the time of year. Alex had to wait perfectly still while her daughter trained her binoculars on what she thought might be a spotted flycatcher.

She never understood where her daughter's patience had come from.

She watched her, crouched down, focused on a faraway black dot. 'Is it rare?'

'Sssh.'

Alex's legs started to cramp. Eventually Zoë gave up and they walked back in the twilight.

William South came out of his front door as they walked past Arum Cottage. 'A word,' he said.

They entered his small wooden cottage. The lights were on inside. He had lit a small fire in the wood stove. On chilly evenings like this, it felt cosy in here. When the wind blew hard, the whole house shook. Alex liked the way it felt a little dangerous, living here at times like that. Tonight the only noise was the spitting of wood inside the stove.

'Anything good?' he asked Zoë.

'Might have been a spotted flycatcher. Couldn't be sure.'

William South put a kettle on his propane stove.

'Those photographs you sent me from Vinnie's house,' he said. 'I was having a look at them.'

'Anything?'

'I don't know. That stuff in the boxes.'

She remembered now, photographing the shoeboxes full of dusty items.

'The labels are all from locations where the badger setts he was studying would be. So I'm pretty sure that's debris from the badger spoil heaps – the stuff the badgers dig out. He was collecting it for some reason.' He opened up his laptop, an old machine that took a long time to wake. 'This one,' he said.

Alex leaned in. Her camera-phone shot of the box full of brown debris, earth-covered lumps.

'What's that?' he said, pointing to a pale oval lying among the other pieces.

She turned to him. 'I don't know.'

'Could it have been bone?'

Alex frowned. On the hob, the kettle started to roar.

'Take a look.'

Alex squinted at the screen. It was the box labelled *Lydd Area & Whiteland Fields*.

'He'd been telling Vera May he'd found ancient remains on the site, but he didn't say what they were. What if . . . ?'

'What if the remains he had found were human bones?'

South and Alex looked at each other; two coppers again, for a second.

'You've been thinking about this all this time?'

'You know. Slow and steady. Not like you.'

'Are you going to be OK on your own for a bit, love?' Alex asked Zoë.

'I'm neglected.'

'I'll look after her,' offered South.

'She can look after herself. I want you to come with me.'

It was only a short drive to Lydd, but it was dark by the time they arrived and a thin rain had started to fall. Alex rang Vera May's bell.

Richard Browne answered. 'Is Vera in?' Alex asked, looking past him.

He called up the stairs. 'Mrs May? The police are here for you.'

'Two minutes,' a voice from upstairs called.

'Found your dream house, Mr Browne?'

'Not yet. You live in Dungeness, don't you?'

Alex frowned. 'How did you know that?'

'Vera May knows your daughter.'

'Of course.'

'That must be a terrible place in winter.'

'That's when I like it most. No tourists. You looking there?'

'I don't think so,' he said. 'I've gone off the idea of moving back. Took me a while to figure it out, but I remember why I left now.'

'Why's that?'

He leaned towards her and whispered, 'It's the sort of people you get round here. They're a bit bloody up themselves, ain't they?'

'Just coming,' called Vera May.

He winked.

Vera May finally arrived at the bottom of the stairs. 'Oh, it's you.'

'I need Vinnie Gibbons's key.'

'I thought you made a copy?'

'It's at HQ. I just need to check something quickly.'

South waited in the car while she let herself into the house and poured all the contents of the shoebox into an evidence bag, then returned the key.

'Is everything all right?' demanded Vera May.

Back in the car, South switched on his phone torch and shone it at the bag. Alex held it, turning the pale circle over in her hands.

'Patella,' said South.

Alex felt its uneven shape through the clear plastic. 'You think? Human patella?'

South looked at it for a while, then spoke quietly. 'Well it's not a badger's, is it?'

She wanted to lean across to hug him, but he wasn't the kind of man who would be comfortable with that. Instead she said, 'You should have stayed a copper, Bill.'

He laughed out loud, and she realised it had been a very long time since she'd heard him do that. 'Well, now you tell me!'

She grinned back at him.

Vera May was still hovering on the pavement in the drizzle, peering into the car. Alex wound down the window. 'You said Vincent Gibbons had said there might be ancient remains on the site? Did he specify what they were?'

'No. He didn't say.'

'Did he tell many people about what he'd found?'

'I don't know. He just mentioned it to me before I went away when we were making arrangements for him to look after my cat – before he disappeared.'

'And did you tell anyone?'

'He said not to start going on about it till he was sure.' There was something about the way she stood on the pavement, hopping from leg to leg.

'But you told your lodger, obviously,' said Alex.

Vera May brushed hair from her face. 'I may have mentioned it. He's in the campaign, you know.'

'And probably a few other people,' Alex said. 'Didn't you?'

Vera May leaned towards the car, still trying to see what it was that was in the bag on Alex's lap. 'We have a steering-group meeting at the George Hotel. I wanted people to know that maybe he had come up with something that could be a big help to us. I mean, it would be rather good news, wouldn't it? No harm in that.'

Alex pressed the button to wind up the window, put the car into gear, leaving Vera May standing alone on the pavement, mouth still open.

FORTY-NINE

The rain brings the worms close to the surface.

The badgers scour the soil around them, sucking up hundreds like spaghetti. For the first time in long weeks, they are feasting.

Belly finally full, the older badger retreats to a secondary sett, one of the shallower holes a little distance from the main one. In the solitary chamber underground, he sleeps, far out of conflict's way, his digging abandoned.

His sleep is disturbed early the next day by the stink of humans. Their noise, too.

They have come, many of them, this time with shovels. Now he wants to be somewhere safer; the main sett is deep, easy to protect. This one is just a shallow scrape in the ground.

He hears metal striking earth above his head and bares his teeth, ready to fight if they come anywhere near his burrow.

FIFTY

'Do you know where Jill is?' A constable stood at the door of the incident room. 'There's a man called French downstairs to see her. Harry French.'

Jill looked up. 'Oh.'

'Is that your boyfriend?' someone said. 'Thought you'd split up.'

'Mind your own bollocks,' said Jill.

Alex exchanged a look with her. 'Tell him I'll come down,' said Alex.

'No, I'll go,' said Jill.

'Sit down,' Alex ordered. 'I suspect this is a work call.'

French's white shirt was creased; his face was red. 'Where's Jill?'

'She's upstairs. Working.'

'Doesn't she want to see me? They've just cordoned off half the site at Whiteland Fields. What's going on?'

'Sit down, Harry,' said Alex. 'We need to talk.'

There was a pair of red plastic chairs for members of the public. She took one and waited for him to join her.

'Why won't she see me?'

'There's an investigation going on.' They had sent the bone away to a lab to try and have it dated. Forensic scientists were arriving this afternoon. They would be sifting through the badger's spoils on the site to see if there were any more bone fragments that had been dug up, and searching for any soil depressions or changes in vegetation to indicate where a body might have been buried.

'They're looking for human remains? This is horrible.' Harry French put his head in his hands, closed his eyes for a minute. 'I was planning on bringing potential investors to the site this week. We are looking for secondary finance right now.'

'Not going well?'

'Confidentially? Any investment on this scale is hard to get. The government talk all this stuff up all the time, saying they want to help developers, but it's pretty desperate. We're that close to being able to do this project, but can't seem to get it over the bloody line.'

'What happens if you don't?'

'I lose a lot of money.' He smiled thinly. 'What was the minister saying to you at the party? We were hoping he was going to make a speech, but then at the last minute he pulled out. You were talking to him, weren't you? Do you know something I don't?'

'No,' she lied.

'I hope to God you're wrong about the body,' he said, laying his head in his hands.

'So do I,' she said.

'How is Jill?'

She looked at him. 'Busy.'

'I've blown it with her, haven't I?'

'You were sleeping with other women.'

'She was not my girlfriend. She made that totally explicit when we first went out. She said it a million times – she didn't want commitment. In no uncertain terms. What does she expect me to do?'

The woman at the desk was pretending not to listen, concentrating hard on writing something in the log in front of her.

Alex lowered her voice. 'Maybe that's not the way she saw it.'

'But it's what she said.'

'You need to work that out with her. I just wanted to explain why we're searching your land.'

'What happens if you find something?'

'Even if we do, it's no reason why it should mean that you can't build on that land. It may just mean some delay, that's all.'

'I'm sure people will be queuing up to buy on a place where dead bodies are buried.'

'We don't even know if there is a body there,' said Alex. 'There's probably nothing there at all.'

She walked back upstairs. She had told French that she hoped they wouldn't find a body buried on the land. But if they did, a lot of things would start to make sense.

'So. What did he say?'

'I'm not your bloody go-between, you know, Jill,' Alex replied.

★

286

'I think you should see something,' said the young woman standing by Alex's desk. 'You know you told us on Friday not to bother any more with the CCTV?'

'Yes?'

'Thing is, when you gave us a date of when you thought the body had been taken away from the back of the caravan site, I thought I'd just have another last look, just on that day, to be sure.'

Before Alex had become sure that the murderer had arrived and left by the farm tracks at the back of the caravan site, officers had gathered hours of CCTV from pub car parks and shop windows, anything that pointed out onto the main road, as well as the security cameras some static-home owners used to protect their properties against vandalism. 'And?'

'I think I have someone who might be Gibbons,' the woman said.

Alex walked to her workstation on the opposite side of the room and leaned over her computer screen.

'I've slowed it down. It's only a couple of seconds long.' She pressed the space bar. The frozen black-and-white picture sprang into life. A man on a bicycle passed the window. She rewound and pressed more keys and slowed it down even more.

'Is that him?' Jill had come up behind her and was peering over Alex's shoulder.

It looked like it was taken from one of the homes on Maple Ridge. The view was out of the main window, onto the paved road.

Again and again, they watched the man peddling past; trying to determine whether it was the dead man, trying to see if it showed a man who had any idea he was heading to his death.

The security guard seemed to be enjoying himself more, now that the site was under investigation.

'You again.' He grinned at Alex like they were old mates as he opened the gate for her car. 'I had some people from the *Kent Messenger* down this morning. Wanted to get on the site. Told them to bloody get lost.' His shirt was buttoned up wrongly, one side higher than the other. 'Park over there.' He pointed towards the other cars, lined up against the fence.

They had cordoned off a large area around the main sett; Alex recognised William South among the figures kneeling down on the ground.

She noticed that a smaller square of land within the main area had been fenced off with metal stakes. Alex's hopes rose. 'They've got something?'

'Don't know,' said the guard.

Alex made her way towards a specialist team. A young man was peering at a laptop, open at a map of the site.

'Have you found something?' She pointed towards the staked-out land.

'Nah. Just building waste. We taped it off because it looks like there's some asbestos dumped in there. Tell you what. It's going to be very hard ruling out that a body is buried here, as much as it'll be finding one. We search for disturbed ground and pretty much the whole site has been dug around over the years. We've been looking for biological indicators . . . different plants, but there's nothing really showing up so far.'

Alex said, 'I was hoping . . .'

'We'll keep looking. Being honest, the best way would be to dig the whole lot up. Which I hear they're going to do anyway. So maybe we should just wait for that.'

South joined her. 'I think we've found all the entrances to the sett. I'm still looking for subsidiary setts.'

'It's not Zoë you're talking to, Bill.'

'This is their territory.' He rotated slowly, pointing to the land round them. 'We haven't got it exactly mapped yet, but we can take a guess. There will be six or seven badgers living here. The main sett is here.' He pointed to the large hole she had seen before when they had watched for the creatures. 'They then have subsidiary setts around them. Badgers sometimes move out of the main sett and move into one of these outliers for a few days. Any one of those holes could have produced the spoil that Vinnie was searching through. I count about fifty different entrances in this territory. But I think I've found most of them, and it doesn't look like there are any bones or any fragments of bone in any of them.'

'What if we don't find anything?'

South scrunched up his mouth in the way he did when he was thinking. 'We found it in a shoebox labelled *Whiteland Fields*, but whether that means it was from here . . . I don't know.'

'Is this a wild goose chase?'

'It might be hard to prove it's not.'

Alex took out a print of a still from the CCTV of the man on his bicycle. 'Do you recognise him?'

South nodded. 'Vinnie. That's his bike, too. A tourer. Is that at the caravan park?'

'There was no bike at his house. And I didn't see one at the caravan park either.'

'Dumped somewhere then?'

The forensic ecologists were packing up their gear for the night, putting plastic boxes into the boots of their cars, when the young man's phone went.

'Sergeant.' He called over to Alex. 'You'll want to hear this.' He put the phone on speaker. 'Say it again.'

'I'd say it's within fifty years,' said a man's voice.

'What?'

'The bone,' the man on the phone said. 'It's definitely human. At this stage I'd estimate it's less than fifty years old.'

FIFTY-ONE

Alex identified herself to the forensic archaeologist on the line.

'Buried within fifty years, or that's when the person died?'

'The latter.'

'Gender? Age?'

'Find me more bones and I'll tell you.'

Compiling a list of the missing was always a depressing experience. The record of people who had disappeared, had been reported to the police, and yet never been found, was a reproach. Over fifty years there would be too many to be useful. They would need to narrow things down more, and the only way to do that would be to find more bones.

But the next day passed, and the next, and there were no bones. The ecologists were joined by a ground radar team who confirmed that the ground was too disturbed to reveal much.

'It's not that we're ruling out that a body might have been buried there,' the young man Alex had spoken to on the first day said. 'But even if that bone came from here, and we're not certain of that, look around. This search area is vast.'

'It has to be.'

'He looked at setts all over the county. How do you know for sure that it came from this one anyway?'

'It was in a box labelled *Whiteland Fields*.'

'I saw the photograph. *Lydd Area & Whiteland Fields*. It was just a patella. It's light. It could have been dug up by mistake and dumped. It could be from anywhere around here.'

She pleaded with McAdam to give them more time. 'I'll have a word,' he said.

At his request, the forensic scientists stayed one more day, diligently digging holes around the piece of scrubland.

Alex's other suggestion was more fruitful: when they dragged Guldeford Sewer to the north of the McKenzies' home, it didn't take long to find Vinnie Gibbons's bike, which emerged from the water covered in mud and weed.

The chances of finding fingerprints or other traces on it were zero, though; they had found none in the McKenzies' home. All that it confirmed was that that was where Gibbons had come to die and that he had come there apparently willingly.

The more Alex knew about what had happened on that day just emphasised how little she really understood. She now knew how, when, and where Gibbons had died, but not why he had been killed, who had been responsible for it, or whether it had anything at all to do with the bone that they had found at his house.

★

On the last day of the search of Whiteland Fields, Alex drove out in the evening and watched the team filling in all the holes they had dug.

'Nothing?'

The young man she had spoken to earlier in the week was sympathetic. 'Sorry. Difficult land. Soil analysis says the whole area has been disturbed too many times over the years to make anything simple. We've done what we can. There might be bones here, but even if there were, fifty-year-old remains aren't going to leave much in the way of vegetation markers. Maybe they'll turn up something when they build the new town out here.'

Except they probably weren't going to build it at all, she thought, and if there were the remains of someone under there, they'd remain hidden.

She sat on the back step of William South's home, drinking tea made how he liked it, too strong and tarry for her taste. She was looking out across the flatland. Zoë was out at the bird traps a quarter of a mile away with some of the people from the bird observatory. She would be taking notes of any birds, maybe helping ring them.

'It doesn't mean he's not there,' said South eventually. 'Or she. Whoever's bone it is.'

'The body might be there, but if we don't find it, it might as well be buried a thousand feet deep. We have no forensics anywhere from the caravan where Vincent Gibbons was killed. I don't even know if that bone is even connected to his death. We have nothing that explains why he was killed or who killed him.'

A figure broke out from among the low trees where the bird

nets were. Alex could have recognised her from anywhere: that boyish slouch of the shoulders as she walked towards them.

'We'll go badger-watching,' he said.

'What revelation have you got for me this time? Another spy lurking in the woods?'

'It's just the perfect time of day. There's a nice breeze too. It'll take your mind off things. You and me.' He paused. 'I just thought it would be . . . you know. Nice.'

'Oh, please. I'm tired. Last time they didn't even bother to show.'

South tried again. 'It'll teach you patience.'

'I don't want patience. I hate patience. I think there's something buried in that field, but the chances of finding it now the search team have gone are zero.'

He looked hurt, she realised, but she was in too bad a mood to consider changing her mind.

By the time Zoë arrived, he was making another thermos of dark red tea for them to take with them to the field, adding sugar this time.

'Anything good?' he asked Zoë.

She shook her head. 'Where you going?'

'Badger-watching. Your mum doesn't fancy it. Want to come?'

'Cool,' said Zoë.

'For pity's sake,' said Alex and watched them leave in Bill's car.

In the incident room the next day, McAdam said, 'Maybe we need to try a completely different angle on this.'

Alex had a packet of crisps open on her desk. She held one in front of her mouth. 'Like?'

McAdam fell silent. Alex put the crisp into her mouth and chewed on it, loudly.

News came in that afternoon of a teenage schoolboy who had been knocked off his bike by a car and killed near Dover. It turned out he had been to the same secondary school as Zoë. They had arrested the driver. Later, downstairs, locked in a cubicle in the women's toilet, Alex found herself crying, unsure why that piece of news had affected her more badly than the dozen terrible things she heard every day.

When she emerged, a woman from Human Resources came out of the next cubicle and smiled at her sympathetically. 'You all right?'

'I'll be fine,' said Alex, looking at her red eyes in the mirror as she washed her hands.

FIFTY-TWO

Even Zoë noticed it.

'Maybe it's the menopause. Jay's mum gets really moody.'

'Oh shut up. I'm not that old,' said Alex.

William South was cooking crab with rice. Zoë disapproved, but promised to eat some of the rice. 'It's Vinnie, isn't it?' he said.

Alex nodded. Zoë and Alex were sitting at the table at the far end, by the window that looked out towards the lighthouses. 'That, and everything. I don't know how much longer I can keep doing this. And I don't know what else I'd do if I didn't.'

South emerged from the kitchen.

'I'm not like you. There's nothing else I've ever done,' said Alex. 'I'm qualified for nothing except for this.'

'It's why you're so good at it,' said South.

She hated it when people were nice to her. 'I just feel used up, to be honest.'

The sun setting behind the power station turned the seakale

that dotted the shingle an impossible shade of green. 'Something will crack. You'll feel better then.'

'I mean,' said Zoë. 'Wouldn't be the worst thing if you left the police, would it? It could be great. There are billions of other jobs.'

'Like what?'

Nobody said anything. The meal should have been delicious, but the crab tasted bitter and Alex wasn't hungry. Zoë picked at her rice.

'What if you just took a week off?' said South. 'You must be due something. You could go and see your mum in London.' Nobody had finished their plateful. He scraped what remained back into the pot and put the lid back on. 'Come and see the badgers. We watched them for an hour last night.'

'I think there's a new male moved into the group,' said Zoë. 'He seems to have taken over.'

'Thanks. I know what you're trying to do, but I wouldn't enjoy it. Really.'

South picked up his plate and took it to the sink. 'It'll take your mind off it. Maybe if you leave it alone for a few days you'll come up with something fresh.'

Zoë looked dubious.

'Please, Alex,' he said.

They parked away from the main gate and knocked on the guard's door. He greeted them as if they were his oldest friends.

'Can I come? I never really seen 'em.'

'What? You work here and you've never seen them?' said Zoë contemptuously.

'Might be easier if folks weren't trying to break in.'

'If you come, you'll have to be quiet,' said South.

The four of them walked the long way around to get on the lee-ward side of the main sett entrance and then they stood amongst the low scrub, waiting.

The sun had gone down, but the sky was a luminous purple grey.

'Where we supposed to be looking?' asked the guard.

'Ssh,' hissed Zoë.

Only when they were still did Alex become aware of how full of noise the air around them was. Crickets buzzed, an evening chorus of birds sang, cars roared up the narrow road towards the A259, heading home after work.

Minutes passed, each one more slowly. The sky darkened a little more. The temperature of the air around them started to fall. She could feel cramp starting in her feet.

It was South who saw the first one. 'There.'

Alex raised her binoculars to her eyes and tried to find it.

'Can I have a go?' said the guard. South passed him the glasses. 'Wow. It's sniffing.'

'Smelling the air to see if it's safe.'

'Oh. Look. More,' whispered her daughter.

'Oh my God,' said the guard. 'They're so cute.'

Zoë tutted.

Alex could see nothing. She removed the binoculars from her eyes and tried to see where the others were looking.

'They're in good condition,' breathed Zoë. 'One female. How many cubs?'

'Two.'

'They're both still alive then.'

Alex found herself feeling jealous of the badgers. Nothing she ever did or said interested her daughter this way. Alex could now see shapes moving on the dry ground in front of the sett. She raised her glasses a second time and found them finally, surprised at how close they really were. One big badger, snout up, anxious, and two smaller ones scampering around, as if happy to be in the open.

'Must be about ten to twelve weeks. Hard to tell,' said South.

'Bloody amazing,' breathed the guard. 'I never seen anything like it.'

The cubs seemed to be taunting each other nose to nose, then scrambling over each other.

'She just rubbed her arse on the little one's backside.' The guard snorted with laughter.

'Scent-marking,' said South. 'It's how they know they're all from the same group. Some people think there may be bacteria in their scent glands that alter the way they smell. By passing it around . . .'

'What? With their arses?'

'Ssh. They have scent glands all over. It's how they communicate. Vinnie used to think there was an entire language there, just communicated by scent.'

'Bloody hell. Big, though, aren't they?'

Somewhere far off a dog barked; a deep, low noise. The three badgers paused, snouts still. After another couple of seconds they relaxed, started tussling each other, nipping at each other's bristles.

Minutes passed without Alex even realising they had, watching the big creatures move, lumbering around each other, crashing through the grass and shrubs. There were moments when they seemed to forget their anxiety about being in the open and moved as if the land were entirely theirs.

But the light was going fast. Alex looked away for a second, wiped her eyes, and when she focused her binoculars on opening them again, they had gone.

She felt disappointed, wanting more.

'Where'd they go?'

'Back down into the sett.'

'They'll be back, won't they?' said the guard, disappointed.

The four of them waited, eyes trained on the lighter earth, but nothing moved.

Alex's cramp returned. She reached down and massaged her leg. 'Are we done?' she said.

'Oh come on, Mum. We only just got here. Give it another fifteen minutes.'

The guard said, 'I'm going to do this every night.' He took South's binoculars again. 'How much are these? Might get a pair myself.'

Stars were pricking into the sky.

The guard scanned the land, back and forth. He stopped, twisted the focus ring, took them from his eyes, replaced them, then said, 'Oh my fuck. What's that?' He lowered South's binoculars again and pointed.

Alex heard her daughter sucking in air. 'It can't be,' Zoë said. 'That's horrible.'

'What?'

'Look,' said Zoë, handing her her glasses. 'By the hawthorn.'

Alex was trying to focus, twisting the wheel. The ghoulish scene sprang into focus for a second, so fast she wasn't even sure she'd seen it, and then was gone again. 'Damn,' she said, twisting the other way until she could see clearly again.

Standing on a different patch of ground, fifteen metres to the right of where the cubs had been playing, was a human skull, soil-stained, propped on top of a small hill of earth, perfectly upright, empty eyes facing them darkly under its pale dome.

FIFTY-THREE

The older badger returns to the new burrow he has dug, passing through a cave of human ribs.

Then stops and waits because the humans are back, right above him now.

Their smell drifts down his newly dug hole.

FIFTY-FOUR

It was sitting on the spoil, right below the entrance, as if it had just materialised there. They stood around for a minute, gazing at it.

'Who did that?' asked the guard. 'I didn't see anybody. You?'

Alex looked over towards the woods, where the man who had watched them had been lurking, but they were empty. 'It can't have just appeared out of nowhere.'

'That's a new opening,' William South said, squatting down. 'They've just dug that. Look. The earth is fresh.'

'You mean the badgers have dug it up?'

'Those are claw marks.' Two fresh, ivory-coloured parallel lines across the side of the skull, where a powerful talon had scratched off old earth.

'It's like the badgers wanted us to see him,' said Zoë and nobody contradicted her. Alex didn't spook easily, but this felt like it had arrived as some mystical sign, offered from the ground.

The guard leaned down to look closer. 'Oh God. There's still stuff inside.'

'Don't touch it,' warned Alex.

Fascinated, Zoë squatted down beside him.

'Jesus. Is that brain?' Without warning, the guard lowered his head and vomited onto the grass at his feet. Though it wasn't a brain at all, Zoë told him later, an arm around his shoulder. It was just a cluster of earthworms, writhing into a knotted mass behind the empty eyeballs, where the badger's teeth couldn't reach them.

The skull; the patella. They were both from here, she was sure of it now. And this time, knowing which sett exit the skull had emerged from would make finding the remains easier.

'How long will it take to get a licence to excavate?' asked Alex.

'Happy now?' asked South.

'I'll be happier when I know we can dig on the site. The body is buried in there.'

'If we step on it, forty-eight hours,' said South. 'See? You were right about it. You just needed to be patient.'

'Oh shut up. We were lucky, Bill. It was a fluke.'

'I think the land was trying to tell us something all along.'

'Oh Jesus, Bill. That's absolute bollocks.'

'Got to admit. It was quite weird,' said Zoë, and turned to the guard. 'You should have something to drink. Settle your stomach. You got tea in your office?'

He nodded; Alex watched as her daughter led the man, whom

four weeks earlier she had been calling a liar and a thief, away to the cabin to look after him.

Two days later the forensics team arrived with their ground radar to map out where the new tunnel lay, and then dug cautiously down towards it. William South stood guard over the sett to make sure that there were no badgers present in the tunnel they were trying to access, ready to trap any animals that emerged from the hole to prevent them attacking the diggers.

'Surprised you're still a single man, seeing you dressed like that,' said Alex, paper cup of coffee in hand.

He was dressed in comically large black protective dungarees and thick leather gloves.

The first hint that they were getting somewhere came late that first morning. 'Nylon,' said the woman from the forensics team, holding up a large scrap of black material. 'Maybe trousers.'

'What's that?' said South, pointing down at the trench they had been digging.

The woman reached down and picked up a coin. 'The pockets must have been cotton. They've disintegrated.'

'What is it?'

The woman brushed off the earth. 'It's a shilling.' She rubbed it on her sleeve, held it up to her eye. 'Dated 1966.'

The first bones emerged from the earth a few minutes later. The body had not been buried deeply. 'Male. Teenager,' said the woman, holding up a complete pelvis.

'That nylon. Could that be school trousers?' called Alex.

'That's what it looks like.'

Alex checked on her phone to find when shillings had gone

out of circulation: December 1990. Assuming the coin had come from the dead boy, that narrowed the window of his death to a twenty-four-year interval. 'I think I may know who this is,' she said quietly.

The digging stopped. The excitement of finding the bones was replaced by something more sombre. Alex called Jill in the incident room.

'That list of missing persons. There was a teenage boy from the 1980s, wasn't there?'

'Hold on,' said Jill.

The diggers had stopped their work and watched her; Alex listened to the clacking of Jill's keys in the distant office.

'Got it,' Jill said. 'Name of Trevor Grey.'

'He ran away from school,' said Alex. 'Didn't he?'

'Did he?' said Jill. 'How do you remember stuff like that?'

She also remembered twisting the binoculars' ring, trying to see what Zoë was looking at, then seeing the skull as it abruptly came into focus, and shivered.

Now there was definitely a body, and they had a good idea who it had belonged to, more officers arrived. Jill came in a car with Gilchrist, though neither of them had any particular reason to be there, except for the fact that they had both been involved in this case and felt the need to be. Tony Skinner, the Wildlife Crime Officer, arrived in a dirty four-wheel-drive.

'How's the baby?' asked Jill.

'Exhausting,' said Skinner.

'Let me show you something,' said South. 'Can we stop for a minute?'

The careful digging around the dead boy's ribcage ceased. The forensics team moved away from the heavily marked trench for a break.

South led the Wildlife Crime Officer over to the new fence line on the far side of the field. Alex saw them staring at a fence post and walked over to find out what South was doing.

'What's the problem?' she asked.

'See that? I reckon that fence post is buried right in an entrance hole,' said South.

It wasn't immediately obvious to Alex; the concrete post looked like any other one, set into the earth, but there was a large patch of bare earth on the far side of the fence, much like the one the skull had rested on.

'Yep.' Skinner squatted down and started taking photographs of the post and the ground in which it sat with his phone. 'The entrance is right where they stuck the post.'

'That's an offence, presumably?'

'Oh yes.'

'I think they did us a favour, though,' South said. 'Because they blocked this one, the badgers ended up having to dig a new tunnel. That's why they started digging up bones.'

'Maybe your boyfriend did us a favour,' said Alex.

'Stop calling him that.'

As the afternoon drifted on more coins emerged. The date window narrowed. The newest was a coin from 1981: *2 New Pence*. 'So it's him, isn't it?' said Jill.

'Looks like it.'

They had broken through into another tunnel now. South

stood ready with a trap, but it looked as if the badgers had retreated further underground, away from the noise of digging.

Trevor Grey. A fifteen-year-old boy who had run away from Thornhead School for Boys, a private school twelves miles away in Winchelsea, in 1984. Reports said he had left his dormitory bed one night and had never been seen again.

'How did he get here, then?' asked the guard.

'He didn't dig himself a hole and lie in it, that's for sure,' said Jill. The discovery of a body darkened the mood; a child's body made it worse. Jill looked up at the sound of another car approaching the gates. 'Shit,' she said.

Alex recognised the driver of the new Audi that had turned in at the site gate; it was Harry French. Dressed in a Barbour and pale trousers, he got out and approached them.

'Hello, Jill,' he said cautiously.

'Hello, Mr French,' she answered stiffly.

'You've found a body then, I heard.' He looked over to where they were building a tent around the trench they had already dug.

'I'm afraid it looks as if we're going to be on your land for quite some time,' said Alex.

'Don't be like that. I'm not that callous. Do you have any idea who it is?'

'Do you?' asked Alex.

French frowned. 'No. Why would I?'

'It's your land.'

'Our consortium bought it five years ago,' he said. 'Was the body placed there before or after that?'

'We can't say yet,' Alex answered. 'Not for certain.'

'Are you Harry French?' They all turned. Tony Skinner was

striding towards them, William South at his side. 'You the owner of this land?'

Harry nodded.

'You understand we'll be charging you for wilfully obstructing the entrance to a badger sett, which is illegal under the Protection of Badgers Act?'

Alex thought she heard the sound of Jill trying to suppress a laugh.

FIFTY-FIVE

Trevor Grey's father was still alive; he sat in a high-backed chair in a nursing home where the television was on so loud, Alex had to lean in close to hear his voice. The TV programme was called *The Nightmare Neighbour Next Door*.

'After it was clear that Trevor wasn't coming home, his mother pretty much drank herself to death.' Ex-army, he still sat straight in his chair, though his hands shook gently all the time she was speaking to him. 'There was never any question in my mind that he was dead. She was never able to accept that. It was something that came between us.'

She had brought a map with her to show him where they had found him.

'Pity you didn't find him earlier, isn't it? You could have saved her all that.'

'Did you have any idea why he ran away?'

'I believe he didn't very much like the school. But many of us don't like the places where we end up.' He looked around himself despondently. The TV kept showing images of a barking dog. 'But we have to get on with it, don't we?' he said.

'He never told you why he didn't like the school?'

'No.' The man picked up a clear plastic beaker from the table beside of him and held it in front of his mouth, the water inside rippling as his hand trembled. Eventually the cup was steady enough for him to bring it to his mouth and drink from it. He replaced it slowly, carefully, on the table. 'He would never talk to me about it. He talked to his mother sometimes, I believe.'

He lapsed into silence.

The family house had been sold. All Trevor's possessions had gone, which was frustrating, as Alex would have liked to have found an old comb or a toothbrush, something they could use to confirm the identity of the boy, using DNA, but proof aside, there was no doubt in her mind that the body they had dug up at Whiteland Fields was his.

'Your wife never talked to you about why she thought he was unhappy?'

'Oh, she had plenty of ideas,' he said, and clutched his hands together to steady them, then looked down at them, as if he wasn't sure they belonged to him at all.

'Such as?' said Alex.

'Oh. All sorts of things. She had never wanted him to go to boarding school. It was me who had insisted on it. I had been there. And I wanted him to go there too.'

'Even though he wasn't happy there?'

'It was nothing to do with the school,' he said. 'She just wanted to blame me for sending him there, that's all.'

Trevor Grey's father seemed uninterested in mourning his

son. A nurse came in and placed a small paper cup in front of him, next to his water. 'Take your pills, Mr Grey,' she said.

'I want a white nurse,' he said. 'A British one.'

'I'm not a nurse,' said the woman. 'I'm a care assistant.'

'The television is too loud. I can't hear myself think.'

The care assistant walked over to the television and put the programme onto mute.

'Not even a bloody nurse,' complained the man. The woman stood by him, waiting.

'He had no reason not to be happy. I was perfectly happy there.'

He lifted a pale green pill out of the paper cup and put it on his tongue, then lifted the cup of water.

As he swallowed, Alex watched his Adam's apple move slowly beneath loose folds of skin, like a mouse shuffling under a cloth.

The school grounds were beautiful, the gentle folds of the land it sat in dotted with copper beeches, cedars and redwoods. The playing fields were empty; children would be in class at this time of day.

At the end of the driveway, new modern rectangles of glass and metal had been barnacled onto a gothic Victorian mansion of red brick and pale stone.

Looking through one ground-floor window in one of the modern blocks, Alex saw ranks of uniformed boys sat at desks. They were all facing to the right, where the teacher must be standing, out of sight. One ginger-haired boy's attention drifted towards her. He looked sideways at her, chewing methodically on his biro, eyes following her as she got out of the car to walk across the tarmac. She heard a raised voice and the boy's attention snapped back to the front of the room.

The head teacher's study was in the older part of the building. The desk was oak, the chair facing it was leather; all intended to suggest the weight of ancient authority. There was a cabinet full of shiny cups, a case full of carefully chosen books.

'The problem is,' said the headmaster, 'we don't have records for that period.'

'No records?'

'It was an entirely different school then, you see. The name is the same but the old school was sold to a trust in the late 1980s. It had been run by a single family up until then and, frankly, it was failing. It was not equipped to cope with the demands of the modern pupil. Plus, there were certain financial difficulties. The trust bought the name and the buildings. Technically, we are now a completely different institution. Few of the staff from that time were retained. It was a *tabula rasa*.'

'You seriously have no records of that time?'

'What you have to understand is that there was no obligation to keep them. The old school operated under its own system. The headmaster kept no staff records at all, in fact, and I understand he took all the pupil records himself when he left. They were quite a muddle anyway, apparently. I know anyone from the state education system might find that strange, but we private schools are often a law unto ourselves.'

'When you say it was failing . . .'

'I think it's fair to say there were education problems. Standards were not as high as they should have been. Oxbridge entries

313

were few and far between. Unfashionable though it is to say, it's all different now. We are very proud of our pupils' achievements.'

Alex leaned forward. 'Don't tell me a private institution doesn't sell itself to a trust and sack most of its staff unless something went extremely wrong.'

'I don't think there was anything in particular.' The headmaster thrummed his fingers on the table.

'Really?'

The man lowered his fingers and spread his hands palms up, shrugged. 'It was simply that the school had fallen behind the times. The owners were elderly. Numbers were falling.'

'Were there any outstanding accusations of child sex abuse?'

The smile vanished. 'I hope you don't intend to repeat that kind of nonsense outside this room.'

Alex looked the headmaster in the eye. She had rattled him. 'It's a perfectly reasonable question. The Independent Inquiry into Child Sexual Abuse has records of hundreds of instances of abuse that took place within the private school system, many of them from the 1980s. If you have no records, how can you dismiss the question as nonsense?'

'It was all well before my time,' said the headmaster. 'I assure you, I have no evidence that anything was wrong with the school.'

'Trevor Grey disappeared from here not long before your trust bought the place.'

'The lack of proper records is very inconvenient, I'm afraid. However, I'm sure the sale of the school has nothing to do with that.'

They locked eyes. 'What about the former staff? Or old pupils from that time?'

'Obviously I can try and dig up a few names and contact details, if that's helpful. I can email them, perhaps,' he said evenly, returning her stare as she passed him her card. 'I suppose this will be in the newspapers?'

'As soon as we have positive identification of the body we'll release his name and the circumstances under which he went missing. We need to try and jog people's memories. Of course, we'll be mentioning the school by name.' Trevor Grey's dirty bones were lying in a box somewhere now. To his father they were just an old argument; to this man they were reputational damage.

'It's inevitable that there will be discussion of the school, and for us it's important there is. As you say you have no records, we have to use whatever means we can to get in touch with former pupils – or anyone who can help us.'

'I assure you, we want to help as much as we can. A former Thornhead boy is dead. Even if we didn't know him personally, that affects us deeply.' He attempted a sympathetic smile. 'Perhaps our public relations officer can assist you?' he suggested.

'No,' said Alex, standing. 'That really won't be necessary.'

They shook hands stiffly. Somewhere outside, a bell rang and the school came alive. The sound of children pouring outside through doors into playgrounds.

She was sitting in the car making notes when a shadow blocked the light. There was a tap on the window.

'Sergeant Cupidi?'

It took a second or two to recognise the woman's face; it was Angela Booth, Gram's girlfriend. She looked angry.

FIFTY-SIX

Alex wound down the window.

'Thought I recognised you,' said Angela Booth. 'Are you here to get me sacked again?'

'I'm sorry?'

'I was let go from the school I taught at. The parents didn't like seeing me in the papers, apparently. I had to find an alternative, so I'm doing some supply teaching here.'

'The reason I'm here is nothing at all to do with you, I promise. Is it your break?'

'Fifteen minutes. I was just going to go out of the gates for a cigarette break. That's not so much of a challenge in a comprehensive school. At one of these –' she waved her hand at the grounds – 'you have to walk half a bloody mile before you're out of the danger zone.'

Alex leaned over and opened the passenger door. 'Get in,' she said.

'Lifesaver. Can I smoke in the car?'

'No, but I can pretend I was just driving through a heavy smoking area and people kept exhaling at me.'

Angela laughed and got in. 'So you really weren't there to talk about me?'

'We've just dug up the body of what we think is an ex-pupil of your school. He ran away from here in 1984.'

'Can't blame him. God knows why parents send their children to these places. It's a shithole.' Alex parked outside the school gates and watched Angela light a cigarette, window wound down. 'It feels naughty, smoking in a police car. So he ran away and got into some kind of trouble?'

'Not easy to tell. There are no records from that time. It beggars belief, but it's not the first time I've come across private schools failing to keep consistent records. They're above all that.'

At the entrance to the school there was a large blue sign with the school's name, and under it, their motto: *Be Still, and Know*.

'It's not like the police did much better,' she continued. 'I've looked through the original notes into the investigation, and there's virtually nothing there.'

'Do you think something bad was going on here then?'

Alex watched the smoke with a twinge of ex-smoker jealousy. 'I don't know.'

'I can't help you, I'm afraid. I'm only here for a few weeks substituting for someone who's on maternity leave. I hate it, but it pays well. Me and Gram are trying to get the money together for a deposit.'

'You're back together?'

She nodded and smiled. 'Like we said, he's a nice boy. There aren't that many of them and I've been through all the alternatives,

317

believe me. I was pissed off at Gram at the time for getting me involved. He's so honest, it hurts. But I figure that's probably a good thing. And it was kind of a sweet thing to do, take me there, even if he was mainly trying to get into my knickers.' She took another puff of the cigarette. 'How was he to know there was a dead body in the freezer? You found out who it was, then?'

'We still don't know who killed him.'

'I always assumed it was the dead husband, killed by a jealous wife. You married?'

Alex watched the smoke curling out of the open window. 'Divorced.'

'Boyfriend?'

Alex shook her head.

'Yeah. Much simpler that way. Gram wants us to get married. I'm not so sure.'

It was true. Alex hadn't had a relationship since she'd moved to Dungeness. As much as she missed sex, it was having someone just to hold her occasionally that she would have liked, but she didn't miss the complications of a relationship.

'I should probably get back,' said Angela.

Alex looked at her. 'Wait. You said you assumed it was the dead husband – in the freezer. What made you think that?'

'All those suits in the wardrobe.'

'What do you mean, "all those suits"?'

'The ones that were on the hangers. In bits. You didn't see?'

'No, I didn't.' The house had supposedly been thoroughly searched by officers, but no one had mentioned the suits.

'Classic. All the backs of the jackets had been slashed. Like someone had gone major stabby on them.'

'No, I hadn't seen that. Why didn't you tell me that last time?'

'You said the man who was killed had nothing to do with the house.'

Alex should have been used to it by now; the way people didn't think the same way a police officer did. Besides, if the police's own search team had failed to mention it, why should Angela have?

Her break had finished. She was going to be late, so Alex dropped her back at the main building.

'Oh God, the headmaster's seen me with you. He's got that disapproving look. He'll want to know why I'm talking to the police. I'm probably going to lose this job now, too.'

'Tell him we're old friends, catching up.'

'He'll definitely sack me then. I don't mind. I hate it here.'

Another bell rang. Angela Booth got out of the car and smiled. Waved, like they were old friends. As Alex pulled out of the long drive onto the main road, a black 4WD seemed to emerge from nowhere into her rear-view mirror. She thought she remembered checking the road before she pulled out into it, and hadn't seen any other vehicles coming. Nor had there been any other junctions from which it could have turned onto the main road.

Unsettled, she checked it in her mirror again, but the car had dropped behind.

Jill had the map out and was kneeling over it on the floor of the incident room, biro in her hand.

She had marked Whiteland Fields on it, and the caravan park, adding a trail following the back route out of the caravan park, up through the fields, then to the B-road, and finally to the A259 towards Guldeford Hall, which was also marked.

'Where's the school exactly?' she said.

Alex squatted down beside her, following the contours and the curves in the road to work out where it was. 'There.' She pointed.

Jill leaned over and scrawled an X directly onto the paper.

'Vandal,' said Alex.

'It's just a map,' said Jill. 'Just a copy of what you've already got on your phone.'

Alex rolled her eyes, then traced her finger from the school to the site in Whiteland Fields, where they had dug out the bones. 'So how did Trevor Grey get from there . . . to here?'

'Walk it?'

'He was running away. He was vulnerable.'

'You reckon someone picked him up?'

Alex looked at the land she was still learning to love; a flat diamond of marsh surrounded by rising hills.

'I was thinking about the red Mazda the gardener saw,' said Alex. 'The woman who had a key. Belinda Utting hasn't been telling us the truth, she knew perfectly well her husband was having an affair.'

'You think she knows who this woman might be?'

Alex didn't answer.

Jill looked at her watch. 'I could go and talk to her before I knock off. I know a little bit about lying.' Alex watched her struggling to fold up the map, like she'd never handled one before.

★

To her surprise, the headmaster of Thornhead School was as good as his word, and emailed her a list of names and numbers. Alex spent a frustrating afternoon trying to contact them. One, a former Geography teacher, had died five years earlier. The school's matron had remarried; Alex only had her maiden name but managed to trace her, only to find that she, too, was dead. She found a number for the third, a PE teacher, but her daughter said he had advanced dementia and was incapable of remembering that time. The fourth was a Mr Lindsay, a former Head of Maths.

Mr Lindsay picked up the phone straight away. 'Oh,' he said warily. 'Trevor Grey. You found him, then?'

'You remember him?'

'A little. Though, as a matter of fact, he was not a very memorable boy.'

Alex pulled out the map and unfolded it again. The house where Lindsay still lived was only a few miles from the 'X' that Jill had drawn onto its surface.

FIFTY-SEVEN

Frederick Lindsay lived alone in a small, square house that sat along the dank Military Canal; built from grey stone, it still somehow managed to absorb the damp of the marsh.

While Mr Lindsay boiled a kettle, Alex looked out onto the weedy water of the canal, wondering how deep it was. It had been dug to stop invaders; an ancient anxiety that ran the length of this coast. The land was full of old fortresses and ramparts. Her own house was built on the site of a Napoleonic gun battery. The low evening light made the water look darker.

'I don't know quite what you expect to discover,' said Lindsay. 'Trevor Grey did not fit in. Some children never do. Unfortunately, he chose to run away from school. He was not a particularly clever child. I can only guess he met someone who took advantage of him, and that it ended badly.'

The house smelt of mud; as if it permeated everything in the building. If there was something primitive about the place, Lindsay didn't seem to notice. He poured tea into a dull green cup and saucer, and presented it to Alex. The cup was cracked and badly washed. Alex left it on the small, precarious table by the side of her armchair, sure that it too would taste of the canal outside the window.

'You said you thought he may have met someone who took advantage of him. What did you mean by that?'

Lindsay felt along the stem of a standard lamp for the switch. The light seemed to make the room's corners darker. There was an ancient marble bust of a man with an extravagant beard standing on a dark wooden column. Its pale shape cast a shadow on the wall behind him. 'You're a policewoman. You must know there are bad people out there who prey on children.'

'Police officer,' she said.

'I beg your pardon?'

'We prefer "police officer" these days. Statistics tend to indicate that the bad people you refer to who prey on children are usually not "out there" at all. Back in your day, schools had plenty of them.'

'Not our school,' he said.

'You know that for a fact?'

'Thornhead's methods were possibly a little old-fashioned by today's standards. We taught good manners and respect. We taught how to be part of the team. It requires work. Of all the animals, the boy is the most unmanageable.'

'I beg your pardon?'

'Plato.' He pointed at the bust, then, unsmiling, added, 'It was a joke, obviously. Greek humour is not to everyone's taste.'

'You taught Trevor Grey?'

He sat back in his chair. 'Yes. As I remember, he was a pretty average pupil. Some ability in the subject, but too easily distracted.'

'Popular, unpopular? Shy, outgoing?'

'Not very popular. He was one of the weaker boys. The ones who tended to try to sit at the back to avoid attention. I made sure his desk was at the front of the class. I always used to do that. It does them no good at all, the quieter ones, to go unnoticed.'

'Do you have any idea why Trevor Grey ran away?'

'I expect he wasn't happy.'

Unhappiness in the young is a powerful thing. She knew that from her own child.

'Why?'

He waved his hand in the air dismissively. 'I can't be expected to see into the minds of every pupil we ever had.'

'Wasn't that your job?'

'Certainly not. I was there to educate them. Happiness can be a consequence of education, but it's not a prerequisite. I was not there to make them happy.'

'A strict school?'

'We were running a school for the elite. For future leaders. Too much freedom is a slavery of its own kind.'

'I suppose that's Plato again?'

He grinned, for the first time. 'Not verbatim. However, I think he said something similar.'

'You believed in the ethos of the school.'

'Very strongly. My father was the headmaster, after all. I went there as a pupil myself.'

'I didn't realise.'

'I had been expecting to take over after he died. Unfortunately, that never happened. We ran into financial difficulties. The climate was much more hostile to private schools in those days.'

'Hostile to Thornhead?' Alex said.

'There is this idea that we just educate the rich. That was never true. We had scholarship people from all classes at Thornhead. Farmers' boys rubbed shoulders with the sons of parliamentarians and entrepreneurs.'

'Trevor Grey wasn't a scholarship boy, was he, though?'

'Paid for by the government. His father was in the army in Germany. But we did our best to mix all sorts. Sometimes it worked, sometimes not.'

'I can't imagine the sons of the posh always liked having farmers' boys in their class.'

'Of course they didn't. And sometimes the lower-class boys resented it too. But we made them respect each other . . .'

'What about friends? Did Trevor Grey have many?'

He gave the question some thought. 'Not really. He wasn't part of any particular gang, not that I remember.'

He stood again, and walked to a cabinet full of books, opening a drawer below it. Even in this dark room, it seemed to be full of rolls of paper. Lindsay pulled one out and unfurled it, and Alex realised it was a black-and-white school photograph. 'Not that one,' he muttered, replacing it and extracting another.

There must have been dozens of them in the drawer; rows and rows of the children he had taught. He leafed through them carefully, unfurling each one, then putting them back as if they were treasure. The tenderness with which he treated them seemed at odds with the dry man who had told her he was not there to make the boys happy. Finally he found the one he wanted and put it onto his dining table, whose ancient walnut veneer had faded badly.

He stood above it, placing items from a silver cruet set on each corner to hold it down; salt, pepper, mustard and vinegar.

'There,' he said, pointing.

A fair-haired boy, sitting smilelessly on a chair, younger boys in front, cross-legged on the grass, others behind him, presumably standing on benches. She recognised him easily from the family snapshot in his Missing Persons file.

'His mother said he was unhappy at school.'

'Mothers sometimes do,' he answered.

'I'll need a copy.'

'I suppose you shall.'

She looked down the row of boys. The line of chairs appeared perfectly straight, but this was an illusion. The old building behind it, which she had visited earlier in the day, was distorted, as if seen in a curved mirror. The photographs were taken with a panoramic camera set on a clockwork mount that panned slowly from left to right.

Trevor Grey looked miserable; most of the other children around him wore smiles. It would be an afternoon out of the classroom, a break from the routine, a chance to muck about. She checked the start and the end of the line and laughed.

'What?'

'Look,' she said.

The same boy stood at both the left-hand and right-hand end

of the line. In both he was grinning broadly. She had heard of this. The boy would have waited until the camera had passed him, then run behind as fast as he could to the far end of the line to appear twice.

'Who was it?' she asked.

Mr Lindsay took one look at the boy and scowled. 'I don't remember.' He didn't find it anywhere near as funny as Alex did.

She looked closer. The boy who appeared twice was not the only person who had been fooling around. At the end that he must have run to, another boy's face was totally blurred. Instead of staying still, he had deliberately moved his head from side to side as the camera had panned past. Instead of eyes, nose and mouth, there was just a grey smudge. Alex ran her fingers back along the rows.

'What about this boy here?' Alex pointed to the boy who sat next to Trevor Grey. While most boys smiled at the camera, this black-haired boy shared Grey's expression.

'Adison,' said Lindsay. 'Revell Adison. Yes, I'm not surprised they were next to each other. Both of them were the same. Quieter ones.'

'Your enemy's enemy is my friend.'

'If you like.'

'You said he didn't have any friends. Can you look again? Are there any others?'

He peered at the photos closely, taking his time. Each face seemed to provoke some kind of reaction in him. 'No. Just Adison. I wonder what became of him,' he said.

Alex asked him to write out the boy's name to be sure she

could get the spelling right. 'Revell was his first name, right?' An unusual name would be useful. It would be easier to track him down. The records for the school had vanished; this was as close as she was going to get. 'If I find him, I'll let you know,' she said.

'Don't trouble yourself.'

When she left, she heard him drawing a bolt across the door behind her, as if relieved to be on his own again.

She sat in the police Skoda in the dark, thinking for a while.

Even if she didn't find Revell Adison, she would find some excuse to come back here. Her visit had unsettled Lindsay. He had more to tell.

The marshland in front of her was dark now. She switched on her engine and the lights came on, shining over the flat field on the other side of the Military Canal. She had a memory of a year before, pulling bodies from water not far from here. She shivered, then reversed out onto the empty road and put the car into forward gear.

Immediately there were car lights behind her. Shockingly, because she hadn't noticed any cars on the road. The second time this had happened that day.

But, this time, as she sped up, the car behind sped up too. She slowed and moved to the left side of the road so it could pass, but the car behind her slowed too.

Conscious of her heart rate increasing, she considered stopping, but she was a woman on her own in a car. If they were someone looking for a road-rage argument, she didn't want any part of it.

It was a while since she'd done her fast-car training, but the reflexes were still there. She accelerated away again fast, and was far enough away from them at the T-junction at the end of Military Road to feel that she might have shaken them off.

But as she turned right, the other car was suddenly behind her again.

On the far side of the canal, she swung immediately left again, accelerating away down a narrower lane alongside the bank. She didn't have to look to know they were still right behind; the glare of their lights filled her rear-view mirror, dazzling her.

Again, she pulled to one side, hoping they would pass. At the first thump on the back of the car, she knew choosing this road had been a major mistake. That was not an accident. They had rammed her deliberately. Whatever car they were driving had better acceleration and more power. She heard brake lights shatter as the second blow on the rear, somewhere behind her driving seat, made the car slew to the right, towards the dark water.

She twitched her steering wheel into the bank in an attempt to recover control of the skidding car, but the road was too narrow. She lost speed the moment her wheel hit the soft verge.

In that second she knew that a third contact from behind would be the decisive one. To control the skid, she had been forced to line her car up perfectly for what was coming.

She felt the other car smash hard into hers, her head cracking back into the headrest with the force of the blow.

The car shook on uneven ground. Branches cracked.

There were leaves on the windscreen, then water.

And then blackness swallowed her and the lights of the Skoda embedded themselves into the mud at the bottom of the canal.

FIFTY-EIGHT

Head-whiplash fuzzy, it took a few seconds to realise that the car had been swallowed by thick black water.

The headlights were deep in mud, the engine weight keeping the front of the car down.

Her first reaction was panic, scrambling for the buckle of her seatbelt and not finding it. To be a police officer was to know too much. Her head was suddenly full. She knew that few ever escaped from submerged cars. She remembered a pale body lying by the side of the water not too far from here. She thought of her mother and of her seventeen-year-old daughter, and howled.

Her feet, she was suddenly aware, were icy cold. The leaking water must be covering them already. She thrashed, still buckled in her seat, overwhelmed by panic and despair.

Next came fury. It had been a cold, deliberate attempt to force her off the road. They had known exactly what they had been doing. They had been trying to kill her. How bloody dare they?

The anger saved her. It felt as if she had years of it, quietly bottled. She stopped wrestling the belt that held her tightly; breathed. Became conscious that her opportunities to breathe were limited. Closed her eyes, shaking from the adrenaline racing round in her blood. This was not the time to lose it.

More seconds passed.

Still trembling, she reached down, found the buckle and released herself, her weight falling forward against the steering wheel, then reached up and switched on the interior light.

The brightness emphasised the darkness that surrounded her. The water enveloping her was deeper than she had imagined it would be, thicker and blacker, but thankfully the rear window was not submerged. The dim ultraviolet of the sky above her shone through.

Time was running out, though, and fast. Freezing water had filled the footwell and was now creeping up her thighs. She wriggled round so that she faced the back of the car, now sloping above her, and clambered over the passenger seat into the rear of the car.

The rear-door windows were submerged, but they were closer to the surface. She took a breath, filling her lungs and pressed the button of the electric window on the left side to open it, waiting for the water to pour in.

Nothing happened.

Either the pressure of water on the glass had jammed the mechanism, or the electric motor had shorted.

She twisted round, tried the other side. Again, nothing.

The only way out would be to break the toughened glass. She turned back, yanked at the headrest of the driver's seat, but it seemed to be stuck. Already the cold, or maybe just the lack of oxygen, was weakening her hands, she realised. She tried the other headrest; this one slid more easily. Wriggling it back and forth, she managed to finally yank it out.

Breaking car glass was not easy; she knew that. Turning to wedge herself against the front seats to get leverage to make her first blow, she fumbled. The headrest slipped from her fingers. It fell into the black water at the front of the car.

'Shit, shit, shit.'

Despair returned.

Her name was Alexandra Cupidi. When she was a child, she had been told by her mother that she had been named after her aunt – Helen's younger sister – who had been assaulted, tortured and murdered when she was just a teenager. Alex had always hated the name, but hadn't dared change it for fear of offending Helen.

She had been named after a dead girl left in a ditch.

Over time, her dead aunt's name had become a talisman. Instead of growing into the name, the name had grown into her. Only after being a detective for a few years did she realise it was why she had gravitated to this work. Murder had named her; it had defined her. And now she was about to be murdered, too.

For a second time, despair turned again to anger. A second time she tried to move the driver's seat headrest, but nothing would budge it.

She swore again, this time furiously, filthily, then swivelled her body and dropped back down into the driver's seat, feeling

333

for the other headrest in the dark of the flooded footwell. She found it, soaked now in cold water, and stood again, crawling up so that her feet were wedged on the steering wheel for purchase, then she rolled over into the back of the car.

As she did so, the whole vehicle shifted. Her stomach lurched. Her weight, combined with the mass of water flooding in, tilted the vehicle backwards towards the horizontal. A black waterline appeared at the back window, lapping against it. The car was going under.

A third time, panic returned, overwhelming her. Pressing one hand against the rear window, she lashed out, whacking at it with the spike. The metal skidded off the glass not even leaving a mark, smashing into her other hand instead. She yelped in pain.

She paused again, concentrated on breathing slowly.

The shakes were bad now. Her head was becoming fuzzy. She knew it was a matter of minutes, maybe less.

Concentrate. She thought of the car that had pushed her into the water, allowing anger to displace fear. She willed herself to think.

The back window was steeply angled, that made it hard to attack. She would have to try and get out through a passenger window. The danger was that the water would rush in at such a speed, sinking the car, that she would never get out. If it tilted too far downwards, or dropped against some hidden underwater obstruction, she would be trapped.

Grabbing the spike with one hand she took as deep a breath as she could, drew back her arm and smashed the other spike against the glass.

Nothing.

Crying now, she sucked in the last of the oxygen, swung her arm back as far as it could go, roared out loud, then swung her arm with all the strength left in her.

PART FIVE

PART FIVE

FIFTY-NINE

Jill was in the shower when she heard the bell.

'Bollocks,' she said, reaching out for the big white towel. 'Who is it?' she called into the entryphone, dripping onto her laminate floor.

There was no answer. She replaced the phone, looked at the splashes of water around her. That would need mopping, she thought, or it would spoil the surface.

She took another towel from the cupboard. One of her luxuries; Egyptian cotton from John Lewis. Cost a ridiculous amount, but worth it.

She kept an aluminium baseball bat in the hallway just in case. Back in the towel, she wrapped her fingers round the handle and lifted it. 'Who is it?'

She put her eye to the peephole, expecting to see some lad holding a tray of cleaning cloths and sponges, hoping to sell them door-to-door.

Harry French was standing there with a bottle of champagne.

She raised her baseball bat a little higher and was about to open the door when her phone rang.

Hesitating, she lowered the bat and walked back to her kitchenette where her iPhone was charging.

The number on the screen was Constable Gilchrist's. Frowning, she swiped. 'What?'

'I just heard it on the Airwave. Your mate Alex's been in some car accident. Think it's pretty bad.'

The towel dropped. 'Oh Jesus Christ. Where?'

'B2080 just by Appledore. There are multiple units heading there now. Are you OK?'

'What's happened?'

'Honest to God. Don't know. Just heard they're calling in units from all over.'

She picked up the white towel, tucked it round her and went back to the front door, baseball bat raised again. She opened it. 'You got your car?' she demanded.

Harry French swayed backwards, away from the baseball bat inches from his face. 'What?'

'Are you drunk?'

'No. Just a bit scared.'

'Then you can drive.'

He had an Audi TT. It was fast.

'I was just hoping you'd come out for a date.'

'God sakes, Harry. Just drive.'

'Sorry.'

'Stop fucking saying sorry.'

It was around ten miles to where Gilchrist had said the accident was; the roads were empty at this time of night.

'Are you OK?' he asked.

'She's my mate,' she said.

'I know.'

After fifteen minutes, they saw a splash of blue light on the horizon ahead.

The road was closed at the junction with Military Road. A traffic officer with a torch said, 'Diversion, mate.'

'I'm an officer,' shouted Jill. Somewhere to the left, through the trees, lights flashed.

'Sorry, mate. No vehicles allowed. Crime scene. You'll have to walk.'

Jill's heart sped. 'What about Sergeant Cupidi?'

'Don't know. I was just told to close the road.'

'What shall I do?' asked Harry French.

Jill ignored him, got out, ran past the parked police car, towards the blue lights.

In the middle of the road, an ambulance, door closed. The road was dark. Jill broke into a sprint, a mistake in this darkness; she tripped on something hard and fell straight onto tarmac, her forehead hitting the ground.

'You OK?' an officer called.

She was panting hard by the time she reached the scene. 'Alex in there?'

A traffic officer nodded.

'How is she?'

'Very bloody lucky, and very wet,' he said, holding a torch that shone onto the roof of a car. The car had settled to the bottom of the canal. Only the curve of the roof was visible now above the water.

'Christ. She was in that?'

He swung the torch around, blinding her. 'Jesus. What happened to you?'

She realised her face was wet and it wasn't all tears.

Alex sat in the back of the ambulance in her bra and pants, covered by a pink blanket, trying to stop the shaking in her legs as the paramedic worked, checking her over.

'No idea of the make and model. From the high position of the headlights it may have been a four-wheel-drive.'

'Road rage?' asked DI McAdam.

'Nope. It was absolutely deliberate.'

She saw the scepticism in his face before the paramedic, an Eastern European man with even stubble, said, 'Look at the light, if you can,' and shone a torch right into her left eye.

'I slowed to let the car past. I pulled to one side of the road. It stayed behind me. It deliberately bloody waited until we were both on a section of road where the canal was right alongside. I moved to the side of the road a second time to let it overtake, and then it deliberately forced me into the canal. They were trying to kill me.'

'They?'

'Gender-neutral pronoun. I never saw them.'

'I've got everyone out looking for a vehicle with any damage at the front. We'll scour the roads for it, I promise, Alex. Whether they meant to kill you or not, we'll get them.'

'They meant to. Swear to God.' The paramedic looked into the other eye.

'So we'll find them,' said McAdam.

'How soon can we get a diver into the car? My notes are in my bag. I'm going to need them.'

'Relax, Alex. There are other officers on the team too.'

'I'm just bloody angry.'

There was a knock at the door. The paramedic put down his torch and opened it a crack and shouted, 'She'll be out in a bit.'

'Who was it?'

'I'm trying to finish up here,' the man complained. Both Alex's hands were cut from scrabbling through the broken window of the rear door. Her clothes were ruined.

The person at the door pulled it open again. 'I just want to see her.'

'For God's sake,' muttered the paramedic, then looked round. 'Christ. You better come in as well, then.'

Jill stood there, blood drying on a wound above her right eye.

The paramedic took one look and said, 'I thought it was just one victim.'

'I just tripped over,' said Jill. 'It's nothing.'

'Let me finish up here, then I'll dress your wound.'

'Bog off. Don't worry about that,' said Jill. 'Look at this.' She lifted her phone and showed a photo of something black lying on the tarmac. 'Tripped over the bastard. Think it came

343

off whatever crashed into you. It's just out there waiting to be tagged.'

Alex sat up on the gurney. It looked very much like a part of a car panel, smashed from the vehicle that had pushed her into the canal.

Alex had no shoes, no clothes. She stood in a pink blanket outside the ambulance with no car to get home in.

'Any nausea, get straight to hospital,' said the paramedic.

'I can give you a lift home, Alex,' said McAdam.

'I don't know if I should go home naked in the car of a senior officer,' said Alex.

McAdam said, 'Oh. Right.'

'Jill can give me a lift.'

Jill's head had been dressed. She had a large white gauze taped beneath her hairline.

'Actually no. I – I persuaded a . . . friend to drive me out here.'

'Would your friend mind dropping Alex home as well?' asked McAdam.

Alex was trying to figure out why Jill was looking so hesitant. 'I suppose,' she muttered. 'Come this way.'

They walked away from the flashing lights, back towards the way Jill had come.

Harry French was waiting in his car, head back against the rest, eyes closed, playing opera on the stereo.

'And you didn't really want to explain to DI McAdam why you'd brought someone who is part of an investigation to a crime scene.'

344

'Kind of,' said Jill.

'Are you two back together?'

'God, no. It was just . . . convenient. I heard you were hurt. I was scared. He was outside my door.'

Alex cocked her head, disbelieving.

'He just helped me out, right?' Jill knocked on the window and French opened his eyes with a start.

They got in the back.

'Jesus. What happened to you, Jill? Are you OK?'

'You all right to give Alex a lift home to Dungeness?'

'Of course.' Harry French nodded and swung the car around. Because the road ahead was blocked, they had to take a small lane that wound through the marshes.

In the car, Alex felt sick. 'Can you slow down,' she asked.

'God,' he said. 'Sorry.' Though narrower, there were still watery ditches on each side of this road.

Alex pressed the button to lower the window and the air blew on her face.

'They said we should take you to hospital if you feel sick,' said Jill.

'I feel fine now.'

'You sure? You've been through all this shit.'

'I thought I was going to die, Jill,' she said. 'I couldn't get out of the car. None of the windows would break, and it was going down all the time. I was cold.'

Jill clutched her arm.

'And when I finally broke the window, and the water came flowing in, I must have swallowed half of it. I thought I was drowning.'

345

Jill tightened her grip. In the darkness, Alex could make out the shape of Fairfield church, long deserted, alone among the flat sheep fields.

SIXTY

Zoë opened the front door and stood, bleary-eyed in a *Hundred and One Dalmations* pyjamas.

'Christ, Mum. What happened?'

'Sorry. I . . . dropped my keys in a canal.'

'To your clothes, I mean. And your hands.'

The hands were bandaged. All she had round her was the pink blanket. Zoë stood aside to let her mother in the door. Jill and Harry French stood in the door, waiting to be invited in.

Alex turned to them. 'I need to speak to Zoë alone.'

Jill looked disappointed. 'Oh. Right.'

'Come on,' said Harry French. 'I'll drop you home.'

'Thank you for the lift, Harry,' said Alex.

'Are you Harry French?' said Zoë.

'Yes.'

Her daughter crossed her arms. 'Harry French from September Homes?'

'Not now, Zoë,' said Alex.

347

Then, resentfully, to Jill; 'I thought you'd dumped him. It's wrong, what he's doing, building on Whiteland Fields.'

'We better go,' said Harry French.

'It's a crime. It shouldn't be allowed.'

'Not now, love.'

Alex watched the car drive away, then turned to her daughter.

'I need to tell you what happened.' And she told her daughter, who listened in shocked silence, about how someone had just tried to kill her, and about how she was worried about her mother losing her mind, and about how, when she finally cracked the glass and she had had to struggle against the force of water with all her might, all she had been thinking about was how much she loved her daughter. The words poured out of her, just as the darkness had poured in.

She was woken by whispering. Zoë had slept in her bed last night; when Alex had fallen asleep, her daughter's thin fingers had been clinging on to her arm, but when she opened her eyes, she was alone.

The whispering was coming from outside the room. Her head ached; she squinted in the morning light. 'Zoë?'

Zoë's voice came from the hallway. 'It's Bill. He wants to come in and see you.'

'He's here? God. Tell him I'm fine.'

'He wants to come in anyway.'

She had showered last night to get the stink of canal water off her skin; had gone to sleep exhausted, with wet hair. She was conscious of how disorderly the room looked. 'Come in, Bill. I'm fine, honestly.'

Next thing he was standing by the side of her bed, skin greyer than usual, fingers knotting each other. 'I'm sorry. This is my fault.'

She sat up on her elbows, brushed the tangle of hair away from her forehead. 'Don't be absurd, Bill.'

'Zoë was right all along. This is much bigger than Julian Epps and his mates. They're idiots, but they wouldn't pull a stunt like that. I was sure it was them.'

'I make my own mind up, Bill. I was stupid for not noticing that someone had been following me.'

He looked around.

'What if I stay here for a bit? I could use the spare room. Just to keep an eye. You know . . .'

She wondered if she could bear someone else sharing their house, even if it was temporary. But he was right. If the person who had tried to kill her was the same one who put the badger on her doorstep, they knew where she lived. 'What if we move in with you? Whoever it is knows I live here already,' she said.

She couldn't help enjoying his discomfort. All his adult life he had lived alone, a single man. 'It's small,' he said.

'Zoë and I can share a bed for a few days. She'd like it there. She loves your house. She's there more than she is here.'

'I guess,' he said hesitantly.

'Settled,' she said. 'Good. Now I need to get up.' And watching him bolt from the room, she smiled for the first time since emerging from the cold canal water.

★

Walking into the station later that morning, people looked at her cautiously, whispered to each other. Everyone had heard what had happened.

In the incident room it was different. The moment she pushed open the door, people started to clap, which was embarrassing, especially as the applause died away as fast as it had started.

'Nice one, Alex,' somebody called out.

Alex's notebook and phone were on her desk, sitting in a ziplock bag by the time she got to work. The divers must have recovered them this morning. She called the crime scene manager. 'What about a photograph? There was a school photograph in the car?'

'Yeah. They have that. They passed it on to the forensics team to arrange for preservation. They were concerned that if it just dried normally, the photograph would be spoiled. You said it was evidence in the Trevor Grey case, yes?'

Alex unzipped the ziplock bag on her desk, smelt the dank rot of the canal she had been in last night and felt her chest tighten.

The notebook was so wet it was hard even to remove from the plastic. When she had finally done it, she started gently trying to unpeel the pages until she came to the last one she had written on.

The blue biro handwriting had leached into the paper but the name was perfectly legible: Revell Adison. Alex googled him but came up with nothing, which was strange. A name that unique usually produced a few hits. He didn't have a driver's licence either; at least, not under that name.

'You shouldn't have come in.' She turned. DI Toby McAdam was standing behind her desk.

'Yes I should. Anything on the vehicle that knocked me in?'

'From the recovered debris, we know it was a black Range Rover Evoque. Other than that, nothing on CCTV.'

Whoever it was could make themselves invisible, thought Alex. It was someone who knew how things worked around here; where the cameras were, and how they could avoid them. She thought of the gates behind the caravan park; the cautious escape route across fields.

'Why don't you go home, Alex? Put your feet up.' There was always something a little stiff and formal about the way McAdam held himself, but he was not the worst of them by any means. 'I think you should see a counselling and wellbeing advisor.'

Alex looked down at the damp notebook in her hands. 'Do you have any concerns about my efficacy as an officer?' she asked.

He lowered his voice. 'That's not what I'm saying, Alex. You've been through a traumatic incident.'

'OK. I will.'

'Good. I'll sort that out for you.'

'Thanks, Toby. I appreciate it.'

He relaxed a little. 'Not a problem.'

'Can you make that next week? This week's a little busy. Week after, maybe.'

'Take some days off,' he said. 'You're owed them. I'm going to insist on it. Seriously, Alex.'

'What did he want?' asked Jill when McAdam had retreated to the far side of the room.

'He thinks I should have some counselling.'

'Yeah. You should.'

'What are you saying, Jill?'

'I'm not joking. I was in counselling half my life. You've been through some shit recently, that's all. You think it doesn't hurt you.'

'I know. I'll do it. OK?'

'Look at this,' Jill said, holding out some printed pages. 'I found a discussion group from ex-pupils of Thornhead on Mumsnet.'

'I thought it was a boys' school.'

'One of the parents started the group. Said she'd taken her child out because of the bullying.'

'Bullying?'

'Was Revell Adison one of the names?'

'No.'

'Maybe he's dead. Or he changed his name.'

'Try the PNC,' said Jill. 'Just 'cause he's got a funny, posh name doesn't mean anything.'

Alex logged on to the police database, not expecting to find anything. 'Bloody hell.'

Jill stood and looked over her shoulder. On the screen was a list of offences that Mr Adison had been cautioned or prosecuted for. 'Well, that's weird.'

Weird because it was an unusual list of offences. If someone had multiple arrests, it would almost always be for the same predictable mix of theft and drug offences. On Adison's record there were four planning enforcement prosecutions, two arrests for criminal damage to property with recklessness and another for a category three common assault.

It listed his address in an old town on the north Kent coast. There was no email address or phone number.

'When are you going to see him?' said Jill.

The towns along the north Kent coast had all seen better days. They declined with the docks. Ill-considered roads rewrote them; industries, shops and populations deserted them. Revell Adison's address was in a place called Windmill Hill, overlooking the Thames estuary. Before the town crawled up the hill, there would have been windmills there, taking advantage of the north wind rising from the river.

Clarence Road had once thought itself better than the rest of the town, looking down on it; a row of early Victorian mansion houses sat opposite a small park and a First World War memorial to the town's dead. A few of the houses were in good condition. The one they parked outside was not.

'I think we're on a wild goose chase,' said Jill. 'It's derelict. Nobody lives there.'

Alex saw her point. Number 38 was dark. Two of the windows on the upstairs floors had no glass in them. So many tiles were missing from the roof that you could see bare eaves.

Alex got out. Adison's house, if it was his, stood out like a sore thumb amongst the others.

A man in his thirties, laptop bag over one shoulder, turned the corner.

'Excuse me,' asked Alex. 'Are you local?'

The man pointed to his house, a little further down the street.

'How long has it been since Mr Adison lived here?'

The man looked puzzled by the question. 'Why? Have they finally evicted him?'

'Evicted?'

'As far as I know, that's where he still lives. He's let the place go to shit, but he's still in there. I don't know how they let him stay. There's no heating in the house. They cut the electric off years ago,' he said. 'We think he lives in the basement. Have you knocked?'

'I thought it was empty.'

'He wouldn't have answered anyway. He never does. He's a nuisance. They should take him away and lock him up.'

Alex and Jill turned back to number 38. The place was a wreck.

SIXTY-ONE

A short concrete path led to the front door. The path itself was clear, but the rest of the garden had disappeared under detritus and rubble. Old sinks, cookers, a washing machine, metal roof panels and a sofa were stacked to the left and had rusted, rotted and decayed, becoming part of a natural landscape. Wheelie bins were ranked in untidy rows to the right, weeds growing over their wheels. There must have been fifteen or twenty of them. Ivy was crawling over an old round-cornered 1950s' fridge. Cracks spider-legged up the house's walls, shattering bricks. Lintels had slipped off the horizontal. Lilacs had found crevices.

'Disgusting,' said Jill.

Alex knocked on the door. 'Mr Adison?'

A passer-by with a small dog paused at the gate. 'Are you from the council?'

'No. We're not,' said Alex curtly. Knocked on the door again.

'He needs help,' said the woman.

'He's never going to answer,' said Jill.

'No,' said the woman, determined to have her say. 'He never answers the door. He only tends to come out at night, anyway. I've lived here twenty years and maybe seen him twice. The man barely leaves the place. There's no electricity or gas in there, or anything. It should be condemned.'

'This is Mr Revell Adison's house?'

'He's lived there all his life. It used to be his parents'. They used to look after him but they're both dead now.'

'Mr Adison,' Alex called up to the broken windows. 'I'm a police officer. We're conducting an investigation into events at Thornhead School where you were a pupil in the 1980s.'

'He lives underground,' said the woman. 'In the cellar. They say he's dug tunnels all around here.' The dog, a terrier, whined and scratched at the pavement.

'We are here to talk to you about what you remember of that time, Mr Adison.' Alex knocked on the door. She hesitated. 'Mr Adison? . . . Are you in there?'

There was no response.

'I told you, he won't come to the door,' said the woman with the dog. 'He's in there, listening to you. He knows you're here.'

'We only want to talk to you about Trevor Grey, Mr Adison.'

There was still no answer, so Alex repeated what she'd just said.

'We're going to need some support to do this,' said Jill. 'He's got to have a key worker in social services somewhere.'

'Wishing you luck with that,' said the passer-by.

And just when they were about to walk back down the path, a voice came from behind the paint-peeled door. 'Trevor Grey?'

The voice was oddly high and reedy.

Alex and Jill looked at each other. 'We believe you knew each other in school,' said Alex.

There was a long pause. Then the voice came again, quietly. 'Do you know Trevor Grey?'

Alex and Jill exchanged a glance. 'We would like to talk to you about him.'

'No thank you.'

'You got him talking, at least. That's a first,' said the woman.

'Please, Mr Adison. It's important.'

'Have you come to arrest me?'

A man who expects to be arrested at the mention of the name Trevor Grey. Alex hesitated, wondering if she should call for local backup. 'What would we be arresting you for, Mr Adison?'

'You're police, aren't you?'

'Can we come inside to talk to you, Mr Adison?'

They waited. After a minute, the door opened by a few inches.

As a police officer, Alex encountered plenty of people with mental health problems. Hoarders were not uncommon, but what she saw here was extreme. The corridors were piled with books, rotting magazines, boxes crammed with vinyl or kitchen implements. The gap between them was narrow and uneven. The passage ahead of them felt more like an underground cave than a hallway.

Adison was a narrow man, thin and wiry; he seemed to fit exactly into the space between the junk. A checked woollen shirt hung off him.

'This way,' he said, and retreated further down the corridor.

It was as if he wanted to retreat from the light into the darker heart of the house.

Alex paused before following him, to take stock of the house's layout. She was somehow not surprised to see that what had probably been a living room, to her right, seemed to be filled, not with belongings, but with earth. By the light seeping in through the closed wooden shutters, Alex could see there were piles of it, from wall to wall, like some bizarre contemporary art installation. It smelt dank and damp. She set off again, following Adison.

At the far end of the corridor there seemed to be a small space kept free of the rubble, vaguely lit from above by a skylight at the top of the stairs. It was not enough space for them to sit down in, only for them to stand, a few inches away from each other.

Revell Adison gave off the greasy, sharp odour of a man who never washed. 'How did you find him?'

Alex gave a meaningful glance at Jill. 'Did you know where he was all this time, Revell?'

'Yes.'

Another shared look, both aware that whatever he said next might be crucial to figuring out what had happened to Trevor Grey.

Alex asked softly, 'Would you like to tell us how you knew?'

'He was in France.'

'Sorry?'

'He went to France. That's what some of us thought. That he was hiding. He was good at French. He went there on an exchange once.'

Jill exhaled. They had been hoping he would give them details of Grey's burial site; of how his body had come to be there. 'You had us going there for a sec, Mr Adison.'

'You thought he'd run away from school and gone to France?'

'Yes. Didn't he?'

Alex's eyes were becoming accustomed to the gloom in here. His face was dark with grime. 'When did you last see him?'

'It was in the summer term. 1984. The night he ran away.'

'Why did he run away?'

Adison's head twitched, but he didn't answer.

'Was he your friend?'

He sniffed. 'Not really. I don't have friends.'

'Did you have any friends at Thornhead?'

He shook his head. 'I didn't choose to go there, you see. My father worked abroad, so I had to board somewhere. I wasn't very happy there. Who told you to come here?'

'Nobody told us, Revell. We have some news for you, I'm afraid. We recently discovered human remains which we think belong to Trevor Grey.'

'So he's . . .'

'We believe he's dead.'

In the dim light, she watched his face. He seemed confused. 'I thought he'd got away. To France.'

'I'm afraid not. If it's his body, and we believe it is, it was found quite close to the school.'

'Oh.' A tear ran down his dirty cheek.

'Got away from what, Revell?'

Adison didn't answer.

'Why do you think he ran away?'

Adison looked down at the bare floorboards dirty with mud. 'Why are you asking me this?'

'We are trying to work out who might have been responsible for Trevor's death.'

'What do you mean, responsible?'

'We believe he was killed.'

He threw his head back and looked up at the ceiling. 'How did you find out where I was?'

He was becoming agitated now.

'A former schoolteacher called Frederick Lindsay told us your name. We were able to track you down through court records.'

'Lindsay?' Another sniff. 'What did he say about me?'

'Nothing very much. Just your name. When we knew that, we were able to find your address through court documents. You have had some trouble with the law.'

'It's my house. I can do what I like with it.'

Jill spoke: 'We're not here about whatever you've done to your house, Mr Adison. We're here to find out what you know about Trevor Grey. Do you remember him?'

Adison scrunched up his eyes. 'I can't talk about all that.'

'Why not?'

'Did something bad happen at Thornhead, Mr Adison? If something did, you need to tell us.'

'Were there instances of sexual or physical abuse you want to talk to us about?' Jill demanded.

'Anything you can tell us about the school would be helpful,' Alex said.

'I don't think so,' said Adison, looking around him. 'I'm quite busy now, you see.'

'If there's anything we can do for you, Revell?'

'I think I would like you to leave now, please,' the man said, his voice rising.

Jill was already edging back through the narrow passageway; she knocked a blackened saucepan onto the floor.

'The earth. Did you dig that out from under your house?'

'It's my house,' said Adison. 'I can do what I like.'

'You should have somebody look at it. It might not be safe.'

'Go now.'

Alex stood her ground a second longer. 'A moment ago, you said you thought Trevor Grey was hiding. What was he hiding from?'

He didn't answer.

Alex was already at the door. 'Is that what you're doing here, Revell? Hiding?'

He nodded. 'Of course.'

'What are you hiding from, Revell?'

'Go away,' he said. Alex took out a card and put it on a pile of old hardback books that seemed to defy gravity. 'That's my number and my email,' she said.

The thin man eyed it, but didn't pick it up. He didn't have a phone or a computer anyway, so leaving the card was probably pointless.

Jill sniffed her coat, wrinkled her nose. 'One more minute in that house and I was going to vom. He's nuts.'

Alex was still stuck inside the sadness of Adison's house. 'Something pretty dark happened in that school.'

361

'It's just horrid. How can people live like that?' Putting her coat on the back seat, Jill got in the car and and sprayed herself with Marc Jacob. 'Whatever it is has happened to him, it's not a fucking excuse for living like that.'

'He's mentally ill, Jill,' said Alex.

'Just because shit happens to you, doesn't mean you have to go like that,' said Jill tetchily. Jill was a woman who lived in a spotless apartment and who seemed to wear new clothes every day. Alex had once caught her using a lint roller on her bedroom floor in case the vacuum had missed any hair.

Jill had been through things too, Alex knew.

They drove out of Gravesend in silence.

After the brief spell of rain, the dry weather was back.

On the way into work the next morning, it looked like high summer already, though it was still only May. When she logged on to her computer, there was an email from the forensics team. The technicians had dried the school photograph that had gone into the canal with her and had scanned it. A JPEG was attached.

Alex clicked on the thirty-five-year-old photograph. She scrolled from side to side until she found the two boys again; Trevor Grey and Revell Adison, side by side. She stared at them, trying to understand what they would need to hide from. Frederick Lindsay was in the front row, looking almost the same age as he did now.

'Come and see,' she said to Jill.

'Is that him?' she said, leaning over.

362

Alex magnified the photograph. Next to Trevor Grey sat Revell Adison – longer hair, clearer eyes, softer skin; barely recognisable from the man they had met the day before.

'Jesus. That's sad,' said Jill.

'Look at that face. He doesn't know what he's going to become.'

The scan was a good one. She zoomed out again.

'I always wanted to go to a school like that. Harry Potter and stuff,' said Jill.

'I don't think there was a lot of magic happening at Thornhead,' said Alex.

'No. Besides, my mother was already a witch anyway.'

'You never talk about her.'

'Nope,' said Jill, and her face hardened.

'Look at this,' said Alex, to lighten the mood. 'See this boy here?' She scrolled sideways to the end of the picture and pointed at the fair-haired boy with the smile. Then she scrolled to the opposite end. 'See?'

'Christ. Is that twins? They made them stand all that way apart?'

'It's the same boy,' Alex said. She explained how the clockwork camera worked, and how the boy must have run from one end to the next, behind the ranks of pupils, popping up at the other end just in time to be captured twice on film.

'There you go,' said Jill. 'There *was* a magic there.'

Alex was glad that at least someone at the school seemed to be having fun. After Jill had gone back to her seat, she zoomed in on the child, first at one end, then at the other, standing next to the other boy with a smudge for a head.

And then back again. Puzzled, she opened up a photo editing programme, selected rectangles of both images of the boy; darkened them a little to highlight the shape of his face.

'Oh shit,' she said out loud.

SIXTY-TWO

She pulled up Howard Roteman's Wikipedia page. 'Jill. Come over here.'

'What do you mean, "Oh shit"?' said Jill.

Alex scrolled down the page. There was a section called 'Early Life and Business Career', which listed a public school in Sussex that he had been at, but there was no mention of Thornhead.

'Is that Howard Roteman?' said a voice behind them. 'He came to a prize-giving at my school.'

Alex turned round. Constable Gilchrist was standing behind them, looking over at the screen.

'You never got to meet him, then,' said Jill.

'*Très amusant*,' said Gilchrist. 'As it happens, I got the Physics prize.'

'Really?' said Jill.

'Don't you reckon that looks like him as a boy?' asked Alex, switching back to the JPEG of the school photograph.

Jill wrinkled her nose, leaned close. 'I'm not sure you could tell from that, though.'

'I know what you mean,' said Gilchrist. 'Those eyes.'

'What are you even doing up here?' Jill asked the constable.

'Know a guy called Julian Epps?'

'We do, as it happens.' They both turned towards the young man in uniform.

'I picked him up for drink-driving last night. He was off his face and had rear-ended this other car in the car park of the Hop Pickers. Said he had some information for you and he'd tell me it if I let him go.' He leaned forward and looked at Alex's screen.

'What was it?' asked Jill.

'I don't know because I didn't let him go,' said Gilchrist. 'I charged him with drunken driving. What's all this about Howard Roteman?'

'Long story,' said Alex.

'We thought Roteman might have been the boy in the photo,' said Jill, looking back at the screen.

'It does look like him, doesn't it?' said Gilchrist.

'But it's not,' said Jill. 'It can't have been him ... unless he didn't want it in his Wikipedia entry because it was a shit school?'

'Hold on,' said Gilchrist. 'I'm sitting with a couple of supposedly shit-hot detectives and they're relying on Wikipedia for their facts?'

Alex and Jill looked at each other. Alex pulled up the revision history, then punched through the pages.

'There,' Gilchrist said. '19:25, 10 June 2015. What was the name of the school?'

'Thornhead.'

'There you go. Thornhead School was deleted from the history by someone who didn't sign in to Wikipedia. They have an IP address of 86.21.26.153.'

'So he went there?'

'Well, according to Wikipedia in 2015, he did. Look. The same IP address deleted the same information on three previous occasions too.'

'What's the betting that IP address belongs to Howard Roteman?' said Jill.

'Or his assistant, the lovely Tamsin Porter.'

'So why wouldn't he want people to know that he'd been a pupil there?'

Alex turned back to Gilchrist. 'Not a word about this to anyone,' she said. 'Do you understand? Not even your mum.'

'Right,' said Gilchrist. 'Got it.' He turned to go. 'One thing.' He paused.

'What?'

'I was wondering if Jill was busy, Friday night.' He smiled. 'Couple of us going out to Cameo.'

'Poor lamb,' said Alex.

'No,' said Jill bluntly.

Gilchrist nodded, smile fixed. 'Another time then.'

'I'm free, though,' said Alex.

There was a second's silence before Gilchrist said, 'Great, yeah.'

Jill said, 'She's pulling your leg.'

'No. Serious. Come along if you like,' said Gilchrist. 'It'll be a laugh.'

'He seems like a nice one,' said Jill, after he'd gone. 'You should go.'

'He was only being polite,' said Alex.

'Yeah. Well. Obviously,' said Jill.

They both looked at the photo again. 'Doesn't necessarily mean anything at all, does it?' said Alex. 'Just that he was there as a pupil and doesn't want everyone to know. It was a failing school with a terrible reputation.'

Two boys, one slightly blurred from getting to his seat just as the camera reached him, in two places at once.

Before she went home, Alex drove to Julian Epps's house and knocked on the door.

'You can't keep away from me, can you?'

'You look like shit.'

'Went on a bender. Big error. Going to lose my licence. Everything's coming up roses, eh?' He stood aside and she went into Epps's living room. The dog stood up, sniffed at her, lay down again.

'You had something to tell me?'

The living room was even less tidy than the last time she'd been here. There was a white plastic takeaway bag on the table, a plate next to it that looked like it had been licked clean by the dog. The woman who tidied up after him had left. He was on a downward spiral. 'I wasn't going to. But when I was off my box last night, I thought maybe we could do a deal. I was off my box, mind you.'

'What sort of information?'

Epps sat down in an old armchair. 'Thing is, I don't wish you any harm at all, but really, I couldn't care less. I was only saying it so the copper would let me go. But he didn't.'

Alex stood, looked around. 'Just tell me.'

'I will do. But just to convince you to get your guys off my back.'

'Nobody's on your back, Julian. I know it wasn't you who left the dead badger at my door.'

'Feels like they are.'

'Can I remind you? You're the one who got involved in badger-baiting, you're the one who nicked a carcass from your workplace, you're the one who chose to drown his sorrows by getting pissed, then getting into his van to drive home and hitting another vehicle instead.'

He laughed, tugged a bit of stuffing out of the arm of the chair he was sitting in. 'Fair play. But you don't really get it, do you?'

'What?'

'They're after you, too.'

'Who are after me?'

'They've been watching you all this time. That day, when I came and visited you, they were there, too. They know where you live. You and your daughter. All of you.'

'What do you want from me, Julian?'

'Just for you to take me for what I am. I'm just like you. You think you're some superior species to the people who live around here.'

'Your chips,' said Alex. 'Your shoulders.'

'No. I know it. You live in Dungeness with all the artsy types. People like me aren't welcome there any more.'

'Oh give over, Julian. Stop wallowing.' Alex grabbed a dining chair and pulled it across the floor. The dog stood up straight away and growled. 'You said someone's been watching me. What do you know?'

'Down, Nigel,' Epps snapped. 'You have to lift the chair. He hates it when you drag it like that. Don't know why. Sit down.'

The dog grumbled, but sat again on the floor.

'You called your dog Nigel?'

'Don't ask.'

'Nigel Farage?'

'Jesus. I wouldn't call a cockroach that. That's what you think we're all like round here, don't you? My dad called him after Nigel Mansell, the racing driver. It was a joke, on account of when we took him out coursing he was so slow he never caught nothing.'

'Coursing's illegal, Julian.'

'Not if you don't catch anything.'

Alex sat down on the chair close to Julian Epps. 'What are you trying to tell me, then?'

'That day I came to see you, they were watching you.'

'They?'

'One man. He was parked just by that pub, the Pilot, sat in his car in the car park with a pair of binoculars.'

'A lot of people with binoculars down our way.'

'This one didn't look like a birdwatcher to me.'

'You don't really know my daughter, do you?'

Epps laughed. 'Seriously, though. He was watching you. You went past on a bike, didn't you, maybe around six o'clock.'

Alex tried to remember; that evening she had been in a bad mood. She had taken a ride out into the marshes.

'He set off after you. And when you came back about an hour later, so did he. See? I got you lot on my back. You got someone on yours, too. They're out to keep us down.'

'What did he look like, this man?'

'Tinted glass. Didn't really get much of a look. Definitely a man, though.'

'And what kind of car?'

'I don't suppose you can do anything about my drink-driving arrest, can you, love? Quid pro quo.'

'You know I can't. It doesn't work like that.'

He scratched behind his ear for a little while as if considering, then said, 'Black Range Rover Evoque.'

And he let that sit there a while, enjoying the look on Alex's face.

SIXTY-THREE

'Will you look at something?' Alex asked her daughter the next morning, before she left for work, in the small kitchen at Arum Cottage.

'Why?'

'I want your insight.'

'Really?' Zoë looked wary.

They had moved the previous evening after dark, bringing their bags down the track to the small cottage while South had hunkered down by the old lighthouse with a pair of night-vision binoculars, keeping an eye out for anybody suspicious who might be watching them. He knew the area like no one else, especially those places a man might try to lurk unobserved.

Alex put her laptop on the kitchen table next to her cereal and opened the folder with the school photo in it.

'Ugh. Imagine that.'

Zoë had hated school. She had left school at sixteen, having done badly at her GCSEs, dropping out of sixth-form college after only a few weeks.

Alex scrolled along the line of boys until she reached Trevor Grey. She pointed. The bandages were off now; there was a single sticking plaster round her index finger. 'This boy here. What do you think?'

Zoë said it straight out. 'He looks desperate.'

'I think he may have been.'

Zoë leaned closer. 'Oh God. He looks so miserable. Look at his eyes. It makes me sad just looking at him. What happened to him?' Her daughter held out a finger and touched the face on the screen.

South leaned over. 'That's the boy who ended up on Whiteland?'

'I'm pretty sure, yes.'

Zoë sat there for a while, her finger on the screen, then took it away and closed the laptop. Alex wanted to give her daughter a squeeze there and then, but just then Zoë had already vanished to somewhere deep inside herself.

Howard Roteman lived in a beautiful house close to the edge of a village under a fold of the South Downs.

Alex and McAdam arrived separately in unmarked vehicles so as not to attract any particular attention. Locals in this Sussex village would be used, by now, to people arriving at all times of day for meetings with the minister. McAdam rarely came out on jobs like this, but Roteman was a government minister. Alex was glad to have him. If there was any comeback, it would not all be on her shoulders.

Alex arrived first and sat in the car, waiting for her boss, checking her phone to see if forensics had made any updates about the dead boy's bones, but there were none.

When McAdam arrived, he parked behind her, and without saying anything more, they walked up to the house, with its whitewashed bricks and pink roses over the door.

The house was warm and well-worn. Dogs had marked the edges of furniture with their presence. The line of cookery books above the huge stove was well thumbed.

'This is Hilary,' said Howard, introducing his wife. She made coffee on the stove in their large kitchen while McAdam apologised for taking up their time.

'Not at all,' said Roteman. 'How is the investigation going?'

'So-so,' said Alex. 'We're not sure exactly what it is we are looking at.'

'I heard you discovered remains on that land.'

'We did.'

McAdam sat silently at the big table. Mrs Roteman put a cup in front of him and poured coffee from a stove-top pot.

Alex said, 'The remains turn out to be those of a former student at Thornhead School, a young man named Trevor Grey.'

'Thornhead?' Roteman sounded shocked.

'Coffee?' asked Mrs Roteman, hovering next to her.

'Please,' said Alex.

She watched Hilary Roteman pour. Some coffee missed the cup and spilled onto the table. 'God, I'm sorry.' She dashed for a cloth.

'It's fine.'

'Some days I'm such a klutz.'

Alex said to Roteman, 'You were a pupil at Thornhead School, and I would guess you would have been there at the same time as him.'

'Would I?'

Hilary Roteman lifted Alex's cup and wiped the table down in front of her.

'Did you know Trevor Grey?'

He frowned. 'I'm afraid I don't remember the name.'

Alex glanced at her boss, then lifted her handbag onto the table. 'What about a face? I have several photographs of him. Maybe they'll jog a memory.' She pulled out pictures from the original investigation and placed them on the table in front of him.

He looked at the photographs carefully, lifting them, one by one, holding them in front of his face. 'Maybe. I don't really know.'

'In 1984 he went missing. There was a search for him. You don't remember anything of it at the time?'

'He went missing?'

'At the time, his parents believed he had run away from school. Though he may have been abducted.'

Roteman looked up. 'If he was there at the time, I would have known him. It wasn't a huge school. It's just that I don't remember. I should explain. Thornhead was a very shitty place. I didn't like it much. My parents pulled me out of there. I haven't spent a lot of time thinking about it, to be honest. I've put it to the back of my mind.'

'Shitty in what way?' asked Alex.

Roteman sighed. 'It was a cruel place. The regime was very

harsh. The head teacher was a very strict man. The private school system had very little oversight at that time. I'm afraid we're only just now becoming increasingly aware of the kind of things that went on in those places.'

'Bullying?'

'Yes,' said Roteman.

'You were bullied?'

There was a long pause. 'Yes. I was.'

Mrs Roteman had left the table and was pretending to be busy at the sink, washing a glass vase, though Alex was aware of her listening to every word her husband said.

'What kind of bullying?'

'Oh, the usual. We were locked in cupboards. There were beatings. The older boys would get you up and force you to swim in the outdoor pool, even when it was freezing. It doesn't sound much but it was fairly systematic. It came from the top, really. The school allowed cruelty. Encouraged it, even.' He looked over at his wife. 'I haven't really talked about it much with Hilary because it was a difficult time for me.'

'What about sexual abuse?'

Roteman pursed his lips and nodded. 'I wasn't a victim of it myself. I'm sure it went on. When you have that kind of regime it brings all sorts of other things with it. It distorts all relationships. In a place of cruelty, any gesture that isn't sadistic can seem like kindness.'

'So it's plausible teachers were abusing children there?'

Roteman looked at her, then his eyes flicked down towards the table. 'I'm sure that was happening, but all I can say is it never happened to me.'

Alex stored up that tiny movement of the eyes. It might be shame; it might be nothing. 'And might have been happening to Trevor Grey?'

He nodded. 'One supposes.'

A bluebottle banged noisily against the kitchen window. 'You said your parents took you out of the school. Why was that?'

'Because of the bullying.'

'Did you make a complaint?'

'I suppose they could see a mile off I wasn't happy there. I was lucky.'

'Are they still alive?'

'Sadly not. I think they regretted sending me there very much.'

Alex looked over at her boss. They had agreed that he should ask the next question, the one that had brought them here. McAdam leaned forward. 'It's a strange thing, for a Minister of Housing to express interest in a murder inquiry. Obviously we took your interest at your word and DS Cupidi was at your disposal. But now we discover that there is a connection between you and the school. Have you been honest with us, Mr Roteman?'

Roteman raised his eyebrows. 'Of course.' Then frowned. 'You think I was expressing an interest in the case because of the murder of this man . . . ?'

McAdam took an A4 folder from his briefcase and scanned his own notes. 'You told Detective Sergeant Cupidi that you were interested in the planning application because of concerns about local politics. Is that accurate?'

'Is this conversation on the record?'

'Sergeant Cupidi said you had indicated that there were political sensitivities around the development.'

Roteman eyed him warily. 'Yes. Confidentially, we are getting a great deal of political backwash about allowing development on greenfield sites in some areas. We're in a lot of shit in places that are supposed to be our heartlands.'

McAdam glanced at Alex. 'However, your initial interest came after we made a possible connection between the land and the death of a Mr Vincent Gibbons.'

'Absolutely. As I told Alex, we are about to make a policy announcement around creating integrated new rural development villages. Because of Lord Michael's interest in the land there were suggestions, largely from Derry, obviously, that we could make this a flagship project, an illustration of our integrated future village policy. My assistant Tamsin picked up on the fact that this investigation was happening and alerted me to it. From what I understand it's possible that Vincent . . . ?'

'Gibbons,' said Alex.

'That this man was murdered because of his opposition to the project. Obviously that could lead to difficulty later on. We are on show all the time as politicians. We can't afford any slips at all. If I had known that there was any connection between this land and my own past, as you're telling me there is now, I swear I wouldn't have touched it with a bargepole.'

Alex drained her cup. 'Is there any more coffee, Mrs Roteman? It's very good.'

Hilary Roteman turned from the washing-up bowl, saw Alex holding up her cup, smiled, and dried her hands on a dishcloth. Alex took the chance to scan her face for any reaction, but Hilary had already turned her back to face the cooker.

'We have checked Wikipedia and *Who's Who*. There is no record of you ever attending Thornhead School.'

Roteman grinned. 'I ended up somewhere much better. Lancing College was a much more convenient place to boast about.'

'Did you delete entries to your Wikipedia page that said you had gone to Thornhead?'

'Yes. I did. Not personally, however. I didn't want to be associated with the place. It's no surprise that it's come up as part of this investigation. It was only a matter of time. Again, it's all about whispers and reputation. It was merely a question of insulating myself from that. It's what we're taught in our media training.' He grimaced. 'To take as much control of our personal narrative as we can.'

Alex reached in her bag and took out her laptop. 'I've got another image we'd like you to look at.'

She started it up and opened the image of the school photograph. It was far too long to fit on the screen. She opened it at the left-hand end, Roteman standing at the very end of the school line.

'Oh my God,' said Howard Roteman.

She scrolled across the JPEG to the far side, Howard Roteman turning up again at the end.

'I don't even remember doing that. Look, darling,' he called to his wife. She returned to the table and watched as Alex scrolled it again from side to side.

'I must have run from one end to the other.'

'How funny,' said Hilary, though she didn't laugh.

'You've never seen this before?'

379

'That was the summer term. I left just a few days after that. I don't suppose my parents really wanted to order the photograph.'

She scrolled back to the part where Trevor Grey sat, unsmiling, next to Revell Adison. 'On the left, that's Trevor Grey.'

He stared at the picture for a while. The bluebottle carried on banging against the window. 'No. Sorry. It's a blank.'

'What about anyone else?' McAdam said. 'Anyone we can contact from that time will be useful.'

Roteman went back to the left-hand end of the photograph, moved methodically across it and remembered a few names; only a few were complete, most would be hard to track down.

Alex drained her coffee. 'One more thing,' she said. 'Do you drive a Range Rover Evoque?'

SIXTY-FOUR

'A Ranger Rover Evoque?' said Roteman. 'We do. Why?'

McAdam's jerk of the head was unmissable.

'What's wrong? Why is that important?'

'What colour is it?'

'Black.' He looked at the two police officers across his kitchen table.

'Can we see it?'

'Is there something you should be telling me?'

McAdam spoke. 'A black Range Rover Evoque was involved in a serious assault on one of the officers in the investigation.' Not naming Alex.

'This is getting quite scary now,' said Roteman. For the first time the politician sounded nervous. 'It wasn't my car. We haven't used it in days.'

'May we see it?'

'When I say we haven't used it . . . my wife drives. I don't.'

McAdam looked him in the eye. 'You are banned from driving, yes. I'm aware.'

Roteman bristled. 'You understand that I let you into my house willingly because I wanted to clear up any suspicion that there was a connection between myself and anything you are investigating.'

'We're very aware of that. And grateful.'

'I'm a public figure. My ability to be an effective one rests on reputation. Innuendo travels fast theses days.'

They had been careful; only a small handful of officers knew of Roteman's link to the school the dead man had come from. McAdam knew Roteman would be on the phone to the Home Office the moment they left the house. 'I'm afraid we still need to see the car,' he said.

Roteman hesitated, then pushed his chair back. 'Of course.'

They left the kitchen by the back door; Hilary Roteman stayed back at the sink while her husband led them to a small gravelled area hidden by yew hedges.

'Needs a wash, I'm afraid.'

The car was covered in a layer of dust. It was parked with its headlights against the hedge. Alex stood back and took a photograph. 'Can you pull it back so we can look at it?' she asked.

'Why?'

'Because we need to examine the front of the car.'

'When was this incident supposed to have happened?' demanded Roteman.

'Can you just move it two or three feet back?'

Roteman got in the car and reversed it, then sat behind the wheel.

Alex squatted down and looked at the right-hand panels. The car had hit something, for sure. A long deep dent ran from just under the right-hand headlamp to the passenger door.

'When did you do that?'

'Hilary did it back in February on the bloody gate hinge.'

Alex squatted down and looked at the dent, then walked to the front gate, and back again. Not only was it at the right height, but there were traces of rust already in the section above the wheel arch. If it had been Roteman's car that had hit her three days ago, someone would have had to replace the panel and then fake the whole dent, to disguise that a missing panel had been changed. Unlikely, if not impossible.

Alex stood up. 'Do you have any other cars?'

'Hilary's little runaround is at the garage being serviced right now, but it's hardly a Range Rover. It's practically a toy. Is that all?' Roteman said, puzzled.

They walked back through the kitchen, shook hands rather stiffly with Hilary and left via the front door.

Outside, on the road, McAdam got into Alex's passenger seat. 'Obviously we still have to bear him in mind,' said McAdam, vaguely.

Alex was digging in her bag for an energy bar. 'I thought you'd like it if he turned out to be a suspect. They'd take the investigation off us within about seven seconds.'

McAdam looked offended. 'We'd be in the worst kind of shit if we were to say he was a suspect at any point and then he turned out not to be involved. We've done what we needed to do. We put the questions to him. He gave us answers. We did everything according to the book.'

'What about his wife?' She pulled out her house keys and her purse, put them on the dashboard, then went a layer deeper.

'What about her?'

'She was nervous. Did you see the way she was picking at her sleeves?'

'I'm not surprised. You make me nervous, Alex.'

She laughed, finally found the energy bar, pulled it out and dusted fluff off it. 'The fact that he has a connection to the land and the school seems like too weird a coincidence.'

'He's a man with fingers in all sorts of pies. He has a lot of connections. What looks like a coincidence can just be a trick of the light. It wasn't his car that hit you, was it?'

'No.' It was true. The dent in Roteman's Range Rover pre-dated the crash that almost killed Alex; besides, the 4WD's windscreen was covered in a layer of dust. It didn't look like anyone had driven it for days.

'A lot of well-off people have Ranger Rover Evoques. Most of them are probably black.' He opened the door and stepped out of the car.

'And a lot of people have Mazdas. Most of them are probably red,' said Alex.

'What do you mean?'

'I'm not even sure myself,' she said, starting the engine.

SIXTY-FIVE

At the Kent border, an impulse made her turn north instead of heading straight home.

She left the A-road and drove up through hamlets that had once been villages and towns. This was the old flatland of Walland Marsh, once rich and busy, now almost deserted. Brenzett, she remembered as she passed through the hamlet, slowing down for a dog walker who glared at her as she passed, meant 'burnt house'; William South must have told her that.

At Appledore she turned again and drove along the narrow lane until she found the place.

The banks of the canal had been scarred, rutted with mud from where they had dragged out the car she had been driving, flattening the spring weeds.

She got out and stood at the bank in the evening light.

She had scrabbled up that bank, scratched and frozen, clawing her way out of the water like some primitive creature. Shivering, she had stood by the side of the road, filthy with dirt.

The first vehicle to pass had been a nervous young man on a motorbike. He had waited with her, unsure what to say to this mud-crusted woman, until, to his relief, the ambulance had arrived.

Green weed floated on the surface; below it the water looked black. She stared down at it. It looked so calm and beautiful; she had never felt so close to death as she had when she was trapped beneath its surface.

She got back into her car and drove on a little further, unable to stop herself checking the rear-view mirror, until she came to the lock cottage.

The technicians had dried out the school photograph. The paper had browned and cracked in places and it was no longer as pristine as it had been, but she had promised to return it to Frederick Lindsay.

She parked, picked up the photograph, went to his front door, and knocked.

There was a light on inside the house, but no one answered. She knocked again, pushed at the door, but it was locked.

To the right of the door was a window. Putting her foot carefully into the flower bed beneath it, she peered into the window of the room in which they'd talked. The desk lamp was on.

She knocked on the glass. 'Mr Lindsay?'

Thistles pushed up through the gravel on the path that ran round the side of his small house. She picked her way around to the rear. Under the kitchen window, a small garden table and chair sat on the narrow canal bank.

She tried the back door. It was open; there was music playing inside. Maybe he hadn't heard her.

'Mr Lindsay. It's Detective Sergeant Cupidi.'

No answer. She went inside.

The kitchen was small, and had a grubby feel about it. A day's crockery sat in the sink, waiting to be washed. Lindsay was someone who lived alone and who didn't have standards to keep up.

'Frederick?'

She stepped into the hallway, looked into the living room where she had sat with him, then into the dining room; both were empty. He had not tidied since she had visited. The dull green cup and saucer sat on the small table by the chair she had sat in.

He had probably just gone for a short walk. It wasn't unusual for people to leave their doors open around here. She never did, but she was a police officer.

She took out her notebook, tore out a page and left the photograph with a message apologising for the state it was in on the kitchen table.

Back outside, she stood on the bank. A pair of swans came paddling up the still water towards her as if expecting something. Lindsay must feed them, she supposed.

The contrast of their whiteness against the dark of the water was stark. Silently they pushed up to the bank in front of her and stared at her. They scared her. She had heard that a swan could break an arm if it lashed out at you. Zoë would probably laugh at that, tell her it was an old wives' tale.

'I have nothing for you,' she said out loud.

As she looked down, she saw that, beneath them, in the water under their big, slowly moving feet, lay something large and pale. Curious, Alex leaned over a little to see what it was. One of the swans dropped its neck, opened its beak and hissed at her.

Through the ripples, she caught a glimpse of a face below the water, then the swans crowded back over it, blocking her view.

'Shoo!' Shocked, she waved her hands at the swans. 'Shoo!'

The swans took this as encouragement, crowding closer, as if she thought they were about to be fed.

She turned round, saw a hoe propped against the wall and lifted it, waving it at them.

Reluctantly the birds paddled away. Alex had to wait until the surface of the water was still again before she could see who was below, staring up at her, eyes blank.

Plato.

The Greek philosopher lay face up about a metre below the surface of the water. Weed drifted across his sculpted beard.

The horror of seeing a face beneath the water gave way to laughter so loud that a pair of moorhens, nesting somewhere in the undergrowth, shot out, feet scrabbling on the surface of the water as they took flight.

Alex stopped laughing as abruptly as she had begun.

She thought of the undrunk tea on the little table.

She peered again into the dark water.

SIXTY-SIX

Busts of Greek philosophers did not have arms. Further out, towards the deeper water among the weeds was a pink hand, with fingers slightly splayed, utterly still under the moving water.

Beneath the weight, face down, pressed deep into the mud below it, lay what she assumed must be the body of Frederick Lindsay.

She called for an emergency response, then she called Bill South. 'I've found another body. Someone I interviewed three days ago.'

She could hear her daughter swearing at South's old cooker in the background. She wished she was there.

'You're alone with the body?'

'Sort of. He's in the canal.'

'Are you sure you're OK?' asked South. 'You sound like . . .'

'Nothing happened to me. I just found him.'

'But he's in the water. Where you almost died. You need to get out of there. It's not safe.'

She could make out his legs now. 'I think I can hear the response units coming,' she said, and ended the call, though there were no sirens yet. It was just her and the noise of the marshes.

She was glad she didn't wear eye make-up any more. She would have gone back into the house and splashed water onto her face, but it was a crime scene now. By the time the first car actually arrived fifteen minutes later, she had managed to dry her eyes enough to get away with it.

McAdam said, 'You shouldn't have been here.'

'I just came to bring his photograph back.'

'We'll give you a ride home if you like.'

The marine unit had arrived and were about to hoist the marble bust off Lindsay's back.

'I want to stay,' she said. 'He was killed by the same people who tried to kill me.'

McAdam stood in a white shirt, arms crossed, as they watched the divers tautening the rope around the bust. 'You can't know that yet. We're not even sure it's him until we lift him out.'

'They came straight back here after they pushed my car into the canal. They killed him.'

'Maybe,' said McAdam.

'Don't you see?'

They had constructed a tripod out of scaffolding poles and were hauling on it now. The recovery team had set up three work lights on tripods around the bank, their glare illuminating the water in which Lindsay lay. The two moorhens were back, paddling anxiously around. Their nest would be somewhere close if the divers hadn't already destroyed it.

'They tried to kill me because they were worried that Lindsay had told me something. Then they came back to kill him. They were trying to obliterate a trail, but all they've done is the opposite. They've shown us that there *is* a trail. That there's something that connects Vincent Gibbons, Whiteland Fields and Thornhead School. They messed up by not killing me.'

The top of the bust's head emerged from the water, revolving slowly. Released, Frederick Lindsay's back bobbed slowly to the surface.

'Are you cold? You're shivering?' said McAdam.

'It's like a crocodile,' she said. 'Hiding the body underwater.' She squatted down on the canal bank, watching the team work. 'I reckon this was a quick fix. Whoever killed Frederick Lindsay came back and killed him the same night they tried to kill me. Everything here is just the same as when I left it. They left me in the water, turned round, came back and killed him. The killing wasn't premeditated so they didn't have time to plan it. Frederick Lindsay was killed exactly because I came to visit him. The killer put the body here and has been waiting for the chance to come back and dispose of it.'

'Like Vincent Gibbons, in the freezer.'

'If you like.'

Once the bust was on the bank out of harm's way, two divers gently rolled the body over. Even under a thin layer of mud, Alex could see Lindsay's eyes were open. When one of the men put a hand gently under Lindsay's head to raise him, water ran from his nostrils and his open mouth.

Torchlight shone briefly from inside the house. A forensics officer had arrived to make a preliminary survey of the scene before the full team arrived, presumably in the morning. 'What do you think it was he told you that was so deadly?'

'I don't think he told me anything at all . . . not directly anyway. But whoever killed him didn't know that.'

The torchlight seemed to fall on Alex's face for a second as McAdam examined her.

'What?' demanded Alex.

'You know very well. If this takes you anywhere near Howard Roteman, the Chief Superintendent needs to know.'

'I know.'

'Does it?'

'What if he's in danger, too? We went to see him this morning.'

In the brightness of the work lights, McAdam's face seemed to grow pale.

'Think about it.'

'Come on,' McAdam said. 'We need to get you away from here. Get you somewhere warm.'

It seemed absurd to be sitting in a normal pub, where people were eating steaks and fish pies and drinking pints of very English-looking ale. They found a table far enough away from everyone else.

'Vincent Gibbons accidentally discovered the remains of Trevor Grey,' Alex said, 'and he was murdered, probably because of what he discovered. Frederick Lindsay and I were both attacked because we might know the connection between Thornhead School and those murders. Anyone else who might know that is either in danger . . . or they're the perpetrator themselves.'

'You think Roteman's a suspect?'

'He's connected. He has to be a potential victim too.' She thought for a while. 'Does he have a specialist protection officer?'

'Roteman is not a senior minister, so probably not.'

'He should probably have one.'

'You seriously think he's in danger?'

'How did they know I was visiting Frederick Lindsay? They've been watching us, and maybe more. They were right there, at the address. They didn't follow me there. I would have noticed on those lanes. It's as if somebody's always one step ahead of us. We have a duty to make sure Roteman's protected.'

'Do you think there's a leak?'

Alex clasped the small coffee cup in both hands, taking warmth from it. The shaking of her hands made little rings in the liquid.

'You look very pale, Alex.'

'I'm fine.'

McAdam took a swig from his diet cola. 'Stay here. I have to phone the Chief Superintendent. We need to pass this up the chain.'

'Good luck with that.'

Alex lifted her coffee to her lips, but her hands were still shaking and some spilled onto her blouse. She cursed quietly, dug in her bag for a tissue to wipe it with. Through the window she could see McAdam standing in the car park, phone at his ear, frowning, listening, nodding.

A large, very drunk woman in a T-shirt came up behind her.

'You look sad. Do you need a hug?'

The woman's T-shirt read: *FAT PEOPLE ARE HARDER*

TO KIDNAP.

'Do you know, that's the very last thing I need.'

'Suit yourself.'

Outside, McAdam was still talking on the phone.

Alex had finished her coffee by the time he returned. 'He says we're to discuss this with no one. Colleagues, friends, family . . . no one. OK?'

Alex nodded. 'What about Revell Adison? He must be at risk too.'

'It's all in hand, believe me. And you. I'm signing you off work now. You've done enough. You've seen enough. Take your mind off this. You need a break.'

And Alex's heart contracted a little more.

SIXTY-SEVEN

When she arrived at Arum Cottage, the house was empty. There was a note from South saying they were out.

There was another note, too, a new one, written on a small rectangle of cardboard and pinned to the bathroom door: *PLEASE LEAVE THE BATHROOM AS YOU FOUND IT.*

She smiled; South was finding cohabiting hard. The bathroom at South's house was small. South had taken Alex's washing things off the edge of the sink and replaced them in her washbag. Alex undressed, had a shower and left the window open to let the steam out. She was looking out of the window across the dark, scrubby land, when she heard her mobile ringing in the bedroom.

She grabbed a towel, wrapped it around her and left wet prints on Bill's floorboards. In the small bedroom, she picked up the phone. Number withheld. She hesitated before swiping the screen. 'Hello?'

'Alex. It's Howard Roteman. I'm sorry, calling so late.'

'I thought you'd call.'

'Did you?' He took a breath. 'They said I might be in some danger.'

She sat on the bed. 'It's just a precaution.'

'It just threw me, that's all. Sorry. Were you in bed?'

'No. Not yet.'

'I couldn't sleep either,' he said. 'Listen. Sorry. Apparently you had an accident. I didn't realise. Sounded awful.'

'It wasn't an accident.'

'This is scary. Jesus. If there's anything I can do.'

'Thanks, Howard.'

A pause. 'Do you really think someone is trying to kill me too?'

Alex heard the unmistakable sound of ice in a glass. 'Are you drinking?'

'A little. It's freaked me out a bit. I get mail telling me people want to kill me all the time. It would be kind of embarrassing if I didn't these days. All of us do. That's just modern politics, in all its glorious vileness, but I've never taken any of it seriously.'

'Like I said. It's just a precaution.'

'What's happened? I'm not an idiot. Something else must have happened if you lot think I need protection. There's an officer parked outside our front gate.'

She thought of Frederick Lindsay's body breaking the surface of the water. 'Something happened, but we can't discuss it yet.'

'Sorry.'

'You'll be OK. Go to bed, Howard.'

She waited for him to end the call. Instead he said, 'There's something else.'

Alex sat on the bed. 'What is it, Howard?'

'When we met . . . I wanted to be honest. I wasn't.'

'Go on,' she said cautiously.

'That photograph. I know one of the names of the boys you pointed out.'

Alex was wide awake now. 'Which one?'

'Revell, his name was. Is that right?'

'Yes.'

'I do remember him. I'll be honest. He was . . . a bit of a weirdo.'

'How come you remember now, Howard? Before, you told us you didn't know who he was.'

'You'll have to forgive me,' said Roteman. 'When you showed me the photograph, I knew right away, but I was kind of shocked by it. It came out of the blue. This isn't at all easy to talk about.'

Alex stood. 'Take your time,' she said.

'When I met you, I said it's not really a time I spend a lot of time thinking about. I think that's a quite common experience with boys from situations like this. We box up our memories and put them somewhere safe. It's always been there, but I've never, ever told anybody.'

She could hear him taking another gulp from the glass. Taking her towelling dressing gown of the hook, she wrapped it around herself.

'I recognised him,' Roteman was saying as she walked out into the living room; a table, a desk, some chairs, shelves packed with South's books on birds and animals. 'I just couldn't face talking about it. Not in front of Hilary, especially. It sounds so stupid. You see, there was a certain amount of roughhousing went on at the school.'

'Bullying.' She looked around the cabin for a pen and paper, opening drawers in his desk.

'Yes.'

Not finding paper, she unhooked a whiteboard from the wall by the back window, laid it flat on the table, wiped the list of birds that had been written on it clean, picked up a felt tip pen and took off the lid. 'It's OK. Take your time.'

'What was your school like?'

'Ordinary state school. I was a police officer's daughter, so it wasn't always easy. You?'

'Oh God. I bet that was nothing like Thornhead. It was utterly Victorian. The masters were strict. The prefects were strict. Everyone was afraid. I suppose that made it easier for someone like him. That's all there is. He was a psycho. I think he may have been mentally ill.'

'Did he bully you?' There was a long pause. Alex nudged him. 'You're talking about the boy in the photograph. Revell Adison.'

'Yes.'

'He bullied you?'

There was no answer.

'Was there a sexual element?'

A long sigh. The sound of more drink being poured.

'We're going to have to interview you formally. You understand that?'

'Yes. Obviously. I know that. It's just that I've never talked to anybody about this. There's still a lot of shame involved. I know, rationally, that none of that was my fault . . .'

'We can arrange that you talk to someone who specialises in abuse. It may make it easier.'

'I know that. But I'd like to explain it to you first.'

Alex held the pen, waiting. 'Go on then,' she said.

She could hear him crying. 'I'm sorry,' he said.

Outside the kitchen window, the light from the power station lit the shingle behind the house. It was never totally dark here.

'In your own time,' she said.

Afterwards Alex checked the time, wrote it on the whiteboard, then photographed the notes she had made, opened the fridge in the hope there might be a bottle of wine in there, but there wasn't. South never had alcohol any more.

She texted Zoë:

You OK?

At the sunken woods. Back soon.

It was gone one in the morning. She couldn't sleep, though. Next she messaged Jill:

Awake?

Jill called back within the minute. 'I heard,' she said. 'You found Frederick Lindsay's body. That must have been vile. I'm sorry.'

'Howard Roteman just called me.'

'Oh shit,' said Jill. 'What about?'

'After we discovered Lindsay's body, McAdam called the Met to make sure Roteman had special protection officers. It's freaked him out. He called me and told me stuff that he hadn't told us before.'

'Like what?'

'Like Revell Adison was a sexual abuser, bully and blackmailer.'

'The weirdo who lives in the cellar?'

399

'They were all at school together. Roteman, Adison and Grey. Roteman said he had a kind of method. It was pretty tame by today's standards. Adison was a prefect, which meant he had his own room. He would persuade boys to talk about their sexual fantasies to him. They were just teenage boys. Some of them would be masturbating when they talked. It was a boys' private school. They were locked away there together. It's so easy for bad things to happen in places like that. But the thing was, Roteman said Adison had a cassette tape recorder and a microphone and he would secretly tape them.'

'Oh,' said Jill.

'Exactly. When he wanted to bully them or humiliate someone, he would play them back a bit of the tape and warn him he was going to play it to the other boys.'

'Jesus. Sextortion existed long before the internet was invented. What kind of bullying?'

'He said some of it was just getting them to give him money, getting them to steal stuff off other kids or from teachers for him, he said. But it was the humiliation that he enjoyed most, by the sound of it. He made them do other things. Sometimes with each other . . . *to* each other.'

'Poor bastards,' said Jill. She sounded wide awake now.

'One way you could get into Adison's good books, Roteman said, was to get other boys to take part. He'd go easier on you if you got other boys to go to his study.'

'What a fucking weirdo. He going to go on record with this? I mean, no wonder Trevor Grey ran away. Beginning to make sense now, isn't it?'

'Is it?' asked Alex.

400

'A teenage child. Vulnerable and upset. Not wanting to go home because he's so ashamed. Easy pickings for anyone who likes harming children. You told McAdam yet?'

'I'm going to call him in the morning.' Alex stared at her notes. 'Why did he call me now, Jill?'

Jill sounded puzzled by the question. 'Like he said, he was freaked out by the fact we said he needed a special protection officer.'

'So why did he tell me that stuff about abuse now?'

Jill's voice was quieter than usual when she said, 'Because that's exactly what it's like, Alex. You feel like you're the one to blame for it. Even years afterwards. You avoid talking about it until you absolutely have to.'

Alex was quiet for a long time. For the second time tonight, it felt like somebody had just tried to tell her something very personal. In the end, she said, 'I just feel I'm being played here, Jill. I just don't know how.'

'Maybe you've been doing the job too long,' said Jill.

'Thanks, Jill.'

'I didn't mean it like that.'

Alex stretched. She heard the key in the front door. 'I need to go.'

Zoë came in, dressed in one of South's old donkey jackets; it looked huge on her. She looked exhausted but happy. 'Who were you talking to?'

South followed a minute later, kicking off his wellingtons in the small porch.

His eyes fell on the whiteboard on the dining-room table,

401

covered in Alex's notes, blue pen crammed across every inch of its surface.

'Sorry. I couldn't find any paper.'

'Mum!' scolded Zoë.

South was already looking disapprovingly down at the floor, still wet from where she'd walked on it barefoot.

SIXTY-EIGHT

Her alarm went off at seven. South was already up, out somewhere. She left Zoë curled up in a ball in bed, made a coffee on South's rickety propane stove, and went outside into the early summer sunshine in her dressing gown. She called McAdam at home, repeated what she'd told Jill, emailed him a copy of her notes. 'We'll need to bring Adison in for questioning.'

She could hear the BBC news was in the background. McAdam cleared his throat and said, 'I have bad news. After we found Lindsay's body, I sent officers round there last night to check on him. The house was empty.'

'Shit.' It was a glorious morning. A pink morning sun lit the lichen that struggled to get a hold on the shingle, deepening its pale green, lending the stones around it a rich pink.

'Maybe he's just gone somewhere.' He was talking in a quiet voice; his wife was still in bed beside him, Alex guessed.

'Hold on. He barely shows himself, that's what the neighbours say. Did they check the basement?'

'Apparently, yes.'

'Have they taken a good look? His neighbours say he dug tunnels under the house. There was earth inside his house that must have come from somewhere. He's mentally ill.'

Alex could hear McAdam's wife asking, 'Is that her again? It's Saturday morning, for pity's sake.'

'You're off, Alex. Forget about this. We'll talk after the weekend. I have to go.'

South returned around eight with mackerel, and fried them with tomatoes and scrambled eggs.

'I've been signed off,' Alex said when he laid the plate in front of her.

'Good.' He put a knife beneath the skin of the fish and lifted its flesh away from the bone. 'I'm glad. You need a break from it. And you need to be safe.'

Her fish's milky eye stared up at her. Revell Adison may have been partly responsible for the death of Trevor Grey, but they were no closer to understanding how he died. And they were no closer to knowing who had killed Vinnie Gibbons and Phyllis McKenzie. 'I feel I was almost there, you know? Just one more push.'

The sun was higher now; outside the window at the back of the cabin, the old black lighthouse cast a shadow across the scrub. 'There's other officers. It's not just you, you know.'

She could hear Zoë stirring in the bedroom they shared. 'I know.'

She emerged from the door in knickers and a T-shirt. South looked away.

'Put a dressing gown on, love,' said Alex.

'What's that smell? It's horrible,' she said.

'I called Helen. I thought we should go and stay with her for a couple of days. We don't see enough of her. Get out from under your feet.'

He chewed on the fish for a minute. 'I'm supposed to say you're not under my feet, aren't I?'

She laughed.

Later, as he stood on the front porch, awkwardly waving as they drove away, Alex wasn't sure if he looked relieved or disappointed.

Zoë slept again in the passenger seat as Alex drove north-west towards London. She had brought a change of clothes, a toothbrush and a book called *A Farewell to Ice*.

When they finally reached the house, Helen didn't answer the door. Alex let herself in with her own key, but there was nobody in.

'Typical,' said Alex.

'Don't, Mum.'

Alex called her, but her mother's mobile rang on the kitchen table. She was boiling a kettle when she heard the front door open. Helen came in wearing a thick winter coat, though the weather was warmer now.

She hugged Zoë.

'Did you forget we were coming?' asked Alex.

'Of course I didn't. And how are you? Are you busy?'

'I'm off for a few days,' said Alex. 'So I thought we'd come and stay.'

'And you can't figure out what to do with yourself?'

'You know me, don't you?'

That afternoon, Alex took them all to a South Indian restaurant on Church Street for a late lunch, and watched her daughter ordering more than she'd ever seen her attempt to eat in her life.

Helen ordered lager. 'Go on, you have one too. You're having a break,' she said.

Alex ordered a half. Just as the food arrived, Alex's phone buzzed.

'Switch it off, Mum,' said Zoë.

Alex picked it up. It was a message from DI McAdam:

Bad news. Revell Adison's body discovered this morning. Suspected suicide.

'Shit,' she said loudly, then apologised to the waiter who was leaning across her with a plate of idli.

'What's wrong?' Helen asked.

'A suspect committed suicide.'

Alex was texting back now.

What happened?

'She's always like this,' said Zoë.

'I know.'

Local police discovered body this morning following your suggestion. Victim was in a tunnel dug beneath the house.

'She has the worst table manners in the world.'

'She's a copper,' said Helen. 'I was married to one.'

Gravesend was not far from East London. In less than an hour she could be at the crime scene.

'Don't you bloody dare, Mum,' said Zoë quietly.

Alex looked at her mother. 'Of course I wouldn't,' she said.

Helen and Alex barely touched their food. For once, Zoë cleared her plate.

'I was thinking we could go shopping afterwards,' said Alex.

'I don't really fancy going into town,' said her mother. 'Not on a Saturday. There's music on at the Shillelagh. I quite often go there.'

'Zoë doesn't really like pubs much,' said Alex.

'I don't mind,' said Zoë. She started telling her grandmother about the new housing estate; about how she had protested against it.

Alex messaged Jill:

Hear the news?

McAdam's text made her anxious; it was just too convenient, Adison dying so soon after Howard Roteman had announced that he was the reason why Trevor Grey had run away.

'I would hate to live in a place like that,' Helen was saying. 'I don't think I could live anywhere else but here.'

'But your house is huge,' said Zoë. 'You can't live there all your life.'

'Why can't I?' said Helen indignantly.

In the kitchen, they made a cup of tea and Zoë told her grandmother that the earth would be unfit to sustain human life soon anyway. 'All right for me, then,' said Helen. 'I don't plan on staying around that long.'

'Gran,' scolded Zoë.

'What's that you're reading?' She pointed at Zoë's book.

'It's about how the world is ending and nobody's doing anything about it.'

'I'm just going outside to make a phone call,' Alex said.

'Go,' said her mother. 'You're annoying me.'

Standing in the cul-de-sac where she had played as a girl, Alex called McAdam. 'What news?' she asked.

'You're supposed to be off. I wish I hadn't messaged you now, but I thought you'd want to know. Nothing suspicious about his death. He hanged himself. No apparent sign of a struggle. He left a note. So that fits with what Roteman told you.'

'A little too conveniently.'

'Leave it alone, Alex.'

'When did he kill himself?'

'It must have been some time yesterday. We've asked around. Nobody has seen anything suspicious. It looks like he just took himself down into this hole he dug and hanged himself down there.'

At around the same time as they'd been finding Frederick Lindsay's body, Alex thought. 'Howard Roteman calls me up and accuses Adison of probably being the reason Trevor Grey ran away from Thornhead. Turns out Adison is dead and in no position to contradict anything he says. What did the note say?'

'"I'm sorry".'

'That's all?'

'There will be an inquest, but I've spoken to forensics. There is absolutely nothing about his death that raises any concerns.'

'So far,' she said.

'Yes. So far.'

She returned to sit in the kitchen, where her mother was watching something gory on Netflix with Zoë. Her phone buzzed again. This time it was Jill:

You heard then? Revell Adison killed himself. It's kind of like an admission of guilt, isn't it? After what Roteman said. Sick fucking bastard. At least he ruined his own life, as well as everyone else's.

'Go home,' her mother said. 'Go back to work. You're spending the whole time looking at your phone. You're obsessed. I can tell. I don't need you here. I'm perfectly fine on my own.'

'I've come to visit,' said Alex. 'Haven't we?' she said to Zoë. But it wasn't like she'd had a lot of choice.

'You don't want to be here. I can tell you don't. Your mind is somewhere else completely. You're like your father.'

Later, washing up in the kitchen while Zoë read in her bedroom, her mother put her hand over hers. It felt small and light. 'OK then. Tell me about what's eating you,' her mother said.

And so Alex told her about the discovery of Vinnie Gibbons's body, then of Trevor Grey's bones; about the dead badger that had been left at her door; about Mrs McKenzie who had been gassed by accident, about the connection with Thornhead School and a bullying case, about her discovery of Frederick Lindsay's body. And finally about Howard Roteman and Revell Adison.

'How awful,' she said, when Alex finally stopped. 'Five people dead. You are so like your father, you know.'

'I miss him,' said Alex.

'Me too,' said Helen. 'More than I like to admit.'

She went to the fridge, pulled out the bottle of wine and filled both of their glasses. They sat in silence.

She was exhausted and fell asleep fast, but woke too early.

The worst thing is that not all investigations succeed. There are many times when you know who did it, but you don't know how to prove it. It's what makes good coppers bad; she knew that. The need to prove something, even when the facts weren't there at all.

The traffic noise was loud and unfamiliar. How had she ever slept with it when she was a child? She missed the sounds of wind and birds; this was not home any more.

She thought about Zoë, sleeping in the attic room upstairs, about seeing the badgers with her. About her talking about the things that you couldn't see. There was so much about all this that was unseen; about how to observe dark things.

It must have been around four in the morning, when the nightclub on the high street beyond the cul-de-sac was chucking out, and the noise of laughing and screaming was hard to ignore, that she sat up in bed, opened her eyes wide, and said, 'Oh.' And after that, she couldn't sleep.

SIXTY-NINE

Neither her mother nor Zoë were awake yet, and they probably wouldn't be for at least another hour. The house was quiet. Since her father had died, her mother had stopped buying decent coffee, so Alex stepped out into the cul-de-sac, closing the door as quietly as she could, turned left and stepped onto Stoke Newington High Street, where a small Turkish cafe had opened on the opposite side of the road. There was little she missed about London, but coffee at this hour of the morning – even on a Sunday – felt like a luxury.

She ordered an expresso, and when she had had her first sip from it, called Jill.

'Where are you?' she asked her.

'In bed of course. It's seven in the bloody morning.'

'Can you do something for me? Can you go into the station, log on to the system and find out what kind of car Hilary Roteman owns? It's either going to be in her name or Howard Roteman's.'

'Why?' she said, and immediately afterwards, 'Can't somebody else do it?'

'You're ten minutes from the station.'

'I was going to have a shower.'

'Call me back as soon as you know.'

'What's this about?'

'Please,' she said.

Then she sat in the cafe, reading the paper. The news was full of arguments about trade deals. Roteman had been right. There was going to be another general election.

She was on her second coffee when Jill called back.

'What's going on, Alex?'

'Go on. Tell me what car she owns.'

'You know already, don't you? A red Mazda.'

The car that had been in the garage on the day she and McAdam had visited the Rotemans' house, the one he had described as 'Hilary's little runaround', was a red Mazda. It's what had struck her at four on the morning: Hilary Roteman's car had been in the garage. The things that you couldn't see.

'What does this mean, Alex?'

'Another favour. Keep this to yourself.'

The cafe was filling with Stoke Newington's sophisticated young professionals, on their way back from early morning runs, ordering yumurtas and avocado on toast.

'What do you mean, keep it to myself?'

'Don't tell McAdam or anyone about what I asked.'

'You're not doing anything dodgy, are you, Alex?'

'No. It's nothing like that. I can't explain right now. Just promise me. We're back tomorrow. Come over and I'll cook something massive, and I'll explain everything then, I promise.'

She ended the call.

It was best that Jill told no one what Alex was up to. Whoever was behind this, they had been one step ahead of them all the time. They had known when Alex had made the connection between the bones on Whiteland Fields and Thornhead School. They had known that she had gone to visit Frederick Lindsay, too. They had known it all.

Tamsin Porter had asked her to keep her posted about how the investigation was proceeding, but Alex had never passed on any operational details. There was a leak somewhere else, so until she had found a way to figure out where that was, it would be best not to tell anyone what she was thinking – yet.

She dug in her bag, pulled out her wallet and found the business card Derry Michaels had given her. Below his office details, there was a mobile number; she tried it.

After just two or three rings, it went to voicemail. He had not recognised the number, she guessed, and declined the call. She texted him instead:

DS Cupidi of Kent Serious Crime. Please call me.

He replied within the minute:

Do you know what time it is?

She texted back:

I need to speak to you. Urgent.

There was no answer.

*

413

The coffee here was just the right side of bitter. She took a final sip, left a tip, then stepped outside and called another number standing on the High Street.

'You again,' Mrs Utting said drily.

'It was Hilary Roteman,' said Alex, above the noise of the buses.

'I know the name, but I don't think I know her personally,' said Mrs Utting. She was listening to something classical.

'But your husband did, didn't he? She was the woman he was having an affair with.'

Belinda Utting was silent for a little while, then said, 'I don't want to talk about it.'

'Your husband was having an affair with Hilary Roteman. She used to visit him at Guldeford Hall. She had a key and knew the code for the alarm.'

'I am going to put the phone down now.' From Belinda Utting's radio came a sweep of romantic strings.

'You knew that, all along, didn't you?'

'I shall call my lawyer.'

'People have died,' said Alex, 'because you didn't want me to know your husband was having an affair.'

'My husband loved *me*,' said Belinda Utting.

When she got back Zoë was still asleep but her mother was up, sitting in the kitchen, drinking tea and reading the *Mirror*.

'You look very pleased with yourself,' said Helen, looking up.

'Do I?' Alex said.

Helen smiled at her. Alex didn't even grumble when her mother lit her first cigarette of the day.

She texted DI McAdam:

Confidential. I can link Howard Roteman to the death of Vincent Gibbons.

When her phone buzzed a second later she expected it to be him. It wasn't.

'Francis Joyce,' said a man's voice. It took her a second to remember him as the CSI who had done the report on the blood in the back of Epps's van; she had only spoken to him on the phone the once.

'You're the one investigating the death of a Trevor Grey, is that right?'

Across the table, her mother looked up. 'Yes,' said Alex.

'And you are also interested in a Revell Adison, recently deceased?'

'That's right,' said Alex.

The man lowered his voice. 'I think we may have something interesting.'

'What?'

There was a pause. 'I think it's better if you take a look. I don't want to prejudice your opinion on what we've found, but I think we'd like your eyes on it.'

'I don't understand.'

'When we were doing due diligence at Revell Adison's house after his suicide, we think we may have found something that indicates that this wasn't a straightforward incident. I'd be grateful if you could take a look at it. Could we arrange for you to come and have a look? I know it's probably impossible at short notice. But it'll only take a minute.'

'Want me to come into Maidstone?'

'It's not there, I'm afraid. Further than that. It's at the house. In Gravesend. I realise that's an imposition.'

'Even better. I can be there in less than an hour,' she said. 'I'm in East London.'

'Really? That's great. One thing,' said Francis Joyce 'We've been ordered to keep investigations confidential. There are security concerns about this case. Due to the nature of the people involved, we're told we need to be careful about who information is being disseminated to.'

Which meant she wasn't the only one with evidence now pointing towards Roteman.

'Agreed,' said Alex. Patterns were emerging from the dark. 'So you don't want me to tell anyone about this?'

'Not for now.'

By the time the call ended, her mother was looking at her with a knowing look on her face.

'I'll be back before Zoë is awake. Within a couple of hours,' Alex promised. 'I'll be right in and out.'

The knowing look changed to a cynical one.

SEVENTY

Alex pulled up outside the empty house and checked her watch. She was early; there was no sign of a police car, marked or unmarked, outside. She figured Francis Joyce, the CSI, couldn't yet have arrived. She looked for somewhere to park and found a space under a small plane tree that was full of pigeons. She'd probably have to clean the car afterwards, she thought.

When she took her phone out from her bag she checked for missed calls. There wasn't one from McAdam, but Derry Michaels had finally returned her call. She dialled him back and he answered straight away.

'What is it, then?'

'Two questions. The day before I met you in the House of Lords, did you have a meeting with Howard Roteman?'

'And a good morning to you, too. I'm not telling you anything before you explain what you were doing at the September Homes launch.'

'I can't,' she said.

'Really? I do enjoy an operational secret, Sergeant.'

'Nope. Sorry.'

He was out somewhere in London. She could hear the city street in the background. 'You know September Homes is in trouble now? They can't get the investment they need. Word is that the Secretary of State is going to overturn planning permission on Whiteland Fields anyway, so the investment they made buying the land is worthless.'

'Please, Derry. I need to know this. Did you have a meeting with Howard Roteman on that day?'

'Not him specifically. It was a House of Lords committee meeting on rural economies. He was there to discuss rural housing.'

'Second question. Did you tell him at any point that day that I was visiting you?'

'What's this about?'

'Please. Just tell me?'

'Of course I didn't.'

'You sure?'

'Absolutely.'

She ended the call. Roteman had claimed Derry Michaels had told him about her visit. That had been a lie. He had been covering up the fact that he already knew.

There was still no sign of the CSI man, Francis Joyce. The place was quiet. She stood on the pavement, contemplating the derelict property. She pushed open the gate. The remains of the tape that had been tied across the door hung down from each side.

Looking closer, she realised the front door looked like it was open, just a crack. She approached it and pushed, and it moved back, creaking slightly in a comical horror-show way.

'Hello? Mr Joyce?'

There was no answer. She stepped inside, out of the late morning sun, into a sudden dark coolness and the house's strange smell of earth. It felt like an animal's den, she thought, as if creatures had lived here, not a human being.

A gust of wind blew through the open door. She thought she heard a noise; a door closing somewhere. It might have just been the breeze.

'Anybody there?'

'DS Cupidi?' The voice seemed to come from under her feet.

'Mr Joyce?' she called. She realised she had never met this man . . . had she? She remembered receiving a text and email from him about the results of blood tests from Julian Epps's van, and speaking to him briefly on the phone. Alex stepped further into the house.

'Down here. I'm in the basement.'

Nothing in the house had changed since she was last here. She passed the rooms full of piles of dirt, navigating down the long, crammed hallway until she reached the door to the cellar.

There was a light on below. Alex hesitated. 'Are the stairs OK?'

'Fine,' said Joyce. 'Come on down. You're part of DI McAdam's team, aren't you?'

'What is it you want me to see?' She peered down, but couldn't see anyone.

'I think we can prove that Revell Adison didn't kill himself.'

Under the house's main staircase, another set of stairs led

down into the darkness. She put her hand against the cold wall and felt her way down towards the bottom of the stairs.

The cellar was musty, the floor bare earth. Francis Joyce stood several feet away, shining the light of his torch at her. She held up her hand to protect her eyes.

'This way,' he said. Only when he shone the torch away did she see that he was dressed in white from head to foot. He was wearing a protective coverall, hood up and mask.

She hesitated. 'Is this a crime scene? Do I need to be kitted out?'

'Don't worry. This part's been swept already,' he said.

She dug into her bag for her own phone, but by the time she had found it and switched it on, he had turned the torch away and ducked into what appeared to be an entirely separate space within the cellar.

'Adison was a mole man,' called Joyce. 'Mentally ill. He dug under the house. The whole lot's going to have to be condemned, I reckon. All that earth upstairs. He excavated it. There are tunnels everywhere. It's as if he was hiding away from the real world.'

She followed him into the next chamber, crouching down to pass through the small doorway knocked into a brick wall. Improvised props held up a lintel. There were more inside, dozens of them, some poles filched from building sites, others just pieces of timber, wedged up against the uneven ceiling.

Revell Adison had dug out this place as a kind of refuge, a place to hide; it was a physical manifestation of his state of mind. A man who had a lot to hide; or a man who was trying to hide himself away.

Her torch shone on a length of rope dangling from the centre of the chamber, and the underground air suddenly seemed cooler.

'Is that . . . ?'

'Yeah. That's where he supposedly hanged himself.' She shone her torch on his face. It was his turn to blink in the light. Bent down, head against the rough ceiling, he held his white-covered arm up in front of his face. If this wasn't a secure crime scene, she thought, why was he still wearing his mask?

'He couldn't have,' she said, looking around. 'There's not enough room for him to swing. What are we really doing here, Francis?'

'Look down,' he said, and focused the beam from his phone onto the floor.

Alex kept her eyes on him. If this was being investigated as a murder scene, why were there no more signs of the team's presence? There were no lights, no markers.

'Go on, look,' he said.

She shifted her eyes to the floor, raised her own phone's beam just for a second – and gasped. Just next to her feet, less than half a metre away, directly beneath the rope, a dark hole opened in the bare earth next to her. It was perfectly round, she realised, and lined with bricks.

'He'd have had plenty of legroom to swing,' said the man. 'If he'd hanged himself, that is.'

An ancient well, she thought, and realised, in that instant, why he had brought her here.

★

In that same moment, she jumped.

Just as he lunged towards her to push her into the hole, she launched herself across it.

Her left hand caught the fraying end of rope above the well, and her weight swung her to the other side, teetering on the edge of the drop.

She was not upright yet. Her body was still suspended over the opening. One hand on the rope, she needed her other hand to stop herself from falling. She had no choice but to drop her phone, so she could reach up and grab the rope with a second hand before she slipped down. For a second, she arched, feet on the other side, just out of the man's reach, as she secured her grip on the small frayed stump. Feet scrabbling, she pressed one hand against the low ceiling to lever herself across, until she was standing again on a narrow ledge on the far side of the gap.

There was the faintest of clatters, echoing in the cave above, as her abandoned phone hit debris at the bottom, somewhere far below her.

There was just enough room on the edge of the well to turn, but not enough to stand up straight. She crouched, knees bent, neck crooked, both arms stretched out sideways and pressing into the rough wall on either side. He was shining his light towards her again, standing on the far side of the well, his back against the opening that was her only chance of escape.

SEVENTY-ONE

She was trapped.

The only thing in her favour was that he could not reach her if she stayed where she was, not without risking her tugging him into the opening. But she could not stand like this for ever, knees bent, forcing herself back against the earth behind her. After a while her muscles would start to cramp.

'Richard Browne,' she said. 'With an "e". Possibly not your real name though.'

He kicked at the earth in front of him. A small stone trickled over the lip of the well, tinkling as it ricocheted off the walls.

He didn't answer.

'How did you know my phone number?' No. That was a stupid question. It would have been easy for him to find her details, she thought. That wasn't really what was puzzling her; it was how he had known exactly which buttons to press to get her here. What he had said about security made him sound like he was an insider with secrets to share. But it also meant that he knew that she had been concerned that there was a leak. He had even mentioned McAdam's name. There had been a leak and it had been coming straight to him.

He had access to emails or phone calls. Or both. Francis Joyce was a real person; she had spoken to Joyce on the phone. Browne had known that, and impersonated him to lure her here. He had known everything.

He held out a hand. 'Come on. I won't hurt you. This is just a misunderstanding.' With his other he leaned backwards and grabbed one of the slender metal poles that had been wedged to hold up the ceiling to brace himself. 'It's OK,' he said gently.

She held her hand out towards his. He stretched a little further.

'Sure it is. Just a misunderstanding.' She could try and grab his hand to pull him in, but he looked stronger, and besides, he was already holding on to something. She was perched on a slope on the edge of a deep drop. If it came to a tug of war, he would easily win.

'Actually, I'm fine here,' she said, lowering her arm.

'Suit yourself.'

She wondered how old the well was. The houses around here were built early in the nineteenth century. It might have been left from some Tudor farm, obliterated by the Victorian sprawl, or to serve one of the windmills that had stood here. 'You knew I was going to be in London, too,' she said out loud, realising that it wasn't just her work situation that he knew about. He had been aware of her exact movements. 'All that pretending it was a surprise that I was in London. You knew all along that I was there, didn't you?'

'Might have done.'

'That was part of it. You chose a place that you knew I'd drop everything and come to. Shit.'

'I've got all day,' said Browne. 'You'll get tired standing there.' He held out his hand a little further. He had kept the evidence gloves on, she noticed.

'Come a little closer,' she said.

He stayed right where he was, arm towards her.

It was a Mexican stand-off. He couldn't reach her without leaning over the well; if she tried to jump across it, he would just stand his ground and force her back into it.

The coverall, the mask and the gloves – they weren't just a disguise. He wanted to leave this place without leaving any trace of himself behind. If they ever did find her body in the well, they'd assume that the impetuous DS Cupidi had come here to explore, and lost her footing.

A terrible accident. Poor, impatient DS Cupidi.

'No?' He held his hand out still.

'Take your gloves off and I might think about it.'

He laughed, because he knew she understood, then shone the phone around the small chamber, presumably looking for some kind of weapon. She felt oddly calm, considering he had just tried to kill her. He said he had got all day, but he hadn't. He had as long as the battery on his phone lasted, and that could not be for ever. Perhaps she could outlast him. It would hurt, though, but maybe she was strong enough. Cycling had built muscle in her legs.

425

The chamber was small. Half a dozen props held the earth above their heads. To her right, another opening seemed to lead to another tunnel, but it was too far away to be useful. To her left, the foundations of an ancient retaining wall had been exposed. The floor was dirty, but bare. She was relieved that there weren't any of the tools that Revell Adison must have used to dig out the place lying about. A shovel or a pick would be enough for him to swipe at her with, but if he left his place on the far side of the well to look for one, it would at least give her the chance to escape.

'Why do you think he dug this?' she asked.

'What?'

'It's pretty amazing, think about it. He dug this place himself, by hand. Why?'

'Because he was mentally ill.'

'Undoubtedly, though I wonder how much your boss was the cause of that. He is your boss, isn't he? Howard Roteman? He was the bully at school, wasn't he? He was the reason why Trevor Grey ran away, wasn't he?'

'The more you talk,' said Browne, 'the stupider you sound.' The man tugged at the prop he was holding. It was firm.

'I don't understand.'

'Nope. You don't understand a bloody thing.'

'Maybe Trevor Grey didn't run away. Maybe he committed suicide, like Revell did. Or didn't.'

'Do you mind talking a bit less?' said Browne.

Alex tutted. 'I was wondering why you didn't just push Revell Adison down the well, like you were going to do with me. But you weren't trying to get rid of him. It would look like he was sorry for what he'd done to Grey if he committed suicide, too. He had to be found, didn't he, in order to throw any suspicion off your boss. I take it Howard Roteman is your boss?'

He laughed. 'That what you think, is it? I was just following orders. Give me some fucking credit.'

Following orders. She thought of the Cymag gas. 'Did you kill Vincent Gibbons too?'

'No comment.' She couldn't see his face against the light he shone at her, but from his voice, she guessed he was smiling.

'I'd lay odds you did it. Or helped, at least. You're a pro.'

'Flattery won't get you anywhere, love.'

'Shame. Pushing me down a well means that the chances are I might not be found.' The thought terrified her. She couldn't let him win. He had definitely killed at least once, maybe many more times. 'You tried to kill me before, didn't you?'

He let go of the pole and tried another one, giving it a shake.

'Wouldn't do that. Whole lot might come down on us.'

'British builders, eh?' he said, giving it another tug. 'The entire British working class. Fucking useless, the lot of them, eh? That's what you think, anyway. Do you honestly believe Howard Roteman is smart enough to have thought of any of this?'

Dust, dislodged by the movement, obscured the light from his torch for a second.

Browne knew he hadn't got all day, as well. He was looking for a weapon, something to dislodge her with.

The third pole he tried was a metal scaffolding pole about half a metre behind him, wedged into the floor. When he grabbed it, she could see it move.

He knelt to put his phone on the floor, light shining up onto the uneven dirty roof of the space they were in, bare earth between boards that held the weight above them. That was her chance. She should jump.

Before she could calculate her move he had swung upright again.

She cursed her indecision, but he was already taking a step back behind the looser prop, eyes fixed on her. He tugged at it.

It moved. The plank to which the pole had been wedged to take the weight of earth above it shifted, then dropped, bouncing down to the ground. The man jumped back a couple of steps, in case it brought down any of the roof with it, but nothing happened.

There was silence for a second.

She should have jumped when she could. Now he was holding a five-foot-long metal pole in both hands, easily long enough to reach across the well.

He approached.

'Don't do this, Richard.'

He ignored her.

'Please,' she said. There was fear now in her voice, but she couldn't help it.

He jabbed it towards her, into the air in front of her chest; a feint to try and make her lose her balance. She tried to bat at it with her right hand, but missed.

She steadied herself, waiting for the next one.

The second time, he hit her shoulder with it, tearing her jacket, but it was a light blow. Again, he edged further forwards. A third stab at the opposite shoulder dug into her skin, but only gently. Every centimetre he moved towards her would allow him to hurt her a little more, but she knew he would want to avoid leaving any marks on her body.

He swung the pole in front of her, taunting her to grab it. She didn't, guessing that if she did, he would use it to yank her into the darkness below her feet, so she let it pass in front of her face.

'Fuck you,' she said.

Changing tack, he lunged again, this time towards her legs. Forced to jump to one side, she lost her footing. Her right shoe slid down towards the drop. Dirt fell into the darkness below her. It took her a second to regain her balance, her heart suddenly racing.

The hope which had kept her reactions sharp started to fall away. It would not be long. She could not hang on for ever.

And then, with no warning at all, something heavy fell from the ceiling and there was total darkness.

Whatever had fallen had landed on Browne's phone, blacking out the light that came from it.

She heard him mutter angrily, though couldn't hear the words.

It was as if his advantage had been snatched from him. For a second time she stood poised to make the leap, but paused, just for a second, to try and judge her jump. To get it wrong would mean disaster.

As she balanced on the edge of the well, she heard a soft creaking, and then, like the noise of small stones thrown onto water, a slow splitting of wood. Some of the props were metal; others were less sturdy. The roof above them was giving way.

And as it did, she jumped into the darkness in front of her.

SEVENTY-TWO

Her face thumped into an upright that still stood. She staggered backwards from the blow, trying to regain her balance, knowing that the drop must be right behind her.

She had jumped to Browne's right. Now she dodged to the left of where she had last seen him, hoping to reach the exit. Instead she tripped over something, sprawling forwards, grazing her skin.

A hand grabbed at her, catching her jacket, feeling for her. Flat on the ground, she kicked hard and found a leg, and realised he was standing between her and the hole through which they had entered this man-made cavern.

There was a crack, louder than anything before.

As she rolled away from her attacker, towards the right, away from the exit, the ground shook. The entire roof had collapsed, rubble thumping downwards with a dull *crump*.

As loose debris followed it, pouring down on her back, she scrambled on her hands and knees towards the second hole she had seen. Miraculously her hands found the edges of the bricks. Not knowing what lay on the other side, she flung herself through it.

And just as quickly it was quiet, and she lay on more bare earth. The only noise was the sound of her own breath, panting in the darkness.

She strained her ears for any sound of movement from Browne, but there was none.

'Hello?'

No answer.

She sat still in the absolute darkness and held her breath. There was a ringing in her ears. And then, faintly, she heard the sound of someone else's breathing.

At first it sounded as if the noise was coming from a long way off, but then she realised that the breaths were slow and very quiet.

'Richard.'

The suck of air continued, each one far apart. There was a reediness to the noise, a sense that the breathing was laboured.

'Are you hurt?'

No reaction at all. No sound of movement.

She had no idea of the scale of the collapse, but where she was, in the next chamber Revell Adison had dug in the earth beneath his house, she at least felt relatively safe.

In the terrifying blackness, she tried to think about what her best plan of action should be. She had put herself in a stupid situation, and was lucky to be alive. She could crawl back into the space next door and hope that Browne was not tricking her, that he was genuinely injured and incapable of attacking her, but that was a risk, and besides, there was no guarantee that what was left of the roof above him was stable.

The alternative was to wait for help, but she couldn't know for certain that anyone was aware of what had happened. Unless there was an obvious sinkhole on the surface, no one might have any idea of what had taken place underground.

And even if people saw that the ground above had moved, they might never venture here to find out what had happened beneath the surface. They would put up danger notices and seal off the area and wait for people who would advise them to stay well clear of the place until it was made safe. She knew how these things worked.

She took a breath and crawled out of the hole in the brickwork, back into the precarious chamber. She was shaking with fear, she realised, unable to stop it.

The flat, earth floor seemed to have disappeared under a layer of rubble. Where Browne had been standing, the layer rose up.

His breathing was close now. She stopped and listened.

Feeling the soil, stone and bricks with her trembling fingertips, she moved forward until she found something soft and warm.

It was a leg, she realised, pressed flat on the ground. She prodded at it, with her hand. It didn't budge. Moving up the thigh, she came to the man's groin, but beyond that, his torso was covered in debris, and on top of that, a timber weighed down by stones and earth lay across his body.

One of the scaffolding planks, she guessed, that Revell Adison had used like a miner, shoring up his strange subterranean world. Browne had killed Adison; now Browne lay wounded under one of Adison's planks. She found a hand next, palm up, sticking out of the debris close to her knees. Warm; still. His breathing continued slowly, but weakly.

'Richard?'

She felt to try and find his face and clear it of obstructions, then realised the breathing was coming from beneath the pile. He was completely trapped.

She forced her fingers underneath the wood, and tried to lift it, but it didn't budge. Feeling along the length of it, she discovered it disappeared under fallen masonry and rubble.

She wanted him alive, if only for her own purposes; he was her proof. She started to pull the dirt off him. Her fingers found something larger than the rest of the spill of earth, something jagged: a broken brick. Shoving and yanking at it, trying to find purchase, it finally came away, only to be replaced by another trickle of dirt from above.

She stopped, waiting for the movement of earth to stop, terrified it wouldn't. Anything she shifted from on top of him simply loosened what was above, risking bringing still more weight down on top of him – on top of them.

This was useless. She needed to get help. Which way was the entrance?

She tried to stand, but the dirt-filled floor was higher now, and she banged her back hard against the low ceiling.

With a sense of horror, she realised she had lost her sense of where she was, where the edges of the chamber were. Gingerly she moved in a crouch, hands in front of her, terrified of tripping, of falling down the well that the trapped man had tried to push her into.

To her right she found a hole in the retaining wall. She guessed it was the one she had just hidden in. In that case, the exit would be in front of her.

On hands and knees, she edged towards it, trying to avoid crawling on top of the man who had tried to kill her, crushing his broken body further, but the uneven floor seemed to rise up steeply. Carefully she tried working her way round it, but every way she tried to approach it was the same. Stones, bricks and earth formed a kind of wall around her.

It dawned on her that the quantity of rubble that had fallen when the ceiling had collapsed had not only flattened her attacker, but blocked her only means of escape.

'Can anybody hear me?' she shouted.

She tried a second time; the same.

'Bollocks,' she shouted as loudly as she could. As if in response, more earth fell from above.

The space in which the man lay was not safe. The roof might collapse at any minute.

In total darkness she edged back into the small hole in the brickwork and sat for a long time. Nobody would find them. The impossible blackness around her made her feel like she was dead already. What time was it, even? She had no way of knowing.

She listened to the slow breathing of the injured man a few feet from her. He had known she was close by in East London. It had been easy for him.

'I am stupid!' she shouted, and slapped her head hard with her fist. 'It was the phone, wasn't it?' she asked.

There was no answer, of course.

'That phone that Jill was given. You've been listening in to every bloody thing she said on it. And everything I said to her.'

The slow rasp of breath continued, barely audible now.

She had thought she was keeping it to herself, not telling McAdam of her suspicions; in fact, she had just made it easier for them.

'Jesus.' Alex slapped herself again. 'Stupid.'

Did that mean that Harry had been involved all along, too? It was him who had given Jill the phone. And there was no way at all for Alex to contact her. And if she lay here, everything would remain buried and hidden, and nobody would know the connection between the deaths of Trevor Grey, Revell Adison, Frederick Lindsay, Phyllis McKenzie and Vincent Gibbons.

She added her own name to the list and screamed again, at her own idiocy.

SEVENTY-THREE

At first, Paul Moore at number 36 had thought the shouting must be coming from the street outside, but when he'd opened the blinds he could see no one, so he returned to his computer, where he was rewriting a press release for a pet-food manufacturer. It took him several minutes to realise that the shouting was coming from somewhere closer.

The words weren't clear, but there was something about them that unsettled him: a sense of desperation and distress. He stood, and started walking around, and realised, with horror, that the shouting seemed to be coming from somewhere beneath his feet; from the cellar. He had seen horror movies. Something bad always happened in the basement.

When he opened the cellar door it was much louder.

'Hello?'

'Help. Please.'

His hand was shaking when he switched on the light. The cellar was a mess. The previous owner had left things that they had never shifted, including a rusting motorbike frame. It was from behind this that the noise seemed to be coming.

'I'm a police officer. What time is it?'

Scared now, he squatted down and peered at where the voice was coming from. A single eye stared back at him.

He gasped; stood up again.

Unsure of what to do, he reached for his phone, but there was no signal here.

'Please.'

He leaned down again, put his hands on the rusting motorbike, and pulled it out of the way.

'Is that a phone?' she demanded. 'Give it to me. Please.'

'No,' he protested.

She seemed angry. He was reluctant to give her anything. He looked at his iPhone. 'There's no signal, anyway.'

'Get a landline then.'

'We don't have one.'

'Jesus bloody Christ. Take a message then.'

He looked at her for a while, then said, 'Just a minute,' and returned upstairs, and sat back at his desk for a minute, wondering what to do. He was not used to situations like this.

She kept yelling. It was really getting to him.

Instead of going downstairs again, he called the police. 'Funny thing. There's a strange woman in my cellar. She's shouting.'

It took a PCSO twenty minutes to arrive. The officer went down, talked to the woman, called the situation through immediately, and within seven minutes fire officers had arrived with jacks to shore up the wall and sledgehammers to punch a hole in the brickwork.

In the meantime, Alex had passed a message to DI McAdam.

Then she was dragged through the hole in the bricks by an officer who apologised as he grabbed her by the upper body and pulled. She emerged into the midday sun, blinking, unable to get her eyes to focus after being so long in the dark.

'What do you mean, I can't go back inside the house?' Paul Moore was whining. 'It's my house.'

'We'll need a structural engineer to assess it before you can go back inside.'

'Sit down, love.' The officer who had pulled Alex out had led her to the wall in front of number 35. He was laying a blanket on it to make a seat for her.

'There's a man in the basement of number 38. He's in a bad way.' Alex was trying to explain to the officer how they could reach him.

They would need specialist teams, she told him. It wouldn't be easy but they had to hurry. Then she begged another phone from one of the officers and called McAdam.

'Is what they said true? You were trapped underground?'

'Jesus, yes. It was horrible.' Alex took a deep breath of clean air, and when she breathed out, it came out as a sob.

'Sorry. You'd been trying to contact me. My phone was off. Are you all right?'

'There's more.' Alex walked away from the crowd that was gathering around the house, far enough for her to be sure that no one was listening in. The paramedic, a young woman who'd arrived on a bike, was following her. Alex took the phone from her ear and said, 'Give me a minute. I just need to talk in private first.'

The woman stopped and let Alex walk on alone until she'd reached the entrance of Revell Adison's sad-looking house. 'A man called Richard Browne tried to murder me,' she said. 'We need to find out how he is connected in any way to Howard Roteman. Roteman's wife had the keys to Guldeford Hall.'

'Christ,' he breathed.

She told him how the man had impersonated an officer to lure her to the house to murder her; and how she was sure that Jill's phone had spyware in it that had been keeping tabs on them for over a week.

'Christ.'

'You need to arrest Harry French too. He gave her the phone as a present.'

'You think all three are in this together?'

Alex didn't answer. Instead she asked, 'What are you going to do about Roteman?'

'I'm going to call the Chief Constable now, and tell him everything you've just told me. It's up to him.'

An ambulance had arrived by now. Alex's next call was to Zoë.

'An hour, you said,' Zoë complained, before she'd had a chance to get a word out.

At a hospital in Dartford they checked her wounds and washed dust from her eyes.

A police car drove her, still sitting in her dusty, torn clothes, from there to the HQ at Maidstone, where someone found a clean tracksuit she could wear; then she was interviewed for an hour and a half.

When they were done with her, she walked along to Interview Room C, where McAdam was still interrogating Harry French.

Jill was sitting on a chair outside, waiting. She looked pale. 'Jesus,' she said. 'They took my phone off me. Apparently it was hacked.'

Alex nodded.

'You seriously think he was in on all this?' said Jill.

'It was that gold phone. That's how he knew where I was, and what we were doing. That's why they were one step ahead. And it was him that gave it to you.'

'And they were trying to kill you?'

'If they had to get rid of me, they'd have had to get rid of you, too, somehow. All our conversations were shared.'

'I must be such a fucking idiot, Alex. Why didn't I see any of that? I mean, he seems OK to me. In spite of everything.'

They sat, side by side, holding each other.

When McAdam heard that Alex was in the building, he halted the interview with French and joined them in the corridor. He, too, put his arms round the sergeant and held her for a second without saying anything. He was an awkward man. Gestures like this didn't come easily.

'How are you doing?'

'Has he talked?' she asked.

'It's early days yet,' said McAdam, 'and we'll have to go over it again, but you know what? I genuinely don't think he knew anything about it.'

'You're kidding?' Alex frowned. 'But he dated her.'

'I'm sure plenty of men would do, given the opportunity.'

'I'm actually sitting here,' said Jill. 'Right next to you.'

'He gave her the phone.'

'It looks like he was tricked into doing it. He talked about his woman troubles with one of his potential investors. It was a local man who had become friendly with him, taken him out for drinks. The investor sold him the phone for next to nothing, said he'd bought it by mistake and it was already paid for by his company anyway. Suggested he give it to his girlfriend to make it up to her.'

'So Harry French is innocent?'

'It looks like it.'

'One of his investors?'

'We're looking for him now.'

A thought occurred to Alex. 'Did he describe him?'

'Around fifty. Somebody local apparently. Dark hair. The details are pretty vague. We're trying to dig out any correspondence he may have had with him.'

'I wouldn't be surprised if we already know where he is,' said Alex. 'What's the latest on the guy who tried to kill me in Revell Adison's house?'

'Right,' said McAdam. 'You think he was Howard Roteman's fixer?'

'Or vice versa. Which one of them was the tail and which one was the dog?'

'French's story seems to stack up. I think he's quite keen on you,' said McAdam to Jill.

'Well, whoop-de-doo,' said Jill.

★

442

At 4.30 that afternoon, Harry French was free to leave. He emerged from Interview Room C looking pale and tired.

'Will you give me a lift home?' he asked Jill.

'Call a taxi,' she said.

'I didn't know anything about the phone, I swear,' he said. 'I was tricked.'

'You didn't even pay full price for it,' said Jill. 'A cheap bloody phone.'

'Sorry,' said French. 'I thought it was legit.'

'Besides, I'm dropping Alex home.'

Harry French, dishevelled and weary, in a crumpled light suit, said, 'Right. I understand.'

'Jesus. OK,' said Jill.

The three of them drove to Ashford in Jill's Fiat 500. She made French sit in the back.

The news came on the radio at around five in the afternoon. '*The Minister for Housing, Howard Roteman, has resigned unexpectedly for what he describes in a letter to the Prime Minister as "personal reasons". The Prime Minister has accepted his resignation, but has made no comment as yet about what lies behind this – yet another blow from a Prime Minister struggling to hold on to control in the run-up to a general election.*'

Police had driven to his house at around four in unmarked cars, McAdam told Alex later. The arrest had been straightforward. He was now sitting in a police cell in Lewes.

'*A man is in hospital, following the collapse of a house in Gravesend,*' the newsreader continued. They had managed to dig him out, but he had severe injuries and was not conscious.

443

'All that stuff Roteman told you about the bullying. He wasn't the victim, was he?' said Jill. 'It was him, all the time. He was talking about himself. It was him who bullied Trevor Grey and Revell Adison.'

'Maybe,' said Alex.

'What do you mean, "maybe"? The whole reason why he wanted to stop the development was that he didn't want anybody to start digging up Trevor Grey's bones. But they came up anyway . . . So you can go ahead now,' said Jill. 'Build your new integrated village.'

'Probably not,' said French, crouched in the back. 'The investment's not there in the current climate. It looks like the Secretary of State was planning to block it anyway. Investors have backed out. We're putting the land back up for sale.'

'You're skint?' said Jill.

'We're going to declare bankruptcy next week.'

'I'm sorry.'

'Really?'

When they arrived at Jill's flat, French asked, 'Do you want me to hang around? I could buy a meal. Take us all out.'

'I really don't think so,' Jill said. And, without saying another word, she got out and tipped her seat forward so he could emerge from the back of her small car.

SEVENTY-FOUR

'As for Richard Browne,' said McAdam, 'the hospital says the high likelihood is that he is quadriplegic, though they won't be able to tell for sure for a few days. His back was broken in several places because of where he fell and the quantity of debris that fell on him.'

'Good,' said Jill.

It was Tuesday, and they were at Alex's house in Dungeness, two days after she had crawled out of Paul Moore's cellar, just over four weeks since Gram Hickman and Angela Booth had found a body in a freezer. McAdam had driven down with Jill for what he described as a social visit, but Alex knew he had come to check up on her. They sat in the kitchen, drinking coffee.

'Bill South looking after you?' McAdam asked.

'What makes you think I need looking after?'

McAdam fidgeted. 'I just want to know you're OK.'

'Go on. Tell me the rest about Browne.'

'His name isn't Browne, for starters. When we visited his room at Mrs May's house, we found a driving licence in the name of Richard Boneville. It's registered to an address in West Norwood. Met Police officers searched the house and found he was paying for a lockup in Crystal Palace. When they went there, they found a motorbike and a black Range Rover Evoque, with damage to the bodywork. The debris we found by the Military Canal was from Richard Browne's car. There were also three containers of Cymag.'

'Bingo. See?' said Jill.

'Plus, two devices which I believe are known as trail cameras. We need to check the serial numbers . . .'

'But you think they're the ones that went missing from Whiteland Fields?'

Roteman had been interviewed by Met officers. He had denied ever having met Richard Browne. He claimed to know nothing about how Vincent Gibbons's body had ended up in the freezer of the house where his wife had been unfaithful to him.

'When can we interview Boneville?' asked Alex.

'So far we've charged him with the murders of Vincent Gibbons, Phyllis McKenzie and Revell Adison, plus the attempted murder of a police officer. We're still looking for any evidence that links him to the killing of Frederick Lindsay. We're talking to him tomorrow at the hospital.'

Alex stood up and fetched her laptop, and opened up the JPEG of the school photograph. 'Show him this,' she said. 'The original is in the evidence locker.'

*

On the Thursday, they interviewed Richard Boneville in the hospital room where they were holding him. Jill turned up at Alex's house that evening with a video recording of the entire interview on a memory stick. 'You will want to see this,' she said.

Alex dug out her laptop and inserted the stick.

His bed was surrounded by monitoring equipment. Propped up with pillows and towels, Richard Boneville wore a neck brace, and his back was being held rigid by a set of metal clamps that ran around his shoulders to his chest. There were monitors and canulas attached to both arms. That his left hand was handcuffed to the bed seemed more of a symbolic act than a practical one. He was paralysed from the neck down and spoke in a whisper, when he spoke at all, having to form words around a tube that ran into his mouth. He seemed uninterested in taking part in the interview; he didn't even look at the two officers or the lawyer, or the doctor who stood at the back of the room, just stared straight ahead.

The officers questioned him about the murders of Vincent Gibbons, Phyllis McKenzie, Frederick Lindsay and Revell Adison. He said nothing. At times, Alex wondered if he could even hear what the officers were saying, he seemed so distant.

'Up to this point, he's like a man who's still buried underground,' said Jill.

And then they showed him a copy of the school photograph, one officer holding it at each end, on each side of the bed, unfurling it in front of him. For the first time he smiled. It was the only move he had made so far. 'Yes,' he said eventually, in his papery voice. 'At the end. The boy with no face. That's me.'

The boy at the end of the line, next to Howard Roteman; the one who had shaken his head as the camera recorded him, erasing his record so that his face was a blur.

'You were right. He was at Thornhead,' said Jill.

'Bunch of bloody snobs,' he said in an almost indecipherable murmur. 'They had it coming. The posh kids made my life a bloody misery when I got there.'

They had had to turn up the sound so high that every medical beep, every rustle of the sheets, every footfall in the corridor outside, sounded deafening.

'He was a scholarship pupil, wasn't he?' said Alex 'One of the poor kids they let in so they could convince themselves they were doing it for the good of society.'

'Cynic,' muttered Jill.

On the video, the officer's voice seemed to boom. 'And Howard Roteman. You knew him?'

Another small smile. 'Ask him about his tape recorder.' And then he closed his eyes and the interview was over.

The arrest of a minister on charges of conspiracy to murder had been the lead on the news for days. In the run-up to an election, the opposition parties were having a field day.

Though few details had been given, journalists had seized on the detail of Thornhead School and the disappearance of Trevor Grey. The papers printed stories. Mostly they were lurid speculation, but there was enough there to embolden a handful of abuse victims from Thornhead. Two other pupils from Roteman's time came forward with tales of being victims of extortion schemes that matched what Roteman had told Alex, except, of course, in their accounts Roteman was not the victim. One of them was an electrical engineer who now lived in Bolton.

When he was interviewed by local police, he said he told them he had evidence that Trevor Grey had never run away at all. Jill sent the audio file by email with a note: *Start at 3' 45"*.

The voice that appeared first was the witness's, Alex guessed.

'His name was Richard Bayliss, not Browne,' said the voice. 'I think his dad was a farmer.'

'Go on.'

'We used to call his sort "oiks". "Oiks" and "toffs". That was the world back then. Sounds ridiculous now, doesn't it? I suppose we were pretty cruel. It was a cruel place.'

'In your own time.'

'Anyway, Roteman had this tape recorder hidden in his room. A little cassette thing. And he had his own room, you see, because he was a prefect. He had, like, porno magazines there that Bayliss had brought. Bayliss had alcohol too, sometimes. Roteman'd invite people in, they'd get drunk and he'd show them the magazines and then get them to . . .'

In the silence, the automatic volume control filled the void with a loud hiss until an officer's voice broke in. 'Can you be specific?'

'He got us to masturbate. And also he egged us on to say stuff out loud. We didn't know he was taping it.'

'Roteman had a tape of you?'

A nervous laugh. 'It wasn't Roteman. He just recorded them. Bayliss was the one who had the tapes.'

'Bayliss had a tape of you masturbating.'

There was a long pause.

'Yes. We were kids. Locked away in the middle of nowhere. Christ, it would be nothing these days. Just swear words, really. It was nothing really. It's difficult to understand now.'

'What did he do with the tapes?'

'If he didn't like you, or if he wanted something from you, he would play you a little bit. He didn't have to say anything else. The implication was that he could make it public. It was how he controlled you. He wanted money from me, so I gave it to him.'

'Bayliss blackmailed you?'

'Yes. Pocket money, really.'

'And you weren't the only one?'

'No. You have to understand, he got a real buzz out of it. It was like he really hated us all.'

They had it coming, thought Alex, listening.

'Why did he hate you?'

'Well, because he was an oik and we were toffs, I suppose. Looking back, it can't have been easy arriving in that place with a working-class accent. Liking all the wrong bands. Not knowing about the right books. I think we were probably awful to him. But all the same.'

'Why did Roteman do it if Bayliss was the one who profited from it?'

There was a laugh. 'You'd have to ask Roteman. I don't know. I always assumed Bayliss probably had a tape of him, too. But Roteman was just as bad. He was a sadist too, I think. I think he enjoyed it that they were controlling all these people.'

'Did Bayliss blackmail Trevor Grey?'

450

'Yes. That was worse. Howard Roteman had Trevor Grey's parents' address, I think. They had been friends once. Trevor Grey's parents were very straight, very strict. His father was in the army.'

'You heard the tape of Trevor?'

There was a long pause. 'I think he knew that Trevor would be easy. Trevor was pretty shy, you know? A bit of a victim. Not many friends. I suppose he must have been thrilled when Roteman pretended to befriend him. Yes. I heard the tape. It was pathetic. You could hear he was saying it just to try and please Roteman. He had some porn mag and was getting him to . . . It was kind of like a naming of the parts. Every rude word Grey knew. And then one day Bayliss said he would send his parents the tape unless Trevor Grey paid him money. I can't remember how much it was, but it was a lot. A lot more than most of us had paid. Trevor was terrified. It would have been absolute shit for Trevor. I'm so ashamed of myself. I never told anyone this ever before. It was easier to pretend none of this had ever happened.'

'Why did Bayliss play you the tape?'

'Grey said he couldn't get the money, or something, so he played it to us in front of Grey. It was the first time he'd done that to any of us. It was awful. And of course we all laughed and laughed. Bayliss encouraged us to be part of the humiliation. I suppose we were scared not to laugh, because he had something on us. And the more humiliated Grey looked, the more we laughed.'

'It's all right. Tell us what happened next.'

'He hanged himself. Like I told you.'

'Trevor Grey?'

'Yes. In the maths classroom. He did it at night. It was me that found him. I was class monitor, so I had to go and clean the blackboard before class. And I walked in there and . . .'

'You saw him.'

'With two school ties, knotted together. From the back of the door that led to the old washrooms. I knew he was dead.'

There was the sound of a man crying; a man trying not to, but being unable to stop.

'Would you like some water? Do you need a break?'

'His lips were blue and his eyes were red. He just hung there against the door, like he was an old coat or something.'

'Who else saw him?'

'I went to tell the master. He told me to go to sick bay and wait there.'

'Do you remember the name of the master?'

'Yes I do. It was Mr Lindsay. He was the maths master. It was his classroom.'

'Frederick Lindsay?'

'Yes.'

'And he saw the body.'

'He must have done. He went in there after I told him.' The man sighed. 'This was, like, eight-thirty in the morning, after breakfast. I waited in the sick bay on my own. I wasn't allowed to talk to anybody. At school assembly that morning, I was expecting the headmaster to say something about it, but he said nothing at all. Lindsay was his son, after all. He must have known. I couldn't believe it. And next thing, there was this rumour that Grey had run away. Roteman's parents arrived that afternoon and took him away. Bayliss was sent home that day too, I think. We never saw them again. It was never explained what had gone on. Nobody even talked about it. We were all just relieved that Bayliss was gone, Roteman too, and that it wasn't us. We never talked about it again, any of us. We were all so ashamed. It was our fault, don't you see? Because we did nothing.'

'Why did Roteman and Bayliss leave, do you think?'

'It's obvious, isn't it? The head teacher knew that they had bullied Grey. Everybody knew it. They asked Howard Roteman's parents to take him out of the school and stuck to the made-up story that Grey had run away. All they cared about was the school's reputation.'

Another voice asked, 'Again, you say "They". Can you tell us exactly who you mean?'

'All of them. The head. Frederick Lindsay. All of them. The people in charge.'

'But you didn't tell anyone.'

'It was our fault, don't you see? We were the ones who made him do it. We were why he killed himself. We were all guilty of it.'

'Why did you wait until now to tell us?'

The man was crying again now, and it was hard to hear what his answer was. Alex played it back a couple of times and decided it was probably, 'I should have stuck up for him.'

The interview was terminated after that. Alex took off her headphones, laid her head down on the kitchen table and closed her eyes.

From the remains dug up from Whiteland Fields, it was impossible to prove that Trevor Grey had hanged himself. Likewise, it would be impossible to prove that staff from the school had removed Trevor Grey's body from Thornhead and buried it on wasteland near Lydd. The head teacher was dead; so was Frederick Lindsay.

For the first week of the investigation, they kept Bayliss's name out of the public domain. The press didn't notice. They were only interested in Howard Roteman.

Three days after Roteman's arrest, his wife Hilary had come in for questioning, with a lawyer at her side.

Another video. Jill sat opposite Hilary Roteman in the interview suite. The bright lighting didn't help, thought Alex, watching it, but the ex-minister's wife looked exhausted; there were dark rings around her eyes and her skin was pale. The press had been camping out outside their house in Sussex.

'Did your husband know you were having an affair with Andrew Utting?' Jill asked.

'There's no way he could have known.'

'We found out.'

'But you're a police officer. He can't have known. He would have . . .' She faltered. 'He wouldn't have forgiven me if . . .'

She was scared of her husband, Alex realised; he was still the bully he had been at school.

'I think he knew,' said Jill.

'How could he? We were always so careful, Andrew and I.'

'How long had it been going on?'

The woman sighed. 'A few years. Almost ten, in fact.' She started to cry; soon she began howling. Jill took a tissue and handed it to her. 'We kept it a secret. When Andrew died, I wasn't able to cry. I wasn't able to go to the funeral or anything. It was all like nothing had ever happened.'

Jill watched her, waiting for her sobbing to subside.

'I actually loved Andrew. I really did. If Howard knew, why didn't he do anything about it?' she asked.

'That's what we were hoping to find out from you. You used to visit Andrew Utting at Guldeford Hall.'

'That's where I first met him. He used to have parties. Andrew knew powerful people. Howard was ambitious. He wanted to know people too. He was keen to go. When we met him first at some Westminster party, Howard practically encouraged me to flirt with him. And then Andrew invited us to one of his house parties at Guldeford Hall. They were always amazing. Everybody drank too much. We always did. The next morning, we all went for a walk. Howard was hungover, so he stayed in bed. We went down to Camber Sands and we just talked and talked and talked, Andrew and me. I fell in love with him there. As simple as that. I was totally, unexpectedly overwhelmed by it. I was like a child. When I got home, I found his mobile number in Howard's phone and started sending him messages. In retrospect, I discovered he was lonely too, like I was. He didn't really like his wife very much. I didn't really like my husband.' She had stopped crying now, but her eyes were red. 'It was easy. You see, Belinda never really liked Guldeford Hall. She wasn't there much. And the higher up the ladder Howard got, the more he was away. I would drive over there, and we'd spend the night together. I loved the place. I loved him.'

'Did you ever discuss divorce?'

'There has always been talk about Howard being a Prime

Minister at some point.' She laughed bitterly. 'Well he's fucked that up handsomely now, hasn't he?' She reached across the table and took Jill's hand. 'He did all this, didn't he? He allowed people to die just to try and cover up his part in humiliating a boy who went on to commit suicide. I'm damned if I'm going to be the loyal wife, claiming he's innocent.'

Jill looked at her across the table. 'You're sure he didn't know about you and Andrew Utting?'

'No. It was our secret. Until he died, and then it was just my secret, and I had no one to share it with.'

'Did you ever let yourself into Guldeford Hall when Andrew wasn't there?'

'Why do you ask?'

'Did you?'

'Yes.'

'So you had a key?'

'Of course.'

'And you knew the code for the alarm?'

'Andrew changed it every six months. It was a condition of the insurance. He would text me the new ones.'

Jill pulled out a photograph and showed it to Hilary Roteman. From the angle the video had been shot at, Alex couldn't see it, but she knew who it was. 'Do you recognise this man?'

'Yes.'

'Who is he?'

'Richard Bayliss. He turned up at our door in Sussex about three years ago. Just after Howard had been made a minister. I didn't like him at all. There was something very off about him. I'm not sure what Howard ever saw in him. He just seemed nervous around him. I wasn't sure he even liked the man, but he seemed to have some kind of power, I suppose. You know Richard was in the car when Howard was arrested for driving over the limit?'

'Is it possible he goaded your husband into doing it?'

Hilary Roteman raised both hands to her face. 'You know? I'd never thought of it like that. I thought it was just him acting like a big adolescent with some old school mate. But now you mention it, yes. I think it was. It was so uncharacteristic of Howard to behave like that. Not that it mattered. He weathered the storm all right. In some ways it made him popular with some of the papers, in fact.'

Richard Bayliss had done it because he could; just to remind Roteman he was still in control. Alex could see Jill thinking this through for a few seconds before she asked, 'Is there any way in which Richard Bayliss could have got hold of your phone?'

So clever, thought Alex, smiling. Jill doing it all now, on her own.

Hilary Roteman frowned. 'Actually, yes. The first time Richard Bayliss came round, he took it by accident. I didn't even realise it was missing. He'd driven off, and then half an hour later he was back, apologising. He said he'd thought it was his and had taken it by mistake.'

That's how Bayliss had known the code to Guldeford Hall. It was all about humiliation. He'd wanted to rub Howard's face in it; that his wife had been having an affair with a rich, glamorous man.'

It was all revenge and humiliation for being the poor boy

let into the rich boys' school. Even completely broken, lying on a hospital bed, facing a long prison sentence, it was clear that Richard Bayliss was enjoying ruining the life of the former minister.

SEVENTY-FIVE

As they searched Bayliss's flat more details emerged.

They found the cassettes in a sealed plastic box hidden under the floorboards. One appeared to feature the voice of Trevor Grey. The tape was much as the witness had described. Alex couldn't bear to listen; these were boys only a little younger than her daughter.

It took longer to decrypt Bayliss's computer. When they did, they found details of a bank account into which Howard Roteman had been paying substantial amounts for the last three years. Bayliss had been blackmailing him, too; just as he had when he was a boy.

In one folder, they found a Word file: a letter addressed to Vincent Gibbons.

Dear Mr Gibbons,
I believe you have an interest in protecting the site known as Whiteland Fields. You don't know me, but I am a metal detectorist.

The correspondent identified himself as a Mr McKenzie. He claimed to have found interesting archaeological remains near to Lydd Airport, and invited him to come and inspect them. He gave his address as a static home on Maple Ridge, in the Golden Sands Holiday Park.

'Why didn't we find the original letter?' Jill demanded.

'Because after he killed him, Bayliss let himself into Gibbons's house with Vera May's key, and took it, so we wouldn't find it. It would have been easy.'

Another folder contained recordings of phone calls between Bayliss and Roteman; more secret tapes. It seemed to have become a compulsion with him, amassing material that could be used against others. Roteman had been terrified by the prospect of the Whiteland Fields development. It was where Frederick Lindsay had disposed of the remains of Trevor Grey to protect the reputation of his beloved school. If the development went ahead, they would find the body.

On one recording, Bayliss proposed going back to the small town he'd grown up in to keep an eye on the development. He asked for more money; and again, when it turned out that a local naturalist had discovered what appeared to be human remains on the site, he demanded still more to get rid of that problem.

A few days later, he reassured Roteman that he had dealt with it. Roteman had seemed relieved, until he told him exactly what he had done – and where he had stored the body: in the place where his wife had been conducting an affair. Roteman had had no idea about his wife's infidelity until then. He pleaded with him to move the body, because it connected him with the murder; Bayliss had laughed.

On another file, Bayliss told Roteman that there was a police officer coming to interview Derry Michaels. 'How do you know that?' Roteman had demanded, unnerved. Vera May would have told him, Alex realised.

But Bayliss didn't say that. 'Oh, I know everything about everybody. Of all people, you should know that by now.'

Roteman's trial was scheduled for the autumn.

One night in June, Alex was woken by Zoë shaking her by the shoulders.

She sat up in bed, blinking. 'What's wrong?'

Zoë looked puzzled by the question. 'You were screaming, Mum.'

'Was I?'

'Yes. It was horrible. Like you were really afraid.' Zoë crawled into bed next to her mother and put her arms around her, squeezing her tight.

Alex said nothing. She had been trapped in the darkness underground. There had been a body pinned beneath the rubble. There had been a well shaft, but she hadn't known where it was.

Zoë soon fell asleep beside her, but it was too hot. Alex went outside, lay on the stones and looked up at the stars, slowly moving, until the sky started to get light.

After an uneasy start, the summer was a hot one. Temperature records were falling. The south-east was dry. There was talk of a drought. It hadn't rained much in May.

Jill came and stayed a couple of nights. She was single again, despite Harry French's best efforts.

'There was somebody screaming in the night,' she said the following morning, sitting at the breakfast table. 'Did anyone hear it, or did I just dream it?'

Alex and her daughter exchanged a glance but said nothing.

The third time it happened, Zoë shook her awake roughly.

Alex was still screaming when she woke, still felt the enormous weight of earth pressing on her chest. It took a long time for her racing pulse to slow.

'It's OK,' said Zoë softly, stroking her forehead. 'I'm here. Everything is OK.'

'Shit,' said Alex. She reached over and turned on the light. 'Can't you smell it? The earth?'

'It's all right, Mum. You did it. You got out of there.'

Awake now, she lay by her daughter, and she thought of Trevor Grey and the misery he must have gone through.

'I was lucky,' she said. 'You took me badger-watching. If we hadn't seen the skull, the whole thing might have gone nowhere.'

She kissed her daughter on the forehead, then looked at her watch. It was four in the morning and because it was almost midsummer, it would be getting light soon.

'That was the weirdest thing, wasn't it? Everyone was ready to give up, and then that skull appeared out of the ground.'

'You should thank them, then,' said Zoë.

'What?'

'You should thank the badgers.'

Alex smirked. 'Don't be silly.'

'I'm serious,' Zoë said. 'You have to thank them.' She got up and went downstairs, returning with a coat on, and a big jar of peanuts. 'Let's go now,' she said.

'No,' said Alex. 'Not in a million years. Go back to bed.'

It was still dark when they got there, but there was a thin line of gold light above Dover. The gate to the fields was left open now. Dog walkers had started using the place again. Maybe it would still be developed at some point in the future if the economy picked up, but not for a while at least.

'Peanuts?' said Alex. 'Seriously?'

'Not too many at once,' said her daughter.

'I feel stupid.' Alex scattered them on the rough ground around the dark entrance holes to the main sett.

'That's enough,' scolded her daughter, and pulled her away.

They lay where they had lain with William South and the guard weeks before, and waited as the gold sky turned silver and the black shapes around them gradually became green bushes and trees.

It was an hour before a badger arrived, trotting back from across the road on its way from trying to find food in the low fields; just a vague shadow of a creature, moving fast through the track they had made in the long vegetation. It paused shortly before returning to the hole it had dug, raised itself on its fore-paws and sniffed the air. Then it disappeared into a hole.

'He didn't even eat them,' complained Alex.

'Ssh,' said Zoë.

Thirty seconds later he was back, cautiously sniffing the air again, then snuffling at the ground around the entrance.

'God. He's scoffing the lot,' said Alex. 'Do you think he's the one who did it?'

'Can't tell. It's too dark to see.'

After that, Alex added unsalted peanuts to her weekly shop. Sometimes she chopped carrots and added them, too. The bad dreams still came, but she was getting used to them.

SEVENTY-SIX

The earthworms were scarce now, and there were fewer bugs than there should be, but the sett was safe. All of them stood a good chance. Two females, two cubs, the young male who had joined their group, and him. Other badgers in the land around them were struggling in the dryness of the summer, but his group were putting on weight. Even the older badger stood a good chance of making it through one last winter.

He found another peanut that had rolled beneath a hawthorn sapling and swallowed it down in a rich gulp, then paused, sniffed the air and paused. Sniffed again.

She was back, lying over there in the grass, perfectly still. He could smell her, though. She was here most nights now, late, long after the other humans had gone to sleep, arriving on her bicycle and feeding them, watching, waiting until the sun rose above the flat land.

People stink.

But he had become used to this one.

Read on for a sample of *The Trawlerman,* the gripping next book in the DS Alexandra Cupidi Investigations.

ONE

Something really, really bad was about to happen.

What it was, Alexandra Cupidi wasn't sure. She was sitting on a cafe bench with a coffee that could have been worse, surrounded in every direction by happy people. The sun was out. Summer bugs dipped in and out of the wild flowers that squeezed their way through the shingle beach. Multicoloured nylon kites flew in a blue July sky.

It was there in her chest; a cold, dark, malevolent slug.

Something really, really bad was about to happen.

However hard she looked around, she could see nothing that would explain what it was that made her so anxious.

The Light Railway Cafe was the terminus for the Romney, Hythe and Dymchurch Railway, close to the house on the promontory in which she lived with her daughter.

It was July, the time of year when the misanthropes, artists, nature-lovers and eccentrics who lived on Dungeness were already tiring of the crowds of tourists who flocked here, disgorging from the comically small train to queue to climb the stone stairs of the old black lighthouse, and to wander around photographing the houses and the locals like they were exhibits, wondering what else you were supposed do here in this strange, flat place.

Bungalows and shacks dotted the scrubby landscape as if scattered there like dice. The Light Railway Cafe was like most buildings here; a hotchpotch of rough rectangles joined at any angle the builder had fancied, held together with paint.

Something was wrong.

It made her skin itch. If only she knew what it was.

The next train was on its way, clattering down the curve of narrow track that ran along the shingle. This one, Alex noticed, was different. It was decorated with flowers; garlands hung from the windows, fluttering as it moved. She squinted through the afternoon sun at it.

Steam from the funnel drifted slowly south towards them, ahead of the train.

There was something comical about the small train. The light railway had been built as a tourist attraction, its terminus this ramshackle cafe. When the war broke out a few years later, the army commandeered the railway to shift the materials needed to build sea defences all along the shore, and the few tourists it attracted then vanished. This small train still ran, driven and tended by disproportionately large men, and dwarfed by this landscape. The huge bulk of the nuclear power station to the west only made it look more like a children's toy, casually abandoned.

Abrupt laughter travelled ahead of the train, carried by a gust of wind. The passengers in the flower-decked carriages were having a party.

'Wedding party,' said someone. They were right. As the tiny train slowed at the Dungeness station, the engine driver blew the whistle – *poop-poop!* – and Cupidi saw the glimpse of white inside the flower-decked carriage. A weekday wedding. The bride emerged first, red hair buffeting in the wind, and then everybody piled out behind her, screaming and shouting, carrying bottles of sparkling wine by the neck. They were drunk, thought Cupidi, joyfully so.

And then a second white wedding dress stepped out of the carriage: a younger woman with short bleached hair; a wedding of two brides.

The wedding party poured out of the station and made their way to the cafe where Alex was sitting.

'Congratulations,' the tourists called out to them.

The red-haired woman, older than she had looked from a distance – late thirties perhaps – smiled a little shyly. 'Thanks.' Women in heels tottered on the shingle. Men moved among them, shirts half untucked, eyes losing focus from drink.

Cupidi recognised one. Curly was local; he had grown up close by in one of the wooden houses. His family had been fishermen here, and he still kept his twin-hulled boat here.

Curly smiled goofily at Alex when he spotted her there.

'Who's the happy couple?' she asked.

'That's Tina,' he said, pointing to the red-haired bride, 'and that's Stella. We're stopping here for lunch.'

471

She had never seen Curly in a suit. It looked wrong. He had the sunburned leathery skin of someone who spent his days here on the beach; his hair was thin, a mixture of pale grey and sandy yellow. 'Can I get you a drink?' He pointed towards the small hut named 'Ales on the Rails'.

The day yawned in front of her. 'Why not?'

She had nothing at all to do today. It was driving her crazy.

They had arranged two of the tables in a single row, the brides at one end, and they had ordered fish and chips, and sandwiches. Cupidi joined them, squeezing onto the end of the picnic table bench seats.

'You ever married?' Curly asked.

'Just the once. Zoë's dad. You?'

'Nobody wanted me,' he said.

'Can't say I'm surprised.'

'Lovely girl, Tina,' said Curly. 'Known her since she was a baby. Worked with her dad on the trawlers. She deserves a little happiness.'

Squeezed on the end of the table, Cupidi looked up towards the two women. They were holding hands across the rickety table, smiling. It didn't look like a little happiness to her; it looked like a lot of it. She felt that familiar pull in her guts; that something was wrong here. Nothing would make this feeling go away.

'Not working today?'

'Off sick,' said Alex.

'Oh. Nothing bad, I hope?'

Alex didn't answer. She picked up the wine Curly had brought

472

her and took a generous swig. The guests chattered. Everything was bright with summer sunshine. She took in every detail, as if looking for something out of place, something that could spoil this prefect day.

She looked at children playing tag in the car park. She looked at a kite shaped like a comma, dipping down over the flat ground, then soaring up again. She looked at lovers, holding hands as they walked by the tiny art gallery by the lighthouse.

And then she saw a woman, a long way off, striding with a sense of purpose.

As the guests chatted, she approached. She was walking towards them at speed.

'Excuse me,' Alex said to Curly. She untangled herself from the packed picnic table and stood. The woman was in her fifties or sixties, dressed in a plain grey mac, gloves still on, as if defying the summer.

Alex's skin prickled. From a distance, Alex could see the sheen of unwiped tears that ran down her face; occasionally she gulped for breath.

By now Alex had left the group she had been with and was approaching the woman as she approached on the concrete track. Alex called out, 'Is everything OK?'

The woman ignored her; strode up towards her, and then straight on past. Alex turned to look where she was heading and saw that she was unbuttoning her grey coat.

Nervous now, Alex ran back towards the group to get ahead of the crying woman, and as she did she saw, tucked into the belt of the woman's dress beneath the open coat, a long, grey steel blade.

Ants were suddenly crawling all over Alex's skin. 'I'm a police officer,' Alex said, voice as low as she could. 'I can help.'

The woman paid no attention still, grasped the handle with her right hand and pulled it out, holding it horizontally out in front of her.

'Stop,' said Alex, louder this time.

The woman blinked, twisted to her right to point the weapon straight at Alex's midriff.

'Shut up,' the woman screamed.

The chatter and laughter stopped abruptly.

Alex stood, arms raised up, drawing her midriff back from the machete in front of her. The edge had been sharpened recently and glittered in the brightness. The woman shook.

'Put it down. Let's talk about this.'

One of the revellers saw the blade and screamed; the scream stopped as quickly as it started.

'Put it down,' pleaded Alex.

Everything was suddenly quiet. The wind seemed to drop. Gulls hung, stationary in solid air.

And to her surprise, the woman did as she had been told, dropping the weapon onto the ground where it clattered on the tarmac.

The woman in grey raised a finger of the hand that had dropped the weapon and pointed it at the red-haired bride.

'Murderer!' the woman screamed. 'Bloody murderer.'

And the red-haired woman, open mouthed, eyes huge, paled; her skin almost as white as the dress she was wearing.

TWO

The wedding party broke up; most of the guests caught the next train back to Hythe, shaken by what had happened. Taxis arrived to collect others, who muttered apologies before they departed. Curly stayed behind with the two brides, who sat close on the bench, arms around each other, whispering together, shocked by what had happened.

The first police car to arrive was driven by a Civil Nuclear Constabulary officer. He was based at the nearby power station. He offered Alex handcuffs and started collecting names and addresses while the woman in the grey coat sat in his car waiting for someone from Kent Police to come and collect her.

'You're the police officer who lives round here, aren't you?' The young CNC officer was new. Alex didn't recognise him.

Curly had brought Alex a fresh glass of wine because he said she looked like she needed one. 'Yes.'

'Weird place to live, isn't it? Right next to that lot.' He nodded at the power station.

'Weird place to work, when there's nothing for you to do,' she answered.

The boy looked hurt; but it was true. The CNC were a heavily armed unit, guarding a nuclear facility that no one wanted to attack anyway. 'You not at work today, then?'

'I have been told to take a little time off for the good of my mental health,' she said.

'Sick leave?'

'Yes.' She held up the glass.

'Unlucky for you; lucky for everyone else here, by the sound of it. Did you know the woman with the machete?'

'Never seen her before in my life,' said Alex.

'Only, some of these people . . .' He looked around. 'They're telling me you stood up and approached her well before she pulled out the weapon.' He looked at his little dark-blue note-book. 'And you had some words with her. Why did you approach her?'

'I'll be honest,' said Alex, 'I have been asking myself exactly the same thing.'

'She was acting suspiciously?'

She had been dressed for the wrong weather, that's all. 'Not really. I just . . .' She tried to think what had made her do it. 'I just knew something really bad was going to happen,' she said.

'That's a copper's instinct, then. Seeing something out of place. Knowing that something was wrong.'

Alex shivered.

'Pretty bloody impressive,' said the copper. 'I'd buy you a drink too, only some of us are still on duty.'

★

Back at the table, Curly lit a cigarette and said, 'Poor cow.'

'You know her?' asked Cupidi.

'Mandy. Tina's mother-in-law. Ex-mother-in-law, I should say. She's not right.'

'Ex-mother-in-law? You mean . . . ?'

Cupidi looked at the woman, stationary in the police car, staring straight ahead, no regret on her face for what she'd just tried to do.

He lowered his voice so the brides could not hear. 'Mandy Hogben. Tina used to be married to her son Frank Hogben. They married young, you know? Tina was eighteen years old. Frank's dead. Died in a fishing accident. Nothing to do with her, but Mandy never believed that.'

'What kind of accident?'

'Fell overboard on a trawler out of Folkestone.'

'Why does she blame Tina, then?'

'Like I said, not right in the head. Not her fault. Just tough on Tina.'

At the other end of the table Tina was crying; her new wife was trying to make fun of her, wiping her tears with her veil.

'Not a great thing to happen on your wedding day.'

'You said it,' said Curly.

'So he just fell overboard?'

'No life jacket. No harness. No chance at all.'

'Why didn't anybody save him?'

'Nobody saw it happen. The other guy on the boat was asleep down below. Came back on deck, engine running, nobody on deck.'

Cupidi thought for a while. 'So how can they be so sure he fell overboard, then?'

'I thought you were off work.'

Alex Cupidi had two more weeks of counselling ahead of her. She would soon be returning to work on what they called 'light duties'. The phrase filled her with dread. 'So?' she demanded.

'If you're on board a trawler one minute, and the next you're gone, that's about the only explanation there is.'

She studied his face for a second. The sun never reached the bottom of Curly's wrinkles, she noticed; little deltas of white skin beneath the reddy brown.

'I used to go out on that boat sometimes,' said Curly. 'It was called The Hopeful.'

'Some name. Did they go back and look for him?'

'You have any idea what it's like to lose a man at sea? Worst thing in the world that can happen. They called out the coastguard and everything. But there wasn't much point. They were in the Channel. It was March. Unless you've got an immersion suit on, you've got ten, maybe twenty minutes in the water and then you're gone.'

'Find his body?'

'No life jacket on. They never did.'

Alex looked round. The woman in the car's face was like iron.

'When was all this?'

'Seven years ago.'

'So his body never turned up in all that time?'

The sound of waves on shingle a long way off. 'That's right.'

Seven years dead; it takes seven years to make a declaration of presumed death. 'That's why they're getting married. They never found the body, so Tina couldn't marry again until now.'

478

Curly didn't answer.

'How long have they been lovers then?'

Curly turned his head and looked at her for a while. 'You've got a bad mind, Alexandra Cupidi,' he said eventually.

At that moment, as if she knew what they were talking about, the dead man's mother turned her head to the left and stared at them, unflinching. In those eyes Cupidi recognised that dangerous kind of emptiness. She was beyond caring what anyone thought.

The younger bride, Stella, stood, picked up a bottle of wine and approached Cupidi with a glass. 'I wanted to say thanks,' she said. Her eyes were an extraordinary bright shade of blue. 'You were cool. She could have hurt you.'

'Not a great thing to happen on your wedding day.'

She handed Cupidi a glass and poured wine into it without asking if she wanted any. 'Well, it's a day we're never going to forget, at least.'

'Sorry about your guests.'

'We wanted to get rid of them anyway. We're on our honeymoon now.'

'Here?' Cupidi looked around. This wasn't the sort of place people usually came on their honeymoons.

'We're staying over there.' She pointed to a low, pale-blue bungalow, the far side of the new lighthouse. 'A whole week. Mostly in bed,' she added with a mischievous smile.

Over her shoulder, Tina sat alone at the end of the table, wedding dress already grubby at the hem. Stella had shrugged off the attack; Tina still looked shaken, her face pale and her eyes red. 'I can't wait,' said Stella.

When Alex looked towards pale-blue bungalow with white-framed windows, she saw also the flashing blue lights of an approaching police car.

THANKS

Thanks to Professor Tim Roper for sharing his phenomenal knowledge of badgers; and to members of the Badger Trust, Dominic Dyer in particular for his help. I'm grateful to ecologists Steve Parnwell and Richard Pash, both of whom encouraged me to write about badgers.

Again, much gratitude to Nick de Somogyi for saving me from my own inconsistencies. Thanks also to Kate Bendelow and Sarah Ward; to Isabelle Grey for the loan of *That Rascal, Fridolin* by Hans Fallada; and to Jon Riley for the title, and so much more besides. Jane, as ever.

Finally to Janet King, Roz Brody, Mike Holmes and C. J. Samson who pointed out that there is no such thing as a 1968 shilling.